REVIEWERS PRAISE MARK MORRIS!

"Skillfully constructed, with a mind-boggling twist."
—*The Times* (London) on *The Immaculate*

"Easily Mark Morris's best novel so far. A real contribution to the literature of the ghostly."
—Ramsey Campbell on *The Immaculate*

"[A] quiet, slow-building ghost story....touchingly earnest."
—*The New York Times Book Review* on *The Immaculate*

"Mark Morris is one of the finest horror writers at work today."

—Clive Barker

"The most stunningly original dark fantasist working in Britain today."

—*Starburst Magazine*

NO LONGER HUMAN

Something terrible was happening to the little girl. Strands of blue lightning were crawling from her mouth and stretching across her face like the shimmering legs of some huge spider. And though her skin was darkening, a sickly white luminescence was leaking from her pupils, as though she was inverting light, turning into a negative version of herself. There was a sound coming from her too—a buzzing and crackling, like a swarm of angry electric bees. As Sue watched, the girl's form seemed to dissolve, to become so alien, so indefinable, that Sue found she could no longer even focus upon it. It was as if both her vision and her mind slid across its surface, making no impression, like a tiny blade on a vast diamond.

Sue whimpered and turned away, trying to keep her swimming thoughts together. Her hand groped across the concrete roof. Tears were streaming from her eyes, blinding her. With a vast effort she closed her hand around the handle of the gun, gritted her teeth to lift it, and screamed a long, rusty scream of pain as she twisted, gun-arm swinging round. With no hesitation she pointed the gun directly into Sam's face....

Other *Leisure* books by Mark Morris:

THE IMMACULATE

THE DELUGE

MARK MORRIS

LEISURE BOOKS NEW YORK CITY

A LEISURE BOOK®

December 2007

Published by

Dorchester Publishing Co., Inc.
200 Madison Avenue
New York, NY 10016

ISBN 10: 0-8439-5893-6
ISBN 13: 978-0-8439-5893-5

Printed in the United States of America.

10 9 8 7 6 5 4 3 2 1

Visit us on the web at www.dorchesterpub.com.

THE DELUGE

ONE

That night she had a dream that the world was shaking itself apart. And then she opened her eyes and found that it was true.

The first thing Abby saw was the silhouette of her dad, Steve, standing in the doorway of her bedroom. He was framed by the yellow light from the hallway, and his lanky form was trembling, vibrating. He put out a hand to steady himself against the door frame.

"Dad?" Abby said.

She sat up, and felt it then. Felt it properly for the first time. The rumbling. The shaking. Almost subliminal. Like some subterranean behemoth powering its way to the surface.

"Dad," she said, hearing the vibration in her own voice, "what's happening?"

"I don't know," he replied.

"Is it an earthquake?"

"I don't know. Maybe."

"But they don't *have* earthquakes in England. *Do they?*" she said, pleading for reassurance, for him to put everything right with a few words.

"No," he said, "not usually. But . . ."

"But what?"

He shrugged. "I don't know. Maybe with the greenhouse effect. Climatic change . . ."

Suddenly she felt angry. He was supposed to comfort her, not fuel her panic. *"Don't say that!"* she snapped.

The lights in the hall flickered, then came on again. For an instant her dad disappeared, sucked into the blackness. Abby gripped the bed, the sheet clasped in her hands. "Dad, I'm scared."

"Don't worry, sweetheart," he said, "I'm sure everything will be—"

The lights went out.

She screamed. For an instant she felt transfixed, paralyzed by the darkness. And then he was beside her, his hand—long-fingered and strong—reaching for hers in the darkness.

She could smell him now too—a reassuring Dad smell of shower gel, coffee, hand-rolled tobacco.

"Why have the lights gone out?" she whispered.

"I don't know, love."

"Is it terrorists?"

"I doubt it. It's probably just an earth tremor. Jiggered the power somewhere. We'll sit tight until it comes on again."

"What if it doesn't?"

"It will."

"But what if it *doesn't?*"

She sensed his face close to hers. He kissed her forehead. "I'll go and find some candles if you like. I'm sure I've got some in the kitchen."

She didn't want him to go, didn't want to be left alone in the dark, but she couldn't tell him that. She wasn't a kid anymore. She was thirteen, for God's sake. She went shopping in town with her mates on Saturdays; wore makeup; drank cappuccino; babysat for little Oliver, her neighbor's son, who kept telling her he would marry her one day.

"Nah," she said, trying to sound casual. "Like you said, they'll probably get it sorted in a minute."

They didn't though. The minutes passed and nothing

changed. They sat huddled in the dark and the rumbling went on, ominous as an oncoming storm. Abby's hand, clenched in Steve's, began to ooze sweat. Her back and neck ached with holding herself so tense.

"Dad?" she said finally.

"Yes, love."

"If it *is* an earthquake, shouldn't we move? I mean, isn't it dangerous being so high up?"

He didn't answer immediately. Then he said, "I think we're safer here than we would be on the ground."

"But what if the building falls down?"

"It won't."

"But what if it does?"

"Then it'd be the first time it had ever happened in England," he said.

"But there's a first time for everything," she said.

"True," he conceded. "But if buildings *are* going to start falling down all over the place, then do you honestly think it'd be safer to be on the streets of Peckham, getting flattened by collapsing masonry, than it would be to be sitting tight up here?"

Abby sighed. "I suppose not. But if this building *does* fall down, I'm blaming you."

"I promise to take full responsibility," he said solemnly.

They fell silent again, listening to the rumbling for a couple more minutes. Then Steve slipped his hand from hers.

"I think I *will* get those candles," he said. "Things won't seem so bad with a bit of light."

"Hurry up."

"I will." He touched her hot cheek. "Don't worry."

"I'm not worried," she said. "It's just . . ."

"Yeah, I know."

It was too dark to see him cross the room, but she tried to comfort herself by picturing it in her mind's eye. She knew that a few feet beyond the end of her bed was a wall, inset with a window that afforded a panoramic view of south London. To the left of that was a flat-pack wardrobe, enlivened by the William Morris–style stenciling she had spent a hot afternoon last summer spraying onto its doors. Much of the wall space was occupied by posters: Johnny Depp, the Killers, Pete Doherty, the White Stripes. She heard her dad clump down the hall and into the kitchen, then the sound of drawers opening and closing.

"Aha!" he exclaimed, and seconds later there came the scrape of a match, followed by a faint haze of brownish light. The light brightened and then a flame appeared at the end of the corridor and bobbed nearer. Abby could see her dad behind the flame, his long, handsome face ghoulish with shadow. He had rammed the candle into an empty beer bottle.

"Is that it?" she joked. "One measly candle?"

"Patience, my little viper," he said.

He crossed to her bedside table and put the bottle on it, moving her lamp so the paper shade didn't catch fire.

"Very classy," she said.

"Nothing but the best for you, my dear." He held up his left hand. There was a bottle attached to each finger.

"Not like you to have beer bottles around," she said, grinning.

"I know. I can't think where they came from."

He produced a half dozen candles of various sizes and colors from his pocket and stuffed them into the bottles. Once the candles had been arranged around the room and were giving off the oddly nostalgic smell of melting wax, Steve folded his lanky frame back onto the bed.

"Funny seeing them all lit up," he said. "It's like being haunted by my lurid past."

"What do you mean?"

"Well . . . the only time I get candles out is when I'm entertaining a lady friend. Each candle is therefore a symbol of a doomed assignation. A beacon of my failure."

"Poor you," said Abby. She knew there was little chance of her parents getting back together, but it still made her uncomfortable and sad to hear either of them talk of other relationships.

"Mind you, that one," her dad continued, nodding towards a chubby red candle, "brings back a few happy memories. Bridget Moxenby that one was. Bendy Bridget, they call her."

"Dad!" exclaimed Abby. "Too much information!"

He laughed. It was a warm, throaty laugh, like shingle shift-ing in a gentle tide. Steve's larynx had been roughened by booze and roll-ups, and by belting out R & B numbers with his band the Hogs in numerous backstreet pubs.

"You should be old enough to know the facts of life," he teased.

"I *do*," said Abby. "I just don't want to know the facts of *your* life."

He was about to reply, then suddenly paused, his mouth half open.

Abby had heard it too—a second sound, which had joined the rumbling. She thought of someone putting a finger to their lips and going *shhh*. Except it didn't sound like one person—it sounded like a thousand. Maybe a million.

"What is it?" she asked.

Her dad looked at her with a kind of wonderment. "It's water."

Instantly Abby realized he was right. It *was* water. The sound of an incoming tide magnified a thousandfold.

"It can't be," she said.

"No," Steve agreed, "it can't. But it is all the same. I'll bet my entire Ray Charles collection on it."

Abby's chest felt tight. She had never experienced dread before, but she thought she was experiencing it now. "What do you think's going on?" she said, her throat suddenly very dry. "Has the Thames burst its banks?"

"No rain."

"What then? A tsunami?"

"I don't know," Steve said, shrugging, and suddenly she wanted to shout at him: Why *don't you know? You're an adult! You* should *know!*

Instead, surprised at how calm she sounded, she said, "What are we going to do?"

"Sit it out," he said. "What else *can* we do?"

Abby watched the candlelight lapping at the walls. She grabbed her duvet and pulled it up to her chin. Steve's face was composed, lips set in a thin line, eyes shining yellow. The rushing sound and the rumbling grew slowly but steadily louder. Abby looked at her watch: twenty to five. Still two hours before daylight.

"Here it comes," Steve said.

Abby didn't need to ask him what he meant. Quite suddenly the rumbling and the rushing of water rose to a crescendo. She felt it in her chest: a pressure. A rapid, feathery drumming. The beer bottles on their various surfaces began to rattle. Something in another flat fell over with a distant crash.

"Dad!" Abby screamed and flung her arms around him.

A bottle worked its way to the edge of her dressing table and fell to the floor. The candle went out before it could set the carpet alight. Two more bottles fell over, and instantly the light in the room changed from a grimy yellow to a sepia brown.

Abby squeezed her eyes shut. We're going to die, she thought. We're going to die.

The certainty of that, in the midst of the shaking and the roaring, went on for a long time. Finally, however, Steve murmured, "Whatever it was, I think it's passed by."

Abby opened her eyes. She was surprised to see that three candles were still burning. She was also surprised to see a crack in the wall directly in front of her, running from floor to ceiling behind her poster of Johnny Depp.

"What was it?" she asked, knowing he had no answer.

"Freak storm? Passing meteorite? Biblical flood?"

"I can hear a cat drinking milk," she said.

She could, too. Or something like it. A great rhythmic lapping sound. A smacking of giant lips.

"Hang on," Steve said. Abruptly, he stood up. She sensed an urgency about him.

"What is it?"

He went to the window, pulled back the curtain and looked out. The glass looked as if it had been painted black. He pressed his nose up against it.

"Dad, what's the matter?"

He turned to look at her. He seemed scared and reluctant, as if he had bad news he didn't want to impart.

"I might be wrong, but . . ."

"But what?"

"I think it's water," he said, "slapping against the side of the building."

She looked at him in bewilderment. "But that's impossible."

"I know."

"But . . . but . . ." She took a deep breath. "So you're saying that part of the building is underwater?"

"Yes."

"How much of it?"

"I don't know. But even through the window it sounds pretty close. Like it's only a couple of floors down."

Dawn came slowly, wounds in the sky splitting open to reveal striations of purple, and then the glimmer of salmon pink light.

Abby and Steve set chairs by the window and watched the sunrise. The first rays reflected on the black solidity beneath the sill of their top-floor flat and became fragmented, glittering shards darting like shoals of tiny fish. As the sun rose higher, it revealed an impossible truth.

"No," Abby breathed.

"Fuck," Steve muttered, a word he barely used around his daughter.

The world was gone, and in its place was water. Thousands, millions, billions of gallons of water. It lapped gently against the upper floors of the few buildings tall enough to have remained visible. Buildings which now jutted from the surface of a new and terrible ocean like a smattering of curious islands.

TWO

.

Fuck, it was cold. Only September, but already it felt like the middle of winter. Max stood on the roof, looking out over the city, and wondered what to do. In truth, his choice was simple. He could either stay up here on top of the hospital in the middle of what felt like a fucking earthquake or he could open the access door on the roof and risk having a bunch of Nazi psychos beat the shit out of him, or worse.

He shook his head. Why the fuck had he let them chase him up here? He was supposed to be smart (didn't Ma always say he was smart?), and yet here he was, like a rat in a trap, nowhere to go but straight into the clutches of the Nazi psychos who had stabbed his brother.

If they were still there. And, to be honest, it was a big if. Twenty minutes ago Max had shouted through the door that he'd rung the cops, and one of the Nazis had said that if they couldn't get to Max they'd get to Noel instead, and this time they'd finish the job. They'd make sure Noel was one fucking nigger who would never run from them again.

Max told himself it was a bluff. Noel was in surgery, and probably would be for a while. And afterwards he'd be looked after—intensive care, someone watching over him all the time. He'd be safe.

Even so . . .

Max wished he *had* called the cops. He'd tried a few times, but on each occasion he'd got the same incredible message: no network coverage. What the fuck was *that* about? He was in the middle of London, for fuck's sake! All he could think was that it was maybe something to do with this freaky earthquake thing that was happening.

Afterwards, unable to use his mobile, he had looked for another way off the building—a fire escape, something like that. But there had been nothing, which was a total fucking piss-off. Wasn't it illegal not to have a fire escape?

He was now sitting against the access door, the hood of his gray sweat shirt pulled over his head. He looked at his watch, the one Mum had bought him for his sixteenth birthday. He couldn't believe that only two hours ago he and Noel had been at Moog's, listening to music and shooting the shit. What was that saying? The past is another country? Two hours ago he'd been happy, and now he was stuck up on this fucking roof and Noel was at death's door, for all he knew.

He thought back to what had happened earlier. The four white guys had been in the playground across the road when Max and Noel had walked past on their way home. Max hadn't even noticed them until Noel said, "Uh-oh."

"What?" said Max.

"Trouble."

The Nazis had shoved open the gate in the chain-link fence that bordered the playground. Soon as he saw them Max knew Noel was right.

"Don't stare, bruv," Noel muttered.

"I wasn't," said Max.

"Oi, niggers," one of the white guys shouted.

Max and Noel ignored him.

"Oi," the guy shouted again. He was heavyset with a stubbly head, bad teeth, a tattoo beneath his right eye. "Oi, I'm talking to you, you black bastards."

Noel and Max picked up their pace. One of the gang threw something. A piece of metal. Max heard it hit the wall behind him.

"Don't fucking ignore me, nigger," Tattoo Face said.

Noel turned to face the guys, walking backwards. "We don't want no trouble, man."

"Come to the wrong fucking place then, haven't you?"

They surged across the street. "Run!" Noel shouted. Max didn't need telling. He turned and sped off. He knew he could outrun these guys easily. He was the golden boy of his local athletics club in Wandsworth; there was even talk of the 2012 Olympics. But that didn't stop him from being scared. Adrenaline was flooding his system, and he knew from his training that if he didn't use it properly, harness the glucose and lipids surging in his blood, then he'd quickly feel drained and jittery. But it wasn't just that. There was also Noel to think of. Noel was two years older and tougher than Max, but he smoked too much weed and drank too much rum and he wasn't as fast as his brother.

Max sprinted a hundred meters, then glanced back. Noel was fifteen meters behind him, and the fastest of the Nazis was lumbering ten meters back from that. Max was using his adrenaline like grade-A fuel. It was making him feel confident, even euphoric. *We'll outrun these fuckers easy,* he thought. He almost felt like laughing.

And then Noel slipped.

Running it back through his head now, Max almost saw it in slow motion. He saw Noel beside the bus stop he himself had passed seconds before; saw rubbish spilling into the gutter from the overflowing bin; saw Noel's foot come down on a KFC box and slide from under him; saw Noel's hand grab for the edge of the bus shelter to keep himself upright; saw Noel go down in a heap, legs and arms still moving even as he fell, trying to propel himself back to his feet; saw Noel succeed in getting to his feet—though not quite quickly enough to prevent the fucking ape behind him from catching up.

What Max *didn't* see was the knife. He saw the guy's arm

come round and heard a thud as his fist made contact with Noel's ribs. But then Noel was running again and the guy was already falling away, his energy seemingly spent in that one clumsy punch. Max waited for his brother, and then the two of them crossed the road and turned down Essex Street. Max would happily have run all the way home, but when they reached the entrance to an alley, a long black throat ending God knows where, Noel thudded to a halt and gasped, "In here."

Max thought Noel was just winded, and told him to keep going, but Noel was already limping into the alley. They hid behind a skip three-quarters of the way down. They remained silent for a minute or so, Max listening for sounds of pursuit. Then Noel said quietly, "You'd better call an ambulance, man."

Max glanced at his brother, surprised. "What for?" he asked.

Noel pulled his jacket open. There was blood all over his shirt and hand. Running down the leg of his jeans. Pooling on the floor.

"Oh, fuck," Max said.

"I'll be okay," Noel told him. Then he turned his head to the side and threw up.

Max traveled with Noel to the hospital, jogged behind the trolley they used to clank his brother up the corridors to emergency surgery. He would have gone into the operating room too if a pretty nurse hadn't stopped him at the door, squeezed his shoulder and said, "Why don't you get yourself a coffee? We'll let you know as soon as there's news."

The waiting area was a big space filled with rows of brown leather seats. It was three in the morning, but there were still people around. There was one gray-haired guy in a red dressing gown whose white shins were knobbly with blue veins, but he was the only one who looked like a patient. The others were ordinary people like him, whose loved ones had been whacked by the big stick of fate on this particular night.

Against a section of wall close to the hospital's main doors were a couple of vending machines—one for drinks, the other for snacks. It was as Max walked across to the drinks machine that he noticed the shaking for the first time. It registered as a vibration beneath his feet, as if there was a vast and powerful engine beneath the floor of the hospital. *Weird,* he thought, punching in the numbers for tea with extra sugar. He looked up as the hospital's main doors hissed open. Instantly a fist of ice clenched in his guts as the Nazi psychos entered the building.

Nothing was said. There was nothing *to* say. Max saw Tattoo Face spot him, saw his expression change from dumb hostility to the invigorated rage of a predator. As the Nazis came for him, he scooped his mostly filled cup out of the drinks machine and hurled its contents into Tattoo Face's face. The Nazi roared as he was blinded by boiling tea. Before he could recover, Max turned and ran.

He ran across the waiting area and turned right at the back of the room. He went that way purely because Noel had been taken left to the operating theatre, and Max wanted to lead them as far away from his brother as possible. The right-hand corridor was full of obstacles—patients, nurses, a discarded wheelchair. Max dodged them with ease, but gathered from the cries of alarm and protest behind him that the Nazis were not so nimble. There came a roar from behind him: "We'll get you, you fucking black cunt. We'll fucking hunt you down."

At the end of the corridor, Max turned right, then left, then right again. Fast as he was, he couldn't seem to shake the gang off, could still hear them on his tail. The corridors were featureless, and aside from ducking through a door with no way of knowing what was on the other side there was nowhere to hide. He rounded another corner, looking for the next turning, the next exit, the next escape route—and suddenly there wasn't one. He had come to what he'd dreaded: a dead end.

Well, not *quite* a dead end. There was a ward in front of him, but even from here Max could see through the open double doors that most of the beds were occupied by old people, mainly women. Whatever happened, he knew he couldn't go in there. If he did, the Nazis would just bulldoze their way in behind him, and if they caught him they'd beat the crap out of him whatever the audience.

He looked around. Halfway down the corridor was a lift and a door into a stairwell. The lift was twenty meters away. He ran towards it. He was almost there when the gang came round the corner.

Shit. Suddenly the lift was no longer an option. As the gang yelled in triumph and came for him again, Max grabbed the handle of the heavy fire door and yanked it open.

He was still on the ground floor, which meant there was only one way to go. He took the stairs three at a time, using the handrail to haul himself up. He'd climbed a dozen steps when the fire door below flew open and the Nazis crashed through it like a tornado.

Max continued to ascend, his only plan being to build up enough of a lead to slip through a door into a corridor without the Nazis knowing. But they were too close to him, their cries tearing at his ears, their footsteps pounding at his heels, and so up he went, and up again, and up once more. He carried on clattering up flight after flight until suddenly, in his panic, he realized there was nowhere left to go.

He was at the top of the building. There were no more stairs ahead of him. There was nothing but a square landing of bare concrete, and a door to his left, stout but old-looking, a chunky key in the lock.

He didn't have time to think about what to do. He crossed to the door and twisted the key in the lock. Feverish with urgency, he pulled open the door and slipped through the narrow gap. He turned back to lock it behind him, and for an agonizing second the key slithered around the lock as if reluctant to go in before sliding home.

Seconds later something crashed against the door from the other side. Max stepped back, expecting to see wood splinter, but the door held. When he was certain that it wouldn't fly from its hinges with a single kick, he looked around. He was on the hospital roof, which was big enough to have accommodated two football pitches with room to spare.

He tried calling the cops, which was when he got the message on his display screen telling him there was no network coverage. He walked around the roof, looking for another way down, only to discover he was out of luck. Finally he decided there was only one thing left to try. He walked back to the access door, which was thankfully still standing. The gang's previously frenzied attack had abated a little, but the threats were still coming, loud and clear and nasty as ever.

"You're one dead nigger," he was told. "You won't get away from us, you little black cunt."

Yeah, yeah, Max thought. But a pulse fluttered in his throat.

"I've called the cops," he shouted, glad his voice didn't betray his fear.

His words were answered with a renewed barrage of blows and threats, which he tried to ignore. "They'll be here any minute," he added.

"Just in time to scrape you off the fucking pavement then, nigger," one of the Nazis replied.

There were a few more kicks and thumps on the door and then Max heard the Nazis talking amongst themselves. He heard—thought he heard—the word "brother." He stepped a little closer, and then jumped as one of the Nazis shouted, "Your card is fucking marked, boy. You're a dead man walking. We're gonna pay your brother a visit and then we'll be back for you. Your fucking brother is one nigger who'll never be able to run from us again."

That had been a while ago. Max had heard their footsteps receding, and since then there had been silence. He'd listened and heard nothing, but even now he wondered if maybe a couple of them had stayed behind and were currently crouching on the other side of the door ready to jump him.

Eventually, trying not to sound nervous, he said, "I know you're still there, you arseholes. And you must be even more stupid than you look if you think I'm opening this door."

Silence. Nothing but the freaky rumble quivering up through Max's feet. After a moment he said, "I can hear you, you brain-dead freaks. I can hear you breathing. Whatever you do to me and my brother, it won't stop you being losers for the rest of your crap little lives."

Still nothing. *Okay,* Max thought, *here we go.* He reached for the key . . .

And turned it just as the lights went out over London.

THREE

"There's no water," Abby said.

Steve would have laughed at that if he could have guaranteed he'd be able to stop. Ostensibly he was calm—sitting by his daughter's open window, smoking a roll-up and watching the smoke drift on the breeze—but beneath the surface was a well of hysteria. He could feel it like a fever beneath his skin, like something wild with directionless energy, wanting to break free.

This water should not be here. His mind recoiled from the impossibility of it; his every instinct screamed at him to curl into a ball and squeeze his eyes tight shut until the world returned to normal.

"What do you want it for?" he called. As if he were asking a normal question on a normal day.

"I wanted a wash." She padded into the bedroom in her lilac nightshirt with COOL CHICK emblazoned across the front. She was a striking girl, tall for her age, with tousled blond hair and plump red lips. Her looks dazzled and alarmed Steve in equal measure. He knew what boys were like, and pretty soon she'd have hordes of them, drooling and desperate, sniffing at her heels. That is, if she didn't already.

Hang on. Reality check. She *would* have had them sniffing at her heels if it hadn't been for this. But now . . . who knew what was going to happen? With London underwater all bets were off. It was terrifying to think that the future was suddenly a blank page, that everything they had taken for granted had been snatched away in a few hours. And even worse was the fact that it had been snatched away by something with no boundaries, no context, no rationale. Because if you couldn't understand what was happening, how could you develop a sense of perspective about it?

Steve had spent the last few hours trying to come up with explanations. What climactic catastrophe could have caused London, possibly even the whole country, to sink beneath the waves? Had the polar ice caps suddenly collapsed like a house of cards? Was that possible? Steve knew about global warming, but like most people he was too caught up in the day-to-day minutiae of his own life to give the subject anything more than lip service.

"Dad?" Abby said. "What shall I do?"

"About what?"

She rolled her eyes. "About having a wash."

"There's some water in the kettle. You could use that. Hang on, though," he said as she turned to go. "Maybe we ought to save our fresh water."

"For drinking, you mean?"

"Yeah."

"What, and not wash?" She screwed up her nose. "That's pretty gross."

He shrugged. "Priorities. Don't worry, it'll probably only be for today. Someone's bound to come and rescue us soon."

"You think they'll send boats?"

"Maybe. Or helicopters."

"Cool." Her eyes shone. "I think I'll still brush my teeth. I just won't use water."

"Good idea."

It was amazing, thought Steve, how quickly the young adapted to crisis. Maybe Abby was simply accepting things on face value, but even so, it wasn't a bad way to be. What was the point of expending energy trying to come up with reasons, theories, explanations? How would that help them deal with practical problems—finding food, water, dry land?

Abby returned ten minutes later, looking pleased with herself. "I found these in my bag," she said, handing him a shiny white package. "I forgot I had them."

"Wet wipes," said Steve. "Aren't they for babies' arses?"

She punched him on the shoulder. "I get makeup off with them. But we can use them to wash our important little places."

She said it so primly that he laughed.

"I went to the loo just now," she said. "The toilet flushed, but the cistern didn't fill up again."

He sighed. "There's some practical stuff we need to talk about," he said.

She perched on the bed. Her narrow jeans made her legs look long and slim.

"All right," he said, "this is the situation. We're surrounded by water, so we're stuck for now. We've got no power, which means we can't cook or listen to music or watch TV. It also means the fridge and the freezer are off, so we'd better eat the fresh food first. I've got tins in the cupboard, so we'll be okay for a while, though we might have to eat soup and beans and stuff cold."

She pulled a face but said nothing.

"But we don't know how long we're going to be here, so we should eat sparingly. The same goes for drinks. There's water in the kettle, plus there's bottled water, orange juice, Coke and booze."

"How long do you think we can make it all last?"

Steve hunched his shoulders. "A week, maybe two."

"That's all right then. We won't be here that long."

"What makes you so sure?"

"We'll have been rescued by then, won't we, dummy? As soon as people realize what's happened they'll send boats and helicopters and stuff."

Steve smiled. It would do no good to express his doubts and fears at present. "Yeah," he said. He flicked the butt of his roll-up out the window and watched it bob away on the flowing water eight feet below.

"I wonder if Mum knows what's happened," said Abby.

"Bound to," Steve said.

"I wish I could call her."

"Phone still not working?"

Abby picked up her lemon yellow mobile from the bedside table. "It still says 'no network coverage.' I thought mobile signals bounced off satellites in space?"

"They do. I think."

"So how come they're not working? Space isn't affected by all this water, is it?"

There were times when Steve realized how little he knew about technology, about how the world worked. "Maybe the signals have to be collected by some sort of receiver on the ground."

Abby swung her legs from the bed and moved across to join him at the window. Instantly Steve raised a hand to hold her back. "I wouldn't."

"I only want to look out of the window."

"I know. It's just . . . I don't think it's a good idea."

She looked at him steadily. "You've seen dead people, haven't you?"

He hesitated, thought about lying, then nodded. "Some, yeah."

"How many?"

"A few."

In fact, it was more like dozens, perhaps even hundreds. Even now, several hours after seeing the first one, his heart still lurched whenever he saw a man or woman or—especially—child float by. It was particularly awful when they were on their backs so he could see their faces. Most of the drowned wore nightclothes, or were seminaked or naked. Some of the bodies were damaged, buffeted by obstacles encountered on their final journey or by the other debris that choked the water—trees, paper, clothes, furniture, bits of houses . . . myriad belongings from myriad lives. Earlier an old woman's body had come to rest below the window, her journey temporarily halted by the building in her path. Steve had watched in horrified fascination as her hand had flailed languidly from the water as if she were halfheartedly seeking help. He had watched her white nightdress billow obscenely up her legs to expose her mottled thighs. He had watched her gray hair spread out like some colorless undersea plant. Worst of all, he had caught glimpses of her face—eyeballs white and glaring, mouth yawning blackly open in a final soundless scream.

Abby was nodding sagely now. "I guess some people are bound to have died," she said.

"A lot, I'd say," said Steve cautiously.

"How many, do you reckon?"

He shrugged, wondered what percentage of London's population had been up high enough to have survived when the wave had hit. Five percent? One? Less? He wondered how much warning there had been, whether the royal family had survived, or the government. He wondered how many landmarks had gone, how many buildings had been destroyed, how many years of history had been obliterated in the space of a few hours. And what of the media, the monetary system, the transport networks, the lines of communication? What of *civilization*?

Steve was aware that his heart was pounding. Pounding with a fear that was almost primal.

"Are you all right, Dad?" Abby asked.

He tried to pull himself together, to smile. "Fine," he said.

"You don't *look* fine."

"I just . . . need something to eat, that's all. What time is it?"

"Half past ten."

"There you are, then. We've missed breakfast."

It felt unreal to be sitting at the kitchen table eating cornflakes. The fridge had only been off a few hours, so the milk was still okay. The cereal made him feel better, but Steve couldn't help wondering when he'd next taste milk after these last couple of pints had gone. *I could murder a cup of tea,* he thought; then inspiration struck him.

"What are you doing?" Abby asked as he crossed the kitchen and dropped to his knees in front of the cupboard beneath the sink. He opened the cupboard door and was delighted to see that the camping stove was still there. He knew that in the great scheme of things this was an inconsequential triumph, but he couldn't help wondering whether this was what their lives would consist of now—a series of little victories, small steps to ease the way.

"Cool," Abby said as he brandished the stove like a trophy. "Does that mean we won't have to eat cold beans after all?"

"It does indeed," said Steve. "And, most importantly, it means we can have a nice cup of tea. I think I've even got some extra gas canisters somewhere."

He made the tea and they carried their mugs into the living room, which consisted of a ratty old settee, an armchair, a wide-screen TV and DVD player with various discs stacked haphazardly beneath them, a state-of-the-art sound system with speakers strategically placed for maximum effect, and floor to ceiling shelves covering every available wall space and containing thousands of carefully alphabetized CDs.

Indicating the walls, Abby said, "Told you to get an iPod."

"Thanks," Steve said gloomily, "that's a big help." It had already occurred to him to wonder when, if ever, he would get a chance to listen to music again.

"What about the shop?" Abby asked.

Steve raised an eyebrow. "I don't think I'll be opening today."

"No, but . . . oh, God, Dad, it'll be underwater. All your stuff!"

He shrugged. "It's just stuff. People are more important."

It was true. The loss of his music shop, less than a mile down the road, was small potatoes compared to all the people who had lost their lives. Even so, Steve couldn't help but feel a pang at the thought of what had become of his Motown concert posters from the sixties, the rare record sleeves that he'd lovingly framed and hung on the walls, and—oh, Jesus— his genuine Jimi Hendrix guitar string, which he'd kept in a polythene zip bag in his little safe below the counter, and which he'd produced now and again for the delectation and awe of likeminded enthusiasts.

Before he could dwell too deeply on his loss, however, there came a knock on the door.

Astonished, Steve said, "Who the hell's that?"

"Postman?" suggested Abby.

"Mr. Marshall?" The voice was shrill, cracked with age and fear. "Mr. Marshall, are you there?"

"It's Mrs. Beamish from across the hall," said Steve. "My God, I'd forgotten about them."

He went into the narrow hallway, breaking into a trot at the renewed flurry of banging. "It's all right, Mrs. Beamish, I'm here," he cried.

Mrs. Beamish was a small, stout woman in her seventies with a jowly face and a feathery busbee of coral-colored hair. "Oh, Mr. Marshall!" she exclaimed as he opened the door, and reached out to enclose his long-fingered hands in her gnarled, arthritic ones. "Whatever's happened? There are so many dead people!"

"Yes, it is a bit grim, isn't it," Steve said. "Listen, Mrs. B, why don't you come in and have a cuppa? I've got Abby here from Scotland. She's staying over for a few days."

"Oh, I can't leave George," Mrs. Beamish said, pulling away. "He's not well, you know. His heart . . ."

"I'll fetch George," Steve said. "Go on, make yourself comfortable."

He escorted her into the lounge, then hurried along the hallway and onto the landing. It was the first time he had stepped out of the flat since the flood, and immediately he was struck by the echoing slap of water from below. The landing was dark—the only illumination came from the diffused daylight leaking from the flat's open door—and when Steve looked over the banister he saw nothing but blackness. Then his eyes adjusted and he realized that the darkness was moving, slivers of light darting and shimmering on its surface.

Water, he thought. *It's water.* Ludicrously, it only now occurred to him that the building would be full of it. With everything else to contend with he simply hadn't considered that beneath his top-floor flat were dozens of others that had been transformed from cosy havens into watery tombs in the early hours of this morning.

He thought of the people who must have met their deaths when the wave struck. There was Nina and her cute-as-buttons daughters, Sapphire and Althea, two floors below; there was Pete Villiers, who made coffee and cleared tables at Starbucks but whose real ambition was to work in the music industry; there were the Lockwoods, who ran an online business selling surf gear and handmade jewellery, and who lavished total and unconditional love on their ten-year-old autistic son, Ben.

All those lives, snuffed out, abruptly and irrevocably. The vast and terrible tragedy of it was suddenly almost too much to bear. Steve felt his mind struggling to shut down those avenues of thought, which threatened to overwhelm him. Telling himself he shouldn't—he *mustn't*—dwell, he crossed the landing to the partly open door that mirrored his.

"Mr. Beamish," he called. "It's Steve, from across the hall."

The voice that answered was a rusty croak. "In here, son."

The old man was lying on the settee, a tartan blanket covering the lower half of his body. Like its occupant, the room was past its best. The pictures on the walls were faded by sunlight, the carpet was threadbare, the furniture lumpy and worn. Even the air seemed old, gray with cigarette smoke and the smell of musty confinement.

"How you doin', Mr. B?" Steve asked. The Beamishes had lived here since the flats were built in 1971. They had chosen the top floor because, as George Beamish had once explained to Steve, "It makes you feel like a king, son, living here. After a hard day's graft you look out your window and see

London, the best city in the world, spread out below you. Our ivory tower—that's what we've always called this place, Mabel and me."

Now George looked up, face wrinkled like an old turtle's. His clenched hands trembled as if he were rattling dice in them. His breath whistled in his throat. Beside him were boxes of pills, an inhaler, a glass ashtray heaped with cigarette butts, and a plastic cup with a drinking straw protruding from its domed lid.

"I'm doing better than most of the poor sods out there," he said, gesturing towards the window. "It's a fucker of a do, this, Steve, ain't it?"

"It is indeed," said Steve.

George nodded and cheerfully croaked, "This'll be the end of me, you know, son."

"Nah," said Steve. "Help's bound to arrive soon."

"And if it don't?"

Then we'll all *be goners,* Steve thought. "It will."

He half carried George to his own flat and deposited him on the settee next to his wife before going back for the old man's paraphernalia. George had not been well even twelve years previous when Steve had moved into his flat. But at least George had still been working then—he had just celebrated his thirtieth anniversary with the London postal service. It was a year later when he had suffered his first heart attack and had to be rushed to King's College Hospital for an emergency bypass. He had been forced to give up work, and in the last decade had had two further heart attacks and four operations, one to remove a benign tumor from his lung. The old geezer took so many pills that, as he had remarked to Steve, "I sound like a baby's rattle whenever I turn over in bed." Despite his health problems, he still smoked fifty Regal a day. High tar, naturally.

When Steve returned to his flat pushing George's wheel-chair, which he had loaded with the old man's medication, he found Abby handing mugs of tea to the two pensioners.

"We need to make a list of what to take with us when we

go," she said. "Food and water and spare clothes and medicine. Stuff like that."

"When we go?" Steve said. "Where do you think we're going to go *to*?"

"I mean when we get rescued. The thing is, what if it isn't the army who rescues us? What if it's just someone in a boat?"

Steve was about to say that the likelihood of them being rescued by a passing stranger was virtually nil, when he registered the light of hope and purpose in her eyes. And he realized she was right. Even if it would take a miracle to get them out of this, they still ought to be prepared for it.

"Good idea," he said. "I've got a couple of rucksacks."

"And I've thought of something else," Abby said. "We ought to paint 'Help' on a bedsheet and hang it out the window. Then if anyone's passing they'll know we're here."

"There's no flies on that girl of yours, is there, son?" George cackled, hands curled like bird talons around his steaming mug.

Steve wished the old man had chosen a phrase that reminded him less of what fate might hold in store for them, but he forced himself to grin. "No, Mr. B," he said, "no flies at all."

FOUR

The dinner-party people were gone. But how *could* they be? They wouldn't have left her behind, would they? Maybe they had attempted to escape on the "raft" (in reality a leaky, splintered door from a barn or grain silo) that had miraculously delivered the little girl to them, soaking and terrified, yesterday afternoon. Maybe all seven of them had tried to get to Sue while she was sleeping and come to grief in the fast-flowing water. . . . No, she could see the "raft," still jutting from the section of roof onto which they had dragged it. Maybe they were all asleep then, out of sight. Maybe they'd seen the blue lightning and had taken shelter under what they could find—the dining table, the chairs—thinking a storm was coming. Sue strode to the edge of her roof and stared across the watery divide, hoping to see a hunched shape, a stir of movement.

"Hey!" she shouted. "Is anyone there?"

No reply. Nothing but the thin hiss of the September wind and the liquid mutter of the water.

Shivering, she pulled her blanket tighter around her shoulders and watched dawn breaking on the horizon. Fingers of salmon light stretched towards the strips of maroon cloud overhead. Any other time it would have been beautiful, but here and now Sue could only wonder how many more dawns she would see, how many days before she starved to death or died of hyperthermia.

She ate breakfast —cheese and crackers, an apple, several sips of water—and thought about the blue lightning. It had been terrible and wondrous. A natural phenomenon or . . . or what? When she tried to figure out what had happened to her world, her mind shied away, like a horse spooked by a snake. She knew the flood defied logic, and yet she tried to convince herself that the Thames barrier had simply collapsed and that the resulting deluge had something to do with global warming. It was a vague theory, but it would do for now. After all, it wasn't as if she *needed* to know how the disaster had happened. All she really needed to concentrate on was how she was going to survive.

She wished the dinner-party people were still there. She had always regarded herself as pretty self-sufficient, but their sudden disappearance made Sue feel lonelier than she ever had in her life. *Maybe,* she thought, *I'm the last person on earth.* She knew it was a crazy idea, but the part of her mind given to wild fancies and childish fears picked at the notion like a scab. She tried to clamp her mind on the thought as if it were a buzzing fly she had caught in her fist. And then suddenly, astonishing even herself, she jumped up, ran to the edge of the roof and screamed, *"Where are you? Where the fuck have you gone?"*

Almost as suddenly as the rage had seized her it seeped away. Sue shuffled back to her little camp in the center of the roof and sank down with a groan. "For fuck's sake, Stark," she muttered, "pull yourself together." Once again she looked across the water at the next roof. The party people and the girl must have gone over the side. There was no other explanation. *Why* they had done so was a mystery, but that must be what they had done.

Was it really only twenty-seven hours since the lights had gone out? Sue had finished her shift at 2 A.M., come home, cooked some scrambled eggs and was watching TV when everything went black. Not long before that the shaking and rumbling had started. Sue had been watching *News 24* in the hope of finding out what was going on. But there'd been nothing. No reports of earth tremors, no news of an approaching wave. The flood had come suddenly and unexpectedly, seemingly catching everyone cold.

The apartment block had filled up quickly, the water level rising by several inches a second. It had been sneaky too, not smashing into the building like a giant fist, but engulfing everything smoothly and rapidly, with a sound that was soothing, even gentle. It was almost as if the water wanted to catch its victims unawares, drown as many as possible before they even knew the deluge was upon them. Sue might have been drowned too if she hadn't decided to visit Stan, the caretaker, who lived in flat 1 on the ground floor.

Stan was the landlord's brother-in-law, and he owned a portable radio that ran on batteries rather than electricity, and which he carried around with him when he was doing odd jobs so he could listen to the test match or football. He was often still awake when Sue came back from the night shift, and tonight had been no exception. As she had passed his door she had seen light leaking from beneath it, heard the murmur of his television. When the power went off and the soft rushing began, she decided to go and ask him if there was any news on the radio, anything that might give them some clue as to what was going on.

She got two floors down in the dark, slowly feeling her way along the walls, when she felt her slippered foot sink ankle-deep into cold water. She jerked her foot backwards with a small splash, and then, heart thumping, crouched down and gingerly stretched a hand out in front of her.

The fact that there was water there at all was alarming, but more alarming still was her realization that it was swiftly rising. Within seconds water was brimming over the step she was standing on and she had to step smartly back onto the next one.

Her mind actually reeled as she realized that if the water had risen this high so quickly, then most of the surrounding area, if not the city, must have been submerged. But that was impossible! An hour or so before, when she had arrived home, the streets had been dry.

She scrambled back up the stairs in the dark, blundered her way to her flat. She hammered on doors as she went, yelling to wake the occupants of the flats that were still above water level. She didn't have time to wait for their responses, however. The water was rising too quickly. She could hear it, gurgling and hissing as it ascended the stairs like something alive.

Her only thought was to get out of the building, and the only way she could do that was to go up. At least there she wouldn't be hampered by ceilings and walls. If the water rose higher than the building, then at least she would be out in the open with a slim but better chance of survival.

First, though, she needed to be as prepared as she possibly could be. For a long time Sue had held a secret ambition to be part of an expedition in which she would be required to push herself to her limits, and to that end she had become an experienced camper, mountaineer and sailswoman in the last few years. Plus she worked out in the gym three times a week and read as much survivalist literature as she could lay her hands on. The only thing she hadn't done was put her theory and training into practice, but if this wasn't the ideal opportunity to do that, she didn't know what was.

Moving around in her dark flat, the water just minutes behind her, she tried to clear her head. One of the main tenets of survival was not to panic. Another was to prepare yourself as thoroughly as possible in the time available, no matter how hopeless the situation might seem. All right, so in the next ten minutes Sue *might* be swept away and drowned in the water that was (impossibly) filling the building. But if she *was* going to die, then at least she would go with the knowledge that she had done all she could to prevent it.

Right, she thought as she groped in the dark for her rucksack and the ten essentials of survival. The list of recommended items varied from person to person, but the general consensus was this:

One: A map of the surrounding area. Well, that seemed pretty irrelevant for a start.

Two: A compass. Ditto.

Three: A torch. She already had a good one in her rucksack, together with spare batteries (she grimaced at her own incompetence in not thinking about that earlier; such fundamental errors could mean the difference between life and death).

Four: Sunglasses. Ha ha. Next.

Five: Food and water. Even as she was running the list in her head she was already making her way to the kitchen, the beam of the torch from her rucksack probing ahead of her. She filled the rucksack with tins and packets and a minimum of perishables, with plastic bottles of water, cutlery, a can opener, and a sharp knife.

Six: Extra clothes. Underwear and socks, hard-wearing trousers that dried quickly (no denim), T-shirts, thermal tops, and rain gear. Plus a blanket and a sheet of plastic, and a good pair of boots which she'd wear rather than pack.

Seven: Matches. Already in the rucksack. Good long kitchen matches. Three boxes.

Eight: Firestarters. Already in the rucksack too.

Nine: Pocket knife. Ditto.

Ten: First aid kit. Ditto again.

By the time she vacated her flat the water was seeping along her corridor like a dark, creeping fungus. She yelled again, but there was no answer from Bob Knott's flat across the corridor. Maybe he was staying at his boyfriend's. Sue hoped he was safe.

She went up onto the roof. There was a biting wind (*A sea-breeze,* she thought), and in the darkness the stars were dazzling. She turned in a slow circle, casting a cone of torchlight before her. Behind her—How far away? Fifty feet? A hundred?—there was another apartment block. And there were people on its roof, a half dozen of them, lit by the yellowish light of flickering candles in glass shades.

At first Sue thought they had fled from the encroaching water just as she had. Then she noticed the table with its white tablecloth, adorned not only with the glass-shaded candles, but also with several empty wine bottles. And she took in the makeshift awning erected above it, and the clothes the people were wearing—the men in tuxedos, the women in evening gowns. And she noted too their general air of garrulousness, of drunken bonhomie. And with a peculiar shock that was half horror, half amusement, she realized that this was not an exodus, but a dinner party. These people had come up to the roof to celebrate something—a birthday, an anniversary, a new job, a promotion. Their presence here was not calculated, but merely serendipitous.

Do they even realize what is happening below them? Sue wondered. They must have heard the rumbling and the rushing of water, felt the ground trembling beneath their feet. "Hey!" she shouted. "Hey!" But she couldn't make herself heard above the water and the raucous laughter of the party people. She waved her torch back and forth, to no avail. Eventually she turned away and sat down.

Oh well, she thought, they would find out in due course. There wasn't much she could do anyway, and if this *was* the end, then she supposed it was better to go in a state of happy inebriation than to sit, hopeless and isolated as she was, waiting for the inevitable. She knew that one of the keys to survival was to keep your head clear and your wits about you at all times. But as she listened to the water creeping up the sides of the building, Sue couldn't help but wish she was on the next roof, guzzling wine and laughing in the face of the apocalypse.

FIVE

My name is Abigail Louise Marshall. I am 13 years old. I was born in London, but now live in a town in Scotland called Castle Morton with my mum, Jackie, and my older brother, Dylan, who is 16. At the moment I'm in London, visiting my dad, Steve, cos it's half term. Back home in Castle Morton I go to St. Catherine's Girls' High School, and am in year 9. My best friends are Chloe Roeves and Martha Newman. My hobbies are horse-riding, swimming, reading, going to the cinema and anything to do with 'Buffy the Vampire Slayer.'

    I've decided to write this diary because something awful has happened and we don't know what's going to happen to us. Last year at school we read Scott of the Antarctic's journal, and this is supposed to be a bit like that. It will tell you about the flood and what happens after, and about how we live and where we go. At the end of Scott's journal he dies, frozen in a tent in the middle of a blizzard. I hope I don't die, but if I do, I hope this diary is found by someone who reads it and maybe learns something about us, and who maybe even tells our loved ones what happened to us (if they're still alive).

It's day 3 after the flood. On Sunday night I woke up and the block of flats where Dad lives was shaking, and we thought there was an earthquake. Then the lights went out and Dad got some candles, and after a while we heard this sort of whooshing noise, and when it got light the next morning virtually the whole of London was underwater. There were only the tops of a few buildings sticking up, including our block of flats. If dad's flat hadn't been on the top floor we would have drowned like all the thousands of other people.

It's horrible looking out the window, and I try to stop myself from doing it. Sometimes, tho, I can't help myself. Every time I look there are bodies going past. Yesterday I saw a body of a baby that was all purple, and sometimes they're not even whole bodies cos things in the water have been eating them. It's totally gross and it makes me feel sick just thinking about it.

There are not just bodies going past, tho, there are other things too. We've seen wood and trees and paper and plastic and twisted bits of metal and parts of buildings, and there have been lots of cars and vans and lorries. Yesterday we saw a big red bus go past, turning over in the water, with all this slimy seaweed sticking to its wheels. And there have been chairs and settees and cushions and TVs and animals— dogs and cats, mainly, but Dad said he'd also seen a horse.

When it first happened I thought the police would come or the army with helicopters or boats and pick up all the survivors. Dad said he had food and water to last us for a week or 2, and he even found a camping stove so we could cook stuff. I thought the worst thing would be that we'd be bored cos we wouldn't be able to go anywhere or do anything. There's no power so we can't watch TV or listen to music. And there's no water in the taps or the toilet, so we can't wash properly or brush our teeth and we have to do our business in a bucket and chuck it out the window.

Me and Dad aren't on our own, tho. Across the landing are Mr. and Mrs. Beamish, who have lived here for years. They're really nice, but Mr. Beamish has got something wrong with his heart and he has to take loads of tablets, and he can't walk very far (he gets about in a wheelchair most of the time). He's still cheerful, tho, but you can tell Mrs. Beamish is worried about him. Yesterday she told Dad that if his tablets ran out then he'd die. But I said to Dad that if our food and *water ran out then we'd all die anyway. Dad laughed and said not to worry, that we would get rescued. I could tell he was only saying that to make me feel better. I think he thinks I don't really know how serious all this stuff is, but I do. I knew that if we didn't get rescued we'd starve to death. But I always thought something would happen, and now it has.*

This morning when I woke up I could tell something was different. Even tho I don't like doing it, I went to the window and looked out. I looked at the next tall building, which was quite a way away, and at first I wasn't sure why it looked taller than usual. Then I noticed a few more buildings sticking out of the water, and suddenly my body sort of jumped, as if someone had put a hand on my shoulder. But I wasn't scared, I was excited, as excited as I'd been yesterday when we saw the helicopter. (Oh, I forgot to mention that. About 4 o'clock yesterday afternoon a helicopter circled the top of our building for about 5 minutes, then flew away. He must have seen our HELP sign, but he didn't land or rescue us or anything, even tho we were leaning out the window, waving our arms and shouting. When he flew away I thought Dad was going to lose it. His face went red and he started swearing. But then he calmed down. He said that maybe the helicopter pilot was on a reconnaissance mission and that he'd gone back to base or whatever to report our position. But the pilot didn't come back. Nobody did.)

Where was I? Oh yes, I was excited by what I was seeing. And the reason I was excited was—Ta da! Wait for it—the water was going down! I went to tell Dad and at first I couldn't make him understand. Then he looked out the window and for about 10 minutes he was really happy. Neither of us knew where the water was going, but it was going somewhere and that was enough for us. Dad said it was as if someone somewhere had pulled a big plug out of a plughole.

"We'll be all right now, Dad, won't we?" I said, and that was when his face changed. From looking happy he suddenly looked worried again, and I could tell he was thinking of stuff.

"Well, it's an encouraging sign," he said.

"But we'll be able to go out now," I said. "If the water keeps going down we'll be able to go out on the streets and get food."

"From where?" he said. "Everywhere's been underwater. The houses, the shops, the supermarkets. All the food will be ruined."

I hadn't thought about that. ▓▓▓
thought that we'd be rescued and ▓▓
wasn't a flood. I hadn't really thought ▓
the water went down and we were still here ▓

"Some of it'll be all right, tho, won't it?" ▓
the packets. We'll just have to see what we can fin▓

The buildings below where the water had been were ▓
looking, as if seaweed and stuff had started to grow on the ▓
to be hard out there, Abby," he said. *"It's going to be total a*▓
There'll be bodies and mud and everywhere will be wrecked."

"But we'll be okay," I said. *"We will, won't we, Dad?"*

He looked at me and smiled. *"Let's hope so,"* he said.

"We could go to Scotland." I said. *"Find Mum and Dylan. Cas-tle Morton's really high up. It'll probably be okay there."*

"We'll have to walk," he said, *"maybe all the way. You do realize that, don't you?"*

To be honest, that was something else I hadn't thought about. *"Maybe it'll be okay when we get out of London,"* I said. *"Maybe the roads will be clearer and we'll be able to get a car. Maybe even the trains'll be working."*

"I don't think so," he said.

"Why not?" I asked.

"I've been thinking about it," he said. *"If it was only London that had been affected, or even the south of England, there would have been signs of a rescue operation by now. There would have been planes and helicopters buzzing around, policemen in boats, but there's been nothing."*

"There was that helicopter yesterday," I said.

"It was privately owned," he said. *"It wasn't an official rescue vehicle."*

"How could you tell?" I asked.

"There was no insignia on it," he said. *"If it had been official it would have said 'Police' or 'RAF' on the side."*

(PS: These might not have been the exact words that we said, but it's more or less.)

(PPS: Dad helps me out with words I can't remember. For in-stance: 'insignia.')

vards Scotland. Dad
way, depending on
now it was as good

I said. "We can't

's something else

h's wheelchair?"

The streets'll be
em on foot."

, but he pulled a

In the back of my mind I just
taken somewhere where there
about what would happen if

I said. "The tins and
d."

black and slimy-
. "It's going
devastation.

Dad went round to the Beamishes to tell them what we were planning and I sat down at the kitchen table and made a list of what I thought we'd need. Dad had a big rucksack, and luckily I'd brought a rucksack with me for the weekend too. I wrote down as much stuff as I could think of, and Dad added some more things. Here's our list:

Food & water
Clothes
Sleeping bags
Tin opener
Sharp knife & other cutlery
Matches
Scissors
Soap, shampoo, toothbrushes & toothpaste
First aid kit
Mr. Beamish's medicine
Tools (hammer, screwdriver, nails, etc.)
Torches & batteries
Camping stove & spare gas canisters
Cigarettes & booze (Dad added that one)

At first I also put makeup and a hairbrush and stuff on the list, but then I crossed them off. Me and Dad filled the rucksacks, and *then the Beamishes came round and we had the biggest meal we'd had for 3 days—tuna fish sandwiches, crisps, biscuits, apples, and hot coffee with sugar but without milk, which I was getting used to now. By 3 o'clock the water was nearly down to street level, and we could see that it was total devastation, just like Dad had said. From up where we were London looked like a muddy tangle of trees and junk and wrecked cars.*

I looked at Dad and I could tell what he was thinking—How was Mr. Beamish going to cope? I admit part of me wished that the Beamishes weren't with us. I felt horrible for thinking that, but I think it was kind of natural to think it too.

At 3:15 Dad said, "Right then, is everyone ready?"

Mrs. Beamish was really nervous. She said, "What if the water comes back?"

"Then we'll have to swim for it, won't we?" Mr. Beamish said, and he laughed in that smoky, crackly way of his.

First thing me and Dad had to do was carry Mr. Beamish in his wheelchair down 20 flights of wet, slippery stairs. "You ready, sweetheart?" Dad said.

I tried not to look scared, even tho I was. "Ready, Dad," I said.

SIX

The crab made him so sick that Max wondered if he was going to die. He curled up in a ball on the roof, pain tearing through his guts. He felt hot and then cold; his sweat smelled pungent and salty. Occasionally he would lean over and open his mouth and a whitish gruel would gout from him and splash on the ground. This was almost a relief, but afterwards he would dry heave so violently that his body would jerk and tears would spring from his eyes. His stomach would feel tight, as if a boa constrictor were coiling around him, crushing his ribs, squeezing the juice out of him.

He didn't know whether it was the crabmeat or his lack of water that brought Noel back to him. All he knew was that, after drifting in the dark for what seemed like days, his eyes opening and closing, he suddenly became aware that his brother was by his side.

"Hey bro," Noel said, in that pseudo–New York/Jamaican patois he adopted sometimes. "Wass happening?"

Max tried to sit up and felt Noel's strong hands helping him, lifting him into a sitting position as if he were as light as a baby.

"I thought you were dead," Max muttered. "I thought everyone was dead."

Noel laughed at the very idea. "Not me, man. Indestructible. Always come back atcha."

"How'd you get out of the hospital?"

"I got up off my bed and walked. Like Lazarus in the Bible."

"But how did you get through the water?"

"I walk on water," Noel said, and laughed again. "No, man, I swam. What do you think?"

"But you're not wet."

"So, I dried. It's a warm day. Breezy. You been out a long time. You don't look good."

"I ate a crab," Max said. "It made me sick."

"A crab." Noel made a face as if he were impressed. "You catch and cook that fucker?"

"Catch, yeah. Cook, no. I tried to light a fire. There's lots of old wood up here. I tried to do it like we used to, remember? Spinning the stick on the wood? But it was too damp. It wouldn't light."

"You should have used a magnifying glass," Noel said. "Remember when we were kids and we used to fry those slugs? Man, they stank when they started to smoke. That's what you should have done."

"I didn't have a magnifying glass."

"That's too bad. Always have a magnifying glass. Box of matches too. First rule of survival." Noel looked around, as if inspecting a piece of real estate. "What you doing up here anyway?"

"Getting sick, mostly," Max said, and Noel guffawed. When his elder brother's laughter had abated, Max told him about the gang. Noel patted his brother on the shoulder.

"You're a hero, man," he said. "You led them away from me."

"Did they find you?" Max asked, suddenly remembering their final threat to him. "They said they were gonna find you and—"

"Whoa, whoa." Noel held up his hands. "Don't fret, bro.

Them couldn't find them dicks in a dark room if them was luminous. Them has been swept away by a mighty wave. The earth has been washed clean."

"And what about me?" Max asked. "Am I gonna die here?"

"Nah," Noel said. "I'll look after you."

"I wanted to stop them," Max said. "I wanted to stop them finding you. I was gonna come down, make sure you were okay. I locked the door, but then the lights went out, and I was too scared to come down in the dark in case they were wait-ing for me. The building was shaking and everything was black and I didn't know what was happening. When the wave came it was like the whole world was being swallowed by black. I thought it was the end, man. I just lay down and waited to die. And then the next day, when the sun came up, I looked out and it was all water, man. I opened the door and I went down the stairs, but after about ten steps there was wa-ter, and I didn't know what to do. It was dark, and there was stuff floating on the top. That first day there was paper and a plastic box like the ones you keep pills in, and other stuff. And I thought of you, man. Down there, in all the water. And it killed me that I couldn't get to you. It made me crazy. . . ."

"Shh," Noel said, putting his arms around his brother. "Tell me about the crab."

"The second day there was a body," Max said. "A woman. She must have floated to the top, up all the stairs. It was freaky. It was like she'd made it up because she could smell me or something. Like she knew I was still alive and she didn't like it. Like she was coming to get me. Her eyes were white. . . ." He began to shudder.

"The crab, man, the crab," Noel said soothingly.

"It was later that day. I was hungry and thirsty. I'd sucked up a bit of rain water off the roof, but that was all. I'd locked the woman in the stairwell, but she bugged me, man. I couldn't stop thinking about her. I thought about her stand-ing up, pulling herself out of the water. I kept thinking I could hear her thumping on the door, trying to get to me. I kept seeing these blue lights far away, crackling like lightning.

When the morning came I wanted to see if the woman was still there. Not knowing was worse than knowing, you know what I mean? So I opened the door, man, and this fucking big crab ran out. I nearly died. I thought it was her. Her hand. Reaching out for me."

"So you killed it?" Noel said.

"Chased that fucker and stomped it to death."

"And the woman?"

"Gone. Sunk back down in the water."

"So you ate the crab?" said Noel.

"Not right away. I couldn't face it at first. I thought it might be okay if I cooked it, so I tried to make a fire, but I couldn't do it. I left it a day. Big mistake. It was attracting the birds by then, and I thought if I didn't eat it the birds would."

"What did it taste like?"

"Like shit." Max shook his head. "There's no way I'd ever eat anything like that again. I'd rather starve."

Noel laughed and patted his brother on the shoulder. "So, what say we have some real food now?"

Max placed a hand on his aching stomach. "Sounds good. Not sure I'd keep it down, though."

"'Course you will. Here." From somewhere, Noel produced a McDonald's bag, from which he took a burger box each for himself and Max, two large bags of fries, and two regular Cokes.

"Wow, man, where'd you get this?" Max asked.

"Nowhere is closed to the Green machine."

"But the water?" said Max.

"No more questions. Eat."

Max ate. He ate like it was the best meal he had ever had in his life—which in some ways it was. Someone had once told him McDonald's burgers were made of assholes and eyeballs, but this one tasted of heaven. It contained the meatiest meat, the onioniest onion, the cheesiest cheese and the relishiest relish that had ever tantalized his tastebuds. He suspected he was drooling like a dog around the bun, but he didn't care. The Coke was a soothing balm on his parched throat. The fizz tingled its way through his system, settled his stomach. After his meal he felt invincible, able to face whatever the world might throw at him.

"What now?" he said.

"Now, little bro, you head out into the big wide world."

"But the water . . ." Max said again.

Noel gestured expansively to the edge of the roof. "Long gone. Take a look."

Max walked to the edge of the roof and peered over the side. To his astonishment he discovered that Noel was right. Where previously there had been a gray ocean, now there were buildings dripping with slime and seaweed, standing in what appeared to be a black swamp of uprooted trees and twisted metal.

"What the fuck, man?" Max gabbled. "Where'd the water *go?*"

No answer. Max swung round, expecting to see his brother standing there, looking smug. But Noel was gone, as was the debris of their meal.

"Noel?" Max said, and then shouted. "Noel, where you at?"

No answer but the whistle of wind across the lonely rooftops, the cries of birds scavenging for scraps in the strange new jungle below.

Max felt bereft. Suddenly all he wanted to do was sink to the ground and weep.

But no. Noel had come to him for a reason, hadn't he? *Now, little bro,* his brother had said, *you head out into the big wide world.*

Max walked to the door that led to the stairwell and opened it. The stairs were coated with silt and mud-caked debris that looked mostly like torn rags. On the fifth step down a fish the length of his forearm was flapping frantically. The stairwell smelled dank and rotten; weed and slime clung to the dripping walls. There were no lights, which meant that after one flight the steps disappeared into an underwater gloom.

Descending the stairs felt to Max like sinking into hell. The steps themselves were slippery as ice. As he headed down the gloom opened out before him, a little vestigial light creeping in from outside. Here and there he saw more fish flapping in the dimness, silver bodies gleaming, mouths agape, eyes boggling.

He encountered the first corpse two floors down. Its arm was lodged in the banister rail, its body twisted into such an unnatural position that it looked more like a loose-limbed doll than a human being. Max thought it was the body of a woman, but it was hard to tell. It was covered in silt, its hair like twigs clumped with mud, its features obscured. He didn't examine it too closely, simply stepping gingerly by, telling himself that *of course* it wasn't going to come alive; *of course* it wasn't going to shoot out a filth-encrusted hand and grab his ankle.

Though he was relieved to put distance between himself and the corpse, stepping over it was only the beginning of his nightmare. Max's hope had been that the fire doors into the stairwell would have remained closed during the flood, containing everything, including the dead—*especially* the dead—inside the main body of the building.

However, he quickly discovered that in many cases the stair doors had been forced and then lodged open by silt and heavy movable objects—lockers, beds, tables, chairs, machinery, stretchers. These objects, together with a million and one smaller items, were strewn everywhere like toys discarded by an untidy child. Intertwined among them were dozens of corpses, most mercifully plastered in mud, which, together with the murky light, obscured many of the grisly details of their individual deaths.

Even so, Max saw enough to fuel a lifetime's worth of nightmares. He saw bodies missing limbs; bodies partially eaten; bodies rippling with tiny crabs that scuttled busily over the bloated flesh of the drowned like the starving given access to a food mountain.

Worse, the closer he got to ground level the more packed with corpses and other debris the stairwell became. Several times he had to clamber over mounds of bodies in order to progress. Whenever he did, crabs scuttled over his shoes and up the legs of his jeans as if crazed by the scent of fresh blood.

On one occasion, climbing over a muddy pile of limbs and torsos, Max unwittingly brought his foot down on the stomach of a child. Instantly the mouth of the corpse gaped open, releasing a gout of foul-smelling water and several thrashing white eels. Max cried out in disgust, and in his haste to get away, slithered over the rest of the mound, dislodging one of the other bodies, which slid after him, limbs flailing as though in pursuit.

Glad though he was to reach ground level, Max quickly realized that his problems were far from over. The thick black silt that coated everything was deeper here, shin-high in even the shallowest of areas, which made progress slow and exhausting. Furthermore, the sheer devastation was utterly overwhelming. For a few moments after emerging from the stairwell, Max could only stand and stare. The hospital he had entered a few days before was now unrecognizable. The curving banks of silt that coated the floor and stretched up the walls to the ceiling made the place look more like a cave than a man-made structure. Loops of dripping weed hung from the mud-caked light fittings. There was so much wreckage, so much that was splintered and smashed and torn apart, that you might almost have believed a bomb had gone off.

And, of course, once again bodies were sprawled everywhere, many with limbs that were twisted and broken and mangled. Some were half buried, arms and legs poking from their shallow graves like macabre plants. *Is this it?* Max thought in despair. *Is this my world from now on?*

He thought of his ma, wondered whether she was out there somewhere, fretting about her boys. He had to get to her, had to make his way home. He trudged along the corridors, the mud clinging to his feet, each step an effort. By the time he reached the reception area, with its big desk and rows of bolted-down chairs, he was exhausted.

Last time he was here, there had been people behind the desk, people gaping at him as he fled the Nazis. There was no one behind the desk now, no one sitting on the chairs. There were just half-buried bodies sticking up out of the mud.

Max waded across to the entrance door, and here was the drinks machine where he had bought the cup of tea he had thrown in the Nazi's face. Next to that was the snack machine. It was glass-fronted and resembled a giant, filthy fish tank in which floated chocolate bars, bags of crisps, packets of sweets. Max was about to walk past when it occurred to him that some of the food might still be okay. Wouldn't the packaging around the crisps and some of the chocolate be vacuum-sealed, watertight?

He grabbed a metal waste bin and with a sucking sound tugged it free of the mud. He hefted it. Half filled with mud it was heavy enough to make his biceps tighten. He was weak and hungry. Despite the burger Noel had given him, the crisps and chocolate inside the machine were making him salivate. Snarling with the effort, he swung the bin at the glass, which shattered, releasing a cascade of water and food. Max jumped back to avoid getting drenched, but slipped in the mud and ended up on his backside.

Soaked and muddy, he clambered back to his feet. He wearily set about picking up the bags of crisps and bars of chocolate with wrappers that had not succumbed to the salt water. He wiped them clean on his clothes and stuffed them into his pockets. He knew the chocolate and crisps would do nothing to slake his thirst and wished there was a machine that sold cans of Coke or bottled water. Despite that he wolfed down three bags of crisps and two chocolate bars, and then was abruptly and copiously sick. Once his stomach had settled he tried again, and this time was able to keep the food down. Then he left the hospital.

Max had seen a whole bunch of movies where the world had ended—blown up in a nuclear war, hit by a meteorite, overrun by zombies or aliens or robots—but none of them could have prepared him for what he witnessed on his slow and terrible journey through south London. The sheer scale of the destruction was mind-boggling. Everywhere he looked he saw mud, seaweed, dead people, dead fish, wrecked cars, uprooted trees, collapsed buildings, splintered wood, smashed

glass and tangles of metal and plastic. There were more personal items too—books, shoes, toys, paintings, tools, chairs,
clothing, crockery, kettles, bicycles—myriad bits from myriad
lives, collected and kept and used and treasured, and now, like
their owners, scattered and broken and dead.

Ten minutes after leaving the hospital, Max came across a
general store that—aside from a crumpled post office van lying half in and half out of its shattered front window—had
remained relatively intact. Though his mind felt battered by
the terrible sights around him, it hadn't allowed him to forget
how thirsty he was. He crossed the road, picking his way
through the ankle-high silt and across several mounds of debris, and entered the building. Inside, a mass of perishable
foodstuffs—cereals, flour, sugar—had combined with the silt
to create a strange-smelling porridge that accumulated in
nooks and crannies where the water had not easily been able
to swill it out. Lying in this was a jumble of food tins—a little
rusty, their labels soaked away—and jars, some smashed, some
not. At the back of the room was a glass-fronted fridge, leaning askew and half filled with muddy water. Max opened it,
stepping smartly back as the water and most of the fridge's
contents gushed out. When it had reduced to a trickle, he
stepped forward and plucked a can of Coke and a couple of
plastic bottles of water from the swamp that had formed on
the floor.

The can was seeping so much rust that he discarded it, but
the bottles seemed okay. He cleaned one as best he could on
his filthy clothes, then broke the seal and brought it to his lips.
The neck of the bottle tasted salty, but the water inside was
clean and fresh. Max gulped two-thirds of it straight down,
then stood for a moment, eyes half closed, relishing the sensation of the liquid sluicing through his system. He picked up as
many bottles of water as he could carry, weighing himself
down with them, and then continued on his way.

He saw the lifeboat another mile down the road. Even in
this incredible new world it looked incongruous, jammed in
the branches of an oak tree ten feet in the air. The tree was in

a small park, between a bandstand and a children's play area. The trees, the swings, the railings around the park, the bandstand itself, all were strewn with slimy, dripping seaweed. A once-white SUV, crumpled as if made of tin, was lying on its roof in the bog that the ground had become. Max thought he could see a shape inside that might be a body, but the vehicle was so packed with mud that he wasn't sure.

He was about to walk by when he heard a groan. It was so faint that he doubted he'd have heard it at all under normal circumstances. Now, though, the city was so silent that every sound—each drip of water, each minute creak of shifting debris—seemed eerily amplified.

"Hello?" he called, a little freaked at the way his voice was instantly gulped by the hungry silence. However, he was rewarded by another sound—not a groan this time, but a creak of movement. His eyes turned to the boat again. Could someone be up there? It seemed crazy, but what didn't right now? Forcing the gate open against the thick black lake that the park had become, Max approached the tree.

He barely even grimaced as his feet sank into foul-smelling mud up to his shins. His sneakers were top-range Nikes, sturdy and strong, but they were wrecked. He could feel water squelching between his toes with each step. Sooner or later he'd have to dry them out or get new ones (though where he'd find a new pair of shoes in this drowned world, he had no idea); otherwise he'd get that trench foot thing soldiers got in the first world war.

But he'd think about that later, once he'd got home and found out what had happened to Ma. He circled the tree cautiously, noting the damage to the hull of the boat where a tree branch had punctured it, working out a possible route up to it should he decide to climb.

"Hey," he called. "Anyone up there?"

There was no answer this time, and Max sighed. He had to go up there. He guessed he'd known that since he'd heard the groan. Anyone who groaned like that wasn't likely to sit up and say hi. Max peeled off his jacket, heavy with water bottles and chocolate, and hung it on a low, slime-smeared branch. He lifted his right foot from the mud around the base of the tree (*shlup!*) and planted it in the crook of a low branch. He grabbed another branch a little higher and hauled himself up.

It was a short climb and relatively straightforward (three days ago Max could have scampered up there in a minute or less, agile as a squirrel), but by the time he came within touching distance of the boat, he was exhausted. He sat for a moment on a jutting branch just beneath the boat itself, clinging to the trunk and trying to blink the dizziness out of his head. "Max Green, you are a fucking pussy," he told himself; then he stood up on the branch and hauled himself the last few feet. He looked into the boat and saw the woman.

"Hey," he murmured.

She was pretty. Slim. Long sandy hair. She was wet and evidently cold, judging by the way she was shivering. She was sprawled across two parallel benches, her feet trailing in several inches of scummy water that filled the bottom of the craft. She was dressed in khaki cotton trousers, a blue sweatshirt and a life jacket. On her feet she had only pumps that had once been white, which made Max think that maybe she had scrambled aboard with little time to prepare for the rigors ahead.

She was alive, but she looked in a bad way. Her ankles, hands and lips were blue; her eyelids were fluttering as if she were having bad dreams.

"Hey," Max said again. "You okay?"

He saw her lips move, but no sound came out.

He leaned forward on the slippery branch and took hold of the boat. The tree creaked alarmingly, as if warning him of dire consequences should he attempt to upset the equilibrium established here. He didn't want to send the two of them plummeting to the ground, but if he left the woman here she'd die, simple as that. Then again, how the fuck was he going to get her out of the boat and down the tree if she was barely conscious? Swaying on the branch, he looked from the woman to the ground and wondered what the hell to do.

SEVEN

Less than three miles in half a day. At this rate, thought Abby, it would take them not weeks but *months* to reach Scotland. The problem, of course, was Mr. Beamish and his wheelchair. It had been a nightmare trying to maneuver him through the silt-clogged, debris-strewn streets. She had lost count of the number of times they'd had to stop to clear the path ahead. On a few occasions—when they had encountered fallen trees or partially collapsed buildings—they had even had to double back to find a different route altogether.

Not that she or Dad would ever consider abandoning the Beamishes. If they did, they'd die, simple as that. All of a sudden the world had become a scary, cruel place. It had never really occurred to Abby how cosseted she was, how much she took food and drink and warmth and health care and housing for granted. She felt ashamed now of all the petty things she used to complain about (if it was too wet to play tennis, say, or if Mum refused to increase the monthly credit on her mobile, or if they'd run out of skinny raspberry muffins in Starbucks), thought what a spoilt brat she must have been. But it hadn't just been her; it had been everybody. No wonder poorer countries regarded places like Britain and America with a combination of envy and hatred.

Of course, Abby had seen programs about famines and earthquakes in other parts of the world, but she had never *seriously* thought what it would be like to be starving or homeless. It was terrifying to realize that from now on they had only themselves to rely on. If one of them had an accident they could no longer call an ambulance or go to a hospital. Or if they were attacked by people who wanted to steal their stuff, they could no longer ring 999 and ask for the police.

If she thought too much about what her life might be like from now on, Abby found her heart starting to thump really hard, found her mouth getting dry. For this reason, therefore, she tried *not* to think about it, tried to concentrate only on the present. Because if the future didn't exist, she reasoned, it couldn't possibly frighten her.

By the time they stopped in front of the big Sainsbury's north of the Thames, just off Tower Bridge Road, Abby was exhausted. She wondered whether *every* day would be as knackering as this from now on.

They had tried to keep to the main roads as much as they could—up Peckham Park Road, on to Old Kent Road, and from there on to Tower Bridge Road, where they had crossed the river—but it hadn't always been possible. It had been Steve's idea, once it became clear that the first part of their journey would be conducted at a snail's pace, to use the supermarket on Prescot Street as their first "base camp."

"We can rest up there for a while," he had said, "have a bite to eat and replenish our supplies."

They still had enough food for a few more days, but Abby knew he was worried that once they moved out of London the pickings might become slimmer—especially if there were other survivors about. The problem, of course, was that they were limited as to what they could carry.

"I could have one of those rucksack thingies," Mrs. Beamish said. "I might be ancient, but I've got the constitution of an ox."

Despite her determined words, however, both Steve and Abby had noticed the old lady becoming increasingly weary as the day had progressed. Over the last half mile, in particular, her pace had slowed considerably. Even so, Steve said blithely, "If we *had* another rucksack we'd let you have it like a shot, Mrs. B, but unfortunately, we don't."

"We'd best look for one then, hadn't we?" Mabel said. "I do want to do my share, you know."

"Tell you what," said Steve, "if we do find a rucksack we'll stuff all the bedding and clothes in it and you can carry that. How does that sound?"

Mabel frowned, but before she could respond, George said, "What the lad is trying to get at is that you're no spring chicken anymore, dahlin'. You're not as useless as me, I'll grant you that, but if you tried to carry what these young 'uns are carrying, there'd be two of us in wheelchairs, and that'd be no bloody use to anybody."

Mabel planted her hands on her hips and scowled at her husband. Steve and Abby exchanged a glance, anticipating fireworks, but then the old lady's face softened. "You're right, as usual, you old bugger," she said. "I just want to do my bit, that's all."

"And you shall, Mrs. B," said Steve. "Believe me, we're all going to have to do our bit if we're going to get through this."

"Yup," said Mr. Beamish. "Group stuntman, that's me. If you want someone to jump off a tall building or dive through a burning hoop, I'm yer man."

Abby gave the old man a hug. "You're our inspiration, Mr. B. You keep us going with your jokes," she said.

George winked at her. "Why are bakers deformed?"

"Don't know," said Abby.

" 'Cos they're all inter-bred," George said, and cackled.

In Abby's opinion the worst thing about the journey so far was not the lack of progress, or even the physical exhaustion; it was the bodies. They were everywhere, snarled among the wreckage like so much flotsam and jetsam. They were a gruesome sight—white and bloated and mud-streaked, many missing limbs, most leaking silt from mouths and eye sockets. Even worse, however, was the knowledge that all these deaths would go unmourned, that these people would rot here, unidentified and uncared for, picked at by birds and crabs and insects.

People as rubbish. Yes, that was what was *most* shocking. It was hard to look upon this battleground of a city that only a few days ago had been teeming, and think of Life Everlasting, of souls ascending to Heaven, of God's creation and love.

The entrance porch at Sainsbury's was a glittering beach of broken glass. The trolleys chained together in their bays were a tangle of metal, coated with slime and weed. Stacked against the side wall of the building, jutting from great drifts of silt, was a crumpled heap of cars, intertwined with a small forest of uprooted trees. As they crossed the mud bath of the car park, Abby's eye was snagged by a variety of objects among the debris—a waterlogged TV; a scattering of what appeared to be office files; part of a billboard, the now pointless advertisement bleached by the sea; a heap of what appeared to be rags, but on closer inspection proved to be a baby in a once-yellow romper suit, one of its hands and half its face missing.

Abby turned away, sickened. Mabel put an arm around her. "We saw some sights during the war," she said, "but this . . ."

Steve crunched his way over the broken glass and peered into the store. "It's a mess in there," he said, "and dark. Got your torch, Abs?"

She swung her rucksack from her shoulder and rooted in it. "Check," she said.

"Okay," said Steve, "here's what I think we should do. I'll go to the left. Abby, you and Mrs. B go to the right. Mr. B, I'm afraid you'll have to wait here."

"That's all right, son," Mr. Beamish said. "I'll stay on the lookout for rampaging Zulus."

Steve grinned. "Okay. Abby, Mrs. B, don't forget, we need vacuum-sealed stuff. A lot of the tins will have no labels, so we'll have to take pot luck. But if you can find some coffee or cereal, that would be good. And we need bottled water. . . ."

"And more pills for George," said Mabel. "And I'll look for a bag so I can help you carry things."

"And what about more dry socks?" said Abby. "Are everyone's feet as wet as mine?"

"If you mean can I feel water squelching between my toes, then yes," said Steve.

"Which isn't good, is it?" Mabel said sternly. "If we plod about with wet feet, a week from now we won't be able to walk at all."

"Supermarkets sometimes have socks and things in sealed plastic bags, don't they?" Abby said.

Steve nodded. "Okay. If you see any, grab them. And pick up anything else you think might be useful. We can always discard stuff later if we decide it's not."

They turned on their torches and ventured into the building. "Be careful, Dad," Abby said as she watched him move away into the gloom, his torch beam bobbing.

"You too," he said. "See you back here in thirty minutes."

Abby and Mabel headed in the opposite direction. Abby's torchlight picked out rows of silent checkouts and a maze of dark aisles beyond.

Abby wrinkled her nose. "What's that smell?"

"Death," said Mabel, who looked apologetic when Abby gave her a startled glance. "I know it's horrid, dear, but I'm afraid it's something we're going to have to get used to. The smell's not so bad at the moment, but it'll get worse. In a week or two we won't be able to visit the cities. There'll be too much disease about."

"Like what?"

"Cholera . . . typhus . . ."

"I thought things like that were caused by rats in the olden days. But they'll all have drowned, won't they?"

"You're thinking of bubonic plague, dear. That was caused by the bite of the rat flea. But you get typhus and cholera from contaminated food and water. And what with all these bodies . . ."

"But if we stick to packets and tins and bottles we'll be okay, won't we?"

"Hopefully. But think of the maggots, the flies, the smell."

"I'd rather not," Abby said.

It was clear that Steve's description of the store as "a mess" was something of an understatement. The floor of the building was a thick soup of black silt, rotting seaweed, the occasional half-buried body and a good proportion of what had once been on the supermarket shelves. Instead of being sluiced out when the wave had come, the contents of the store had been pretty much contained within the walls of the building. As a consequence, crushed boxes, torn cartons and dented tins, together with the smashed remains of bottles and jars and the spilled and scattered contents of what they had once contained, were mixed in with the mud, the stench of which was incredible. Though Mabel had described it as the smell of death, it was actually far more than that. Lingering beneath the brackish, putrid stink of salty decay were myriad other smells—vinegar, alcohol, sour yogurt, pasta sauce, coffee, washing powder, decomposing vegetable matter . . .

As the overwhelming stench of it all hit her, Abby gagged and bent over double. "Are you all right, dear?" asked Mabel.

It was the determination not to let anyone down that made Abby nod fiercely. "I'll be fine."

As though to prove it, she slithered over the nearest checkout, coating her jeans with a layer of filth that came almost to her knees. Mabel followed more slowly, teeth clenched in a grimace.

Abby directed her torch up the nearest aisle. "How will we find anything among that lot?"

"With a lot of patience and a strong stomach, I should think."

"But it's hopeless."

Mabel gave her a look of such fortitude that Abby felt ashamed. "Beggars can't be choosers."

"I suppose not," Abby said. "Sorry to be a wuss."

Mabel squeezed her hand. "*I* should be apologizing to *you*, pet. I know how much easier it would be for you and your dad if you didn't have us old codgers holding you back."

"You're not holding us back," Abby said. "We're a team, aren't we?"

"It's sweet of you to say so, dear. But I know it's not easy, what with that bloody wheelchair and two extra mouths to feed."

"The way I see it," said Abby, "is you saved us from Adolf Hitler in the war, and now we're saving you from the flood. We're just returning the favor."

Mabel laughed. "Oh, what a poppet you are!" She gestured ahead. "Well, where shall we start? Wines and spirits, home baking or pickles and sauces?"

"I don't think it matters," Abby said, "though I definitely *don't* want to start at the fish counter."

Wading through the sludge was hard and the pickings few and far between. After ten minutes Abby and Mabel had accumulated nothing more than a dozen muddy tins, a vacuum-sealed bag of muesli, a jar of coffee and a plastic bottle of what appeared to be limeade, but might, once they got it into the daylight, prove merely to be lemonade contaminated with sea water. By this time Abby's thighs were aching with the exertion of wading through the vile-smelling sludge and she was pouring with sweat inside her fleece. Her back, in particular, was soaking beneath the rucksack.

They worked on doggedly, and found several more tins, a packet of noodles, a sealed bag of pasta and an unbroken jar of blackcurrant jam. As each new item was unearthed, Mabel cleaned the muck off as best she could and stuffed it into Abby's rucksack.

Eventually they reached the stage where the rucksack was so full that Mabel could no longer refasten the clips with her arthritic fingers. Abby shrugged herself free of her burden, shuddering at the breeze that instantly turned the sizeable patch of sweat on her back to icy water, and together she and Mabel struggled with the fastenings for a moment before managing to secure them.

"My word, that weighs a ton," Mabel said, placing her hands beneath the rucksack as Abby hauled it back on to her shoulders. "Your poor spine."

"I'm okay," Abby muttered, "though if we find anything else we'll have to carry it in our hands."

"We haven't found any pills for George, have we?" said Mabel. "I suppose we'll have to find a proper chemist's for those. And remember, we still need dry socks. Oh dear, we're in a bit of a pickle, aren't we?"

"We've got spare socks in the rucksack," Abby said, "and a couple of towels. We can build a fire tonight and dry everything out. We'll be all—"

Suddenly she stopped.

"What's the matter?" Mabel asked.

Abby's voice dropped to a whisper. "I heard something."

Together the two of them stood motionless, alert for the slightest sound or movement.

After a minute or so Mabel murmured, "Perhaps it was just your father moving about. Why don't you call him, pet?"

It was a sensible suggestion, but Abby felt oddly reluctant to draw attention to herself. "I will in a minute," she said. "I just want to check it out myself first."

She waded through the filth, the torch beam lurching before her. Tiny crabs on the surface of the muck scuttled away from the light. Their presence—not just here, but everywhere—had given her the creeps at first, but they were so ubiquitous that she was now becoming used to them.

She reached the central aisle and swept the torch in a wide arc left and right. Nothing moved. She turned back to Mabel, who was plowing through the mire behind her, when she heard it again.

Instantly she swung back, torch beam lurching. "Did you hear that?"

"What, dear?"

"A splash of water."

"Perhaps something's leaking somewhere," Mabel suggested.

"No, it was like . . . like someone scooping water out of a basin and letting it fall again."

Mabel gave her a long look, and at last she said, "Where did it come from?"

Abby indicated right with the torch. "Over there, I think."

"Then let's investigate," said Mabel.

The two of them crept forward, though there was little chance of stealth. The mud squelched beneath their every step, and slurped hungrily each time they pulled free of it. They moved past the confectionary aisle and what had once been the bakery section. Abby glanced at the empty shelves and wondered whether she would taste fresh bread or cake ever again. She halted when she heard another splash of water, and glanced fearfully back at Mabel. It was clear from the expression on the old woman's face that she had heard the sound too.

"Sounds like someone having a bath," Mabel whispered.

Abby directed her torch beam towards the freezer section, where waist-high bays had once contained bags of frozen vegetables and ready meals. A dark figure was standing there, and she leaped in shock before realizing it was simply one of a dozen or more pillars that marched down the central aisle, stretching from floor to ceiling.

She smiled shakily. "I'm getting jumpy."

Mabel cupped her hands around her mouth. "Who's there?" she called.

No answer. The two of them moved forward again. They were halfway up the aisle, freezer bays flanking them on both sides, when another splash, the loudest so far, sounded no more than four feet to their left.

This time Abby almost slipped in the mud, the torch beam swinging wildly. *"It's coming from in there!"*

Mabel took the torch from her and plodded forward. When she was right beside the bay, she stared down into it, bending at the knees for a closer look. She remained in that position for several seconds before breathing, "My goodness."

Abby's voice was flinty with trepidation. "What is it?"

Mabel beckoned her. "Come and look."

"Can't you just *tell* me?"

"It's better if you see," said Mabel. "It's quite safe."

Nervous, Abby plodded forward. Taking back the torch, she peered into the freezer bay and realized that it was full of murky water. For a few seconds she saw nothing; then a dark shadow slid by just beneath the surface, suggesting a sleek torpedolike shape the length of her forearm.

"It's a fish," she said.

As if to confirm this, the fish's tail broke the surface, then slapped back down into the water.

"It must have been left behind after the flood," said Mabel. "If we caught it we could end the day with a lovely fish supper."

"We've nothing to catch it *with*," Abby said, "and I'm certainly not going to stick my hands in there."

Mabel gave a wistful sigh. "All the same, it's a nice thought. I could just manage a bit of fresh fish."

Abby smiled and squeezed Mabel's arm. "Maybe we can find a couple of tins of sardines or something."

Mabel gave her a rueful look. But before she could comment, the wall not twelve feet away from them split open and an apelike figure burst through.

Abby screamed and spun, the torch beam veering in a wide, erratic arc. Light spilled over the figure, causing it to hiss and throw up its hands. Abby's first thought was that some black, simian demon had leaped at them out of a solid wall. She swiftly realized, however, that the figure was no nightmarish creature, but simply a man—small, wiry and dressed in the filthy remnants of what must recently have been a smart business suit. His hair was sticking up in muddy tufts, his eyes were wild and his spectacles were hanging askew on his face. Furthermore, she realized that the section of wall from which he had emerged was not actually solid, but composed of wide, vertical strips of mud-smeared plastic, each of which overlapped the next and evidently provided access to some kind of warehouse or storage area.

Realizing that she was blinding the man, Abby jerked the torch downwards, out of his face.

"Sorry," she said, "you made me jump."

"Abby!" The voice boomed somewhere to her left, making the little man spin towards it with a slackly startled expression. "Are you all right?"

Abby was still shaking, but recovering quickly now. "Fine, Dad," she called. "We've found someone."

"Who?" The lurching, brownish light of his torch beam approached through the aisles.

"A man."

"Alive?"

"Yes." She almost laughed as she said it. She had begun to think that she, her dad and the Beamishes were the only survivors in the city.

"Is he alone?" Steve shouted.

Abby blinked. It hadn't occurred to her that the man might have companions. "Are you?" she asked.

The man stared at her. His head had been darting back and forth between Abby's voice and Steve's, and now his lips began to move, though in an odd way, as if he were not so much attempting to reply as to merely imitate her actions.

"You okay?" said Abby, stepping towards him. She felt a restraining hand on her arm.

"Careful," murmured Mabel. "He's like a coiled spring, this feller. I don't think he's quite all there."

"He's just scared," said Abby. Soothingly, she said, "We're not going to hurt you. We're friends."

The man's voice was a rusty croak, as if he hadn't used it for days. "Monsters," he said.

Abby glanced at Mabel. The old lady raised her eyebrows. "No," Abby said, "we're friends. What's your name?"

Absently the man raised a hand to push his glasses back on to his face, leaving a smear of mud on the lens. "Seen them out there," he babbled. "Monsters."

"There are no monsters," Abby said. "There's only us."

The man looked agitated, anguished. "Seen them," he almost sobbed. "Coming for me. Coming . . ."

Abruptly the intermittent, diffused light from Steve's torch strengthened and he appeared around a corner to their left. The man leaped back, slithering in the mud, as Steve pinioned him with torchlight. The man's face was a chalky, stricken mask, his eyes black pools, his hands jerking.

"Dad," Abby admonished, "you're scaring him."

"Sorry," said Steve, lowering his torch.

The word was barely out of his mouth when the man let out a piercing shriek, the echo of which careered around the store. He delved into his pocket and the next moment was brandishing a long kitchen knife with a serrated blade. He waved it back and forth in front of him as though slashing at unseen assailants.

Abby took a step back, the sticky mud and the weight of her rucksack causing her to stumble. Mabel steadied her, but Abby's mouth was suddenly too dry to mutter her thanks.

"Hey!" Steve shouted, but this only caused the man to slash the air in an even greater frenzy.

"*I see it now!*" he screamed. "*You won't catch me out! Oh, no! I'm too clever for that!*"

"Hey," Steve said, his voice low and urgent, "come on, calm down. We don't want to hurt you—"

"You're *them!*" the man hissed. "I know what you can do. I've seen it."

Steve glanced at Abby and Mabel. "Who do you think we are?"

"You're *them!* I've seen you out there. I know what you can do. *Get away from me!*"

He screeched out this last sentence as though Steve had taken a lunge at him. Steve raised his hands and said, "Hey, calm down, feller. We're going. No need to get excited." He indicated to Abby and Mabel that the three of them should retreat.

"We can't just leave him, Dad," Abby said.

"We can't take him with us either," Steve said. "Look at him."

The man looked more bestial than ever now—eyes wide and glaring, teeth bared, standing in a half crouch with the knife held out before him. If it wasn't for his muddy spectacles, filthy suit and neatly knotted tie he would have resembled a caveman from some old dinosaur movie.

"But he'll die," Abby said, her voice cracking with desperation.

"Not our problem," Steve muttered, but he looked a little shamefaced.

"There's nothing we can do for him, pet," Mabel said reasonably. "His mind's gone. He'd only be a danger to us."

Abby knew they were right, but it was still awful to think of the man here on his own, terrified and deluded, living like an animal among the filth. She felt sick and hollow as they backtracked to the far end of the aisle. Steve, who had slipped down the parallel aisle so he wouldn't have to get close to the man, met them there.

"You all right?" he said.

Mabel nodded, but Abby stared at the ground.

"Abs?" Steve said gently.

Still refusing to meet his eye, she murmured, "I hate it. We can't live like this. Why can't things be back the way they were?"

"Hey," he said, putting his arms around her, "I know things are horrible at the moment, but we'll be okay. I promise."

Angrily, she said, "You don't know that. There's no one to help us. Nearly everyone's dead. The only person we've met wanted to kill us. What if other people want to as well?"

"They won't," Steve said. "This was a one-off. That guy's lost it big time."

Abby shook herself free of his embrace. "You don't *know* that!" she snapped. "Who's going to stop people doing horrible things if they want to?"

"Abby's got a point," Mabel said quietly. "I hate to say it, Steve, but I really think we should arm ourselves. As well as looking for food, we ought to look for weapons."

Now Steve sounded angry—or at least resentful. "We'll talk about it later." He shone his torch back down the aisle. The little man with the knife had gone. "Come on," he muttered, "let's get out of here."

EIGHT

"There it is again," Marco said, pointing. He sounded annoyed. "What the fucking hell is it? Tell me that."

Dr. Gregory Nichols, erstwhile consultant pediatrician, leaned back and closed his eyes. With his thumb he caressed the glass he was holding and debated whether to even bother answering the question. Not for the first time he wished he had survived the flood alone, and wondered what Marco's response would be if he were to suggest they go their separate ways.

"Are you even listening to me?" Marco demanded.

Greg knew without looking that the younger man had turned from the window and was now glaring at him.

"Of course I am," he murmured. "Do I have a choice?"

"What do you think it is, then?" Marco asked, though what he actually said was, 'Wotcha fink it is, den?' Greg found Marco's London accent both contrived and tiresome, and after five days he was beginning to feel that listening to the young man's voice was akin to being thumped over the head with a rubber mallet.

"I really have no idea," he responded wearily. "Does it matter?"

" 'Course it matters," Marco said with a scowl. "It might have something to do with this wave thing."

Greg took a small sip of malt, relishing it, knowing that soon it would be gone and that if he wanted more he would have to go out scavenging.

"Even if it is," he said reasonably, "there's very little we can do about it."

Marco grunted. "Don't like it, that's all," he said sulkily. "Fucking unnatural, it is."

Greg chuckled inwardly. Unnatural. That was certainly one way of putting it. His word for it, though—well, not the blue lightning; he had no idea what *that* was—would have been *cleansing*. He knew that countless lives had been lost, and that a tragedy of Biblical proportions had been visited upon the earth (or at least upon their cosy corner of it), and yet, for him personally, the flood had come almost as a blessing. His life had been in such chaos, his mind in such terrible turmoil, that the wave, the tsunami, whatever one wished to call it, had come almost like a proclamation from on high. In one fell swoop his problems had been—quite literally—swept away, rendered insignificant by the natural catastrophe that had overtaken them. And ironically, rather than making preparations to die in a land of abundance, he was now doing his utmost to survive in a world that, he had no doubt, would soon be ravaged by hunger, disease and lawlessness. Oh, yes, Greg was under no illusion that these were the halcyon days, the days of languor and indulgence, to be enjoyed—as thoroughly as one was able—before the real battle began. Not that such a thing could be explained to one-note dunderheads like Marco. Creatures such as he could no more grasp the intricacies of the human psyche than they could grasp the colors of a rainbow. No, at some point Greg knew he was going to have to jettison the boy. Prolonged exposure to Marco's unceasing banalities would, in the boy's own parlance, "do Greg's head in."

For now, though, he was useful. He was young, strong; he had already made an adequate (if complaining) laborer, and

Greg had no doubt he would make an equally adequate body-guard if and when the situation arose.

Together the two of them had spent most of the time since the water had abated removing corpses from the flood-damaged lower floors of the hotel. A grim task, but—as Greg had constantly had to remind his companion—necessary to their well-being if they were going to continue to use the hotel as their base. They had kicked down door after spongy door and carried the bodies down the hotel's many stairs—once sumptuously carpeted in a deep maroon plush, but now a squelching mudbath littered with stinking weed and dead sea creatures. At first the two of them had treated the dead respectfully, even (in Greg's case) tenderly, but by yesterday morning, during which time the corpses had been out of the water for eighteen hours or so and had begun to bloat and discolor almost in front of their eyes, they had been forced to quicken the process, to roll or even toss the bodies down the stairs in their haste to add them to the growing pile outside. And by dusk yesterday any compassion or respect that Marco, in particular, might have initially felt for the dead had long gone. In fact, he had become so densensitized that he seemed, at times, even less human than the heaps of spoiling meat that had once been fellow guests and hotel staff members. In one objectionable instance he had dangled the body of a child by its foot above the central section of the stairwell before letting it drop eight or nine floors to the ground below. As the body had impacted with the floor and split apart, he had even let out a whoop and punched the air, his face shining with glee.

Greg had remained silent on that occasion, but the second time Marco had overstepped the mark he had expressed himself more forcefully. Over the course of the past few days, Greg had discovered that, despite being the senior member of their unlikely partnership by some thirty-five years, he was by far the more motivated and energetic of the two. Marco was lazy, slothful, and although his body was reasonably muscular for now, there was also a fleshiness to it that seemed to indicate that in the not too distant future what was now a bearlike physique would rapidly dissolve into sagging layers of fat. He slept long hours, and took as many breaks as possible, which actually suited Greg fine. The older man relished whatever time he spent alone. Time merely to bask in his newfound serenity.

Early mornings were the best. For the first three after the flood, he had woken to the whisper of moving water, to the gurgle and splash of it impacting with the side of the hotel. On the fourth day, once the water had drained away, he had woken to the dawn chorus, and had particularly loved not the song of the birds themselves—though that had been fine enough—but the way it had eventually dwindled to a silence more profound than he had ever known.

And as well as the silence, Greg loved too the pearly, roseate quality of the dawn light, which seemed particularly beautiful after the curious pyrotechnics of each of the previous post-flood evenings. Yesterday, Thursday, he had got up and— basking in his solitude—descended through the sodden dankness of the hotel, pushed through the double entrance doors on the ground floor, and turned left, away from the growing heap of corpses in the street, to take the morning air.

So liberating had his walk been yesterday, in fact, despite the devastation all around him, that Greg had been looking forward to repeating it again this morning. However, after performing his ablutions—washing himself with soap and bottled water, applying deodorant, brushing his teeth, combing his thinning hair, carefully trimming his neat gray beard— he had exited his room only to discover that Marco was actually up and about before him.

The door to the younger man's room (or rather, suite—and indeed the suite that Marco had appropriated had once been the bridal suite, prompting Greg to wonder how many of the couples who had begun their nuptials here were still together, still happy, still *alive*) was standing open. This was unusual, for although Marco had smashed the lock from the door in order to gain access to it a few days earlier, he was in the habit of jamming it shut when he was inside.

"Marco?" Greg had called, first hovering in the doorway and then venturing over the threshold. The room had been dim, the curtains drawn, the air fusty (Marco was not as particular about his personal hygiene as Greg was), but it was immediately apparent, even before Greg entered the bedroom beyond the sitting room and noted the empty bed with its rumpled, grubby-looking sheets, that the young man was not at home.

Perhaps, thought Greg, his companion had turned over a new leaf. Perhaps he had woken uncharacteristically early and had decided to make a prompt start on the day's grisly task. Perhaps he had even taken Greg's advanced years into consideration and had been determined to spare him some of the arduous labor of hauling what amounted to slabs of putrefying meat down corridors and stairs to the growing human mountain outside.

Perhaps . . . but Greg doubted it. It was more likely that the boy had woken up hungry and had gone foraging for food. He decided to head down to the fifth floor, which was where he and Marco had ceased work yesterday, to see whether there was any sign of the young man.

It was here, entering a room whose door had been kicked from its hinges and was now lying half in and half out of the corridor, that Greg encountered Marco, trousers round his ankles, pimply backside exposed, yanking down the pants of a dead girl perhaps fifteen or sixteen years old. The girl's flesh was a marbled purple-green color, her stomach distended with gas, her face bloated and blackened almost beyond recognition.

As Marco tossed the girl's filthy pants aside and stepped forward, Greg blurted, "What the hell are you doing?"

It was evident that Marco had no inkling he was being observed. He leaped away from the bed onto which he had hauled the girl as though doused with scalding water.

"Fucking hell!" he yelled, pulling up his trousers and spinning round. "What you sneaking up on me for?"

Greg could barely believe the gall of the man. "I was hardly 'sneaking up,'" he snapped. "Besides which, I think that's somewhat irrelevant, don't you?"

Marco zipped his fly. The thick black brows on his wide, olive-skinned face crunched into a scowl. He glowered at Greg, but said nothing.

"All right," Greg said after a moment, "I'll ask again. What the hell were you doing?"

Marco snorted. "Who are you? My fucking dad?"

"No. Thank the lord."

"Then keep yer fucking beak out!"

Greg sighed. Outwardly he was calm, but inwardly his stomach was crawling with revulsion. "Aware as I am of our present radically altered circumstances," he murmured, "I'm afraid that necrophilia is one thing I simply can't ignore."

"Necra-what?" said Marco dangerously.

"Just answer me one question, Marco. Were you or were you not about to have intercourse with a four-day-old corpse?"

"Intercourse." Marco sniggered like a six-year-old.

Voice still icily calm, Greg said, "All right, you moron, I'll bring it down to your level. Were you about to fuck the stiff?"

The grin fell from Marco's face. "What I do is my own fucking business. It's got fuck-all to do with you."

Greg licked his dry lips. "You disgust me," he said quietly.

"Yeah? Well, tough shit. You might not have noticed, granddad, but the world's gone down the fucking plughole. We've got to take whatever we can fucking get now."

Greg regarded Marco's hulking form almost contemplatively. Then, at last, he waved a dismissive hand.

"You're quite right, of course," he said. "Conventional morality is a redundant concept in this brave new world of ours." He stole another glance at the bloated corpse. "Well,

I'm off for some breakfast. I'll leave you to assuage your particular appetites in your own way."

He was gone for over an hour. He walked the mud-caked, debris-strewn streets of Mayfair and Soho almost blindly, bypassing the dead as if they were nothing but sacks of rubbish, once even stepping over a severed arm as if it were a branch blown from a tree. Already the streets were beginning to smell bad. Greg wondered whether the rats had drowned with the people. He hoped so, though they were hardy buggers, with fierce survival instincts. If even a few had survived, the city would be overrun in weeks. It was a terrifying prospect. The birds were bad enough. Wherever you looked you could see pigeons, gulls, even garden birds like sparrows feasting on human flesh, and also on the ubiquitous red crabs that themselves were making a meal of the city's population. All at once, by dint of the fact that their numbers had remained relatively unaffected by the disaster, birds were the top of the food chain; nature had been turned on its head. Greg wondered how long the remains of the human race could survive in such a world.

He walked up to Buckingham Palace—a muddy ruin, its ground-floor windows hidden behind banks of black silt, the railings that surrounded it dripping with raglike weeds. There was a crumpled red bus lying in the driveway, and half of what appeared to be a caravan nestled beneath the famous viewing balcony like a giant smashed egg.

He tramped over to the National Gallery, which was hard work because, Hyde Park being so close, the streets in this area were choked with more than their fair share of uprooted trees and vegetation. The Gallery looked as though it had been hit by a bomb. The whole left side of the building had caved in. Greg thought of what the place had once contained. All that history, he thought, all that human creativity and endeavor simply wiped out. Part of him felt he should have been devastated by the loss, but the strange thing was, it didn't seem to matter. With as good as everything and everyone gone, who would be left to acknowledge it, or care? What was the legacy of the human race but a trivial indulgence?

Back at the hotel he breakfasted on tinned rice pudding, courtesy of the well-stocked, though extensively flood-damaged kitchens, then crossed what had once been the opulent marbled lobby, complete with Corinthian columns, to the staircase. Halfway up the stairs he encountered Marco, red and sweating, dragging the body of a woman in his wake. So lathered in mud that she appeared to be made of tar, the woman's dirt-encrusted hair trailed behind her like a mass of roots and her head bounced off each squelching step.

"How are you getting on?" Greg asked bluntly.

"Finished floor five," Marco muttered.

"Good work," Greg said. "I'll give you a hand."

For the rest of the day the two men worked mostly in silence, doggedly clearing corpses from the hotel and adding them to the growing mountain of rotting flesh farther down the road. It was late afternoon, the daylight beginning to lose its luster, when they swung the last corpse onto the pile.

Greg stepped back, plucking away the soap-smeared handkerchief that he had been wearing over his nose and mouth to combat the smell.

"Task complete," he said. "Well done, Marco."

"Yeah. You too," Marco said dutifully. "I'll get the fuel."

Greg nodded, standing upwind of the sickening miasma of what would soon become probably the largest funeral pyre that London had seen since the days of the Black Death. The smell of the dead was on his clothes and he wondered whether he ought to burn those too. He watched the birds circling above the heap of flesh until Marco returned with the two plastic canisters of fuel they had salvaged from a petrol station the previous morning.

Together the two men walked around the pile, splashing petrol onto limbs and torsos and heads. Greg tried not to look at the people he was dousing, tried not to think of them as anything other than disease-ridden waste that needed to be neutralized.

When they had finished, Marco lit a match and unceremoniously tossed it onto the pile. The gulls wheeled away with shrieks of protest as the fire took hold. The flames spread quickly, obliterating limbs and features, melting skin as though it were plastic. Within a minute the air was filled with the angry sizzling of hot fat, with boiling clouds of thick black smoke and the stench of rancid barbecue. Marco stood and watched, eyes gleaming. Greg turned away, wanting to bathe and rest, desperate for something to take the taste of decay from his mouth.

As the day darkened, the fire became a beacon, bestowing the surrounding wreckage with an odd, jerky life. Marco seemed fascinated by it. Even later, when they were enclosed in the sanctuary of their top-floor suites—each a pantheon of classical 1930s style, all chrome fittings and etched glass he kept shuffling into Greg's sitting room and over to the window, his gaze drawn by the flickering light as a baby's might be by glittering shapes or bright colors.

Irked by the younger man's presence, Greg eventually asked, "Can't you watch the fire from your own window?"

"Can see it better from this one," Marco muttered.

"But what's to see? If you've seen one fire you've seen them all."

Marco gave him a strange, slow-eyed look. "This is our fire," he said, "and it's got people on it."

It was only when the blue lightning returned, dancing and snapping at the horizon, that his attention became distracted. As if the lightning had been designed to annoy him, he muttered, "Don't like it. It's fucking unnatural."

Greg wished he had something to listen to. Something with earplugs. What he wouldn't give for a bit of Stravinsky. Eyes closed, he tried to imagine the music in his head.

Then Marco said, "There's someone down there."

Greg's eyes snapped open. "What?"

Marco pointed through the glass. "There's someone on the street. By the fire."

"Are you sure?" But Greg was already pushing himself from his seat, despite his stiff joints and aching muscles. "Where?"

Marco pointed again. "There, look."

And there he was. With the fire behind him the figure looked strangely thin, oddly insubstantial.

Despite his desire for solitude, Greg felt suddenly excited. "Come on, we'd better go down and meet our guest."

"What if he ain't friendly?" Marco said.

"Why shouldn't he be?" Greg retorted.

Marco shrugged. But he picked up the quarter-full Scotch bottle before following Greg from the room. By candlelight, the two of them made their way down to the ground floor. By the time they reached the lobby Greg felt breathless and dizzy. He couldn't remember when he had last done so much physical labor in so concentrated a period.

Though the fire was dying it was still burning brightly. The smell of charred meat was sickening. The heat from the fire, even from halfway down the street, made Greg's eyes sting, his cheeks redden.

"Hello?" he called. "Is someone here? We saw you from the upstairs window."

"Be careful, Doc," Marco said. "If he's hiding, it's probably 'cos he ain't friendly."

"Or it could be because he can see you waving that bottle about," said Greg irritably. "For God's sake try not to look as if you're itching to club someone, can't you?"

Marco sighed, but did as Greg asked.

Turning back towards the fire, Greg called, "Please show yourself if you're there."

A dark shape extracted itself from the far side of the fire and stepped forward. Marco raised the bottle again, but Greg pushed his arm down. "Come forward," he coaxed, "to where we can see you."

The figure hesitated, then took several cautious steps forward. As he stepped from the dazzle of the blaze into the gentler illumination, Greg saw that he was a boy, perhaps seventeen years old. He was slim, black, good-looking, but his clothes were filthy and he had a wary look in his eyes.

"Hello, young man," Greg said softly. "My name's Greg and this is Marco. What's your name?"

The boy scrutinized them for what seemed a long time, and then he cleared his throat and said, "Max."

"Pleased to meet you, Max," Greg said. "Can we offer you anything? Food? Something to drink?"

"Help," Max muttered. "I need help. I've got a sick friend. If we don't help her, I think she'll die."

NINE

I didn't tell you what we did after we met the man in the supermarket, did I? It was getting dark when we came out, so we looked around for somewhere dry to stay, but we couldn't find anywhere. In the end we broke into somebody's house and slept in their front room. There weren't any bodies around, thankfully, but loads of stuff had been swirled about by the water and was lying around all broken and jumbled up. Me and Dad cleared it all out, then pulled up the soaking wet, muddy carpet (which was not easy, let me tell you) until we'd created a big enough space on the floor for us all to sleep. The floorboards were a bit wet and stinky, but not too bad. Dad put plastic sheets on the list of things we needed, cos he said finding dry places to sleep would be virtually impossible for the next few weeks. Anyway, like I said, we all slept on the damp floor in our sleeping bags, and the next morning we woke up stiff and achy. My shoulders and legs were killing me from carrying the rucksack and tromping through all that mud. Mr. and Mrs. B looked even worse than I felt, but they didn't complain. Mr. B's breathing was really bad, like his throat was full of gravel or sand, and he kept putting a hand on his chest. I could tell Mrs. B was worried about him, but she didn't say anything.

We had breakfast—jam sandwiches, using the last of the bread, which had started to go a bit dry round the edges (boo-hoo, bye bread)—and set off. Dad plotted a route in the A–Z, which would have taken us up Kingsland Road through Shoreditch and Hoxton, and then up Stoke Newington Road, towards Tottenham. It seemed straightforward, but when we tried it, it was impossible. If it had just been me and Dad we'd probably have found a way through, but there were so many wrecked cars and collapsed buildings that there was no way we could get Mr. B through with his wheelchair.

So we had another look at the map and Dad decided that we should head west along the river, past St. Paul's Cathedral and towards the houses of Parliament and Buckingham Palace. It was a bit of a roundabout route, but he reckoned that if there were any other survivors they might have headed somewhere like that, or if there was any kind of rescue operation that might have been where it was taking place—somewhere big and well-known. So that's what we did, but because we'd wasted so much time earlier, by 4 o'clock we'd only gone about a mile from where we'd set off that morning. We were all shattered and fed up, so we decided to bed down for the night and set off again the next (i.e. this) morning, so that's what we did. It was tough going like before, but we made a bit better progress. Dad wanted to make it to the A5 cos he thought the road would be clearer, and from there we could stick to the main roads, at least until we were out of London. Mrs. B plodded on, and Mr. B slept a lot, even when the wheelchair was being jolted along, sometimes even when me and Dad were having to lift him over stuff. We were kind of getting used to things like the crabs and the birds eating all the dead bodies by this time. I mean, it's still horrible, but we just try not to look at it.

It was about 5 o'clock when Mrs. B saw the smoke.

"Do you think someone's done it to attract attention?" she asked.

"Could be," said Dad.

"We've got to go there, Dad," I said. "We've got to see."

"I agree," he said, "but let's be careful."

We decided to go to where the smoke was, because Dad said if there was a chance of meeting up with people who could help us we should take it.

"What if the people there are nice and everything, but they don't want to come to Scotland?" I said.

"Then we'll go on without them," said Dad. "But at least it'll give us more options. And it'll give Mr. and Mrs. B more options too."

I hadn't thought about that, but he was right. I couldn't really see Mr. and Mrs. B making it to Scotland with us. So if we could find someone nice to take them in, then that would be best for everyone.

By the time we got to where the fire was it was dark, and I mean REALLY dark, not just getting dark. We hadn't traveled in the dark before and it was freaky without streetlamps and lights from buildings and cars and stuff. We all had torches, but when you shone them around you couldn't help thinking that things were moving in the shadows just outside the light. The thing was, wherever you looked there was movement. The little red crabs were everywhere, and they made a horrible noise that I hadn't noticed in the daytime, a sort of rustling. The sound of lots of little legs scuttling about.

The dead bodies looked worse in the dark too, but that was probably because we couldn't help looking at them, because until we shone our torches on them we didn't know where they were. It was their faces that were the worst, their open mouths and eyes, the way they looked all sort of slack. And most of them had these awful purpley-black blotches on them where the blood had collected under their skin, and they had crabs crawling all over them, over their faces and through their hair.

Okay, I'm going to stop writing this stuff about the dead people now cos I'm REALLY starting to freak myself out. I'm writing this by candlelight, and there are brown shadows moving on the walls, and the hotel keeps creaking, which Dad says is cos it's drying out.

One GOOD thing about the dark was that the blacker it got the more we could see the glow of the fire in the sky. We followed it, a bit like the wise men following the Star of Bethlehem to Baby Jesus, but we weren't sure how close we were until we actually came round a corner and there it was.

We could tell straightaway that the fire had burned down a lot since it had been lit, but it was still crackling away. It smelled weird, *kind of meaty, like the hog roast we have at school every Bonfire Night, but not as nice. I didn't really think about it until Mrs. B suddenly said, "Are those people?"*

I thought she was talking about somebody standing behind the fire, and then I noticed she was looking into the fire, and so I looked INTO the fire too, and you know when you look at something, and at first you can't tell what it is, and then suddenly you can? Well, I looked and I saw this charred stick sticking out of the flames, and suddenly I realized that the stick had a hand on the end of it, the fingers all black and curled up like the legs of a dead spider. And once I'd seen the hand, I suddenly saw other things too, skulls and legs, and I realized that what I'd thought were logs were bodies, and they were all burning and giving off this smell like burned meat.

I could taste smoke in my throat, and I thought about swallowing tiny bits of all the bodies in the fire, and suddenly I puked my guts up all over the road.

"I know it's horrible," Dad said, "but at least someone's decided to make a go of it."

I was bent over with my hands on my knees. The rucksack felt like an animal sitting on my back. "What do you mean?" I said.

"I mean it looks as though someone's decided to lay down roots," he said, "otherwise why would they clear the area? You certainly wouldn't do this if you were just planning on staying for a day or two."

Suddenly I realized what he was on about. Seeing all the bodies had made me think that something really bad was happening here, like someone was killing people and burning them or something. Dad must have realized what I was thinking, cos he smiled and said, "I think you've been watching too many horror movies."

I suppose it was kind of weird, him smiling when he was standing right next to a load of burning bodies, but hey, this is the kind of world we live in now.

"I reckon all these stiffs came from yon hotel," Mr. B said.

We all looked at the hotel he was pointing at. It was a big posh place, surrounded by office blocks, which sort of stood back from it, as if the hotel was a king and they were its subjects.

"Could be," said Dad.

"I'm sure of it," said Mr. B. "It's the tallest building round here,

ain't it? If anyone had survived in these parts, where would they likely have come from?"

I looked up at the hotel and saw that, like all the other buildings, the walls were covered with greeny-black slime that had been left behind when the water went down. But the top floor wasn't. There was a tide line and above that the walls were white again.

Dad nodded. "We'll check it out. Mrs. B, would you mind waiting with Mr. B in the lobby?"

Mrs. B nodded and gave us a tired smile, and we went into the hotel, Dad pushing the wheelchair. Then me and Dad went up the stairs. They were wet and muddy, but you could see from the way the mud had been squashed down in the middle that they had been used a lot in the last few days. It was hard going, especially with the rucksacks, and after a few flights the tops of my legs were aching. It was creepy too. Dad kept calling out hello, but nobody answered. Our torch beams kept overlapping, making circles of light in front of us. It reminded me of Mulder and Scully investigating some deserted old building in 'The X-Files.' I kept expecting to suddenly shine my torch onto some horrible face in the darkness—the face of a demon or something.

At last we got to the top, and cos no one had answered Dad's shouts I wondered whether the people here were lying in wait for us. Maybe they were mad like the man in the supermarket, I thought. Or maybe they just thought it would be easier to kill whoever came by in case that person was out to steal what they'd got.

It turned out there was no one around, tho. There were 6 suites on the top floor and they were really luxurious. Each one had a bedroom, a sitting room, a bathroom and a little kitchen. We worked out pretty quickly that 2 of them were being lived in and the others weren't.

"Must have gone for a night out," Dad said. "Nice meal, perhaps a visit to the theater."

"And a taxi home?" I said.

"Oh, I think so, don't you?" Dad said with a grin.

We went back down to tell Mr. and Mrs. B what we'd found. But just as we got to the bottom of the stairs, the hotel doors opened and

3 people came into the lobby carrying a woman on a stretcher made out of a door.

For a few seconds we all just looked at each other, shocked. At one end of the stretcher was a black guy, quite nice-looking, a few years older than me, and at the other end was a tough-looking man of about 25 who had an Italian look about him, like Joey from 'Friends.' The third man, who was holding the door open, was tall and thin with a gray beard. He had glasses on a chain round his neck and was wearing a gray jacket and a shirt and tie, as if he still had a job to go to or people to impress.

It was the man with the beard who spoke first. "Good evening," he said.

I started to giggle. It was so freaky hearing someone say something in such a polite voice. I put my hand over my mouth, but I couldn't stop.

Everyone looked at me. "I'm sorry," said the man with the beard, raising his eyebrows. "Did I say something amusing?"

"You took us by surprise, that's all," Dad said. "We haven't seen anyone to speak to for nearly a week."

"Yes, there are few of us about," said the man with the beard, "but I'm afraid formal introductions will have to wait. This young lady is suffering from hyperthermia and dehydration."

"Is there anything we can do to help?" Dad asked.

"We need to transport her to the top floor, so I'm sure an extra pair of hands will be most welcome," said the man with the beard.

I'd got over the giggles now and felt bad that the man might have thought I'd been laughing at him. "We've just been up there and seen where you live," I said. "It's very nice."

The Italian-looking man said, "Been poking around, have you?"

I looked at him and he stared back at me, and the look in his eyes made me uncomfortable. I know I'm only 13, but I'm not as innocent as older people usually think. I recognized the look he gave me, like he hated me, but wanted to sleep with me at the same time. I looked away from him and tried not to shiver.

"Not at all," said Dad sharply. "We saw the fire and worked out that someone must be living here. We just came by to say hello and perhaps suggest pooling our resources."

Dad, Marco and Max (we didn't know their names then, but it makes it easier) carried the girl upstairs. Me and Greg (that was the name of the man with the beard) followed, and Mr. and Mrs. B stayed down in the lobby, tho Dad told them he'd be back for them in a minute.

"What's her name?" asked Dad, nodding at the shivering girl on the stretcher.

"Libby," said Max.

"Is she your girlfriend?" I asked.

He laughed as if he was embarrassed. "Nah, I just found her. She was in a boat up a tree."

"Really?" said Dad.

"Yeah, man. She must have been floating about for a few days. When the water went down, she went down with it," said Max.

"So how did you get her down?" Dad asked.

"It wasn't easy," said Max. "She was too heavy to carry, so I found a load of mattresses, yeah, and piled them up under the tree, and then I just dropped her onto them. They were soaking wet and muddy, but they broke her fall, you know?"

"Very resourceful," said Greg.

"How long have you been looking after her?" Dad asked.

"Couple of days," said Max. "I've tried to keep her dry and give her food and water, but she was in a bad way when I found her, and she don't seem to have improved much. She's come round a few times, spoken to me a little bit, but every time I think she's getting better, she'll go off again, you know?"

The men got Libby upstairs and Greg crushed up some paraceto-mol in water and made her swallow it. He said she was feverish, but thought she'd be fine.

"We're going to have to be very careful about illnesses from now on," he said to us all a bit later. Dad had unpacked the camping stove and we'd made some coffee and were sitting in Greg's suite. "We can't take coughs and colds and minor infections for granted, like we used to. We'll need to really look after ourselves, raid as many chemist shops as we can find and build up a good supply of drugs, as well as things like vitamin supplements to complement our diet. It's unlikely we'll be eating very much—if any—fresh fruit and vegetables in the

coming weeks and months. Our immune systems are going to take quite a hammering and there will be greater risk of contagion and infection. Diseases suppressed for years are likely going to rear their heads again before too long. If we're going to develop communities, which I think is inevitable, we're going to have to have quarantine areas for the sick." He rubbed a hand across his face and I could see it was trembling. "I don't want to be alarmist," he said. "It's just something I've been thinking about a great deal. We're all in shock at the moment, trying to cope the best we can. But in a strange kind of way this is actually the honeymoon period. The real trials are ahead of us. Long-term survival is going to be very tough. Very tough indeed."

Greg seemed pleased to have us around and said we were welcome to stay in the empty suites. He and Marco and now Libby all had one each, so Max took another, me and Dad shared one and the Beamishes shared one. Once we were settled and we'd changed our wet socks and Dad had cleaned our boots and stuffed them full of bits of an old T-shirt to soak up the damp, we got some food on the go. The tins had no labels so we opened some at random and ended up making a sort of stew with corned beef, baked beans, sweet corn and lentils (a bit weird but quite nice). After we'd eaten we told our stories—Dad first, speaking for us and the Beamishes, then Max, then Marco (who hardly said anything—I found out his family had owned a restaurant and that he'd been a hotel porter and that was it) and then Greg. When it was his turn he was a bit quiet at first and then he said, "All right, cards on the table. I don't suppose any of it matters now anyway."

(Before I start I ought to say that Dad helped me a lot with this next bit. I couldn't remember some of what Greg said or what words he used, so Dad helped me fill in the gaps.)

"If the flood hadn't come I'd be dead now," Greg said. "It's ironic. Maybe millions have died because of this awful disaster, and here I am, possibly the only person who is still alive because of it."

We all looked at each other, but nobody said anything. We were sitting roughly in a circle, apart from Marco, who was sitting on the window ledge, looking out at the blue lightning.

"That's right," Greg said, nodding, "I came here to kill myself. I know you're thinking. What a bloody selfish bastard, leaving *the mess for somebody else to clear up. But I didn't want my wife to find me, and so I came here. Might as well go out in luxury, I thought, rather than in some grotty place with rising damp and cockroaches. Besides, I wasn't planning on leaving much of a mess, or even one at all. It was simply going to be a bottle of whisky and a few dozen sleeping pills. I'd have been found tucked up in bed in my pajamas. Nothing too alarming for the maid. Nice and peaceful.*

So why was I going to do it? The simple answer is that I didn't want to cope with my life anymore. I used to have a good life. I was happy and rich. I had a good job, a wife who I loved and who loved me. We had marvelous friends, holidays abroad, wonderful dinner parties. We went for walks in the country and played golf at weekends. No children, but that was something we'd accepted long ago, and as we'd grown older it had actually become an advantage. It had given us more time for ourselves.

Then about 5 years ago, my wife, Iris, began to forget things. Words for everyday objects. Or she'd go out and leave the front door wide open. We joked about it, but in the back of my mind I suspected it was Alzheimer's, and of course I was right. I won't go into details, but since those first symptoms presented themselves she's become progressively worse. When I took her to the residential home on Sunday, the day I checked in here, and said good-bye to her, she had no idea who I was. The woman with whom I had spent 35 mostly happy years was dead and gone.

All in all, the last 5 years have been a bloody nightmare, but Iris's illness is not the real reason why I decided to kill myself. I'd be a pretty poor doctor, and an even worse human being, if it was. No, her illness was simply the catalyst for a whole series of events—or at least one particular aspect of it was. You see, Iris has never been much of a sleeper. Even when she was well, she would be a night owl, pottering until the early hours and still up before me each morning to put the kettle on. But since her illness she's been worse, sometimes getting up several times a night. And if I wasn't there to put her back to bed she would eventually find her way outside. So, as you can imagine, I was on tenterhooks all the time, far too anxious to get anything like a good night's sleep. The upshot of all this, of course, was that I was being ground down, both physically and mentally.

This latter stage—the chronic sleeplessness—has been particularly bad for about a year now. Because of it I was finding it increasingly hard to concentrate, and starting to make mistakes at work. Only little ones, but in my job there is no room for error. I'm a consultant pediatrician, you see. WAS a consultant paediatrician."

He paused and took a swallow of water. No one said anything. After a moment he put his bottle down and carried on.

"One morning, 3 months ago, I set off for work. It had been a bad night and I was like a zombie. I should never have been driving. I hit a child. She was 6. She was with her mother, but she saw her friend across the road and ran out without thinking.

I was told that it wasn't my fault, but on top of everything else I couldn't endure the thought of trying to live with the guilt of what I had done. I knew in my heart that if I'd had my wits about me that child would still be alive."

Suddenly he gave a hard, sharp laugh that made me jump and said, "Or until the flood came and reduced both our individual pasts and our collective past to an irrelevancy, the child would still have been alive." He spun a hand above his head, as if demonstrating how the past had swirled away like smoke and didn't matter anymore.

"So I came here to end it all. But the flood beat me to it. And the flood really DID end it all. But in so doing it made my intended gesture seem trivial somehow. In an odd way it made me realize that there was no point in dying. Or at least no point in dying by my own hand. It even made me start to think that maybe I had done that little girl a favor. I had saved her from this. From the horror of possible survival."

Nobody seemed to know what to say and for the next minute or so there was a funny sort of silence. Mrs. B walked over and gave Greg a hug. He didn't exactly hug her back, but he didn't pull away either.

Everyone had forgotten about Marco, over by the window, until he said, "There's another fire."

"What?" Dad said, jumping up and rushing over. I stood up too and went to stand by Dad. Marco gave me another one of his creepy stares, but I stared back at him and this time HE looked away.

The blue lightning was going crazy tonight. You couldn't tell whether it was coming up out of the ground or down from the sky. It danced around like a living thing. It reminded me of one of those *glass balls with electricity inside that follows your movements when you put your hand on it.*

We'd talked about it earlier, when we were cooking. In fact, me, Dad and the Beamishes had talked about it a few times, but nobody had any real idea what it could be. Dad said he thought it was some sort of random electrical discharge (whatever that meant), Mr. B said he thought it was something to do with the crazy weather or pollution, and Mrs. B wondered whether it was something to do with the army, maybe some new weapon that had got out of control. We didn't know whether IT had caused the flood or whether the flood had caused IT, or even if it was anything to do with the flood at all.

Anyway, the new fire. The city was so dark that it was hard to tell how far away it was, or how big. It was closer than the blue lightning, but it still wasn't much more than a glow in the darkness. To us it looked about as big as a candle flame. If I put my thumb over it on the window I could just about blot it out. I got the feeling it was somewhere high up, like on top of a building or something. But it wasn't just a burning building. Dad said he was pretty sure it was a signal, a beacon for others to see.

"Man rediscovers fire," Greg said. "The city is coming back to life."

"We ought to go there, man," Max said.

Dad looked at his watch. "I agree. But not now. It's impossible to tell how far away it is. Let's wait till tomorrow."

"What if the fire isn't there tomorrow?" Mrs. B said.

Dad said, "If it isn't it isn't. But somehow I think it will be."

"Yeah, and it'll be just as impossible to tell how far away it is tomorrow," Marco said, as if Dad was stupid.

"Not if they light up at dusk, or even before, it won't," said Dad.

I thought that Marco was going to punch Dad, but then he pulled a face and turned away.

"So who wants to go on a little expedition tomorrow?" Dad said. "I think we should keep the numbers down. Say, a nice, tight band of 3."

"Yeah, count me in, man," Max said straightaway.

The 3 oldies looked at Marco, as if he was the other obvious choice, but he stayed silent. Suddenly afraid that Greg or Mrs. B would volunteer and I would be left here with him, I said, "Yeah, me too."

Dad winked at me and suddenly I realized that he had got the 3 he wanted. Marco might have been tougher than me and Max, and more able to help out if things turned nasty, but it was clear Dad liked and trusted him about as much as I did.

TEN

Sue hefted the Glock in her hand and wondered at what point she'd be tempted to put the business end in her mouth and pull the trigger. Maybe she never would. Maybe she'd get used to this way of life which she already thought of as the three S's—solitude, scavenging, survival. Maybe in time she'd come to like her own company so much she'd even discourage whatever human contact might happen her way. She pictured herself five years from now as some wild hillbilly with rotten teeth and mad eyes, pointing a Heckler and Koch at fellow survivors and shouting, "Get orf moi land."

The image made her smile. Well, almost. Because however okay she'd been in the past, living on her own, she *really* craved some company now. The loneliness was starting to get to her; that and the sheer fucking boredom. And there was something else too, a dull, enervating weight in her belly and bones that she had come to recognize as fear caused by uncertainty and the unknown.

She'd done okay, however, for all that. Better than okay. In the three days since the flood water had abated, she had made herself a new home on the top floor of an office block, a half mile from where she had previously lived; she had scoured the local retail outlets, stockpiling food and water and medicines and various household goods; she had undertaken an expedition to a police station four miles away, which she knew housed an armory that was not as secure as it might have been, and had liberated six Glock 17 9mm self-loading pistols, four Heckler and Koch 9mm carbine rifles and as much ammunition as she could carry in a sack made of a dried-out duvet cover; and finally she had built a bonfire on the roof of her old apartment block out of whatever she could find that was not so saturated that it wouldn't light when doused with paraffin.

Last night she had lit her fire for the first time, and for a couple of hours had been in a celebratory mood, watching the flames leap high. She had even toasted a bag of marshmallows she had found two days earlier and had been saving for the occasion, washing them down with gut-warming slugs of Glenlivet. It was only when her fire had started to dwindle that she had looked south, towards the river, and had seen a second fire.

Immediately she had scrambled to her feet and rushed to the edge of the roof. Ridiculous though it was, she had felt an urge to leap up and down, to wave her arms and yell. She wondered whether this second fire had been lit as a response to her own. She waited for hours, until her own fire had gutted to almost nothing, wondering if they would come. But they didn't. No one did. She sat there until there was no more warmth in the embers, until the manic blue lightning on the horizon was superseded by the first pale talons of dawn. Then she plodded the short distance back to her new home and crawled into her cocoon of bedding, wondering if the fire-maker would come tonight; wondering whether *she* should go to *them*.

She slept for three hours, until her own sense of urgency woke her, and then, eating breakfast—a vacuum-packed bag of dried apricots—on the hoof she set about collecting material for bonfire number two.

She lit it late that afternoon, just as the light was seeping from the unseasonably bright sky. Her muscles ached, her hands were rough and sore with splinters, and for the first time since showers and baths had become a bygone luxury, she could smell herself—the sour smell of her own sweat. As the damp wood began to spit and pop, Sue retreated to her little camp forty yards away and sat down, her back against the brick wall of the central stairway block.

She opened her rucksack and took out a tin she knew from its shape contained sardines or mackerel or pilchards. She ate the fish cold with a fork, and then she delved into her rucksack again and extracted three further tins, their labels soaked away. These would comprise the surprise element of her evening meal. She was becoming used to opening tins and taking pot luck, eating whatever they contained. The first tin she opened tonight contained macaroni and cheese, the second, oxtail soup and the third, coconut milk.

She put the macaroni and soup tins close to the fire to warm through. While she waited she sipped the coconut milk and took the Glock apart again. Her aim in the police had been to become a weapons operative, perhaps even to eventually lead an armed response unit. She had found herself stymied in her career course by the incipient sexism that persisted even in the dynamic, forward-thinking metropolitan police force of the twenty-first century. As a result, her firearms training had been minimal. Most of what she knew about guns she had learned from the Internet. Even so, she had successfully managed to strip down the weapons she'd procured, dry them, clean them and put them together again. She had tested them out in the cavernous interior of a B&Q store that was a silt-caked jungle of splintered wood, mangled metal and shattered fixtures and fittings. She had fired into the gloom, half expecting one or more of the guns to blow up in her face. The noise had been deafening. A thousand fat birds, which had been feasting on the neighborhood dead by day and nesting in the rafters by night, had exploded upwards in shock. Now Sue carried a Glock at all times, handling it constantly like a talisman.

The other guns were back at the office block, carefully wrapped and concealed behind a stack of office chairs in a stationary cupboard. When she was there she spent most of her time taking them apart and putting them back together again, like a child with a favorite jigsaw.

She ate her food, put the gun back together again, and settled back to wait. She watched the blue lightning start to flicker up from the horizon, like a living force rising from the earth, attracted by the darkness. She wondered whether she'd ever again see an airplane leaving a vapor trail across the sky or whether she'd look out across London and see it aglow with house lights and streetlamps and the headlights of growling traffic.

Eventually she dozed—and dreamed. In her dream she was running through London's busy streets, trying to warn people about the oncoming disaster. It was a variation of a dream she'd had several times over the past week. On each occasion she had reached such a pitch of desperation that she eventually woke, floundering in her bedding, instinctively reaching for her gun.

This time, however, it was not the dream that woke her. It was the sense that she was not alone.

As ever, her first response was to strengthen her grip around the reassuring weight of the weapon in her hand. Her eyes felt hot and gritty, as though full of embers, her face half baked, the skin dry and stretched. She extended the gun in front of her and rubbed at her eyes with grubby fingers.

"Who's there?" she called. "Step out where I can see you."

There was a scrape to her right, like someone dragging something across a rough surface. Her head snapped in that direction, the gun swinging like a compass needle. She had the impression that someone was standing around the corner of the central block, pressed up against the brickwork.

"No use sneaking up on me," Sue warned. "I'm armed." Then, realizing that this might be the wrong tactic, she said, "I'm not going to hurt you."

Another few seconds, and then a dark shape sidled around

the edge of the wall. Sue tensed, then relaxed. Peering at her curiously was a girl, maybe six years old.

"Hello," Sue said, "where have you come from, then?"

The girl just looked at her, wide-eyed.

"What's your name?" Sue asked, lowering the gun, then placing it on the ground, out of sight.

When the girl didn't answer, Sue said, "Shall I tell you my name?"

The girl gave a brief nod.

"It's Sue. Which is an okay name, but I'll bet you've got an even nicer one. Do you want to tell me what it is?"

The girl whispered something, but it was lost in the crackle of the fire.

"What was that, honey?"

"Sam," the girl repeated.

"Is that short for Samantha?"

She nodded.

"And are you on your own, Sam?"

Another nod; then the girl's wide-eyed gaze shifted to the fire, as though she had never seen one before.

"Did you see my fire from the ground?"

"Yes."

"It's nice and bright, isn't it? Do you want to sit next to me and get warm?"

For a moment the girl appeared to be weighing up the risks. Then she sidled across to Sue and sat beside her.

"There," Sue said, "that's better, isn't it?"

The child looked so lost that Sue's heart immediately went out to her. She had always believed she didn't have a single maternal bone in her body, yet she felt an urge now to put an arm around this tiny scrap of a thing, infuse her with human warmth and comfort.

She didn't, though. She didn't want to terrify the poor thing by coming on too strong, too quickly. For the time being she contented herself with merely sitting next to the child, reveling both in her silent company and in the undeniable proof that she wasn't the last human being left alive on

Earth, after all. She looked down at the little girl again, and suddenly it occurred to her that she had seen her before. Sue wondered why she had not realized it immediately, why it had taken until now for the penny to drop.

"Sam?" she said.

The little girl looked at her, eyes wide and gleaming, face solemn.

"Sam, what happened to you when the water came?"

At first Sue thought the little girl wouldn't answer, that perhaps her memories were too painful. Then she said, "I don't know."

"You don't know?" Sue said. "You mean, you don't re member?"

Sam didn't reply, merely gazed at Sue with her huge liquid eyes.

"Do you remember being rescued?" Sue persisted. "Do you remember sitting on the door in the water, and the people on the roof rescuing you?"

Still no answer. Nothing but a petulant shrug.

"There were six of them," Sue said. "They were wearing nice clothes. They'd dressed up for a party. . . ."

Sam's face was still unreadable.

"Do you remember the people?" Sue asked gently. "Do you remember what happened to them?"

A frown wrinkled the girl's brow, but still she didn't respond. Sue had to clench her fists to prevent herself from shaking the girl by the shoulders.

Perhaps the party people had set the fire, she thought suddenly. Despite what Sam had said about being alone, perhaps they were on their way here now, stumbling through the mud and over the rubble, bedraggled and filthy, still wearing their dinner-party clothes. Perhaps Sam had run on ahead, eager and excited to find the big fire they had all seen.

"I'm hungry," the girl announced suddenly. Sue felt a momentary flash of irritation, but then nodded, a little ashamed.

"'Course you are, sweetheart," she said. "Let's see what we've got here, shall we?"

She turned to where the rucksack was propped against the wall. There were some snacks in there—not much, just dried fruit and chocolate and crackers in cellophane packets.

"Do you like—" she started to say, and then all at once she felt incredibly strange. Not faint or sick (though there were elements of both sensations), but rather as though she were being drawn out of her body, or more specifically as though a hole had opened in the base of her spine and her life essence was being tugged out like some thick, viscous rope of matter.

She gasped and tried to turn, but all at once her body felt immensely heavy, as though gravity had suddenly increased and was crushing her down. With an intense effort she twisted her head on a neck that felt like drying concrete. She felt as though the skin on her back was stretching, tearing, as though her bones were being bent out of shape like the bars of a cage. Through her darkening vision she saw Sam and the blue lightning. Except the blue lightning was no longer up in the sky.

It was coming out of Sam's mouth.

Something terrible was happening to the little girl. Strands of blue lightning were crawling from her mouth and stretching across her face like the shimmering legs of some huge spider. And though her skin was darkening, a sickly white luminescence was leaking from her pupils, as though she were inverting light, turning into a negative version of herself. There was a sound coming from her too—a buzzing and crackling, like a swarm of angry electric bees. As Sue watched, the girl's form seemed to dissolve, to become so alien, so indefinable, that Sue found she could no longer even focus upon it. It was as if both her vision and her mind slid across its surface, making no impression, like a tiny blade on a vast diamond.

Sue whimpered and turned away, trying to keep her swimming thoughts together. Her hand—vast and cumbersome as an anvil—groped across the concrete roof. The pain in her back was excruciating now. Tears were streaming from her eyes, blinding her. With a vast effort she closed her hand around the handle of the gun, gritted her teeth to lift it, and screamed a long, rusty scream of pain as she twisted, gun arm swinging round. With no hesitation she pointed the gun directly into Sam's face and pulled the trigger. She had a confused impression of something black and jagged, like overlapping chunks of slate, beneath a halo of thrashing blue-white light filaments. And then the thing—no longer remotely resembling anything that might once have been a little girl—uttered a shrill, utterly inhuman screech, and was gone.

Sue sank to the concrete, her body seeming cold and boneless, as though she were a puddle of melting ice. Had she killed the thing? Or at least driven it away? She hoped so, because she had nothing left in her. A black cloud suddenly rushed forward to engulf her, and this time she did nothing to resist it. She floated in blackness for a while. And then she felt something beside her, touching her arm, and she burst into consciousness, gasping and screaming, scrabbling for her gun.

"Hey," she heard a voice say, "it's all right."

She tore open her eyes. For an awful moment she thought the girl was back again, looming over her, and then she saw that this was an older boy, his dark skin glowing with a chestnut hue in the firelight. He looked alarmed. He licked his lips.

"What?" she barked. She couldn't think of anything else to say. Her hand flexed, but there was no gun there.

"Are you looking for this?" another voice said. Her eyes flickered to the right and she saw a man—tall, thin, stubble, long hair—standing behind the kneeling black kid, holding her gun.

She couldn't prevent herself from making a futile clutching motion towards him. "Give it," she said.

"We saw your fire," said a third voice. A girl's. Sue flinched, then realized this couldn't be Sam. Her gaze shifted again and she saw the girl crouching to her left, long blond hair falling forward. She was very pretty, this girl.

"We're friends," the black kid said. "We saw your fire."

"Friends," Sue repeated.

The black kid grinned. "Yeah. Good fire, by the way."

"Thanks," Sue whispered. Then she burst into tears.

ELEVEN

"A monster?" scoffed Marco.

Sue looked as though she'd like to throw her coffee in his face. "I'm telling you, she wasn't human."

Marco rotated his finger at the side of his temple. "You're going loco, lady. Too much time on your own." He waved a hand dismissively. "I ain't got time to listen to this shit. I got better things to do."

"Like what?" croaked George. "Polishing your python?"

Marco was stalking from the room, but now he swung back, raising an index finger. "Fuck you, old man, or you'll be out that window, wheelchair and all."

"Oi," shouted Steve, "that's no way to talk to your elders."

"He started it," Marco snarled, clenching his fists.

"Grow up, Marco," snapped Greg. "Ever since our friends have arrived you've behaved like a toddler who won't share the sandpit."

Abby laughed. Marco looked daggers at her. "Yeah, well," he said, "that's because I don't see the world through rose-tinted glasses."

"What's that supposed to mean?" asked Steve.

"It means we've worked to get this place fit to live in, and you lot just saunter in and take over."

"We're not taking over," Steve scoffed. "We came to offer the hand of friendship. God knows, there are few of us left in this bloody city. Better to band together than struggle on alone, don't you think?"

Marco said nothing, simply glared at him like a boxer trying to psyche out his opponent.

Steve shook his head, a wry smile on his face. "Sorry, mate, but I left the playground behind years ago. Look, if you don't want us here, we'll find somewhere else to live."

"Of course we want you here," Greg said.

Marco snorted and left the room.

"That young man has an attitude problem," Mabel said.

"He'll come round," Greg sighed. "So, come on, Sue, tell us about this monster."

It was Sunday lunchtime, almost a week since the lights had gone out across London. After Steve, Abby and Max had calmed Sue down the previous evening, she had led them back to the office complex where she had made her home. They had oohed and aahed at her impressive stock of provisions, and the men had been particularly taken by the guns.

"May I?" Steve asked after Sue had opened the door of the stationary cupboard and revealed the rifles propped in the corner.

"Be my guest," Sue said.

Steve had examined the rifle with the awe and reverence of a child with an expensive new toy. "Is it loaded?"

Sue shook her head.

Steve cradled the weapon in the crook of his arm, striking a somewhat self-conscious pose.

"You've never handled a gun before, have you?" Sue said.

Steve flushed. "Is it really that obvious?"

"To be honest, yes." Sue glanced at Max. "How about you?"

"Hey, I'm a black kid from the ghetto. What do *you* think?"

Sue raised her eyebrows and Max smiled. "Never even seen a real gun before," he admitted.

Sue gave him an unloaded Glock to handle. Like Steve, Max was self-conscious at first, but soon he was holding the weapon high and side-on, like a yardie on a crime show.

"You want some, motherfucker?" he said to an empty chair across the room. Then he spoiled the effect by turning and grinning shyly. "Sorry about my potty mouth there, guys. Got a bit carried away."

He offered the gun to Abby. "You want a go?"

Abby grimaced as though he were offering her a tarantula to hold. "No thanks."

They spent the night with Sue and returned to the hotel the next morning. Sue needed little persuading to accompany them. They each loaded their rucksacks with as many essential items as they could carry; then they set off, knowing they could come back for more if needs be.

Sue told Steve about the girl on the way back to the hotel. Out in the open, he noted she seemed nervous, her eyes darting everywhere, and he asked her what was wrong. After ensuring that Abby and Max were out of earshot, and then prevaricating for a while, she eventually told him how Sam had appeared, and how she had turned her back on the girl and felt the pain in her spine.

"Pain?" Steve said. "So are you saying she stabbed you?"

"No." She seemed irritated by the assumption. "It was weirder than that."

"Weirder how?"

She looked at him a long moment, then put a hand on his arm and said, "Hang on." She shrugged off her rucksack, then pulled up her wax jacket and the layers of clothing beneath to show him her back.

"Fuck," Steve said.

There was a weal or burn mark at the base of her spine that was the size of a side plate. It seemed composed of a series of concentric circles of angry, blistered skin, giving the impression that someone had tried to burn the shape of a whirlpool into her back.

"Has this been treated?" he asked.

"I've put antiseptic cream on it and taken some paraceto-mol. I guess the wound should be dressed really, but"—she shrugged—"I couldn't do it on my own."

"You should have told me about this last night," Steve said. "I don't understand why you should want to keep it a secret. Is it professional pride? Are you embarrassed this girl took you unawares?"

"No, nothing like that."

"What, then?"

She allowed the clothes to drop back down, concealing the wound, wincing a little as the material made contact with her skin. "The girl . . . changed," said Sue. She seemed to have difficulty forcing the word out.

"Changed?" said Steve. "How do you mean?"

Bit by bit he eked the story out of her. And when she came to tell it for a second time, later that day, she was even more hesitant, more apologetic, more embarrassed.

Afterwards Greg steepled his fingers to his lips. Max looked at Abby, raising his eyebrows as it to say, *Jesus, what do you make of that?*

Sue sat back and rubbed at her eye sockets. "It's okay. I'll get my coat," she said.

"Pardon?" said Greg.

"Never mind, it's a joke. Look, I'm sure none of you know what to say. I don't think I would. And I don't blame you for not believing me."

"Nobody here has said they don't believe you," Steve said quickly.

"That man in the supermarket talked about monsters," Mabel said. "You remember, Abby?"

Abby nodded. "He thought *we* were monsters, didn't he? You don't think . . ." She tailed off.

"Go on, dear."

Abby looked around the room. "Well, suppose the man in the supermarket had seen the girl—or even someone else—change into one of these things. If he knew people could change, he wouldn't trust anybody, would he?"

"So what we talking about here?" Max said. "Werewolves or something?"

"The girl didn't change into any sort of *animal*," said Sue.

"What then? Aliens?"

Sue scowled and flapped a hand. "Oh, I don't know! It's bloody ridiculous!"

"You saw it," said Max.

"I know," Sue said. "I know and I'm sorry, Max. It's just . . . well, I'm finding it difficult to accept myself. It doesn't fit into my world view."

"What do you think, Greg?" Steve asked.

Greg puffed out his cheeks. "I'm not sure what to think. Every instinct tells me that Sue was mistaken in what she saw. On the other hand, we find ourselves in extraordinary times. Who is to say that the flood is the culmination of our experiences, that there are not yet further wonders in store?"

"Don't believe I'd think of a man-eating monster as a wonder, Doc," George wheezed. " 'Specially if it was biting me head off."

Mabel, whose response to Greg's quiet authority was a respect bordering on reverence, lightly slapped her husband's knee.

Greg chuckled. "Alas, the wondrous does not always translate as benign."

"So let's suppose that Sue saw what she saw," said Steve. "What do you think we could be up against, Greg?"

"I'm not sure I'd even care to speculate. Young Max's suggestion seems as good as any."

Max looked surprised. Abby felt a chill go through her. "Aliens?" she said. "Are you serious?"

"Aliens? Escaped government experiments? Terrorist weapons? Human beings infected by this curious lightning we see each evening? Who knows what's lurking out there? As I said, we live in extraordinary times."

Everyone seemed a little stunned by his words. Somewhat guardedly, Steve said, "Okay, then I guess we should be asking what we're going to do."

Greg spread his hands. "In what sense?"

"Well, the way I see it we've got maybe three options. We can either get on with things here and choose to ignore it; we can go looking for this girl and, if we find her, bring her back here and—I don't know—observe her under controlled conditions; or we can just get out of town."

"And go where?" said Sue.

Steve stole a glance at Abby. "Well, Abby and I have talked about heading up to Scotland. My ex-wife and son live up there, and we want to see if we can find them. It's an emotional crusade, granted, but I reckon it makes practical sense too. Pretty soon the big cities will be nothing but charnel houses. The streets are going to stink and there'll be a real danger of contagion."

"So what makes you think it'll be any better in Scotland?" Sue asked.

Steve shrugged. "I don't *know* that it'll be any better, but it can hardly be any worse, can it? Castle Morton, where my ex lives, is on pretty high ground, so I guess it's more likely that people will have survived up there."

"I reckon it's the same everywhere," said Max gloomily. "I mean, we ain't seen no planes, have we? If it was only London got flooded, we'd have been rescued by now."

"We saw a helicopter," said Abby, then blushed as everyone looked at her. As if she felt she needed to justify herself, she said, "It was only a little one. It was about five days ago, before the water went down."

"Did it have any insignia?" asked Sue.

Steve shook his head. "Privately owned."

"What did it do?"

"Just hovered around a bit, then flew away."

Max said, "But that proves my point. If people were still alive in Scotland, they'd have sent planes and shit."

"No one in Castle Morton owns a plane or helicopter," Abby said. "There are a few boats, but why would anyone bother to sail down here?"

The door to Greg's suite opened. Abby looked up, expecting to see Marco, but it was Libby who entered. She looked around sleepily, pushing a handful of hair back from her face.

"How are you feeling, my dear?" Greg asked, moving forward to take her arm.

"Still a bit weak and wobbly, but . . . better." She looked around, half smiling. "What's this? War conference?"

Steve's laugh was more fulsome than the quip deserved. "Kind of, yeah."

It was evident to Abby that her dad was rather taken by this woman from the boat. There was no reason why he shouldn't be—Libby was close to his own age, maybe midthirties, very pretty and graceful. Even so, Abby couldn't help feeling a bit weird about it. She guessed that seeing her dad showing interest in other women was something she would have to get used to.

Libby's fever had broken in the early hours of Saturday morning. By nine A.M. she had been sitting up in bed, taking small mouthfuls of porridge, washed out but able to recount what she remembered of her ordeal. Her boyfriend, Tom Lionel, had apparently been a dot-com millionaire, and the two of them had been on his yacht, enjoying a few days' sailing around the south coast, when the sea had succumbed to a series of surges of such force that the boat had been tossed around like a toy. Libby and Tom, who had been asleep below decks, had managed to launch the lifeboat just before the yacht had begun to break up. Libby's mind was a blank after that. She had no recollection of what happened to Tom.

"We've been wondering what to do for the best," Steve told her.

"Steve believes we should head north to Scotland," said Greg.

"His wife lives there," said Max.

"Ex-wife," Steve quickly corrected.

Libby looked around as if wondering whether she should offer an opinion. Then she shrugged. "It sounds reasonable."

"Maybe we should vote or something." suggested Max.

"Me and Dad are going anyway," said Abby. "Aren't we, Dad?"

For a moment Steve seemed undecided; then he nodded.

"Count me in too, if that's okay," said Max quickly. "Like

you said, Steve, things are gonna get real bad here real soon. Only thing is . . . I gotta go home first. See if my ma . . . well, see if I can find her, y'know?"

"Sure," said Steve. "I'll go with you if you like. We could go this afternoon. Unless you'd rather go alone?"

Max shook his head and mumbled, "Nah, man, I'd appreciate the company. Cheers."

"Can I come too?" said Abby.

Max tried not to look too eager, but he couldn't quite manage it. "Sure," he said.

TWELVE

So after lunch we set off again. We didn't take much with us cos Max only lived a couple of miles away in Notting Hill, and so we were hoping we could be there and back before it got dark.

I sort of wanted to go and sort of didn't. It was horrible out in the streets, and part of me just wanted to lie on my comfy bed and listen to my iPod. But I didn't like the thought of Dad going off somewhere without me. And I definitely didn't want to be left here with that creepy Marco about, not if Max was gone too.

I like Max a lot. He's funny and kind, not to mention quite fit (and you'd better not be reading this, Max!), tho a sad thing about him is that Dad says he's in denial about his mum. I mean, Max has talked about going home quite a lot, but before today he hadn't actually done anything about it, even tho it's not that far away. Dad says that deep down Max must know that his mum couldn't have survived, but for every day he puts off going to find out, he can tell himself that maybe she's still alive.

"So, why does he want to go now?" I asked Dad when Max was out of the room.

Dad shrugged and said, "You can't put off the inevitable forever."

The journey was as horrible as ever—wreckage and mud and dead people and crabs and birds. Outside a pub called the Black Cap was a big pub sign, and hanging over it, like a bag of dirty washing, was the body of a woman.

She was swollen and purple. Her hands hung over one side of the sign and her legs over the other. Her muddy hair hung down too and covered her face (thank God), and her clothes were just brown rags stuck to her body.

The crows were eating her. That was the worst part. I know the woman was dead, but in some ways it reminded me of a gang attack, and that made the whole thing really upsetting. There were about 8 crows in all, and they were screeching and swooping around the woman, dive-bombing her, jabbing her with their beaks. Sometimes 1 or 2 would land and they'd take a few pecks out of her like she was a slab of meat (which I suppose to them she was) and then they'd fly off and swoop around again.

I've seen lots of awful stuff over the past week, but for some reason the crows eating the woman really got to me. I don't know why. Maybe because the woman was hanging over the sign, maybe because the crows were vicious, almost like they were celebrating the fact that she was dead and they could do whatever they liked to her, or maybe because we were on our way to find out what had happened to Max's mum and I suddenly thought that this time last week this woman was probably a mum or a wife or a sister or a daughter, a person with a normal life going along thinking about normal stuff, like her husband or her kids, or what she was having for tea that night, or what she was doing at the weekend, or what was happening on 'EastEnders.' I bet she didn't think that in a week's time she'd be dead and hanging outside a pub, being eaten by crows. It was sad and sick and it made me want to cry.

"How do you think she got up there?" Max asked.

"Probably the same way Libby's boat ended up in the tree," said Dad. "When the water went down she settled there. I'll bet there are bodies on flat roofs all over the city."

We carried on. There were more bodies, but none of them affected me like the hanging woman did. Most of them were just lying in the mess as if they were becoming part of it all—which in a way they were. Sometimes you only knew there was a body there because the crabs were crawling all over it. We kept our eyes peeled for the girl who attacked Sue, or anything else unusual (Dad and Max had brought guns just in case), but we didn't see anything.

Notting Hill, where Max lived, looked like it had been a nice place once. He lived a couple of streets from Portobello Road, which was lined with shops and cafés and restaurants that must once have been full of color and life, but which were now just wrecks covered in slime and seaweed.

The houses on Max's street were joined together with little yards or gardens at the front. There were trees in rows on the pavement, and those that hadn't been torn out by the flood had seaweed and rubbish (mainly long dangling brown loops of stuff that could have been clothes or paper) hanging off their branches. There were a few bodies among the wrecked cars and other junk, and I tensed, thinking Max was going to recognize one of them, but he didn't.

"That's my house," Max said, pointing.

"It looks nice," I said, thinking straightaway how dumb the words sounded.

There was half a billboard on the roof and I hoped it wouldn't come down on us when we tried to get the door open. Before we could even get to the door, though, we had to lift a tree out of the way whose roots were sticking up in the air like a load of black tentacles.

When we lifted it, hundreds of the little red crabs came pouring out of the hole we'd made as if they had a nest under there. Some of them ran over my feet, which made me scream, but at least I didn't drop the tree. I looked down into the hole and saw a body, or bits of one, half-buried in the tangled muddy stuff below. I saw a hand and half a face that looked as if it had no eyes (though they could have been full of mud) and some bones, ribs I think, which were visible because it looked as if the crabs had eaten all the flesh around the chest and stomach. I looked away quickly and concentrated on what I was doing with my bit of the tree.

"Right," Dad said, "how are we gonna do this?"

"I'll go in," Max said. "You don't have to."

"Do you want us to?" Dad said.

Max shrugged and looked away. "Nah, it's all right, man."

I knew what Max was thinking. On the one hand he didn't like the idea of being in there on his own, in case of what he might find, but on the other he didn't like the idea of maybe getting upset in front of us.

"How about we come in with you, but if you want us to go we'll come back outside and wait for you here?" I said.

Max still looked unsure for a few seconds, then said, "Yeah, okay. Thanks."

Although he had a key, the wooden door had swollen with the water and he and Dad had to give it a few kicks before it opened. We jumped back as a wave of water came out, bringing a few things with it—a packet of toilet rolls, a cellophane wrapper filled with a green wet lump of mouldy bread, a wastepaper basket, a cushion, some lumpy stuff that might once have been newspapers or magazines, a black shoe and some other stuff too that I can't remember.

Max picked up the shoe and wiped a layer of mud off it with his thumb. It was a woman's slip-on shoe, black leather with a low heel.

"This is my ma's," he said.

Dad put a hand on his shoulder. "Are you ready for this?"

Max didn't look like he was, but he nodded. "Yeah, man."

We went in. The carpet was like a swamp, the muddy water swirling around our boots. Straightaway I knew (and I'm sure Dad and Max did too) that things were going to be very bad here. We'd only taken a few steps when the smell hit us. Unless you've actually smelled a rotting body it's impossible to describe how disgusting it is. Think of all the rotten things you've ever smelled—meat, fish, cheese, eggs—and then times that by a hundred. It's a thick sort of smell, like a big, greasy cloud of gas. It's hours now since we were in Max's house, but I still get whiffs of it, as if it's in my clothes and skin and hair, and every time I do it makes me want to puke.

I DID puke in Max's house. I couldn't help it. As soon as that smell hit me I turned my head and hurled up the wall. I didn't have time to go outside and do it in the garden. I felt really bad, like I was the rudest person ever, but then Max bent over and he puked too, right between his feet.

Dad took some rags out of his pocket and handed one to me. I *thought it was to wipe my mouth, but he told me to tie it around my face.*

"Sue gave them to me," he said. "She said we might need them."

The rag smelled of something nice, like lavender or something. It didn't make the disgusting smell go away, but it made it bearable.

When we all had our rags tied over our faces, Dad said, "You know the signs here are not good, don't you, Max?"

Max pulled a face as if he didn't want to hear it, but he nodded. "Yeah, man."

"Look," said Dad, "why don't you 2 wait here and I'll see what's what? You don't have to put yourself through this."

Max, tho, shook his head. "I have to see. Even if it's bad I have to see it with my own eyes."

"You sure?" Dad said.

Max nodded.

"Okay," said Dad. "Come on."

Whenever I see people on telly whose houses have been flooded or burned down or whatever, I always feel really sorry for them. I always think of the things they've lost that can never be replaced (photographs and family heirlooms and stuff) and how terrible that must make them feel. And I think of them having to build their lives up again from nothing, having to find a place to live and stuff to put in it. Not just basic stuff like carpets and curtains and furniture, but all the little things we collect over the years that remind us of places we've been or things we've done.

It's weird, but none of that material stuff now seems to matter. When I said this to Dad, he said, "That's because sentiment is a luxury we can no longer afford." What he meant is, sentimental things are fine when the world's okay, because the memories that go with those things exist in that world. But when the actual world's gone, when there's something much bigger to worry about, then the sentimental things aren't worth anything anymore. You can't live on them. You can't keep warm on them. And when nearly everyone's dead except you, the only REALLY important thing is that you're still here. It's like Dad and his Jimi Hendrix guitar string. If that had been nicked a couple of weeks ago he'd have been devastated. But losing it now isn't all that important. It's just a little thing. And we don't have time for little things anymore. There are too many big things to think about.

It was like that with Max too. If I'd gone through his house with him in the normal world and it had been trashed by vandals or burglars, I'm sure he would have been gutted. But the fact that all his and his mum's and brother's stuff was wrecked just wasn't important anymore. Finding his mum was the only important thing. Even though we were 99% sure she was dead, all Max wanted was to find her. Then he could cry for her and close the door on that part of his life and move on, or whatever.

As we expected, we DID find her on the upstairs landing, and she WAS dead. She was lying on her front with her right arm above her head as if she was reaching for something. Her body looked shrunken and twisted, and there were white things moving all over her.

Dad said, "Jesus," and Max made a noise that was half a gasp and half a word. I turned away, feeling sick.

Then Max started whispering over and over, "Oh God, Ma, oh God, oh God, Ma."

"What do you want to do?" Dad said, but Max didn't answer. Dad put a hand on his shoulder. "Max, what do you want to do?" he asked again.

Max was half crying, his voice breaking up. "We've got to bury her, man," he said.

"Are you sure?" Dad said, as if he didn't think it was a good idea. Max looked at him angrily. "I ain't leaving her here!" he shouted.

"Okay," Dad said, and it sounded like the same voice he'd used in the supermarket when he'd been trying to calm down the madman. "If that's what you want, that's what we'll do."

Then Dad came over to me and said quietly, "I want you to wait outside, Abby."

I didn't argue. I went down and waited in the garden. A few minutes later they came out carrying Max's mum's body in a filthy wet duvet. I could see from Dad's face that things had not been good up there. Max looked shocked, as if he'd seen something so bad he was in a daze.

We found a bit of the garden that wasn't too swampy and cleared the rubbish out of the way, and then Dad and Max dug a hole, using *part of a mangled car bumper, taking turns to scoop out great chunks of sloppy earth. When they'd finished they picked up Max's mum's body, still wrapped in the duvet. I went across to help, but Dad said it was okay, they could manage.*

They put the body in the hole, then filled it in again. Then Max went down on his knees beside the grave, his legs folding under him as if he was so tired he couldn't stand up anymore. His knees sank into the mud but he stayed there for a while, his head down and his hands clenched together, as if he was praying. A couple of times his shoulders shook like he was crying, but I didn't hear him making any sounds.

At last he got up, the mud making a slurping noise as he pulled his legs out of it, and walked over to us. He'd taken the mask off his face and tears were running down his cheeks. He wiped an arm across his face and then he looked at us.

"There ain't even any f***ing flowers, man," he said, and he sounded really angry. "There ain't no f***ing flowers in this f***ing world anymore."

"Why don't you put the shoe on the grave?" I said. It was on the path where Max had dropped it earlier.

He didn't answer, and I thought maybe it was a really stupid thing to say. But then Dad said, "It was something that belonged to her. It's more personal than flowers."

Max looked across at the shoe and then he went over and picked it up. Without a word he walked back to the grave and put the shoe on it really carefully, right in the middle. Then he kissed his fingers and touched the shoe and walked back to us.

"Let's go," he said.

THIRTEEN

They turned the body over and recoiled, Max expelling a childlike scream. His mother's face was gone, eaten away. In its place was a hollow of bone and rotting flesh, seething with maggots. More maggots, engorged on putrescence, spilled from the red-black wound of her stomach. As though crazed by blood and galvanized by their feast, the maggots began to twitch and then to *leap,* to flow upwards, fastening themselves to Steve's clothes, pattering his face and hands like raindrops. He felt them wriggling in his hair, attaching themselves to his flesh like leeches. He reeled away, batting at them, snatching handfuls of them from his clothes. He could feel their fat little bodies bursting beneath his fingers, coating his hands with a sticky liquor that smelt of rot. He felt them seeking the orifices of his face, exploring his ears and nostrils, forcing themselves between his lips, probing at the corners of his eyes. . . .

He thought he might have screamed as he snapped awake, though he wasn't sure. If he *had* screamed, then no one had heard it, no one had stirred. He looked around the former classroom they had converted into a dormitory for himself, Max, Marco and Greg. It was pitch-black—no streetlights, nor even a glimmer of moon. But he could hear the deep breathing of sleeping men, Greg's gentle snores. He shuddered, like a dog shaking off the rain, then reached towards his rucksack for his torch.

Dealing with Max's mum's body had been grim, but Steve had done his utmost to hold himself together for the boy's sake. It was only later, walking back to the hotel, that the effects had hit him. He had begun to shake as if his central nervous system were under attack. When they got back to the hotel he had shut himself away for an hour, trying, not for the first time, to come to terms with the way the world had been tipped on its head. Tonight's dream had been an exaggeration of what had happened, but not a wild one. Steve had certainly never seen so many maggots, and particularly not ones that appeared so lively. Indeed, it was the fact they had seemed almost *aggressive* that he had found so repellent. Careful as he and Max had been not to touch the corpse, they had still discovered maggots beading them throughout the enshrouding of it, had had to keep swiping away the wriggling little lumps of life that managed to find their way onto their sleeves and thighs, even their shoulders and lapels.

Making sure that his torch was pointing upwards, he turned it on. The water-stained ceiling squashed the beam into a white pool of illumination that cast definition around the room. Steve glanced over to where Max was curled in his sleeping bag. If Steve was suffering nightmares, then God only knew what Max was going through—though for the moment he appeared to be sleeping peacefully.

Steve shucked off his sleeping bag and rummaged in his rucksack for his tin of tobacco and his rolling papers. He slipped on his still-damp boots, grimacing at the clamminess he felt against the soles of his feet; then in a T-shirt, sweater, boxer shorts and boots, he made his way out of the room.

Plodding down the corridor, torch beam probing ahead of him, it occurred to Steve that they could not have found a more eerie place to make camp than this secondary school in Dollis Hill. Schools in general were weird places—full of life by day and mausoleums by night. The thought that most, if not all, of the children who, until just over a week ago, had come here every day were now gone forever made the place seem eerier still. If ever there was a building where the spirits of the dead might congregate, then this was it.

He shivered and entered a classroom at the far end of the corridor. Spooked by his own thoughts, he forced open the water-swollen door of the stationary cupboard in the corner to ensure that there was nothing lurking inside, ready to leap out at him. On this side of the building, the room was intermittently lit by flashes of the blue lightning out on the horizon. Steve's torchlight crawled across chairs and desks, which had been strewn about as though by a mob of unruly children, the wood they were constructed from softened and darkened by water. He found a chair that was cleaner than most and easy to tug from the tangle of furniture and equipment. He guessed this room had once been a language lab, judging by the two laminated posters, bleached and wrinkled, that still clung to the walls. He wiped clots of silt from the seat of the chair and set it beneath the window. Then he sat down and rolled himself a cigarette.

He wondered how long it would take them to reach Scotland. How far away *was* Scotland? Five hundred miles? Today they had traveled about five miles, working their way mainly up the A5, through Paddington and Maida Vale, Kilburn and Cricklewood. Sue had spent Sunday afternoon building a kind of sedan chair out of dried-out planks of wood salvaged from the surrounding streets. This had been used to lift Mr. B's wheelchair over the tricky bits, and overall it had worked pretty well. He, Abby, Max, Marco, Sue and Libby had taken turns carrying the old man in half-hour stints. The day had been uneventful aside from one major blowup between Sue and Marco. It had started because Marco had grunted something about Mr. B being a burden when it had been his turn to carry the old man's wheelchair.

The only person who didn't seem to take offense at Marco's comment had been George himself.

"You're right, old son," he said, "I *am* a burden. I wish there was somethin' I could do about it, but there ain't. So if you decided to leave me behind, I wouldn't be able to blame yer."

"Don't you worry, Mr. Beamish," Sue said. "If anyone's going to be left behind, it's him."

Marco sneered. "Oh yeah? I'd like to see you try."

"Oh, I don't think you would," Sue said dangerously.

With an arrogant shake of the head, Marco said, "You ain't the law no more, girl. You might think you are, but you ain't."

"Believe it or not, I'm well aware of that fact," Sue said. "What I *am*, though, is a member of a group of people who need to work together to survive. Do you understand the situation we're in here, Marco? Has the significance of what we're facing not just today but possibly every day for the rest of our lives penetrated that tiny brain of yours? Because I don't think it has."

"Fuck you!" Marco snarled. "I don't need to listen to this shit."

"I rather think you do, Marco," Greg interceded quietly.

"Fucking hell," Marco said, "you're all in this together."

"We're not *in* anything, Marco," Steve said, "except deep shit. Sue's right. We need to work as a team, help each other. You included."

"Might have thought *you'd* have your fucking say," Marco said. "Well, you're not my fucking boss, pal, and you never will be."

"Grow up, you moron!" Sue yelled suddenly, making Abby jump.

"Yeah, man, shut your mouth," Max said.

Marco looked wildly at each of them—and then he swung the Heckler and Koch he had been carrying from his shoulder. He didn't exactly point it at anyone, but he held it as though he would be prepared to if provoked.

Libby took a step backwards. Mabel gave a little scream. George said conversationally, "What you gonna do, son? Put me out of my misery?"

Before Marco could respond, Sue said evenly, "If you point that at any of us it will be the biggest mistake of your life."

"Oh yeah?" Marco said.

"Yeah," said Sue, and turned to Steve. "Knew it was a mistake giving him a gun. Knew he wouldn't handle it responsibly. It's just lucky I didn't give him any ammunition."

She swung her own Heckler and Koch from her shoulder and tapped the stubby magazine that was loaded forward of the trigger. Marco stared at her weapon, then his own, and saw the empty space there. His face turned a deep crimson. He hurled the gun to the ground.

"Fuck you!" he screamed, then turned and stomped away.

"Oh dear," Mabel moaned.

"Marco," Greg called, and started to go after him.

Sue, however, held up a hand, as though halting traffic. "Let him go."

"But we can't leave him to his own devices," Greg said. "I doubt he'd have the resources to survive on his own."

"He'll catch up," Sue said.

"How can you be so sure?" asked Libby.

Sue turned and gave her a hard smile that failed to reach her eyes. "Trust me."

She was right. A couple of hours later Marco reappeared, silently tagging on to the back of the group. No one said anything. No one spoke to him until half an hour later when Steve and Abby were coming to the end of their stint carrying George's wheelchair and it was time to hand over to someone else. Then Sue called, "Hey, Marco, you want to help me with this?"

Abby braced herself, but Marco gave an abrupt nod and plodded forward. Steve looked at Libby and raised his eyebrows and was rewarded with a wink and a smile.

So. At their present rate of progress it would take them one hundred days to reach Scotland. Three months traveling. That would take them past Christmas and into the New Year. Steve wondered where they would spend Christmas

Day and how they would cope with the tumbling temperatures as winter approached.

"Penny for them," a voice said behind him.

He spun so violently that his cigarette went flying out of his hand. Silhouetted in the doorway was the figure of a woman. A crackle of blue lightning revealed it to be Libby, her skin and hair limned in blue. Her laughter was light, but with an underlying throatiness that Steve found incredibly sexy.

"Sorry," she said, "did I make you jump?"

"No, no," he said, spying the glowing ember of his dropped cigarette and plucking it from the damp floorboards. He grinned. "My hair hasn't turned white, has it?"

"Well . . . perhaps just the tiniest bit gray. Mind if I join you?"

"Not at all," said Steve. "Pull up a pew. On second thought, you have this one, and I'll get another for myself."

He hauled another chair from the silted tangle of wood and metal. As Libby sat he saw her cross her arms and shudder.

"Cold?" he asked.

"Not really. It's just that creepy lightning. It gives me the shudders."

He set his chair opposite hers, wiping the seat with his sleeve. "Yeah, I know what you mean. It's like an omen or something, isn't it? But the bad thing's already been and gone."

"Maybe there's worse to come."

"Now *there's* a cheery thought." Steve took a pull on his cigarette. "Do you smoke?"

"No."

"Don't blame you. Disgusting habit." He dropped the stub and stamped on it. "So, I'm guessing you couldn't sleep?"

"I've done enough sleeping recently. I've already missed a lot of the fun."

"Yeah, it's been a riot." He smiled at her and she smiled back. "So, what did you do before you got shipwrecked?" he asked.

"I was a primary school teacher in Canterbury. You?"

"Retail baron slash rock star," he said, and grinned at her skeptical expression. "I owned a record shop in Peckham and played in a band."

"Did you sell your own records?"

"*Sell* is stretching it a bit. *Stocked* would be more accurate."

She laughed again, uncrossing her arms and moving her hands up and down her denim-clad thighs.

"I love your laugh," Steve said, then held up a hand in apology. "Sorry, that sounded like a cheap chat-up line. I just meant it's nice to hear someone laugh again. There hasn't been enough of it recently."

"So, what's *your* story?" Libby asked. "I know you and Abby are hoping to find your wife—"

"*Ex*-wife."

"*Ex*-wife and son in Scotland. But how did you survive in the first place?"

Steve told her. It had been only five days since he, Abby and the Beamishes had set out on their journey, but the three days they had spent trapped with water swirling around them already seemed like ancient history.

"How did you get together with this boyfriend of yours, if you don't mind me asking?" Steve said. "I mean, where do you *meet* dot-com millionaires? And are there any female ones you can introduce me to?"

Another laugh. Steve was loving the fact that this gorgeous woman was finding him so amusing.

"We were both members of the same gym," she said. "Our eyes met across the elliptical trainers."

"Painful," said Steve. "Had you been going out for a while?"

"No. This was only our second date. I usually take things a bit slower, but it's not every day a bloke asks you to spend a few days on his luxury yacht." Suddenly she looked down at her hands and her voice grew quieter. "Poor Tom."

Steve wondered whether he should reach out to her. In the end he simply said, "Shall we talk about something else?"

She gave him a watery smile. "It's okay. It's not like Tom and I were really close. He was just . . . a nice guy, you know. Not really my type, if truth be told, but nice all the same."

He knew it was crass, but Steve wanted to ask, *So, what is*

your type? And he wanted her to reply, *Well, if I'm honest, some-*
one like you. And then he would lean forward and kiss her
softly on the lips. . . .

"So, what are *your* plans?" he asked. "Long-term, I mean?"

She shrugged. "I haven't thought that far ahead."

"Any family *you* want to track down?"

"My dad died when I was five and my mum died four years
ago. They were elderly parents. My mum was forty-four
when she had me. I was a mistake."

"A welcome one, I'm sure."

She smiled a little wistfully. "Yes."

Steve was about to speak again when someone screeched,
"Help! Help me!"

"That's Mrs. B," Steve said, jumping up so quickly that his
chair clattered against the wall. He grabbed his torch from the
windowsill and raced across the room, followed by Libby.

Mabel was standing outside the door of the classroom she
was sharing with George. Her hair was a frizzy halo in the
torchlight and her fists were clenched. She winced beneath
the light and called in a quivering voice, "Who's that?"

"It's Steve, Mrs. B." He turned the torch round and shone
it on himself. "What's up?"

"George woke up with chest pains," she said, "and then he
just collapsed."

"Get Greg," Steve said to Libby. She nodded and hurried
away. Steve ran past Mabel and into the classroom. His torch
beam swept across the empty wheelchair, the metal frame of
which reflected light in slick white flashes. He heard George
before he saw him, his breath liquid and tortuous, as though
he were gargling mud. The old man was lying on a mound of
crumpled bedding atop a plastic sheet on the floor, and he did
not look good. His face was reddish blue and his lips a livid
purple, as though he were being throttled.

Steve's mind was racing. He thrust his torch at Mabel, who
was hovering behind his left shoulder, and tried to sound
calm. "Could you point this down at George so that I can see
what I'm doing, Mrs. B?"

She nodded and took the torch, but seemed to fumble it, as if her hands were numb with cold. For a moment Steve was terrified she would drop it and that it would break, forcing him to try and resuscitate George in the dark. Then she got a grip on it, pinning her ailing husband in the spotlight. Steve tried to remember the basics of the first-aid course he had taken ten, twelve years ago. First check the mouth for obstructions, make sure the patient hasn't swallowed his tongue. . . .

He dropped to his knees, peering into the old man's mouth, smelling the smoky sourness of his breath.

"Could you shine the torch down here, Mrs. B?" he said. "I want to check that George's air passages are clear."

The light became whiter, more concentrated. Under its harsh scrutiny the old man's purpling flesh looked ghastly, as though veins and vessels were erupting everywhere, suffusing the paper-thin sack of his skin with escaping blood. The light turned his mouth into a frothing red wound. Steve tried to blank his mind, then clamped his mouth to that of the old man's. He pinched George's nostrils shut with his left hand and tugged the man's lower jaw wider with his right. He blew air into the old man's mouth, trying to ignore the foulness of George's breath and George's foamy, curdled saliva mingling with his own.

The couple of minutes before help arrived seemed like an eternity. Steve was wondering whether to attempt heart massage (remembering his instructor's comment that you couldn't be halfhearted, that sometimes you had to go about it with enough force to crack ribs) when Libby, Max and Greg entered the room.

"How is he?" Greg asked, lowering himself gingerly to his knees.

"Not good," Steve said. "I've given him mouth to mouth, but he doesn't seem to be responding."

He moved aside to allow Greg access. After a quick examination, Greg said, "He's arrested." He glanced at Mabel. "Mabel, has George had his medication today?"

She nodded, her face fearful. "Yes. He's been taking it religiously. I make sure of that." She hesitated. "Is he going to be all right?"

Greg glanced at Steve and said, "We're doing all we can, Mabel, but I'm afraid George is very ill."

"Oh dear," she moaned.

"Look, Mrs. B, why don't you give the torch to Libby?" Steve said. "Max, will you get the stove going, make Mabel a nice cuppa?"

"Sure," Max said.

"I want to stay," said Mabel.

Greg had tilted George's head back and had already started artificial respiration.

"I don't think that's a good idea, Mrs. B," Steve said. "You might find it upsetting."

"I want to stay," she said more firmly.

Steve shrugged. He certainly wasn't about to argue with an old lady in front of her dying husband. He sat back on his haunches and watched Greg working on George, feeling dismal and helpless.

"There's no response," Greg said finally. "Steve, can you give me a hand here?"

"Sure. What do you want me to do?"

"Can you move round to the other side and keep going with the artificial respiration while I start with the chest compressions?"

"No problem."

"Keep it as regular as you can. One breath every four seconds."

They kept going for the next ten minutes, until Steve was feeling breathless and dizzy and Greg was dripping with sweat. Finally, exhausted, Greg straightened up, head rolling back on his shoulders. "It's no good," he gasped. "He's gone."

"Oh no!" Mabel wailed.

"Ain't there *nothing* you can do?" Max asked bleakly.

"Not unless you've got a defibrillator and a source to power it with," muttered Greg.

"Shit, man," Max said.

Steve rubbed his hands over his face, then looked around bleakly. At some stage Abby had entered the room and was now trying to console a sobbing Mabel, even though she herself was weeping. The torch was drooping in Libby's hand. Behind her stood Sue and Max. All three wore expressions of abject despair. The only member of the group who was not present was Marco, who—Steve thought with a sudden surge of anger—was no doubt still curled up in his sleeping bag, warm and cosy and lost in his dreams.

FOURTEEN

Nobody felt like sleeping. At first light they wrapped George in the duvet he'd died on and buried him at the edge of the football pitch round the back of the school.

It was a dismal day. A light rain was falling from a cement gray sky—the first since the flood nine days earlier. Steve and Marco dug the hole, using shovels they found in the caretaker's lockup. The ground was marshy, but ironically this made the digging tougher than it would have been had the earth been baked hard. Each time they removed a spadeful of muddy soil, the hole immediately filled up again with filthy water.

But at last they were done. Everyone filed out as they lay George to rest. Steve said a few words (like it or not, it seemed the position of leader—or at least spokesman—of the group had been foisted upon him almost by default); then they filed away, leaving Mabel to say her private good-byes to the man with whom she had shared the past fifty-two years of her life.

Not that he wanted to make an issue of it today of all days, but since Marco had crawled from his sleeping bag that morning, Steve had been monitoring his behavior closely. And so far he had been impeccable. He had seemed shocked, albeit in a subdued way, when informed of George's death.

"I was dead to the world. Someone should have woke me up," he mumbled.

"You wouldn't have been able to do anything," Sue said.

"Even so . . ." He glanced at Mabel. "Sorry about George," he said. "And sorry for what I said yesterday an' all."

It was a subdued party that set out later that morning on the next leg of their journey. They left the wheelchair behind, of course, but took one of the shovels with them.

It was around midday when they heard the strange clattering that at first none of them could identify.

"What the hell's *that?*" Max said, swinging his gun from his shoulder, as if he believed the sound was the prelude to some form of attack.

The rest of them had stopped and were looking around too. "Sounds like a motor," said Sue.

"There, look!" Abby was pointing at the murky sky, excitement in her voice. At first Steve saw nothing but birds, wheeling high like flecks of ash. Then he saw the glint of light on metal.

"It's a helicopter," Libby breathed. There was wonder on her face. She glanced at Steve in gleeful hope. "Does this mean we're saved?"

"I don't know," Steve said.

"I would advise caution," Greg muttered.

"What makes you think he might be hostile?" asked Sue. Steve noticed that her fingers were resting idly on the butt of the Glock in her belt.

"I didn't say that. I just meant perhaps we oughtn't to get our hopes up," Greg said.

"It's not an official aircraft," said Sue. "Looks like a Robinson Raven, or a Raven Two. R44, I'd say."

"What does *that* mean?" asked Steve.

"R44, as opposed to an R22. Four-seater, not a two-seater. Like a family saloon."

"You know a lot about helicopters," Max said.

Sue shrugged. "Not a lot, but I know Robinson is an American company, and I'm pretty sure UK emergency services don't have any—but I might be wrong. We're more likely to use McDonnells or Eurocopters."

"So that helicopter might have come from America?" said Abby.

Sue smiled. "Not unless it was able to refuel somewhere over the ocean. No, I'd guess it's a business helicopter, privately owned. Is it the same one you and Abby saw, Steve?"

Steve shrugged. "It looks about the same size. And it *was* white."

As the helicopter drew closer, shedding rain and scattering birds, Abby, Libby and Max began leaping up and down, shouting and waving their arms. Sue and Steve waved too, though more sedately. Greg, Mabel and an uncharacteristically quiet Marco simply stood and watched the machine approach.

It was obvious the pilot had seen them. Not only did he circle them several times, but at one point—although he was little more than a silhouette—he distinctly raised an arm.

"He waved to us! Did you see that?" Abby cried, her face shining with rain and excitement.

"Do you think he's looking for somewhere to land?" asked Max.

But after circling them several more times, the helicopter began to move away.

"Hey!" Max shouted. "Hey!" Hampered by his rucksack and by the MP5 over his shoulder, he began to run after the helicopter, only realizing how pointless it was when he slipped and went down on one knee. "Shit," he said.

"Looks like he was on reconnaissance only," said Sue. "He would never have been able to take us all anyway."

"Do you think he'll come back?" Libby asked.

"I wouldn't count on it," said Steve.

They plodded on, and by early afternoon they reached the tangle of roads where the A5 passed under the A406 North Circular and the M1 began. Steve hoped that once they were on the motorway progress would be quicker. He was hoping, in fact, that they could up their mileage to a still-comfortable ten a day—though that would depend on whether the older members of the party could sustain such a schedule. He was hoping too that there wouldn't be too much debris on the road because of how light the traffic would have been at the time of the flood—though who knew how far and wide the country's snatched-up flotsam and jetsam might have been carried before being dumped back down like the accumulated crap from God's garbage can?

There *was* a danger, naturally, that the farther they walked the *slower* they would get, due to people picking up injuries en route—muscular stresses and strains, cuts and blisters. Also supplies might be harder to come by as they moved out of the city, and then of course there was the good old British weather.

So many factors to take into account, so many imponderables, so much that could go wrong. When it came right down to it, Steve thought, all they could *really* do was plow on and hope for the best

Although they no longer had George's wheelchair to cope with, it was, ironically, *because* of George that progress had been slower than usual that day. Unsurprisingly, the death of her husband had hit Mabel hard and she had been shuffling along as though hauling a huge burden behind her. Of course no one had pilloried her about it, and in fact they were *all* tired, borne down by sleeplessness and grief. It had taken the appearance of the helicopter to raise the level of conversation above more than the occasional murmured comment.

As Steve had hoped, the motorway, with its wide lanes, was much easier to negotiate than the congested London streets. There was still a huge amount of debris, but it was scattered over a wider area and therefore easier to weave in and out of. As they started up the long road towards Scotland, Steve sensed a definite lifting of spirits and a willingness to pick up the pace. Hoping that Mabel wouldn't find it a struggle keeping up, he dropped back to keep her company.

"How you doing, Mrs. B?" he asked.

She looked up and gave him a watery smile. "Oh, pretty awful, to tell you the truth. In fact, I've just been wondering why I'm even bothering to go on."

Steve wasn't sure how to respond at first. Then he said, "Well, I suppose we go on because there's no other alternative."

"You know what I've been thinking?" she said as if he hadn't spoken. "I've been thinking what difference would it make if I sat down here and never got up again. Because my life's over now, Steve. It's as over as the lives of these other poor souls." She indicated the dead bodies decomposing among the silt and debris.

"I can understand why—" Steve began, but Mabel interrupted him.

"Our lives, mine and George's, were over the minute that bloody wave came along. This world's not for the likes of us old codgers. You and Abby and Max and the rest of you . . . you're young, you might make a decent go of it. But I don't want this, Steve. I don't want to have to struggle at my age. And I don't want to be a burden either."

"You're not a burden, Mabel," Steve said, "and you never will be."

It was only when she smiled again that he realized how much she had aged even in the past week. "It's sweet of you to say so, dear," she said, "but I know you're all having to go slowly because of me, and that's not right."

"I don't think anyone's got much energy today," Steve said. "We're all upset about George."

"I know, dear." Her voice broke on the last word and she began to sob, her shoulders shaking uncontrollably. Steve wrapped his arms around her and held her until her tears subsided a little. Then he kissed her tenderly on the forehead.

"I never had a grandma," he said. "My dad's mum was killed by a bomb in the war and my mum's mum died of septicemia the year before I was born, so I never knew either of them. But if I *had* had a gran, I'd have loved her to have been like you."

Mabel thumped him lightly on the chest. "Go on, you daft beggar. Save that silver tongue of yours for young Libby."

"It's true," Steve said. "You're one of the reasons why this bloody world is still worth living in."

Mabel was silent for a moment, then said, "We'd better get walking again, or the others will be leaving us behind."

"I don't think we'll lose them," said Steve. "It's straight on till morning from here."

They resumed their interminable trudge. The layer of silt on the road stretched as far as the eye could see.

"You and young Libby seem to be getting chummy," Mabel said.

Steve blushed. "I like her. She's a nice girl."

"She's a *lovely* girl," Mabel said. "And she likes you too."

"You think so?" Steve felt a wriggle of pleasure in his belly.

"I *know* so."

"Why? Has she said something?"

Mabel was about to respond when, thirty yards ahead of them, Greg suddenly cried out, spun around and collapsed to the ground.

Instantly Steve heard a whooping sound off to his left. He turned to see several scrawny figures appear at the top of the litter-strewn banking and come tearing down in great lolloping strides towards them. One of the figures was carrying a crossbow, which made him think ridiculously of wagon trains in the Wild West being ambushed by Indians. Ahead of Steve, Abby and Libby started running towards the crumpled figure of Greg, and he saw Sue drawing her Glock, Max swinging his MP5 from his shoulder.

Steve drew his own Glock and said, "Mabel, get behind me."

"What's happening?" she said.

"It's an ambush," he replied, aware even as he spoke the words how crazy they sounded.

A gunshot cracked in the air with a sound like an exploding firework. Steve saw one of the attackers fall down the banking and for an awful moment thought that Sue had shot him.

Then he saw the others either sliding to a halt or diving for cover and realized they were taking evasive action. Having fired a shot into the air, Sue now lowered her gun and pointed it at the gang.

"Come any closer and I'll blow your fucking heads off!" she yelled.

The kids looked at one another, evidently bewildered and scared. Now that Steve could focus on them he realized they were a sorry bunch. Thin, filthy and dressed in rags, they ranged in age from thirteen to about twenty. There were five of them, four boys and one girl. It was the oldest boy who was holding the crossbow. Greg was lying motionless, an arrow protruding from him. From where he was, Steve couldn't see which part of his body it had penetrated.

In a plaintive voice the girl on the banking called out, "We're hungry."

"Tough shit," shouted Sue. "Now drop the bow and get the fuck out of here."

"We only want some food," one of the boys shouted.

"Then you should have thought about asking nicely before you attacked us. Now I haven't got time to argue. One of our party is injured and needs treatment. If you haven't all disappeared in ten seconds I'm going to start shooting. And that is no idle threat."

The teenagers immediately scrambled back up the banking like frightened mice and disappeared over the top. The older boy looked at Sue sullenly for a moment, then hurled his crossbow and arrows to the ground and stomped away.

"I'm going to see if Greg's all right," Steve said.

"You go," said Mabel. "I'll catch you up."

Steve ran across to where Libby and Abby were crouching beside Greg. Sue, gun still drawn, told Marco to fetch the crossbow. To Steve's surprise Marco obeyed the order without question.

"How is he?" Steve asked.

Abby looked ashen. Her hands and clothes, and Libby's too,

were covered in Greg's blood. Steve saw they had been trying to staunch the flow with a towel from Abby's rucksack.

"The arrow's gone . . . right through him," Abby said.

"Let me see."

Steve crouched down, and immediately winced. The arrow had passed through Greg's arm and lodged itself in his rib cage. There was too much blood and torn clothing to see how deeply it was embedded in his chest. But it was not beyond the realm of possibility that the tip of the arrow had smashed its way through his ribs and punctured his heart.

As if confirming his fears, Libby said bleakly, "I think he might be dead."

FIFTEEN

Abby moaned and drifted awake. She was more exhausted than she had ever been in her life and yet she was finding it impossible to slip into the REM sleep her body craved. It was partly the stench of death suffusing the hotel in which they had been forced to spend the night; it was partly her anxiety for Greg; and it was partly the awful memories of the past few days, playing in her mind like a repeating film reel.

By the time they had managed to staunch the gush of blood from Greg's wounds, she, Dad and Libby looked like they had finished a shift at the local abattoir. While she had been ministering to Greg, Abby had been concerned purely with the task in hand. It was only afterwards, once the bleeding had been stymied, that revulsion had surged through her and she had reeled away, retching at the hot, coppery smell on her hands and clothes. She had dumped her rucksack on the ground and had torn off her "new" wax jacket (chosen from Sue's impressive stock of salvaged clothing), and hurled it away from her. Even as the jacket was sailing through the air, trailing blood like a fresh animal pelt, Abby had stooped and plunged her hands into the silt at her feet. She had rubbed her palms back and forth in the dirt, coating them, hiding the blood, trying to rid herself of its stickiness.

Dad, Marco, Max and Sue had carried Greg five miles to the next rest stop. It had been raining and Greg had been mostly unconscious, the rain falling on his upturned face. Towards the end he had begun to writhe and mutter, his lips as gray as his beard, his skin deathly pale. Abby wondered how much blood he had lost, and whether, in the world before the flood, he would have been given a transfusion. There was no chance of that now, of course. No transfusion, no operation, not even crisp clean sheets or central heating. The best they could do was milkless tea, painkillers, bottled water and disinfectant.

Exhausted and soaking, they had taken refuge in the Days Hotel at London Gateway a couple of junctions up the M1. The hotel had been half occupied at the time of the flood and it stunk to high heaven with the rotting dead. Gagging, Libby had put her hand—Greg's blood still under her fingernails—over her mouth and had said, "We can't stay here."

"Beggars can't be choosers," Sue had said grimly. She had opened a small zip pocket in the side of her rucksack and extracted a thumb-sized bottle of Albas Oil, a few drops of which she had sprinkled on each of their cuffs. "If it gets unbearable, breathe this in," she had said. "We'll try and find a bunch of unoccupied rooms close together."

It was clear that no one had been in the hotel since the flood. The fixtures and fittings were strewn with mud; the carpets were saturated and layered with silt; the air was thick with flies, which were instantly attracted to Greg's bandaged but still seeping wounds. The former occupants, now in a state of such putrefaction that they were boiling with maggots and coming apart like rancid cheese, were mostly confined to the rooms they'd been sleeping in when the disaster had struck.

The group found four unoccupied adjoining rooms on the third floor, spread out their plastic sheets and bedding, opened the windows to let in some air, and settled down for the night. One of the rooms was given to Greg and whoever was watching over him. Everyone had elected to sit with him for at least an hour to monitor his condition. Abby took the first watch and then crawled down into her sleeping bag, trying to distance herself from the stink and the mess and all the horrible things in the world. She was asleep as soon as her eyes closed, but it was not a restful sleep. She tossed and turned, and when she *did* finally wake up some hours later, her body felt as though it had been never still, as though she had run a marathon. She had no idea what time it was. The battery on her phone had died days ago and she never wore a watch. It was pitch-black. The air was stifling despite the open window. The stench of putrefaction was so strong that she couldn't help but imagine that the dead were in the room with her. So vivid was the image that she swung out an arm, half expecting to connect with a soft, bloated face. Something moved close to her, and a shard of fear pierced her gut. Then the room was bathed in a flickering flash of blue-white light as lightning streaked on the horizon, and she realized that the movement had just been Sue, turning over with a soft grunt.

Abby needed some air. Real air. Air from outside. She didn't relish the thought of creeping through the hotel in the dark, but she honestly thought that if she breathed any more of the hotel's poisoned air she'd puke.

She struggled fully dressed out of her sleeping bag and hastily dragged on her boots. She rummaged in her rucksack for her torch, then tiptoed out of the room, wincing each time the plastic sheet crackled beneath her feet.

The smell of death was worse in the corridor and she breathed in the smell of Albas Oil from her cuff. It helped. Not much, but a bit. She switched on her torch, illuminating a carpet caked with filth, and mold-blotched walls from which strips of sodden wallpaper lolled like thick red tongues. The door to the room where Greg was sleeping was slightly ajar and the flickering glow of a candle flame was discernible through the gap. Abby briefly toyed with the idea of popping in to say hi to whoever was on duty, but then it occurred to her that it might be Marco.

She crept down the stairs and eventually reached the lobby,

which she had been dreading because there were two bodies there. The air was so rank she felt as though she could cut a hole in it. One of the bodies was underneath a big window on the left, and the other was over by the reception desk, its arms above the black, festering pile of gunk that had once been its head. Abby had tried not to look at the bodies closely when they entered the hotel, but she hadn't been able to help glancing at them. She had seen enough to tell from their filthy clothes that both of them had been women, and that the one under the window was wearing a string of pearls around her neck.

At least by knowing where the bodies were, she could direct her torch away from them, leaving them in the shadows. Then again, *not* being able to see them was in some ways even worse. The worst thing of all, though, would be if she shone her torch onto one of them and it *wasn't* there. Try as she might, she couldn't help imagining doing that very thing, and then hearing a sludgy snarling noise behind her. What if she spun round and the dead thing was right behind her, its flesh greeny-black and maggots falling out of its eyes. . . .

That did it. She bolted across the lobby, torch beam veering wildly, breath like a hacksaw in her throat. She reached the main doors, the glass still miraculously intact, and blundered out into the night. Immediately a barrage of cold rain and wind hit her, making her head swim so violently that she thought she was going to faint. She crouched down just outside the door, hunched over, hair hanging limply across her face. The torch dangled between her hands, its beam pooling in the silt at her feet. She took a deep breath, and another, retched suddenly, then felt the nausea begin to pass. Already her fears from moments before seemed foolish enough to make her smile. She glanced at the blue lightning and started to straighten up—and a hand snaked round from behind her, clamping over her face and cutting off her breath.

SIXTEEN

"How is he?"

Libby's head jerked up as Max entered the room. She hadn't realized she'd nodded off until he spoke. She glanced guiltily at Greg, but he was still sleeping peacefully. "Must have phased out for a minute there," she said. "Um . . . what did you say?"

Max smiled. "I was just asking how Greg is."

"Oh. Okay, I think. He woke up earlier and we had a little chat. He was drowsy but lucid. The main thing is to keep the wound free from infection. If we can do that hopefully he'll be fine. How about you? How you doing?"

Max shrugged. "Better than Greg."

"I didn't mean physically. I meant . . . with your mum and everything."

Max glanced away, and for a second—despite his broad shoulders, his athletic frame, the fuzz of dark beard on his chin—he looked boyish, vulnerable. "Okay," he muttered. "It's just something I gotta live with." He nodded at Greg. "So, what were you and the doc talking about?"

"Oh, the usual. The latest cinema releases, what Victoria

Beckham is wearing, where we're going for our holidays . . ."
She laughed at Max's expression. "You should see yourself.
You look so superior. No, Greg asked me what had happened,
where we were; then he became very practical. He asked me
if the wound was clean, how much blood he had lost, what
medication he was being given, and whether I could see his
fingers moving."

"And could you?" asked Max.

"Yes."

"That's a good sign, ain't it?"

"I suppose so."

Max looked down at the pale, gray-bearded man with
something like affection. "He'll be okay, the doc. He's a
tough old boy."

Libby said good night and left the room. Max looked at his
watch—5:05 A.M. He wondered what the next day would
bring. He guessed they would probably have to stay here another day or two to give the doc time to recover. It was frus-
trating making such little progress, but there wasn't much
alternative. He was settling back in his chair, wishing he had
something to occupy his mind—a book or a pack of cards, or
better still a Game Boy—when the door opened and Libby
reentered the room.

"Have you seen Abby?" she asked.

"No, why?"

"It's just she's not in her sleeping bag. Seems a bit odd,
that's all. Where would she have gone?"

Max shrugged. "Toilet?"

"No, I've just partaken of the facilities myself," said Libby,
referring to the two his and hers buckets they used at night,
"and she's not there."

"Well, maybe she couldn't sleep. Maybe she wanted some air."

"Maybe," conceded Libby, "but it seems a bit weird. Do
you think we should look for her?"

"I dunno. We shouldn't leave Greg, should we?"

"Actually," said Libby, "when I said 'we' I kind of meant
'you.' I don't fancy creeping around in the dark. I thought

maybe I could sit with Greg for five minutes while you have a quick look round."

"Okay," Max said wearily, and pushed himself to his feet.

He was gone maybe ten minutes. She heard the thumping squelch of his footsteps a couple of seconds before he burst into the room.

"I think someone's taken her." He panted out the words.

Libby felt her guts clench. "Why? What have you found?"

"Outside the main doors . . . a torch, still turned on . . . and there are drag marks in the mud . . . and footsteps that I'm sure aren't ours." He took a deep breath. "I'll get Steve and Marco. You tell Sue. Mrs. B can sit with Greg."

Libby nodded, but Max didn't see it. He was already running from the room.

SEVENTEEN

At first she thought it was the kids, but it wasn't. It was the man from the supermarket. Though small and skinny, he was strong. Abby fought furiously, tried to rake her heels down his shins, but he held her tightly, his filthy hand crushed over her mouth and nose with such force she could barely breathe. After a minute or so her head began to swim and she started to panic. She felt herself losing coordination, her chest becoming tight.

I'm going to die, she thought. *Oh God, I'm going to die.*

Then the man shifted his hand from her face to tighten his grip on her arms, and she whooped in a great lungful of air. He half carried, half dragged her along the silty ground, scampering away with his catch like a spider with a fly.

When he was out of sight of the hotel, he hooked his leg around hers to scoop her feet from under her, then slammed her facedown onto the ground. As her chin connected with the road, Abby's teeth clacked together so hard she might have bitten off her tongue if it hadn't been curled at the base of her mouth. The silt helped cushion the impact, though her chin would be bruised in the morning—assuming she was still alive then. The silt was cold and sticky and foul-smelling, but it was the least of her troubles. Worse was the fact that the man was now clambering onto her back, pressing his weight down on her.

He's going to rape me! Abby thought with a bright flare of panic. She raised her head from the silt with a sucking sound. "Don't," she begged. "Please . . ."

The man ignored her. He was muttering to himself, but Abby couldn't make out the words. She gasped as the man yanked her arms behind her back, and then again as something bit into her wrists, forcing them together.

When he hooked a hand into the belt of her jeans and hauled her to her feet, she felt almost relieved. He gave her a little push, still muttering, the words coming out of his mouth in a breathy cascade.

"You-walk-walk-forward-don't-run-keep-walking-don't-try-don't-run-don't-try-to-change-I'll-kill-you-I-mean-it-I'll-kill-you-if-you-try-just-walk-I-can-you-know-I-can-kill-you. . . ."

She stumbled ahead of him in the darkness, sliding in the silt, tripping over unseen objects in her path. Her captor was clearly deranged, keeping up a ceaseless and often incoherent stream of babble, his movements quick, birdlike. He directed her onto the motorway, up the banking and across a water-logged field. The rain was coming down hard now, droplets exploding softly on her scalp, diluting the silt, which ran down her neck and dripped from her throbbing chin. In the darkness the downpour was visible only when the blue lightning ripped apart the night sky in sporadic flashes, whereupon it was revealed as an endless torrent of silver arrows.

Beyond the field was an estate of identical pale-stoned houses with pan-tiled roofs. Though they were still technically in north London, somewhere between—where was it Dad had said?—Edgware and Elstree, the darkness and rain and the lack of life made it seem like the back end of nowhere.

Abby thought about everyone back at the hotel, curled up in their sleeping bags, and wondered when she would be missed, how far away she would be by then, how the hell Dad and the others would even *begin* to start looking for her? She was scared of provoking this man, but she was even more scared of not knowing what was going to happen to her, and eventually she blurted, "Where are you taking me?"

He didn't answer. He just kept muttering to himself. Abby felt a rush of desperation, and then a welcome flare of anger. She stopped walking and turned round, her hair plastered to her face, her hooded sweatshirt heavy with water.

"Where are you taking me?" she yelled.

He bared his teeth at her. He looked more simian than human. His tie had gone. His glasses too. A thought skimmed across Abby's mind: *How good is his eyesight?* He seemed to have no trouble negotiating the darkness—as if, by shedding the trappings of civilization, he had awakened long dormant senses and instincts.

"I'm not moving till you tell me why you're doing this," she said.

He pointed at her. His hands were crusted with that was running in the rain. Two of his fingernails were overlong, while the others were ragged and broken.

"Been-watching-you," he muttered. "Been-following-you-you-don't-see-me-you're-not-as-clever-as-you-think." He waggled his head, raindrops flying from the knotted clumps of his hair. "Know-what-you-are-seen-you-but-you-don't-see-me-know-what-you-are-you-don't-fool-me."

"What I am? What do you mean, you know what I am? What am I then?"

"You know," the man crooned, like a teasing child with a secret.

"I don't, actually," snapped Abby, "so you'd better tell me."

His eyes grew big. "Monster," he hissed. *"Changeling."*

Abby thought of the story Sue had told them—the little girl who had become something else. "Have you seen them?" she asked. "Have you seen them change?"

Abruptly his face creased with rage. "Don't-fucking-play-games-can't-play-games-with-me."

"I'm not playing games," said Abby, "and I'm not one of them. But someone in our group saw a little girl change into something else. Is that what you saw?"

The supermarket man clapped his hands to his ears. "Not-listening-not-listening-to-you."

"Okay," she said, "so you think I'm some sort of monster—which I'm *not*, by the way. But if I *were* one of those things, what would be the point in capturing me? What do you get out of it?"

The man removed his hands from his ears and an expression of childlike cunning appeared on his face. "I-got-you," he muttered.

"But what's the *point* of having me?" said Abby. "If I'm one of these monsters why don't I just change into whatever it is they're supposed to change into? And if we're *all* monsters, then won't you just have made all the other monsters angry by capturing me?"

It was like trying to fire a gun with a crooked barrel. Her bullets were simply not hitting the target. Abby decided that if reason wouldn't work, then she would have to try threats.

"Listen, you idiot," she said, trying to sound angry rather than scared, "we've got guns, yeah? And if my dad thinks you've hurt me, or you're *going* to hurt me, he'll shoot you. So why don't you just . . . stop all this? We can help you."

The man stared at her, the rain running down his face, his ragged clothes plastered to his body. All at once he struck Abby as pitiful rather than frightening, and for a second she thought she might have got through to him. Then he gestured towards the houses, which resembled ice sculptures under the blue lightning. "You walk."

Abby felt like weeping with frustration, but she clamped the emotion inside, scared that if she started she might not be able to stop. She splashed ahead of him once again, blinking rain out of her eyes, and eventually they reached a gate at the edge of the field. The man darted forward and pushed it open, beckoning her through. He ushered her across a road to the line of houses on the opposite side. Up close, Abby could see that the pale stone walls of the houses were streaked with silt, the pan-tiled roofs caked with sandy mud and debris. There was the decomposing carcass of a cow in one boggy garden, its legs sticking up in the air. At the edge of the field a green delivery van seemed to be growing out of the mud, and a child's tricycle hung from the branches of a bedraggled tree.

The man directed Abby through the estate, and finally ordered her to halt in front of a corner house in what must once have been a pleasant cul-de-sac. He scampered ahead of her and opened the door.

"Inside," he said.

They went in and he directed her to a ground-floor room leading off the hallway. The place stank of moldy carpets and stagnant water, though thankfully not of human decay. It was pitch-black between lightning flashes, and Abby moved hesitantly, unsure whether the squelching sound when she walked came from her boots and socks or the carpet beneath her feet.

"Stand-against-the-wall-over-there," the man said.

"I would if I could see it."

"Stand-over-there," he repeated.

The lightning flashed, giving her a glimpse of the room. She moved over to the wall, which was cracked and trickling with water. The man scuttled over to what she could only think of as a nest in the corner and scrabbled about. Moments later he produced several stubby candles and a matchbox. He lit the candles and the room came to flickering life.

He had made no concessions to homelyness. Instead of shifting the debris out of the way, as Abby's group did whenever they stopped somewhere, the man had simply left it where it was. Thus items of furniture were strewn about and the room's other contents were little more than a muddy, shattered mess of plastic, glass, wood and wiring spread across the floor. The plaster ceiling bulged in several places, as though about to collapse at any moment. But at least the glass in the windows was intact, and judging by the smell the house appeared to have been unoccupied at the time of the flood—which was probably why the man had chosen it.

"Sit-down," he said, waggling a hand at her.

"I'd rather stand."

"Sit-sit-sit-sit-sit."

Abby sighed. "Have you got anything I can sit *on?*"

"Sit," he said again.

"I'm not a dog," she said, but she squatted on her haunches, cold and wet and miserable.

The man seemed oblivious to the conditions. He hunkered down in his nest, watching her, his eyes glittering in the candlelight. Water dripped off Abby's clothes. She felt the shivers starting deep in her belly, and tried not to succumb to them.

"Well, this is nice," she said.

The man said nothing. Abby swallowed, refusing to be intimidated.

"So, what happens now?" she asked.

The man delved into a bag and produced what Abby thought was a muddy bar of soap. When he wiped it on his wet sleeve, however, she realized it was a chunk of vacuum-packed cheese. He produced a knife with a serrated blade and hacked at the wrapping until he could peel it off with his fingers. He munched the cheese, watching Abby as though daring her to try to take it off him.

"Aren't you going to offer me any?" she asked.

Again he flashed that cunning grin. Spraying clots of cheese, he muttered, "Can't-fool-me-don't-need-it-do-you?"

"I need to eat too," Abby said.

The man shook his head. "No-no-don't-eat-what-we-eat-oh-no-no-I-know-that-yes-I-do-oh-yes-yes-yes."

"So what *do* I eat then?" Abby demanded.

"Us."

"What are you on about?"

"Us-us-I-know-I-know-I-seen-it."

Abby thought for a minute, wondering what to say, what to do. Weren't people in hostage situations supposed to try to get to know their captors, build up a rapport with them?

"What's your name?" she asked.

The man glanced at her, his jaw working rapidly. He reminded her of a chimpanzee in a zoo, nibbling fruit and watching the visitors.

"You must have a name," Abby said. "Mine's Abby. Abby Marshall. I'm thirteen years old. I live with my mum in Scotland, but I was visiting my dad in London when the flood came. My dad's called Steve. He owns a record shop. He's in a band—the Hogs. They're quite well-known. They've done CDs and stuff. They play old people's music, rhythm and blues and that. Some old musicians are still pretty cool, though, aren't they? Bob Dylan and Johnny Cash and the Beatles. What sort of music do you like?"

She kept up a stream of chatter, giving the man as much information as she could think of. She kept throwing in the odd question too, but he didn't answer any of them. She tried not to be discouraged by his silence. She hoped his taciturnity was a sign that he was listening to her. The man ate half his cheese, then produced a plastic bottle of water, which he drained in less than a minute, gulping it as if it was the first drink he'd had in days.

"Thanks for offering me some," Abby said. "I'm quite thirsty too, you know."

"You-lie," he muttered, and pointed at her. "You-lie-you-lie-you-lie."

Abby glared at him. "My name is Abby Marshall. I'm thirteen years old. And you are making a big mistake."

She rested her head against the wall, feeling a sudden wash of despair. She was wet, cold, filthy, hungry, thirsty, scared and miserable. She could hardly believe that less than two weeks ago Dad had met her as she got off the train and taken her shopping in Oxford Street. He'd bought her two new tops and a pair of jeans from Diesel. They'd had a latte in Starbucks, and later they'd had something to eat in All Bar One. The place had been full of young city types with smart suits and trendy haircuts, sipping wine or foreign beer out of bottles. Entranced by the buzz and glamour of the city, Abby had told Dad that when she was old enough she wanted to move down, maybe go to London University, get a job in publishing or the media, something like that.

She didn't realize she'd fallen asleep until she jerked awake. She was immediately aware of two things: It was daylight and she was shivering. When she moved she became aware of a third thing: a sharp, glassy pain in her shoulders. She might have cried out if she hadn't glanced across at the supermarket man and realized that he was asleep and snoring quietly.

She couldn't believe her luck. He might have tied her hands behind her, but he hadn't tied her legs. He really *is* mad, she thought. Mad and careless. Using the wall behind her, she pushed herself into a standing position. Pins and needles immediately sprang to life in her legs, the tingling gradually worsening to a muscle-spasming crescendo.

Gritting her teeth, she took a couple of experimental steps forward. Though her legs felt unlike her own she forced herself on. Half a dozen steps later she was at the door and he was still snoring. She had to turn her back to the door to manipulate the handle with her numb fingers. It took a few goes, but she kept calm, and eventually the handle turned. She tugged the swollen door open, gritting her teeth at the sound it made, like a wet rip, as it dragged across the carpet. When the gap was wide enough she slipped through and hurried along the boggy hall carpet to the front door.

This door was harder to open because of the Yale lock above the handle at chest height. To manipulate it she had to turn her back to the door, bend over double and raise her arms behind her as high as she could. After several attempts she managed it, twisting it open and unlocking it. She turned the door handle and was pulling the door open when a howl of fury ripped through the silence of the house.

Frantically she squeezed through the gap between door and frame, and started to run. But the ground was swampy underfoot and without her arms to balance her she slipped several times, only just managing to keep upright. It was like running in a dream, wading through treacly mud. The man roared again, a muffled, echoey sound—and then he burst from the house.

Abby's terror seemed to sap the strength from her legs, but

she kept running. He roared again, much closer now, and Abby screamed, veering from side to side in the hope of evading capture. But then something got tangled in her legs and she fell, desperately twisting onto her side to avoid her already bruised chin hitting the ground. Her momentum caused her body to skid several feet, like a kid on a homemade soap slide on a summer's day. Filthy water arced up on either side of her. And then she was being pulled roughly over onto her back.

The supermarket man loomed above her, blotting out the daylight. He was snarling and grunting like an animal, his dirt-streaked face twisted in fury. In his hand he was clutching the knife that he had used to saw through the plastic wrapping of the cheese. He raised the knife, and with a clarity born of terror, Abby saw the muscles knotting in his sinewy forearms, the sleeves of his gray jacket and once white shirt hanging in ragged loops.

As he brought the knife slashing down, Abby squeezed her eyes shut and screamed.

EIGHTEEN

Hearing the scream, Libby's body clenched like a fist. Instinctively her finger jerked on the trigger of the crossbow, releasing the arrow, which flew across the street and straight through the upper glass panel in the front door of the house opposite. The glass collapsed inwards with a shrill jangle, but Libby didn't see it; she was already looking around, trying to pinpoint the source of the scream.

"Hello?" she called. "Is anyone there?" Feeling self-conscious and horribly exposed, she yelled, "Steve? Sue? Max? Can *anyone* hear me?"

The second scream was so shrill, so bloodcurdling, that it was like a punch to the gut. Libby felt her legs go weak. "Bloody hell," she moaned. "Bloody hell, bloody hell." Though her hands were trembling, she managed to reload the crossbow just as Sue had told her; then she began to shakily run towards where she thought the sound had come from.

How long since she and the others had split up to, as Sue put it, "maximize the search area"? Twenty minutes? It was certainly no longer than that. They had arranged to rendezvous after an hour, and because Libby didn't have a watch

Sue had promised to give her a five-minute warning by firing a shot into the air.

Libby wished she could do that. She hadn't envisaged this scenario when she'd suggested she have the crossbow because she was too nervous to carry a gun. Sue had tried to impress upon her that the only difference was that they had less ammunition for the crossbow, but Libby had been insistent.

She ran through several streets, feeling like one of the ill-prepared, ragtag soldiers she used to see on the news, scuttling through the dusty streets of some battle-scarred town on the other side of the world. She ran around aimlessly for five minutes before realizing how pointless it was. She was sweating and breathing in deep rasping gulps, not because she was unfit, but because she was stressed to the eyeballs, overdosing on adrenaline.

The two screams had sounded so close that Libby had half expected to stumble across some atrocity in the middle of the street. The sounds had certainly seemed to come from outside, but that didn't mean the screamer still was. Whoever had made the girl (Libby *thought* it was a girl) scream could easily have dragged her into a house or a shed. The girl and her tormentor might be in *any* of the houses Libby was passing; there was simply no way she could search them all.

She walked on, calling Abby's name, trying not to tell herself it was hopeless. She came to a left turn, which a metal street sign, rusted by salt water, informed her was Lurgan Drive. Beneath the name of the road were the words "cul-de-sac." Libby began to stroll down it, holding the crossbow out in front of her, head moving from side to side as she scanned each house for signs of occupation. "Abby!" she shouted every ten seconds or so. "Abby!"

She reached the bottom of the road and was walking past the corner house when a metal wastepaper bin, rusty and dented, arced out of the large front window in a glittering crescendo of shattered glass and landed with a splat in the mud of the front garden.

Even before the rain of glass had stopped falling, Libby

was diving for cover behind a blue Citreon that was upside down in the middle of the street. Her nerve endings sizzled with shock; her heart thumped wildly. She took a few seconds to gather herself, and then she popped her head out to see what was happening.

She half expected a bullet to go zinging past her face, but there was no movement, no sound, from the house. Through the jagged hole in the front window she could see only an indeterminate mass of shadow. She tried to call out, but her throat was so dry that at first she could make no sound. She swallowed, licked her lips, tried again. "Abby!" she called in a croaky voice. "It's me, Libby! Are you in there?"

Nothing. No scuffs of movement, no bumps or bangs. If whoever had screamed was the same person who had thrown the bin out the window, she'd guess they were now being restrained—or perhaps had even been dragged out the back door while Libby was crouching behind the car.

She *had* to act. She knew that. She couldn't just stay here, hiding. *Shit,* she thought. *Shit, shit, shit.* She had never had a fight in her life. Violence was anathema to her. She had even taught primary because she hadn't thought she'd be able to handle the stress of teaching teenagers.

"Come on, Libby," she muttered to herself, "you can do this." She sidled around the edge of the Citreon, eyeing the house, then scuttled across to the dubious cover of the lamppost beside the silted-up garden wall. She was panting and her heart raced in her chest. She didn't feel like a soldier; in fact, she couldn't remember when she had ever felt so uncertain about what to do. She jumped as something cold splashed on her cheek, then realized it was water from last night's rain dripping off the slimy strings of seaweed draped over the craning neck of the lamppost overhead.

She tried to order her thoughts, to formulate some kind of plan. But all she could think of to do was enter the house and check out every room. But what if she was attacked? Would she be able to pull the trigger of the crossbow, actually shoot someone? On the other hand, what if Abby suddenly popped up from nowhere? Would Libby be able to *stop* herself from pulling the trigger?

"Okay," she muttered, "here we go." She broke cover and ran up the drive, her feet squelching in the mud. She reached the front door and tried it. Locked. *Shit. What now?* She thought of the front window. Could she climb in without cutting herself to ribbons? She decided to check it out, hurrying from the door to the window. She paused at the side of the window, then jabbed her head forward to peer into the room.

It was empty, but there were recent signs of habitation. A sleeping bag, a discarded plastic bottle. Triangles of glass were sticking out from the frame of the broken window. There was one above her head the size of a guillotine blade. She could knock it out, but that would make a noise. Then she noticed the smaller windows on either side. The frames were ill-fitting, saturated by seawater. She got her fingers under the edge of the closest one and tugged on it. To her surprise it parted like wet cardboard and the window swung open.

She hauled herself onto the sill and climbed into the house. *Okay*, she thought, *so far so good*. She crept across the room towards the door, listening. Hearing nothing, she pushed the door slowly open. She began to edge out into a hallway that stank of mold, the carpet like waterlogged turf. . . .

And a hand shot round the edge of the door and yanked the crossbow from her grasp!

Libby squealed, partly with shock and partly because the weapon had been snatched from her so roughly that she felt as though her right forefinger had been dislocated. She stumbled forward, almost slipped on the soggy carpet. She turned to see a filthy, ragged man pointing the crossbow at her face. She put up a hand, knowing that if he fired, the arrow would pass straight through her palm and embed itself in her skull.

"Please . . ." she begged.

"Sit down!" the man screamed at her. *"Sit-down-sit-down-sit-down!"*

Libby slid to the hall carpet, filthy water seeping through the material of her trousers. Behind the man, lying on her front, was Abby, hands and feet tied, gagged by a filthy strip of cloth. Libby saw the look in Abby's eyes and felt ashamed and full of despair. She had failed, succumbed with barely a whimper. Too late she realized she should have left a sign for Steve and the others, some indication of where she was. The man grabbed her arm in a painful, clawlike grip. He was mumbling, his voice so low that the words were like gravel shifting in his throat.

"I'm sorry," Libby sobbed, "I can't tell what you're saying."

The man leaned over her, baring his teeth. A string of drool escaped from his lips and spattered on her arm. Libby wanted to wipe it off, but was too scared.

"On-your-front," the man muttered. "Lie-down-on-your-front-now-*now!*"

"Okay," Libby whimpered. "Okay." She did so, and the man pulled her hands roughly behind her back and tied them with something that felt like damp cloth. He did her legs too, pulling the cords so tightly she gasped in pain. Water soaked through the front of her clothes, chilling her from head to foot. The man rolled her over and within seconds the back of her was soaked too. She barely had time to register he had something in his hand before he was stuffing it into her mouth.

It was a lump of cloth, sour and salty, slick with some sort of oil or slime. Instinctively she tried to spit it out, but before she could the man flipped her deftly back onto her front and tied another strip of cloth around her mouth, pulling it tight around the back of her head, snagging strands of her hair.

She started to panic. She couldn't move or breathe. She felt her heart crashing, her gorge rising. *Oh God, what if she was sick? She would drown in her own vomit!* She strained her neck to look up, and her eyes met Abby's.

Abby was looking straight at her, and immediately Libby knew, just by the expression in the younger girl's eyes, that Abby was urging her to stay calm. Libby closed her eyes, took deep breaths through her nose. Their friends were out there, she thought. *Steve* was out there. And in twenty minutes, when she didn't turn up at the rendezvous, they would realize something was wrong and they would come looking. And this time there would be three of them searching a smaller area. It would only be a matter of time before she and Abby were found and rescued.

The man dragged them, one at a time, into the front room with the broken window. He dumped them against the wall, then sat on a heap of filthy bedding in the corner, the crossbow across his knees. With his filthy hair and ragged clothes, Libby thought he looked like something from *Lord of the Rings*, some hideous troll or demon.

She glanced towards the broken window. Abby must somehow have thrown or kicked the bin through it to attract her attention. Unless the man had done it to lure her into the house. He could have been watching her walking up the street, could have seen that she was alone. She wondered whether he knew or had guessed that she had not come here on her own. She wondered whether Steve and the others would consider the possibility that she had been overpowered, the crossbow taken from her. It would be awful if they sauntered up the street and the man shot one of them before they realized what was happening. If anyone was injured or killed because of her she would never forgive herself.

All at once she realized that the shimmer of sunlight on the jags of glass protruding from the frame were not random. They were dancing in a pattern; not merely gleaming on the glass, but also flickering around the room.

Libby knew immediately what it was: Someone was using a lens to direct sunlight into the room. She turned to look at their captor, and saw that he had noticed the light too. His head was darting around like a cat's, following the light's erratic movements as if it were a butterfly. Slowly he rose, picking up the crossbow. He scuttled across to the broken window in a crouch, then dropped to his knees against the wall beneath the sill. He raised his head slowly, peering over the sill at the street outside. Hefting the crossbow into a firing position, he rested it on the sill, evidently prepared to let fly should he detect the slightest movement. Libby and Abby looked at each other, wondering what was going on. They were still wondering when a man they had never seen before silently entered the room, ran across to their captor and buried a meat cleaver in the back of his head.

Blood and watery stuff gushed out of the massive wound that the cleaver made in their captor's skull. His head shot forward like someone in a car crash, and his face was impaled by jagged shards of glass sticking out of the window frame. The newcomer yanked the cleaver from the man's head with two swift tugs, like someone removing an ax from a sinewy tree stump. The man's body fell back into the room, leaving blood and shreds of his face on the broken glass.

Libby was rigid, unable to comprehend what she had just seen. Her body and mind felt frozen by the awful brutality of the violence. She stared down at their captor, lying face up in a pool of his rapidly spreading blood. Less than a minute ago he had been alive and now he was dead.

Beside her Abby was whimpering, trying to bury her face in the wet sleeve of Libby's jacket. Libby felt compelled to watch as the murderer calmly wiped his cleaver on the dead man's jacket. When he turned to face her, raising the weapon once more, Libby tried to scream, but again could make no sound. The man saw the terror in her eyes and lowered the cleaver, simultaneously raising his other hand in a placatory gesture.

"Don't worry," he said. "I was just going to cut you free. Is that okay?"

Libby stared at him, then nodded. The man sliced through the cloth at her feet and ankles and did the same for Abby. Then he carefully cut through the knots of their gags.

"Better?" he said.

Libby nodded. She pulled the filthy cloth out of her mouth and spat until she could no longer taste it.

"Give yourself a moment," their rescuer said. "Let the blood start flowing again."

He saw Libby glance at the body of their captor, and said, "Sorry you had to see that, but I needed to make sure. He had a long-range weapon; we didn't. I'm afraid there's no room for niceties no more."

He was tall, with straight black hair and a beard that looked as though it had been growing since the flood. He wore a long black oilskin coat and he spoke with a blunt Yorkshire accent.

"Who are you?" Libby asked in a small voice.

"Nobody special. Just survivors like you."

The man walked to the window and waved his arm slowly back and forth.

"How many of you are there?"

"Half a dozen, all told. You'll meet most of us in a minute."

Sure enough, moments later Libby heard boots clomping into the house. Three men entered the room—a skinny boy of about seventeen with lank dirty blond hair, a man around fifty with neat, back-combed gray hair and startlingly dark eyebrows, and a sharp-featured, handsome man in his midthirties with an almost military haircut. All three men were wearing identical coats to their rescuer, and Libby couldn't help thinking that it made them look like Nazi officers from some old war film.

The handsome man glanced at the body. "Nice work, Geoff," he said. "Are you two ladies all right?"

"We will be," Libby said, "once we get out of here."

"Of course." The handsome man beckoned the boy over. "Todd, give the ladies a hand, would you?"

The boy shuffled forward and stretched out a hand. He looked to Libby as though she could pull him over with a sharp tug, but he was stronger than he appeared. As she stamped life back into her feet, he extended a hand to Abby, but she remained hunched against the wall, her hands over her head.

"It's okay," Libby said, and crouched beside the younger girl. Suddenly *she* was the one who appeared to be coping better with the situation.

"Come on, Abby," she said, "let's get out of this horrible place."

Abby lowered her arms and peered up at her. Her chin was

bruised and her tears had left clean lines down her grubby cheeks. "I've never seen anyone killed before," she said.

"It was a first for me too."

With Libby's help Abby shakily got to her feet. Flanked by the four men, they left the house to its grisly, now permanent occupant and walked out into the sunshine.

"Thanks for rescuing us," Libby said. "We need to find our friends now."

She saw a look pass between the bearded man and the handsome one and suddenly felt uneasy.

"We've got a nice place," the handsome man said, "not far from here. Why don't you come back with us for something to eat, give yourselves time to recover?"

Alarm bells were jangling in Libby's head, but she tried to keep her voice light.

"That's kind of you, but our friends will be wondering where we are."

The older man spoke for the first time. His voice was rich, almost melodious, and he had a West Coast American accent.

"We'll find your friends for you. You can *all* be our guests."

Libby licked her lips. "Um . . . thanks, but I don't think so. Abby needs to be reunited with her dad as quickly as possible."

The bearded man sighed, as though disappointed with her response.

The handsome man raised the crossbow he had picked up, and pointed it at the girls.

"I'm afraid we're going to have to insist," he said.

NINETEEN

"Over here!" shouted Max.

Steve and Sue came running. It had been over three hours since Libby had failed to show up at the rendezvous point and Steve was getting frantic.

"What is it?" he asked.

Max pointed at the house with the broken window.

"Oh, hell," said Sue. "That looks like fresh blood."

"We've got to go in there," said Steve, moving towards the house.

"Steve, stop!" Sue shouted, going after him.

"I've got my gun, haven't I?" he retorted.

"Yeah, and they might have them too," she said. "Remember, if they've got Libby they've got the crossbow."

Steve glowered at her a moment, then nodded. "You're right. Sorry. So what do we do?"

She beckoned them across to the shelter of an upside-down Citroen in the middle of the street. "We keep under cover as much as possible. And we overlap, taking turns to advance in short bursts. That way when one of us is moving the others are covering him. Understand?"

Steve and Max both nodded.

Sue went first, raising an arm when she was in position. A minute later all three of them had reached the front door of the house unchallenged. She indicated they should stand with their backs to the wall on either side of the door; then in one swift movement she darted forward, shoved the door open and jumped back.

No one attacked them; no one fired at them; there was no sound from inside the house at all. Sue peered around the edge of the door to check that the hall was clear, and then, gun held in front of her, entered the house.

They found the body in the room with the broken window.

"Gross," said Max with the weary disgust of one who had seen many gross things recently.

Sue briefly examined the body. "This happened not long ago."

"Who is he, d'you reckon?" Max asked.

Steve had been looking dispassionately down at the body. Suddenly his eyes widened. "Hang on, I recognize this bloke. We met him in London about a week ago. Mad as a hatter. Threatened us with a knife."

"Small world," Max said.

"Is it?" said Sue. "I wonder."

"What do you mean?"

"Personally I reckon it's too much of a coincidence that he's here." She tapped her head. "Suspicious copper's mind. It's more likely he's been following us. He probably took a liking to Abby, and first chance he got, he grabbed her."

"You think Abby did this to him?" Steve said.

Depends what he *did to* her, Sue thought, but didn't say. "Abby and Libby together maybe. There's no sign of the crossbow. And no sign of the weapon that killed him either. From the look of him I'd say he was whacked with a pretty big blade."

"But if they got away, why didn't they come looking for us?" said Max.

Sue pursed her lips. "That's what bothers me." She examined the dead man's boots, peered at various marks on the floor. "I think someone else has been here," she said finally. "Someone's walked in the blood, left prints all round this area, and then again, over here. They're not ours, and they're not the dead guy's, and they look too big for the girls."

"So someone else killed him?" said Steve.

"I'd say it's a strong possibility."

"So someone came in here, killed this guy, then took the girls with him?" said Max.

"It's only a theory," Sue admitted, "but it *would* explain why the girls haven't come looking for us."

"There'll be tracks, won't there?" said Max. "Outside in the mud, I mean."

Steve was already out the door.

"Be careful where you put your feet," Sue called after him. "You don't want to obliterate anything."

Finding the tracks was not difficult. They hadn't noticed them before simply because all their attention had been focused on the house.

"There's more than three of them," Sue said. "Five or six, I reckon."

The tracks stretched along the road before turning right at the next junction.

"Let's go," Steve said, and set off. Sue fell into step beside him.

"I know how eager you are to find the girls, Steve, but if we do catch up with the people who've taken them—"

"*When* we do, you mean," he said.

"Okay, *when* we catch up with them, you do realize we'll have to proceed with caution? For the good of everyone we can't just go running in like bulls in a china shop."

Steve looked momentarily irritated; then he saw the concern on her face. "Yeah, I know," he said. "Don't worry, I won't be a liability."

Following the tracks was easy for a while. They wound through the estate, heading north, before following the line of a main road for perhaps half a mile, then veering to the left through what had been a new and still developing retail complex. After crossing another main road, however, they petered out on the edge of an area of boggy meadows and hills studded with clumps of trees too sparse to be termed woodland.

"They must have gone across there," Sue said.

"Then let's get after them," said Steve.

She glanced at her watch. "It's almost one now. We've got about four hours of decent daylight left. This is where it gets hard. They could have gone off in any direction. Keep your eyes peeled for any clue."

They climbed the fence into the field and splashed forward through the waterlogged meadow. The hillside ahead of them was a shimmering green-black, and choked with all manner of debris—bricks, garden furniture, plastic bags, bottles; there were even dead fish floating belly up in the ankle-deep water.

They plodded on for an hour or so, mostly silent, not even commenting on the occasional decaying body jutting out of the sludge. The sky had darkened again since the bright promise of that morning's sunshine, gray clouds massing like tanks. Max felt a drop of rain splash his forehead and looked up. Beyond the next clump of trees, the upper branches of which were starting to thrash in a gathering wind, he saw a thread of smoke.

He glanced to his right, where Steve and Sue were trudging determinedly forward, heads down.

"Hey!" he said, and pointed. "Hey, guys, look!"

The two of them looked up.

Sue squinted, then clenched her teeth in a grin. "That could be it," she said.

"How far away, do you reckon?" Max asked.

"A mile maybe? Hard to tell."

In fact, it was more like two. Twenty minutes after spotting the smoke they appeared to be no closer to it. Then they moved into a dip where the water came up to their shins, and when the land rose again to crest the long slope of a tree-lined hill, there it was, on the next undulation of hillside: a squat, sturdy farmhouse of dark, rough-hewn stone, flanked by barns, the wooden walls of which were black with water damage, but still defiantly upright.

They crouched behind trees to observe the farmhouse, but aside from the black smoke curling out of the chimney there were no other signs of life.

"Our best bet is to make our way round to the left here," said Sue. "That way we can keep under cover of the trees all the way round to the big barn at the edge."

Steve nodded. "What do we do when we get there?"

"We draw them out," said Sue. "But let's get there without being spotted first. Be careful in the woods. There might be someone on guard. There might even be booby traps."

"Such as?" Max asked.

"Trip wires, maybe. They might even have dug pits if the ground's not too boggy."

"You really think they might be that organized?" said Steve.

"Who knows? But let's not underestimate them. They could be ex-paras for all we know. Then again, they might just be a bunch of kids."

They moved off, keeping low, scanning the way ahead. They encountered no hazards, no guards, no booby traps. Their only hairy moment was when a flock of crows burst from the branches of a tree to their left amid a clamor of flapping wings and raucous cries. Max spun, gun coming up, finger squeezing the trigger . . . then he turned and grinned sheepishly at Steve and Sue's tense, wide-eyed faces.

Five minutes later they reached their destination, the trees thinning out as they followed the line of a now half-collapsed and water-rotted wooden fence. The fence bordered the mud bath that had once been a farmyard at the side of the house. Steve, Sue and Max approached the building in a half crouch and hunkered down out of sight, conversing in whispers, the side of the big barn at the left-hand edge of the property, no more than twenty meters away from them.

"So how do we draw them out?" asked Steve.

"Fire," Sue said, routing through her rucksack. With a grin she produced matches and fire lighters. She was about to say something else when an ear-splitting scream shattered the silence, freezing the smile on her face.

TWENTY

Abby thought about smashing the window and jumping down to the yard below. Might it be possible the men *wouldn't* hear the breaking of glass? Might it be possible she *wouldn't* injure herself falling the twenty feet to what was probably stone beneath the ankle-deep sludge? Might it even be possible she would be able to find her way back to the hotel and bring Dad and the others back to rescue Libby?

She hoped Libby was okay. As soon as they had arrived the two girls had been separated. Abby still wasn't sure she liked Libby that much. She found her to be attention-seeking and wimpy, maybe even a bit manipulative—though that *could* simply be because Dad liked her, and Abby still couldn't get used to the idea of him being with anyone but Mum. But, like her or not, Abby didn't actually want anything *bad* to happen to her. What kind of a bitch would it make her if she did, especially as Libby had tried to rescue her from the supermarket man?

She walked back across the room and looked out the window. The room was at the back of the house, and the window had locks on the bars, so you couldn't open it. Below the window was a yard bordered by a row of falling-down sheds covered in sea slime. Beyond that was a boggy field, after which the ground dropped away and then sloped up again. It would have been a nice view once, but now the ground was muddy and waterlogged and covered in rubbish. It looked, she thought, like Glastonbury after the fans have gone home. It suddenly struck her that there would be no more Glastonburys, and it had always been her ambition to go there. Abruptly she felt like weeping, felt tears prick the backs of her eyes, then start to tumble down her cheeks.

Footsteps. There were footsteps creaking along the landing towards her. She gave an almighty sniff and wiped her grubby hands across her face; she didn't want to be found crying. She moved across to the bed, which, like the rest of the room, smelled musty and damp (though the sheets looked dry and clean) and positioned herself so she could step behind it, use it as a flimsy barrier if need be.

The door opened and a man came into the room. She hadn't seen him before. He was young, slim, not too tall, and yet there was a presence about him, a sort of *charisma,* which she wasn't sure whether she liked or not. He was good-looking in an ordinary sort of way, and was wearing a gray hooded top and jeans, which made him look like the lead singer in an indie band. He had watchful eyes, blue and unblinking, and Abby got the feeling that he was physically very sure of himself, which made her uneasy. Despite being aware of her *own* physical assets—her tallness, her blondness, her prettiness—Abby felt awkward and childlike in his company.

"Hi," he said. He had an ordinary voice, with perhaps just a trace of a northern accent. "My name's John."

The only item of furniture in the room apart from the bed was an office chair with a metal frame and a cushioned seat in pale green plastic. John picked it up, positioned it closer to the bed and sat down. He leaned forward, elbows on knees, hands loosely clasped.

"You're nervous. There's no need to be nervous. Why don't you sit down?"

Abby hesitated, then lowered herself onto the edge of the bed, feeling like a deer in the company of a predator, mesmerized and wary at the same time.

"What's your name?" he asked. Easily, casually, as if they were a similar age.

"Abby," she said.

"Do you understand what's happened to the world, Abby?"

She shrugged. "I think so."

"Then you'll know how special you are. How special we all are. We're the survivors. The one in a thousand who've lived through the worst disaster the world has ever known."

"How do you know it's one in a thousand?" Abby asked, wishing she didn't sound so timid.

He smiled. "I don't. It might be one in five thousand. Or ten."

"Maybe it's just us," Abby said. "Britain, I mean. Maybe the rest of the world's okay."

"Maybe," he said, "but I don't think so." He leaned back. "You know it's our duty to survive, don't you?"

She pulled a face. "I suppose so. I mean . . . that's what we're doing, isn't it?"

"I'm not talking individually," he said. "I'm talking about the human race. It's our duty to make sure the human race survives. So far we've just been coping, coming to terms, concentrating on the basics—food, water, shelter, warmth. But we've got to move on from there; we've got to look ahead. We've got to be strong, and we've got to be ruthless, and we've got to make sacrifices. There's no point eking out a living for ourselves and then having nothing to hand down to future generations. Sooner or later the shitty resources we've got left are gonna dry up—if you'll pardon the pun—and then where will we be? So we've got to make things happen. We've got to learn how to grow food and make tools and reclaim what we can. Everyone has a role to play. Do you understand what I'm saying?"

"I'm not sure," said Abby. "I mean, I think so. But what's this got to do with me?"

John smiled. "We're all blokes here. There's no women. If we're gonna build a community, expand, we need women. Do you see what I mean?"

Abby's stomach turned over. "But . . . you just took us," she said. "Kidnapped us. You can't do that."

He half laughed, as if she had said something charmingly naive. "That's what I mean. That's what I was saying before. You've got to be ruthless. You've got to make sacrifices. Look, we're not bad blokes, Abby, but we're realists. We know what needs to be done, and in the absence of any sort of authority we know *how* things need to be done."

"But . . ." Abby felt her voice failing; she struggled to overcome it. "You can't just take us. You *can't*. I was with my dad . . . my friends. You can't just take me away from them. . . ."

Despite her distress, he was still looking at her with an expression of indulgent amusement. "Listen," he said, "I know where you're coming from. Family ties are important. I think it's great that you and your dad survived, and the last thing I want is to split you guys up. So here's the thing—your dad and the others you've been traveling with will be given the chance to join us. We'll send out a delegation and explain where we're coming from, and if they want to help us expand the community, great. If they don't"—he shrugged—"no big deal. They'll be free to move on peacefully. Do their own thing."

"And me and Libby too?"

He grinned, shook his head, as if she had failed to grasp some basic principle.

"You and Libby have to stay. You're important commodities. We need you here."

"Commodities? What do you mean by that?"

John shrugged. "All right, it's a shitty word. You're people, not things. But that's the way it's *got* to be. You've *got* to have babies, Abby. It's your duty. And because the infant mortality rate is going to be high due to the lack of medicine and facilities, you've got to get cracking as quickly as possible, have as many kids as you can."

"But I'm only thirteen!" she wailed, close to tears again.

"Do you have periods?" he asked.

She couldn't answer. Could only stare at him, stricken and scared, her hand over her mouth. He looked at her with his gentle, intense eyes, and as the tears started to spill down her cheeks once more he said softly, "If you have periods, then you're ready. I'm sorry, Abby, but you are. All the old rules and regulations, all the old morality, it's pointless now. Survival is all that counts. Propagation and progress." He stood up and walked towards her. Abby ran round to the other side of the bed, cramming herself into a corner.

"It won't be bad, Abby, I promise," he said. "I won't hurt you."

He stepped up onto the bed and reached a hand towards her.

TWENTY-ONE

As soon as Steve started rising to his feet, Sue dropped everything back into the rucksack and grabbed his arm. She yanked at his sleeve, pulling him off balance, forcing him to drop onto one knee. "You promised me you wouldn't be a liability," she hissed.

He glared at her. "Didn't you hear that? That's Abby and Libby in there."

"So what are you going to do? Kick the door in and start shooting? You'll probably hit one of the girls, get shot in the chest by the crossbow and lose us the element of surprise."

There was another squeal from the house, and then very clearly they heard a girl yell, "Get off me!"

Steve squeezed his eyes shut. "That's Abby," he moaned.

"So *listen,*" Sue said. "Let's not waste any more time." She paused for the briefest of moments. "Are you with us, Steve?"

He opened his eyes. "Yes, yes."

"Good. I don't want to have to repeat myself."

She outlined her plan. As soon as she finished speaking, Max moved off to the right, on a route that would bring him in line with the front door. Sue and Steve ran in half crouches across the twenty meters of open ground to the side of the water-ravaged barn. Even as Steve was flattening himself against the slimy black wood, Sue was moving along the wall, carrying her rifle diagonal across her chest, muzzle pointing upwards. She reached the corner, peered around it, then indicated to him that the way was clear. A few moments later they had tugged the barn door open and were inside, Sue immediately stepping to one side, out of the light, making herself a less obvious target.

She leveled her gun, sweeping it left and right, but the barn was unoccupied. Along the left-hand wall were stacks of plastic storage boxes full of supplies—tins, bottles, jars, tools, clothes and other items salvaged from the wreckage of the flood.

"They're well organized," she said. Already she had slung her gun over her shoulder and was crouched in front of her open rucksack.

Steve routed through the boxes, scurrying from one to the next. "There's not much to burn here," he said.

"I don't think we'll have too much trouble," Sue said. She lifted a two-pint plastic milk container filled with clear liquid out of her rucksack.

"Is that petrol?" Steve said.

She nodded. "Thought it might come in useful. When I was on my own I had this idea that I might find a workable vehicle, or at least one that wasn't so wrecked that I couldn't strip it down and get it running again. Pipe dream, I know, but I grabbed some petrol on the off chance."

She hurried over, unscrewed the cap and started splashing the petrol over the plastic boxes.

"But where did you get the petrol *from?*" Steve asked.

"I found a tanker on its side when I was out looking for stuff. The cabin was a mangled wreck and the tanker itself was dented but still intact. I managed to puncture it and filled up a bunch of plastic containers, most of which I had to leave behind. But I grabbed a couple just in case, and they've been in my rucksack ever since." She straightened up. "There, that should do it. I'd stand back if I were you."

Steve retreated to the door of the barn. Sue lit a match and tossed it almost casually towards the center of the plastic boxes. The eruption of light and heat was soundless and shockingly sudden. One moment there was only the tiny flicker of the tumbling match, and the next the flames were surging upwards and outwards like a fire genie released from an ancient bottle.

"Don't just gawk at it, get into position!" Sue shouted, running towards him. With the heat at their backs and the stench of burning plastic already stinging their nostrils, they scurried across to the line of trees opposite the barn's entrance and plunged between their dark and twisted trunks.

Seconds later they heard the clash of breaking glass from the direction of the house. "Nice shot, Max," Sue murmured. Turning to Steve she said, "Get ready, but remember, wait for the right moment."

He nodded, face grim.

"Here they come," she said.

From their vantage point among the trees they saw the farmhouse door open. A young man came out. He was skinny, almost scrawny, despite his thick sweater. He looked around nervously, then moved over to the broken window and examined it.

"Anything?" someone shouted from inside the house.

The boy gave a quick shake of his head. "Can't see any—" Then he looked to his right and saw black smoke gushing from the door of the barn.

He froze, like a cartoon character, mouth dropping open. Then he spun and almost slipped, waggling his arms like a panicking child.

"The barn's on fire!" he yelled.

The farmhouse door flew open. A bearded man ran out, followed by an older man with gray hair. Bringing up the rear, almost casually, was a man with close-cropped hair and a bony face. This man was carrying the crossbow and his eyes swept across the row of trees bordering the farmyard, as if he knew Steve, Sue and Max were there and was simply pinpointing their location.

Sue remained still, resisting the urge to shrink farther back into the trees as the man seemed to look directly at her. She knew that any movement, however slight, would be more easily detectable than if she was motionless. For a moment the man stood his ground, ignoring the anguished cries of his colleagues. Then, as if he knew little could be done and that it was pointless expending energy by trying, he strolled across the yard to the burning barn.

As soon as he turned his back the three of them broke cover. Max and Sue raised their rifles, while Steve, who preferred a handgun, kept his weapon pointing at the ground.

"Drop your—" Sue said, but before she could complete her sentence the man with the crossbow turned and fired. The bolt passed through the four-foot gap between Steve and Sue and missed Max's head by inches. Steve instantly raised his gun and shot the man. He fell without a sound, blood gushing from his shoulder. Steve looked down at him curling in pain, and he felt a strange combination of revulsion and vicious glee at what he had done.

The other men, running around near the entrance to the barn, desperate to save their supplies but driven back by the fire, turned at the sound of the shot. The skinny boy was so startled by the sight of the three armed attackers that he dropped to the ground, hands shielding his head, as if he had taken a bullet himself.

"That's a good idea," Sue said. "Why don't you all do that?"

When the men simply stared at her, she shouted, "Down on the ground! All of you!"

"It's muddy," said the older man in an American accent.

"So have a nice hot bath later," said Sue. "Now lie on your bellies or I'll shoot your fucking legs from under you."

The men complied. Sue, Steve and Max moved forward,

Sue kicking the crossbow out of the reach of the injured man as she did so.

"How many of you are there?" she asked.

None of the men said anything.

"If you don't answer I'll kill all of you and go in there shooting," said Steve.

Sullenly, the bearded man said, "Six of us."

"Two more in the house?" said Max.

"Well done, Einstein."

"Whereabouts?" asked Sue.

"Fuck knows," said the bearded man. "I'm not psychic."

"Whereabouts are they *likely* to be?"

No one answered. Sue pointed her gun at the skinny youth, who whimpered in fear. "You. Tell me or I'll shoot you in the leg."

For a moment it seemed the skinny kid was too scared to speak. Finally he whispered, "Den will be . . . in the kitchen and . . . John will be upstairs."

"Shagging your women," said the bearded man.

Steve strode forward, aiming his gun at the bearded man, his arm stiff as iron.

"Don't let him goad you," Sue said calmly. "You'll only have to live with it afterwards."

Steve stood for a moment more, breathing hard. Then he lowered his gun. "I'm going in."

"You sure, man?" said Max.

"I can handle two of them," Steve said.

Sue seemed to weigh up the alternatives, then gave a swift nod. "Okay. But be careful. Take your time. They're unlikely to have guns, but they may have bladed weapons."

Steve nodded, already moving off. He entered the farmhouse, pushing the door open with his foot. The front door led into a sitting room. The walls and ceiling showed signs of flood damage, and nails along the edges of the floor with threads of material still attached showed where a carpet had recently been pulled up. The boards of the wooden floor were

blackened and warped, but dry. The embers of a fire still
glowed in the hearth and a variety of candles, currently unlit,
had been placed around the room. Items of mismatched furniture were arranged so they faced the fire. The upholstery
looked worn but clean, as if it had been scrubbed and left to
dry in the fresh air. Even so, there still lingered a trace of the
dank, fishy smell that clung to the inside of every building
Steve had entered since the flood—every building which
wasn't suffused with the stink of rotting flesh, that was.

The farmhouse was silent. Even Abby's cries had ceased.
Were the two men who had remained in the house aware of
his presence? Had they immediately assumed that the fire was
evidence they were under attack? Steve couldn't believe that
the two men in the house hadn't worked out what was happening by now. What would *he* do if he were them? Lie low
in the hope of ambushing the enemy? Hide on the off chance
they wouldn't be found? Flee out the back and lose themselves amongst the trees? Threaten the hostages and initiate a
standoff?

All were possibilities. It depended what kind of men they
were. Desperate to know whether Abby was all right, Steve
had to fight an urge to shout her name. The skinny kid had
said that one of the men would be in the kitchen, the other
upstairs. The staircase was on the right-hand wall of the sitting room. He presumed a closed wooden door in the back
wall led to the kitchen. Steve's instinct was to run straight up
the stairs, but he knew the sensible thing was to check the
kitchen first. Raising his gun, he strode across the room,
turned the handle of the kitchen door and flung it open.

The kitchen was dominated by a large wooden table. Lying on
the table was a naked human body chopped into several pieces.
The head was at one end, mouth gaping open, a nub of bone jutting from the meat of the severed neck. The limbless torso was in
the center, lying in a pool of blood so dark and plentiful that it
was trickling over the sides of the table and splashing on the
stone floor. The torso had been slit open and the skin pulled
back, exposing the ribcage. Plastic buckets under the table were

GET UP TO 4 FREE BOOKS!

You can have the best fiction delivered to your door for less than what you'd pay in a bookstore or online—only $4.25 a book! Sign up for our book clubs today, and we'll send you FREE* BOOKS just for trying it out...with no obligation to buy, ever!

LEISURE HORROR BOOK CLUB

With more award-winning horror authors than any other publisher, it's easy to see why CNN.com says "Leisure Books has been leading the way in paperback horror novels." Your shipments will include authors such as RICHARD LAYMON, DOUGLAS CLEGG, JACK KETCHUM, MARY ANN MITCHELL, and many more.

LEISURE THRILLER BOOK CLUB

If you love fast-paced page-turners, you won't want to miss any of the books in Leisure's thriller line. Filled with gripping tension and edge-of-your-seat excitement, these titles feature everything from psychological suspense to legal thrillers to police procedurals and more!

As a book club member you also receive the following special benefits:

- **30% OFF all orders through our website & telecenter!**
- **Exclusive access to special discounts!**
- **Convenient home delivery and 10 days to return any books you don't want to keep.**

There is no minimum number of books to buy, and you may cancel membership at any time. See back to sign up!

*Please include $2.00 for shipping and handling.

YES! ☐

Sign me up for the Leisure Horror Book Club and send my TWO FREE BOOKS! If I choose to stay in the club, I will pay only $8.50* each month, a savings of $5.48!

YES! ☐

Sign me up for the Leisure Thriller Book Club and send my TWO FREE BOOKS! If I choose to stay in the club, I will pay only $8.50* each month, a savings of $5.48!

NAME: _____

ADDRESS: _____

_____

TELEPHONE: _____

E-MAIL: _____

☐ **I WANT TO PAY BY CREDIT CARD.**

☐ **VISA**   ☐ **MasterCard**   ☐ **DISCOVER**

ACCOUNT #: _____

EXPIRATION DATE: _____

SIGNATURE: _____

Send this card along with $2.00 shipping & handling for each club you wish to join, to:

Horror/Thriller Book Clubs
1 Mechanic Street
Norwalk, CT 06850-3431

Or fax (must include credit card information!) to: 610.995.9274. You can also sign up online at www.dorchesterpub.com.

*Plus $2.00 for shipping. Offer open to residents of the U.S. and Canada only. Canadian residents please call 1.800.481.9191 for pricing information. If under 18, a parent or guardian must sign. Terms, prices and conditions subject to change. Subscription subject to acceptance. Dorchester Publishing reserves the right to reject any order or cancel any subscription.

JOIN NOW!

filled with loops of grayish intestine and other offal. One contained hands and feet with shattered bones splaying from the severed ends. Stacked in a gory pile at the other end of the table were the limbs of the corpse, chopped into portions like joints of meat.

The scene was so appalling that for a few seconds Steve couldn't quite accept what he was looking at. He was so shocked that he initially failed to react when the man in the blood-soaked butcher's apron stepped from behind the door.

The man was big, with a craggy face and thinning hair. He was holding a meat cleaver in his blood-caked hands. In the instant before he raised the cleaver, Steve noted that he had a tattoo of a bird—a raven perhaps, or an eagle—on his hairy, blood-speckled forearm. Then the cleaver was swinging towards him, and Steve flung himself to one side, his right shoulder connecting painfully with the door frame.

An instant later that pain was superseded by the greater pain of the cleaver blade slicing into his flesh. It was only a glancing blow, but it cut through several layers of clothing into the fleshy part of his arm beneath his left bicep. Even as he was twisting away, the blade passed through his flesh and whacked across the side of his ribs like a club. Steve staggered backwards into the sitting room, aware of a wet burning sensation in his left arm. He tried desperately to stay on his feet, but his legs somehow became tangled up with one another and he fell backwards, his view of the man suddenly replaced by a swooping flash of water-stained ceiling. His fall was partly broken by an armchair, which skidded backwards, propelled by his momentum. For one awful second Steve was sprawling and helpless on the ground. He raised his head in time to see the man swinging the cleaver back over his shoulder for a second blow.

Reacting out of sheer terror, Steve drew back his right leg and pistoned it forward in a clumsy kung fu kick, the bottom of his boot connecting with the man's left thigh. The man gasped, his upper body jerking forward, the arc of his swing interrupted. For a moment it seemed his legs would buckle, but then he straightened stiffly, his teeth clenched in pain. Steve scrambled back a few more feet, and as the man raised the cleaver again he shifted his weight from his right elbow to his back, pointed the Glock at the man, and pulled the trigger.

The sound of gunfire was obscenely loud in the small, carpetless room. Even more obscene was the way the right side of the man's head suddenly exploded backwards in a spray of red meat. The man didn't fold gracefully like in the movies; he went down like a sack of cement. For several seconds after pulling the trigger, Steve could only lie there, shaking and weak as though with fever, watching as the pulverized remains of the man's head slid slowly down the wall.

A sudden stifled cry from upstairs got him moving again. He scrambled to his feet, instinctively putting his left hand down to the floor to push himself up. Though the hand was numb, the upper part of his arm felt like it was on fire, and he screamed in pain. He looked down and saw that his left side was soaked in blood. He felt sick and dizzy, but he had to move. *Had to.* Suddenly the front door of the farmhouse crashed open behind him and Steve spun round, pointing his gun.

"Don't shoot!" yelled Sue. *"It's me!"*

Steve lowered the gun. Sue's gaze swept around the room. "Fuck," she said.

"He attacked me," Steve mumbled. "I had to shoot him. . . ."

"I know. Where are the girls?"

"Upstairs, I think."

Without another word, Sue ran for the stairs, gun raised high. Steve went after her, leaden-footed, shaking his head in an attempt to clear it. The upper floor smelled of mold and damp, though there had obviously been a concerted effort to clean the place up. There were four doors on this landing, all closed. Instead of sneaking about, trying each in turn as Steve would have done, Sue took up a position against the banister where she could cover all four.

"If there's anyone here, come out with your hands up," she shouted. "There are two of us and we're armed. We don't want to hurt anyone, but if you show any aggression towards us, we won't hesitate to shoot. We only want our friends back—then we'll go."

There was no response. Sue glanced at Steve. "You okay?"

He wasn't, but he nodded. "Fine."

"I'm going in," she said. "You stay here, cover the other doors. Don't come after me unless I call you or you hear shooting."

"Okay."

Sue edged up to the nearest door and put her ear to it. Hearing nothing, she took a couple steps back and booted it open. She was inside, gun sweeping in an arc, even before the door had fully swung inwards. Within seconds she was out. "Bathroom," she said. "Major shithole."

It was the same procedure with the second door. As soon as she entered this room, however, she yelled, *"Get away from her! Let the girl go and lie on the floor! Do it! Now!"*

Despite what she had said, Steve ran into the room. There was a bed to the right of the door, and a young man was sitting on it almost casually, Abby kneeling on the floor between his legs with her back to him. He had one hand over her mouth and the other resting lightly on her shoulder. His legs were wrapped around her arms, rendering her immobile.

"Now, I said!" Sue screamed, but the man ignored her.

"Let my fucking daughter go," Steve barked, his voice dredged from the smoky depths of his lungs.

The young man looked at him, not defiantly, but almost quizzically.

Steve pointed his gun at the man's head. "Let her go or I'll kill you like I killed the man downstairs."

The young man sighed and raised both hands. Abby struggled free from the constraints of his legs and slumped forward. Beneath the screen of her dirty blond hair she began to gag. Concerned, Steve took a step towards her, but Sue stuck out an arm.

Steve watched as Abby raised a trembling hand and pulled something from her mouth. It wasn't until she dropped it on

the floor that he realized it was a sock. He looked at the man
and noticed that one of his feet were bare.

"You fucking animal," he muttered.

The young man rolled his eyes. "Oh, grow up," he said
mildly.

"I told you to lie down," Sue said.

The man regarded her with an unsettling calmness.
"Where do you want me? Bed or floor?"

"On the floor, on your front," Sue said.

The young man took his time in satisfying her request.
When he was prone, Steve hurried forward and dropped to
his knees beside Abby.

"Hey," he said softly.

She let out a sound like a soft sob and clung to him so tightly
that his bruised ribs flared with a pain he tried not to show.

"Are you okay?" he gasped.

She nodded against his chest. "I knew you'd come," she
whispered.

"None of them . . . did anything to you, did they?"

She shook her head. "No. Not like you mean. He was going to though. He said I had to have babies. He said it
was . . . my duty."

Steve glared at the young man. "You sick little fuck," he
snarled.

The young man raised his head to look at him. There was
disdain on his face.

"You really don't live in the real world, do you?" he said.
"You have no inkling of what's required to survive. For your
own good I'm going to tell you a few home truths. Number
one, women have to have babies. If we're going to survive as
a species and claw our way back to anything like a reasonable
way of life, then we need to repopulate this planet, starting
now. If we fall back on social niceties, on redundant concepts
of what's *civilized* and *moral,* we'll die out within a generation
or two. Number two, animals are extinct, which means the
only meat we've got now is each other. It's not *nice,* it's not

civilized, but it's fact. Law of the jungle. Survival of the fittest. Accept it or perish."

Steve shook his head. "You *are* sick."

"No, mate," the young man said, "I'm realistic. You, on the other hand, are living in cloud cuckoo land." He laughed suddenly. "Why don't you ask your mate there? She knows I'm talking sense. I can see it in her eyes."

Steve looked at Sue, who glanced away guiltily. "All I want is to find Libby and go," she said. She jabbed the young man in the side with her foot. "Where is she?"

"Two doors along," the man said, "but it's a pity you have to leave. By pooling our resources we might have had a nice little community going here. You might have stood a chance."

"We'll take our chances without you, thanks," Steve said. He helped Abby to her feet.

For the first time she noticed the blood coating his side. "God, Dad, what happened to you?"

"I'll be fine," he said. "Let's go and get Libby."

Together they moved towards the door. Sue lingered a moment. "Don't you move," she said to the young man. "Don't you come after us."

"You sure you don't want to stay?" he asked.

Sue bent over him, her voice low. "I'd rather die than live the kind of life you're proposing."

"Then that's exactly what you'll do," he said.

She shuddered and left the room, slamming the door behind her. Steve and Abby were already outside the room at the end of the corridor, where the man had told them Libby was.

"Libby," Steve said, "are you in there? Answer me if you are."

He turned at Sue's approach. "There's no answer. The door's locked though." He indicated the key.

"It might be a trap," Sue said.

"That's what I was thinking."

"All right, flatten yourselves against the wall there. Steve, give me your gun and take mine."

"What are you going to do?" asked Abby.

"I'm going to be careful."

They did as she asked. As quietly as she could, Sue unlocked the door. She carefully reached out, twisted the door knob, then shoved the door open, squeezing herself back against the frame as it swung inwards. There was no sound, no movement from inside the room. They couldn't see much from their position—just part of the floor, the right angle where two walls met, the edge of a window. Sue lowered herself onto her stomach and crawled forward. As soon as she was round the edge of the open door, she pointed her gun into the part of the room they couldn't see from outside.

It seemed to take an age before she said softly, "It's okay, you can come in." She was rising to her feet as Steve and Abby moved forward to join her. At first glance Steve thought the room—bare of everything but a double bed—was empty. Sue glanced at him, pointed at the bed and mouthed, "Under there."

Steve moved forward, but Sue again raised a hand. "I'll deal with it," she said, and passed him her gun.

She walked up to the bed, then knelt down and peered underneath. "Hey, Libby," she said in a softer voice than Steve thought her capable of. "It's Sue. I've got Steve and Abby with me, and Max is outside. We've come to take you home."

Steve thought of the water-damaged hotel, stinking of corpses, where they had spent the night. He wouldn't have called it "home," but in this brave new world of theirs, he guessed home was wherever your friends and family were.

There was a whimper from beneath the bed, and then Libby's tearful voice asked, "Where are the men?"

"They're not going to hurt you," Sue said. "You're safe with us now."

Libby crawled from beneath the bed and shakily climbed to her feet. Like Abby, she was filthy and her face was streaked with tears. She looked at Abby, wide-eyed and haunted. "Did they . . . hurt you?" she asked.

Abby shook her head.

"Thank God," she whispered. "Thank God." Then she slumped and Sue grabbed her to stop her from falling.

Steve dreaded asking the question, but at the same time couldn't help himself. "What did they do to you, Libby?"

The expression on her face was answer enough.

They left the house, Steve and Sue deliberately positioning their bodies so that the girls wouldn't see the dead man in the room downstairs. Max was still standing over the three men lying in the mud outside the burning barn. The fire had really taken hold now, and looked as though it might spread if it wasn't dealt with quickly. The barn was a blackening shell, collapsing in on itself as the inferno raged. Max turned his sweating face towards them and his relief was plain to see. When they got close enough to hear him over the roaring flames, he nodded down at the man with the shoulder wound and shouted, "He don't look good."

Sue examined the man quickly. "He's unconscious," she said. "He's not dead."

"He's losing a lot of blood."

"That's his problem," she said brusquely. She stood up and strode forward to address the three men lying in the mud. "I hope you've learned your lesson. We didn't come here looking for trouble. We only came to get our people back. Because of what you did, you've lost your supplies and one of your people is dead." She nodded at the unconscious man. "And he might die too if you don't do something about it. I think I speak for all of us when I say that we don't like the way you live your lives. But that's up to you. It's got nothing to do with us. All I want to say before we go is don't come looking for revenge. Because we're the ones with the guns and if we see you again, we won't ask questions. Is that understood?"

None of the men said anything.

"I *said* is that understood?"

"Yeah, yeah," snarled the American man. "Now get out of here."

Sue stared at the men for a moment, contempt on her face. "I sincerely hope we never meet again," she muttered.

TWENTY-TWO

"How's your arm?" Libby said.

Steve looked up. He had been so preoccupied with his own thoughts, and with the sheer hard work of putting one foot in front of the other when all he wanted to do was stop to ease the grinding pain in his side, that he hadn't realized she had fallen into step beside him. The farmhouse was over half an hour's walk behind them, and up to now the long plod back to the hotel had been undertaken mostly in silence.

"Not too bad," he lied. "The paracetomol that Sue gave me has helped a bit."

"You don't look good," Libby said.

"Oh, thanks," he said. "I always thought I had a certain rakish charm."

She almost smiled at that. "You look pale, feverish."

"I'm not feeling brilliant," he admitted, "but neither is anyone else. Nice cup of tea and a lie down, that's what I need. It's been a long day."

"Tell me about it," she mumbled.

Lowering his voice so that only she could hear, he asked, "How are *you*, Libby? Really?"

"I'll survive," she said, so quietly he could barely hear.

"Do you want to talk about it?"

"No." Her answer was abrupt. She gave him a sidelong look. "Sorry, Steve, but no. I'm not ready."

Daylight was draining from the sky when the hotel finally came into view. By now Steve's limbs were prickly and tender, as if hot glass were pulsing through his veins, and though he hadn't said anything, he didn't think he could have gone on much longer. He hoped the blade hadn't been rusty or dirty. The thought of getting a blood infection was pretty frightening.

All seemed quiet as they arrived, squelching and muddy, on the forecourt of the hotel.

"Wonder how Greg is," Max said.

"I expect Marco's been making him mugs of cocoa and reading him bedtime stories," said Sue.

There were a few halfhearted grunts of amusement, but no one was really in the mood to laugh.

They entered the hotel, each of them covering their noses and mouths. "I'd forgotten how fragrant this place is," Sue said.

Trying to ignore the rotting bodies in the foyer, they went upstairs. The third floor was so quiet it might have been deserted.

"Hi, honey, I'm home!" called Sue.

There was no response.

"Please, no more shit today," murmured Max, taking a firm grip on his rifle.

"Anyone around?" called Sue. "Marco? Mabel?"

Silence. Sue was about to say something when Abby held up a hand. "Shh."

"What is it?" asked Max.

"I can hear something. Listen. A kind of . . . fizzing noise."

After a few seconds Max nodded. "Yeah, I hear it too. It's like them things Ma used to take for her stomach."

"Alka-Seltzer," said Steve, and almost unconsciously murmured the slogan from the TV commercial: "Plink, plink, fizz."

"It's coming from the end room, isn't it?" said Libby.

"Greg's room," confirmed Sue. "Max, with me?" He nodded. She looked over her shoulder at Steve. "Are you up to this, Steve? You look terrible."

"I'm fine," he lied, and held up his gun.

"Nice and slow," Sue said. "It might be nothing."

They approached the room—Sue, then Max, then Steve, bringing up the rear.

The door was very slightly ajar. "What *is* that noise?" whispered Sue.

"Radio static?" suggested Steve.

"I'll push the door open and we'll enter quickly in single file, okay?"

They nodded.

She held up three fingers. "Three, two, one." Then she pushed the door open, entered and pointed her gun at the bed.

Steve couldn't ever have imagined that he would see anything worse than what he had already witnessed that day. However, the sight that met his eyes when he stepped into the third-floor hotel room was so horrific, and so unbelievable, that it felt as if all the blood left in his body were draining into his boots. He heard a thump as his gun slipped from his nerveless fingers and hit the floor, and the room began to sway around him.

Beside Greg's now empty bed, Mabel—dear, sweet, brave Mabel—was being . . . the only word that came to Steve's mind was *absorbed*. Her tongue, horribly swollen and purple, was lolling from her open mouth; her eyes, glaring from their sockets, were red with ruptured blood vessels. Her body was folded almost in two, so that the tips of her toes were almost touching her chin. Her dangling arms flopped and twitched like those of a marionette. It was as if she were being sucked into an industrial mangle, as if the back of her jacket had become snagged in its metal rollers and she were being pulled inexorably in. But this was no machine that was killing her. This was . . . what? Some kind of animal? Above the rhythmic and almost gentle fizzing sound it made, Steve could hear Mabel's bones cracking, could see her flesh splitting open. Could see blood and other . . . *stuff* spattering the carpet beneath her, forming an ever-widening pool.

The creature itself. The *thing*. Though Steve was staring right at it, it almost defied the eye. It appeared to be a shimmering blue-black color, its flesh—if it could be termed as such—possessing an almost metallic sheen. It had no recognizable form, but was instead simply a mound, a *bulk,* perhaps roughly the size of a one-man tent. It seemed composed of a mass of jagged shapes, like overlapping beaks or loosely fitting scales. At the outer edges of its "body" were hundreds of hair-thin tentacles, or filaments, that moved languidly, like hair underwater. Indeed, the creature itself seemed to be shuddering, rippling, *breathing* constantly. Steve watched as with one final, hideous crunch, Mabel's body crumpled like a Coke can before folding completely in two, and then disappeared into whatever passed for the creature's maw.

There followed a silence—a stunned pause of perhaps two seconds—and then Sue and Max started firing. The noise was incredible in the confines of the hotel room. Bullets tore into the creature and gouged huge chunks of plaster out of the wall behind it. The creature let out a nerve-shredding, metallic bellow, like the scream of a buzz saw, and started to move, to *flow,* towards them. It was evident that the bullets were hurting it, though there was no blood, no ichor, no discernible sign of physical damage. The three of them scattered before the creature's advance, Max and Sue diving to the left, Steve— despite his injury—throwing himself to the right. The creature made no move to attack, simply passed between them, a shimmering, crackling presence, more suggestion than shape. As it flowed through the door and into the corridor, Sue screamed a warning to the two girls.

"Get out of its way! Open the nearest door and shut yourselves in! Don't move till we tell you!"

Afterwards. Blood on the carpet. Silence apart from Max's too-rapid breathing. Steve lay, swimming in the treacly misery of his own pain, traumatized by what he had seen, thinking that the legions of the drowned had been the lucky ones, after all.

Abby fell to her knees on the carpet beside him. "Dad," she whispered. She put her arms around him, lay her head on his chest. "Dad, Dad . . ."

The rustling of movement. The sound of people stirring, rising, attempting to pull themselves back together. Max's breathing slowing, becoming a series of shuddering breaths. Sue's voice, low and shell-shocked: "That's it. Easy. Deep breaths."

Then Max's voice. High and raw. "What *was* that thing? *What was it?*"

Sue again: "It's like the thing I saw in London. The little girl."

"But what *the fuck was it?*"

"I don't know."

"It killed Mabel. It just . . . *it fucking gobbled her up, man!*"

Steve felt Abby stiffen. He opened his eyes and saw her sit up, horror and incomprehension on her face. "What do you mean, it killed Mabel?" she said. "Mabel's not dead! She's not!"

There was silence. Then Sue said softly, "I'm afraid she is."

"No!" wailed Abby. She looked at Steve. "Tell me it's not true, Dad! Please tell me Mabel's not dead!"

"I'm sorry, sweetheart," he whispered.

Abby let out a wailing scream, then collapsed across him, her body heaving with sobs. Steve wrapped his arms around her and held her tight. His arm and ribs were burning with his daughter's weight, but he didn't care.

There was a thumping from farther down the corridor. Then Libby's muffled voice. "What's happening? Can I come out now?"

"You can come out," Sue shouted wearily.

"Where's Greg?" asked Max in a dull voice. He was slumped against the wall beneath the window, his gun across his knees, looking exhausted. "And where's Marco? Do you think that thing ate them too?"

Then a new voice, weak, from low down: "I'm here."

Sue looked around. "Greg? Where are you?"

"He's under the bed," said Libby, who had just entered the

room. She saw the blood on the carpet. "Oh, God. What happened?"

No one answered. Max and Sue were scrambling across to the bed, delving under it, reaching for Greg.

"Gently," Sue said. Together they eased Greg out. He was on his back, his injured arm clamped protectively to his side, hand curled like a claw on his chest. He was white-faced, sweating. Steve wondered whether this was what they would *all* be reduced to sooner or later, hiding from the monsters, cowering under the bed like children.

"Has he gone?" Greg asked in a rasping voice.

"Has who gone?" said Sue.

"Marco."

"We ain't seen Marco, man," said Max. "Only you and . . . and Mabel."

Greg shook his head. "No, no, *it* was Marco. The thing that attacked Mabel. It was Marco and then it wasn't. It *changed*."

They stared at him in disbelief, and then quietly Sue said, "Oh my God."

"You mean . . . that thing was Marco all along?" said Libby.

"Not *all* along," Sue replied, "but you remember how aggressive Marco was before he stomped off, and then how quiet he was when he came back?"

"You think it wasn't Marco who came back?" said Max. "You think it was that thing?"

Sue nodded.

"But that's impossible," said Libby.

"Try telling *him* that," said Max, nodding at Greg. "Try telling Mrs. B."

Abby raised her head from Steve's chest. Her eyes were red from crying.

"But that means that thing's been living with us," she said. "Living amongst us."

Sue nodded grimly. "Which means we can't trust anyone anymore." She glanced around the room, her eyes briefly resting on every one of them. "Not even each other."

TWENTY-THREE

Sunday, 15th October

I know I haven't written anything for a while, but that's because since we lost Mrs. B 10 days ago, everything's been pretty much the same. We've been walking during the day, scavenging food where we can (I'm SO SICK of food out of packets and tins that I'd give anything for an apple or a banana or a fresh piece of chicken) and finding somewhere to sleep at night. Although the motorway has been clear enough for us to walk around obstacles, progress has been slow cos Greg's injury has really knocked him for 6. Before, he was quite a fit old man. In fact, I wouldn't even have called him "old," even though he's about 70. But since he got shot he HAS seemed old. He walks slowly cos of the pain in his ribs and he gets tired quicker and he can't use his arm properly. We're not having to carry him or anything, but we're not going as quickly as Sue and Max would like to.

Sue's pretty patient tho. She knows people are injured and she's good at encouraging them. She's tough, but she's quite kind. I like her. Also, she usually seems to know what to do, which I suppose comes from being a policewoman.

She's sort of now become the leader of the group. Before, I would have said Dad was the leader, even tho he's never been the sort of person who likes organizing things and making big decisions. Since he got hurt, tho, I think he's happy to leave decisions and plans up to Sue. His injury doesn't slow him down as much as Greg's does, but I know it hurts him and makes him feel more exhausted at night than he would be normally. Usually, tho, after a few painkillers and a good night's sleep he's OK again.

I hope he'll recover properly. The cut on his arm is gross and it doesn't seem to be healing very well. Greg says that's just cos the wound was so deep. He says there's a lot of flesh to knit back together, but that it should get there eventually. But it keeps bleeding and leaking this sticky, watery stuff. Every night Libby changes his dressing, and then Greg's. She's like Florence Nightingale (and I don't mean that in a bitchy way. Libby is OK, but she still gets on my nerves sometimes). The problem is we haven't got any bandages, so we're having to make do with strips of cloth or whatever we can find—it's hard sometimes to find things that are clean enough. Greg has told Libby to put lots of disinfectant on the wounds cos he says we have to be careful of "secondary infections." I can tell from Dad's and Greg's expressions that the stuff she uses stings like hell, but they don't make too much fuss.

Food is getting a bit harder to come by, the problem being that even when we DO find loads, there's only so much we can carry with us. Also, the places where you can find food on our route, like motorway service stations, have often had people there before us. It's not a MAJOR problem at the moment, but it is getting a bit more of a worry. I know Dad and Sue have talked about it quite a lot.

Walking-wise, we're managing about 10 to 15 miles a day, which has brought us up to just south of Sheffield—the last big town we passed was Chesterfield at Junction 30. Weird to think that before the flood we'd have done this journey in 2 hours in the car.

It's not all bad, tho. Some things have got better. For one thing we haven't had much rain since we left the hotel where Mrs. B died, so the ground has dried out a bit. The mud on the roads has now gone dry and crusty, so it's easier to walk on (a bit like black sand). Even inside the buildings it's dried quite a bit, tho most places stink cos all the carpets and furniture and stuff are going rotten with damp. Plus there's furry mold growing on everything, like the stuff that grows on old bread or cheese.

The dead bodies don't smell as bad as they did either, and they don't look as bad as they did. They've now gone past that horrible swollen-up phase, where they all went black and disgusting, and now they've sort of shrunk. They look more like skeletons now, except not REALLY like skeletons cos they've got this brown leathery skin wrapped around them. Their eyes have gone—dissolved or been eaten or whatever—and their lips have shrunk back so you can see all their teeth. Also there aren't as many flies around as there were, which Dad says is mainly thanks to the weather. He says if this had been summer it would have been worse, but we've had a couple of frosty days, so lots of them have died out.

Also there don't seem to be as many crabs around as there were before. Maybe the cold and the dryness has killed them too, or maybe now the bodies are turning to old leather there isn't as much for them to eat.

The only creatures that DON'T seem to be dying out are the birds. There are loads of those, and some of them, the gulls especially, are really vicious. If we're eating outdoors they'll hover around, and sometimes they'll swoop down and snatch things like crisps or biscuits out of your hand. Max got bitten on the hand when a seagull stole a piece of fruitcake he'd been eating. It was cool, tho, cos he was so mad he took a shot at it—and hit it! It was a total fluke, a one in a million chance, but that night we had roast seagull and rice for supper, which was TOTALLY delicious. If someone had told me 3 weeks ago that I'd think roast seagull was one of the yummiest things I'd ever tasted, I'd have thought they were mental.

Since Mrs. B died, we haven't seen any more monsters, or even any signs of any. I don't know how many there are or where they've come from (the blue lightning?), but knowing there are things on earth that can imitate human beings so well that we can't tell the difference is pretty freaky, and has made all of us really nervous. We haven't seen that many people over the last 10 days, but we've seen a few, and most of the time we've kept our distance from them. We've tried to warn some of them about the monsters, or find out whether they've seen them too, but now we don't bother. Most people think we're nut-

ters, or lying, tho we did meet this one man who was traveling with a boy about 10 who I think was his son, and as soon as he saw us he and the boy ran to the central barrier and climbed over it.

It turned out a man in Leeds had made friends with them, and then one night he'd changed and almost got the boy. The man (Colin) and the boy (Oliver) had got away by throwing a chair at it, which Colin said had seemed to confuse it. His story was bad news to us. We'd been hoping that the aliens (which is what we've started calling them) were only in London.

"Where are you headed?" Sue asked him, and he told us he was going to London.

"You don't want to go there," Max said. "That's where we've come from. There's nothing there but lots and lots of dead people."

Whatever we said, tho, we couldn't change Colin's mind. He thought there'd be more food in London, more "resources" as he put it, and he said that he thought that was where people would head for, and where any kind of rescue or aid operation would be centered. He thought we'd made a mistake by leaving there. He said he didn't know what the situation was like in Scotland, but it was just as bad in Leeds, so he didn't see why any other part of the country should be any different. Greg told him the usual thing about big cities being rife with disease, but nothing would change his mind. Dad said later that sometimes when someone gets an idea in their head, they'll cling to it no matter what, even if other people tell them that it's wrong.

So we said good-bye to Colin and Oliver and we went our separate ways. As they walked off, Sue said, "I don't fancy their chances."

"Maybe we should have given them a gun," said Max.

Sue, tho, shook her head. "S****y tho it sounds," she said, "we can't give away our most valuable resources. We're living in a selfish world now. There's no room for charity anymore."

Dad let out a big sigh and said, "So, what does that make us?"

Sue had a really serious look on her face. "Survivors," she said.

Guns. That was another thing I wanted to talk about. After Mrs. B got killed, Sue said it was time we all learned how to handle and fire a gun. I didn't fancy the idea, and neither did Libby, but I guess both of us knew that it made sense. For one thing, I didn't want people having to look out for me and protect me all the time, and for another, we had more guns than we were using—in fact, we'd brought 4 rifles and 6 pistols with us, which meant there was enough for one each plus 4 left over—and because me and Libby had been weird about touching them, it had meant Dad, Max, Sue and Greg had had to carry them strapped to their rucksacks, which wasn't fair, as they're not the lightest things in the world.

So me and Libby and Greg had lessons from Sue in how to hold the guns and load them and fire them, and now all 6 of us carry one. I hope I never have to use mine, but I suppose it DOES make me feel a bit safer. As Sue said, a gun is more a deterrent than anything else. She didn't think we'd come across many people who also had guns, and so as winter came along and food got scarcer, they might prove our most valuable resource. She said our guns would probably PREVENT violence rather than cause it, because we'd only have to show them to potential attackers to make them leave us alone. So now Sue and Max carry the rifles (which are Heckler and Koch 9mm carbine machine pistols), and the rest of us carry handguns (which are Glock 17 9mm self-loading pistols).

I think that brings everything up to date. I've pretty much got over what happened to me 10 days ago, tho I'm quite nervous of strangers now, and I get a bit more jumpy at night. I haven't had too many bad dreams, tho I think all the walking helps, cos by the time we crawl into our sleeping bags at night we're all exhausted.

Dad and Libby have got really close, which I find a bit hard to take sometimes. I had a talk with Sue about this, and she said that Dad was the only constant left in my life, that he was my rock, and that it was only natural that I should see Libby as a threat. But she also said that I would always be Dad's number one priority, and that I should cut Libby a bit of slack. She said that one of the men in the cottage had raped Libby, and that Libby was doing an incredible job of holding herself together and trying not to become an emotional burden for the rest of us. She said Libby was secretly terrified she might be pregnant, and that she needed someone to cling to as well, and that the person she had chosen was Dad. She told me that Dad was doing a fantastic job trying to help Libby through it all, and that we had to find love where we could nowadays. Then she went quiet on me (she was a bit drunk, to be honest—she'd had a load of wine) *and she admitted that she was gay and that she had a bit of a crush on Libby herself, but knew that nothing would ever come of it. She asked me if that was a problem, and I said no, it was no big deal. I gave her a hug and for a minute she didn't seem tough at all. She seemed just as frightened and confused as the rest of us.*

Tonight we're sleeping at Woodall Services, in what used to be the main café/restaurant area. We've got into a routine now when we stop somewhere. Dad, Max and Sue will put on gloves and clear any bodies out of the area, and me and Libby (and Greg if he's up to it) will clear away any other rubbish until we've got a big enough space to sleep on. Then we'll put down our plastic sheets and our bed rolls and our sleeping bags. We'll look around for food and then we'll set up the gas stove—which we all (except Greg) take turns carrying—and then we'll brew up some water and have some tea or coffee and get some food on the go. We'll light a few candles and then we'll talk for a bit, and the adults will maybe have a drink if they've found some booze, and then we'll turn in, usually about 9 or 10 o'clock. Someone will always stay on guard, and we'll do hourly shifts. Me and Greg always do one hour each, and the other 4 divide up the other 6 hours or however long it is between them.

Oh, one last thing before I go to sleep. Remember what I said about food being harder to come by now? Well, when we got here the vending machines had been raided and virtually all the edible stuff we usually find had gone. So tonight we came to a decision. We've decided that tomorrow morning, Sue and Max will get off the motorway at the next junction and go into the nearest town to find some food. We did talk about all going together so we could carry more, but we decided that it would be best if just Max and Sue went, cos a) they'd be quicker, and b) we wouldn't all want to be totally weighed down by food anyway, cos that would just slow us down.

So that's what's happening. Max and Sue are heading off at about 6, and the rest of us are having a bit more time than usual to rest and get our strength back. We're a bit nervous about splitting up the group, even for a short time, but we've all got guns, so hopefully we'll be OK.

And now I'm going to rest my aching legs and my blistered feet for a few hours. And by the end of tomorrow, hopefully, we'll be a little bit nearer to Scotland and to seeing Mum and Dylan again.

Night-night, world.

TWENTY-FOUR

"Whoa," said Max. "Look at that."

Sue came to a halt beside him. In the hour since leaving the service station at six A.M. the pair had made excellent progress. They had walked five miles in the slowly breaking dawn light, passing through two villages that had yielded nothing but a few odds and ends from a couple of local convenience stores. They could have spent their time going from house to house, salvaging what they could from pantries and kitchen cupboards, but they had decided to press on, find a town with a decent-sized supermarket in which everything would be centralized, rather than scrabbling through a ton of filth for the sake of a few scraps. They were now heading for the ex-mining town of Whitthorpe, which lay six miles east of the service station in which they had spent the night.

Whitthorpe was not a big place—it was basically a quartet of housing estates surrounding a main shopping area—but it was sizeable enough to merit its own Safeway or Sainsbury's. Max and Sue were on the outskirts of the town, where its biggest houses were situated, when Max stopped beside a gate that led into a large paddock. The paddock was positioned be-

tween two postwar properties that would have looked impressive before the flood, but which were now crumbling with
water damage and filthy with caked-on silt.

It was not the houses that had drawn Max's eye, however.
Lying in the paddock between them were the remains of a
vast creature, almost undoubtedly a whale. It was virtually a
skeleton now, its rotting flesh picked from its bones by insects
and birds. Even so, in this muddy, litter-bedecked field in the
middle of England, the carcass of the once majestic creature
still remained an astonishing sight. Bathed in the salmon red
light of dawn, the scene reminded Sue of the cover of the
kind of science fiction novels she had read in her teenage
years. Seeing the whale was like looking upon the remains of
an alien creature lying beneath the fiery skies of a distant
planet.

"Wow," she breathed.

Max looked at her and nodded. "Yeah, I know."

They stood, as if in homage, for several more seconds; then
Sue repositioned her gun, shifting its weight. "We'd better
get on."

They trudged on towards the town, the countryside falling
away behind them, the houses becoming more plentiful. Max
kept his gun poised and looked constantly left and right, alert
for the slightest sound or movement.

The silence was unnerving. Even now, three weeks after the
flood, he couldn't get used to it. He would have given just
about anything to hear the bustle of a London market or the
rumble of traffic or the roar of a football crowd.

Or music. God, what he wouldn't give to hear some *music*.
He wouldn't care what kind either. Even the gospel stuff his
mum used to listen to, and he and Leo had hated, would be a
godsend.

What became evident to both of them as they entered the
town proper was that even without the devastation caused by
the flood, Whitthorpe would have been a grim place. The
colliery had evidently been the heart of the community, and
now that it had closed, the town had become little more than

a collection of empty shops, boarded-up businesses and run-down housing. After negotiating a labyrinth of narrow, debris-choked streets they came across the common. Emerging onto a pavement beside what they guessed was a main road, they saw a spiked metal fence adorned with slimy beards of seaweed and streamers of shredded paper, ringing a vast patch of what might once have been grass, but was now merely a lake of mud scattered with the usual wreckage of cars, uprooted vegetation and smashed household items. Hefting his gun in one hand, Max said, "What's that?"

"What?" asked Sue.

"That pile of stuff over there."

Sue squinted into the rising sun. "Dunno. Town bonfire? Does it matter?"

Max shielded his eyes. "I think it's people," he said.

"What?" Now Sue was shielding her eyes too. After a moment she said, "Fuck, you're right. It's a heap of corpses."

"What's going on, d'you reckon?"

"Clean-up operation? Maybe a bunch of survivors have banded together, made this their base."

Max glanced at her. "Reckon we should check it out?"

She thought about it a moment, then said, "Come on then."

They crossed the road and climbed over the fence. The common covered a large area, and the heap of bodies was maybe eight hundred yards in from its perimeter. They were within two hundred yards of the mound when Max stopped.

"Look at the bodies," he said. "There's a funny sort of . . . blue gleam."

Sue shielded her eyes once again. "You're right. It's like they've been scattered with blue jewels or something."

Max looked around at the buildings surrounding the common. "I don't like this," he said. "Something's not right."

"Apart from the fact that everyone's dead and monsters are stalking the land, you mean?" Sue smiled. "Come on, let's check this out, then find some food and fuck off."

They edged closer to the heap of corpses, their guns raised

and ready, as if they half expected the dead to suddenly rise up en masse.

They were maybe twenty yards away when Sue murmured, "Oh, fuck."

"What?"

"I know what these things are." She swallowed. "They're eggs."

Sure enough, the bodies were encrusted with hundreds, perhaps thousands, of blue "eggs." Each one was a quivering jellylike sac, and looking closer, Max realized that within every semitransparent coating he could see the suggestion of squirming, shadowy movement.

He wrinkled his nose in disgust. "That's gross, man."

He jabbed one of the sacs with his rifle. A thin, colorless fluid gushed out, followed by a trickle of lumpy black liquid. The shadow inside the sac convulsed for several seconds, then became still. Max didn't feel any better for having killed the thing. He watched, sickened, as the sac deflated.

"We should torch the lot," he said bleakly.

"Uh-oh," said Sue. "We've got trouble."

Max looked up. Around the common, doors were opening and people were coming out. There were men and women both young and old, even the occasional child. The one thing they had in common were the expressions of grim intent on their faces. They began to march, almost in unison, towards Sue and Max, apparently unconcerned by the guns that they carried, seemingly prepared to overwhelm them by sheer numbers.

"Run!" Sue shouted.

Max's face was taut with fear. "Where?"

"Back the way we came. There's a gap in the ranks."

"Not much of one."

"It's all we've got. Come *on!*"

They ran, weighed down by their boots and guns, their feet slithering in the mud. The townspeople closed in on all sides, marching inexorably, faces set.

Sue and Max were less than two hundred yards from the fence when the first wave of townspeople reached them. Max swung round, gun raised.

"Back off!" he screamed.

"Halt or we fire," Sue shouted, wondering not only whether she was capable of gunning down civilians in cold blood, but also how many she could kill before they engulfed her and tore the weapon from her hands.

She was both relieved and surprised when her order was obeyed without question. As one the townspeople clumped to a halt, though they continued to stare balefully at the intruders.

"We don't want any trouble," Sue said. "What happened was an accident."

There was no response. The townspeople remained still as statues.

"Why don't they answer?" Max hissed, glancing about nervously.

"I don't think they're human," said Sue.

"You mean they're all . . . those monster things?"

"Either that or they're being controlled in some way."

"Fuck, man," Max breathed.

"I think they're like . . . antibodies," said Sue. "Or . . . what are those things that travel to the site of a wound? Endorphins. They're like endorphins, flowing to the injury, protecting the body."

Max was still trying to cover every direction with his gun. "So what happens now?"

"Now we go."

"Easy as that?"

"Let's see." Sue raised her voice again. "Is anyone going to speak to me?"

Silence.

"Okay," she said. "My friend and I are going to leave now. We won't hurt you if you don't hurt us. Deal?"

At first none of the townspeople moved or spoke, and then those that had closed in took a few steps back, creating a clear path to the perimeter fence.

"I think that's our cue," said Sue.

Max nodded. "Let's go. These guys give me the creeps."

Once they had put the town a mile behind them, Max gave the barrel of his gun a pat. "Think they'd have let us go if we hadn't had these with us?"

"I don't think I want to find out," Sue said.

TWENTY-FIVE

"It seems the evolution of our mysterious new species has entered the next phase," Greg said once Sue and Max had told their story.

"There were hundreds of those eggs, man," Max said quietly.

"Thousands," Sue said.

A somber silence descended upon them. "So?" Abby said. "What do we do?"

"I think . . ." Greg steepled his fingers to his lips, then seemed to come to a decision. "I think we should talk to them."

"Talk?" said Libby.

"You mean go back there?" said Max.

"Yes." Greg nodded decisively. "What have we got to lose?"

"Our lives?" said Max.

"But they could have killed you and they didn't."

"They killed Mabel," Libby reminded him.

"One of them killed Mabel," corrected Greg. "But who's to say that wasn't a rogue element? Or perhaps their initial period of aggression has now passed. How do we know they haven't now evolved into intelligent, reasoning creatures?"

"I still say we should keep away from 'em," said Max.

"That may soon become impossible," Greg said. "I think we have to assume, Max, that the situation you happened across in Whitthorpe was not an isolated one. It's a reasonable hypothesis that similar activity is taking place throughout the country, perhaps even the world."

"You mean they're spawning?" said Steve.

Greg nodded. "It would seem so."

"We're fucked then," said Sue. She raised a hand. "Sorry, Abby."

"What for?" Abby said. "I'm not a kid. What I've seen over the past few weeks is a million times worse than hearing someone say the F-word."

"If we're in such a dire situation as you believe, Sue," pointed out Greg, "then that brings me back to my earlier point. What have we got to lose? Based on your evidence I would surmise that in a very short time, whatever's left of humankind will be not only outnumbered but overwhelmed by these creatures. And if they *are* predatory, as you fear, then I'm sorry to say that our days left on this planet are very much at a premium. So rather than run and hide, why not face that uncertainty sooner rather than later?"

"Take the fight to them?" said Max.

"They say attack is the best form of defense," muttered Sue.

"I'm not advocating a military campaign," said Greg.

"No, but it's always best to be prepared," Sue argued.

"We've got guns," said Steve. "What else can we prepare ourselves with?"

"Petrol bombs," she suggested.

"Forgive my ignorance," Libby said, "but don't you need petrol for petrol bombs?"

"We've got petrol," said Sue. "Gallons of it. There's a petrol station right outside."

"Yeah, but it's been underwater," Max said.

"So?"

"Won't the water have got in? Contaminated the petrol or something?"

"No reason why it should have. Those underground tanks

are sealed units, tight as submarines. They have to be. They're full of thousands of gallons of highly flammable liquid, remember."

"But how do we get to it?" asked Steve. "Surely the pumps won't still be working?"

Sue drained her coffee mug and stood up. "Let's see, shall we?"

TWENTY-SIX

They stashed most of their stuff at the service station and set off just before midday, their backpacks containing nothing but petrol bombs and light provisions.

"I can't believe we're going back there," Max said to Abby.

"Are you scared?" she asked.

"Nah." He glanced at her and smiled. "A bit. You?"

"Terrified," she admitted. "What do you think's going to happen, Max? Long-term, I mean?"

"Who knows? Let's just get through today, shall we? Not think too far ahead."

"Live for the moment?" she said.

"Yeah, man. It's all we got now, isn't it?"

She sighed. "I can't believe there was so much I was looking forward to a few weeks ago."

"Oh yeah? Like what?"

"Just little things. The new Faithless album. My friend Myleen's birthday party, which would have been . . . oh, God, last weekend! And when I was in London my dad was going to take me to *Billy Elliot*. We had tickets and everything."

"Bummer," said Max. "Did you get a refund?"

"We tried ringing the box office, but no one answered," she said, deadpan.

He tutted. "Can't get the service these days."

"I know," she said. "What *is* the world coming to?"

They looked at each other and sniggered. Then Max said shyly, "Can I ask you something, Abby?"

"Depends."

"If the world was, say, still normal, and I asked you out . . . what would you say?"

"I'd say no," she replied without hesitation.

"Really?"

" 'Fraid so."

He swallowed. "Why's that?"

"Because Dad would kill me."

Max looked hurt, but tried to make light of it. Adopting a Jamaican accent, he asked, "Is it because I is black?"

"No," said Abby, "it's because you is seventeen and I is only thirteen. But ask me again in three or four years. It might be all right then."

"Okay," he said, "I'll do that."

On the outskirts of the town he told her to close her eyes, and didn't let her open them again until he had led her around the corner and stood her in front of the paddock containing the remains of the whale. Despite the trepidation they all felt, they still allowed themselves a moment to view the spectacle. When they finally—reluctantly—moved on, Sue said, "Okay, guys, we're getting close now. Keep your eyes peeled and your ears . . ."

"Pricked?" suggested Libby.

"That's the one."

They followed the route that Sue and Max had walked earlier, but didn't see a soul. "Reckon they're watching us?" Abby whispered to Max.

"Who knows?"

Eventually they emerged from the maze of streets and came in sight of the common. Everything was as it had been earlier that day—the mound of corpses in the near distance, the houses fringing the vast, litter-strewn patch of mud, betraying no obvious signs of life. Abby nervously scanned the encircling windows, so dark within their white frames that they looked painted on to the buildings. She half expected to glimpse ghostly faces melting back into the shadows, but she saw nothing.

They crossed the road and hovered on the pavement beside the fence. "What now?" asked Steve. "Head for the center or go round the outside and knock on a door?"

Sue delved into her rucksack and pulled out one of the carefully packed petrol bombs. "Let's negotiate from a position of strength."

"You aren't going to *use* that, are you?" Abby asked nervously.

"Only if I'm forced to."

She and Max scaled the fence and helped the others over. Steve winced as Max grabbed hold of his injured arm. "Sorry, man, I forgot."

They tramped across the mud towards the corpses. As soon as they were close enough to see the egg sacs glistening among the bodies of the dead, Libby turned away. "I feel sick."

Abby joined Greg, who had walked right up to the heaped corpses and was peering intently over the top of his spectacles at the substance coating them.

"Fascinating," he said. "Obviously the dead are here to provide sustenance for the newborn."

"What now?" said Steve. "Do we just stand here and wait for them to come out?"

"I could fire a shot into the air . . ." suggested Sue.

Steve nodded. "Go for it."

Sue pointed her rifle at the sun and pulled the trigger. The gunshot was oddly muted in the still air.

"Can anyone hear us?" she shouted. "We were here earlier. We've come to talk to you."

At first nothing happened, and then, almost in unison, doors opened and the inhabitants of Whitthorpe emerged, same as before. They filed through a gate on the far side of the common and began to tramp across the mud, a ragtag army, unhurried but well drilled. Libby huddled closer to Steve. Sue held the petrol bomb casually in her left hand, as if it were a pint of milk she had bought at the local shop.

"Shall we tell them we come in peace?" Abby said. "That's what they always say in the movies."

The townspeople clumped to a halt some twenty yards from the six survivors and regarded them, no expressions on their faces. It struck Steve that this was like a standoff in a Western—high noon in Whitthorpe. Instead of the Magnificent Seven he and his friends were the Motley Six.

"Hi," he said, suddenly realizing that maybe they should have elected a spokesperson and decided exactly what they were going to say. "A couple of us were here this morning. We've come back because we want to talk to you. We want to . . . well, basically just find out who you are and what you're doing here. . . ."

He tailed off, hoping the others weren't as dissatisfied with his words as he was. It was only as he had started talking that he had realized what an odd, even unique situation he was in. What did you say to people who might or might not be monsters or genetic mutations or space aliens in disguise? Everything that came to mind sounded like a dopey rehash of lines from some dumb science fiction movie. What he really wanted to know was whether the earth and what was left of its inhabitants were under threat, and, more specifically, whether by coming here he and his friends had strolled unwittingly into the lions' den.

A man broke away from the rest of the townspeople and approached them. He was about fifty, tall and portly, with graying hair and rimless spectacles. He was wearing a white shirt under a maroon sweater, blue jeans and black walking boots. He looked like a civil servant relaxing at the weekend, like the sort of man you would pass in the street and not look at twice. The only unusual thing about him was the unnerving blankness of his expression.

"You've come to talk?" he said.

Steve nodded. "Yes."

"But you have guns. You don't need guns to talk."

"We weren't sure what kind of reception we'd get," Sue said.

The man regarded her. "That's reasonable."

"So who are you?" Steve asked.

The man spread his arms. "We are the people of Whit thorpe."

"With all due respect, we know that's not true," said Greg.

Abruptly the man smiled. "Perhaps *you'd* like to tell us who we are then?"

"We don't *know* who you are," said Greg, "which is why we're here. We believe you're a new species to us. We've seen what you really look like, but we can't identify you—hence our curiosity."

"I see," said the man.

"So?" Sue said. "Who *are* you?"

Again the man spread his arms, as if to show he had nothing to hide. "We are just like you. Our aspirations are the same as yours."

"Which are?" Steve asked.

"To survive."

"And how do you intend to do that?" Greg asked.

"In any way we can."

"By using us as food, you mean?" said Sue, nodding at the mound of corpses.

"Your dead are a source of nourishment," admitted the man, "but we didn't kill these people. The water did that."

"But who brought the water?" asked Steve. "Was that you?"

"The water has always been here," said the man.

"That doesn't answer the question," growled Sue. "Did you cause the flood?"

The man's stare was impenetrable. "No."

"I don't believe you."

The man shrugged. "That's your perogative."

"What plans do you have for the survivors of the flood? For people like us?" Sue said, beginning to lose her cool.

"Why do you assume we have *plans*?"

"Do you intend to wipe us out?"

"Of course not. We're the same as you."

"You're *not* the same," Sue snapped. "We've seen what you're really like. One of your . . . *kind* killed our friend, and another one nearly killed me. I've still got the scars to show for it."

"I can't answer for all of my *kind*," the man said, emphasizing the word in a way that seemed almost mocking, "just as you can't answer for all of yours."

Sue glared at him, chin thrust forward pugnaciously.

"Where do you come from?" Steve asked.

"Why is that important?" said the man. "What would you do with that information if we gave it to you? Would you attempt to use it against us?"

"Of course not," said Steve. "We're not like that."

"Then what are you *like?*"

"We're just . . . people. We want to get by. Survive. Live a quiet life."

"Then do that. We're not stopping you."

"But you will," said Sue, "when you're strong enough."

"Strong?" said the man. "What's *strong?* You've got guns, we've got information. Who's the stronger?"

"Oh, I think you are," said Greg.

"Then give *us* the guns and we'll give *you* the information," said the man, and suddenly he was smiling again. "So you see? We *are* the same, after all. You ask us who we are? Why don't you just hold up a mirror to yourselves?"

"You're *not* us," Sue muttered. "*We* haven't attacked you."

"He killed one of our young," said the man, pointing at Max.

"That was a mistake," said Sue.

Still smiling, the man said, "Now who's lying?"

"This is *our* world," Sue shouted like a petulant child.

The blandness of the man's voice made Sue sound like the unreasonable one. "It's ours too," he said.

TWENTY-SEVEN

"We didn't handle that well," said Steve.

They were back at the service station, sitting around the camping stove. It was late afternoon and the sky was already darkening. As they had trooped back from Whitthorpe, gray clouds had ganged up on the sun. Minutes later a blustery wind carrying cold, stinging rain had blown up out of nowhere. By mutual consent they had decided to stay at Woodall another night and strike out for new pastures the next morning.

"We asked the right questions," Sue said bitterly, "but they didn't give us any answers."

"At least they didn't kill us," said Libby. "That's got to be a positive thing, right?"

"The only reason they didn't kill us was because we were armed and right next to their precious eggs."

"That's one possibility," said Greg.

"Oh, come on. Don't tell me you believe that 'We're just like you' bullshit? Humans and monsters living in perfect harmony?"

"Not harmony, perhaps," Greg said, "but mutual ambivalence may be possible."

"You mean it might be they just don't care about us?" said Max.

"Exactly. We're of no consequence to them. Perhaps they regard us in the way we regard . . . I don't know . . . cats, for instance."

"As cute little fluff balls they want to keep as pets?" said Abby.

Greg smiled. "Well, perhaps cats is not the best example."

"I still think they're out to get us," muttered Sue.

Libby sighed. "And why's that?"

"Well, why else would they make themselves look like us if not for the purpose of infiltration? It's a hunting tool. They do it to confuse us, catch us off guard. It makes us easier prey."

"Maybe on this planet our shape is just more practical," said Libby.

Greg was about to offer his opinion when something hit one of the windows of the service station restaurant with enough force to make them all jump.

Sue and Max were first on their feet, Steve a split second behind them. All three pointed their guns in the direction of the sound, but the day was now so dark that they could see nothing but their own candlelit reflections on the rain-speckled glass.

Libby said, "Maybe it was just a bird flying into the glass, confused by the candlelight."

"Better to be safe than sorry," said Sue. She reached the window, cupped her hands around her face and peered into the gathering dusk.

"Can you see anything?" Abby asked.

"There's something on the window here, a mark of some kind, but I can't make it out. Could someone bring me a torch?"

Libby unfastened Sue's rucksack, pulled out her torch and carried it to her.

"Thanks," Sue said, and turned it on.

The mark on the window proved to be a smear of sticky liquid, slightly more viscous than the rain, which was already diluting it. Sue frowned and touched her fingertips to the inside of the window. "If I didn't know better I'd say it was saliva."

"Looks like dog slaver," said Max. "My aunt Leanne had a long-haired retriever and a patio door into her back garden. Wilson, her dog, was always making marks like that on the glass. Used to drive Aunt Leanne mental." The trace of a wistful smile flitted across his face.

"But there aren't any dogs around anymore," said Sue.

"Just because we haven't seen any doesn't mean there aren't any," Libby said.

"But the only people who survived were the ones on the top floors of hotels and apartment blocks. Dogs aren't allowed in places like that."

"In some flats you're allowed to keep pets," said Libby. "It's not beyond the realms of possibility that some survived."

"Could you pass the torch?" Steve asked.

Sue handed it over, and Steve pressed it up against the glass, forcing ochre light to spill weakly into the shadowed world beyond. Everything at ground level—every building and tree, every overturned vehicle, every chunk of debris—was now melded together, as if blackness had seeped up from the earth and absorbed it all. The sky above was a smoky violet, deepening to near-black at the horizon.

The torchlight washed across the blackness, plucking out vague shapes. What made Libby gasp, however, were the half dozen or more pairs of eyes, gleaming and milky, that reflected the light back at them.

"You were right, Max," said Sue in disbelief. "It's a pack of fucking dogs."

"They must have been attracted by the candles," said Steve.

"Or the smell of food," added Max.

Sue glanced at Greg and Abby, who were still sitting beside the camping stove. "Quick, blow out the candles."

As Abby scrambled to do so, Libby said, "Where can they have come from?"

"Who knows?" said Steve.

"As long as they move on, I don't care if we never find out," said Sue.

The candles were extinguished now, the air full of blue-gray smoke and the smell of hot wax. Steve switched off the torch too, and suddenly they were plunged into blackness. Libby couldn't decide what was worse: not knowing where the dogs were or seeing the baleful glow of their eyes in the darkness. She snaked out a hand, seeking the warmth of Steve's. For a moment she imagined touching sleek fur, a cold, wet snout, the bristly fuzz of a muzzle curling back over sharp teeth. She shuddered and then she found Steve's hand and clutched it gratefully.

There was something about the dogs that bothered her. Something about the lean muscularity of their barely glimpsed shapes in the darkness. It had been troubling her since the torchlight had picked them out, but it was only now that she realized what had been preying on her mind.

She pressed her mouth to Steve's ear. "I've just thought of something."

His hair, longer than it had been when she had first met him, brushed her cheek. "What?" he whispered.

"The dogs. What kind would you say they were?"

"I don't know. They looked like guard dogs. Dobermans or something."

"That's what I thought too," she said, "but don't you think it's weird that they're *all the same?*"

He went very still. "What are you suggesting?"

"I don't know," she said. "It's just odd, that's all."

They lapsed back into silence, each pondering their own thoughts. Libby wondered how thick the glass of the windows was; whether, if the dogs were still out there, she would be able to hear them. She wondered how long they would wait here in the pitch-blackness until someone decided it was safe to relight the candles.

And then, from somewhere over to her left, she heard the soft pad of footfalls.

Gooseflesh spread across Libby's shoulders and crawled down her back. She huddled closer to Steve, wanting to ask him whether he had heard the sounds too, but she was too terrified to speak. She had thought, back at the farmhouse, that if she could get through what was happening to her she would be able to endure anything; there would be no need to be afraid ever again. But she was wrong. Fear never went away. It just kept changing and coming back.

She gripped a fistful of Steve's grimy sweater as she heard a low, threatening growl from somewhere close to where Greg and Abby had been sitting. Next moment the torch that Steve had used minutes before clicked back on, releasing a cone of light that punched through the darkness. Illuminated in the light was a dog, which, for the brief second it stood there, seemed to Libby as big as a lion. Its fur was black and sleek as oil, its eyes an eerie combination of pearly white blindness and a penetrating and devilish fire. It seemed to absorb the light, or perhaps even to repel it—and then, with a flash of teeth, it leaped.

Libby screamed as the dog launched itself, snarling, towards Greg and Abby. Abby dived for safety, scattering mugs and toppling the unlit camping stove with a trailing foot. Greg's reflexes, however, were not nearly as quick as hers. He could do little but half raise an arm before the dog was on him.

The attack was so swift, so savage, that Libby could later remember it only as a sequence of images flash-framing through her mind. She saw the dog in midair; Greg's head snapping back; a sudden jet of red in the torchlight; the dog lunging and pulling back, something ragged and dripping blood hanging from its jaws.

Then the shooting began—Steve, Sue and Max all firing simultaneously. Libby pressed her hands to her ears, mouth wide open to reduce the pressure, but it still seemed her brain was being squeezed tight by the sheer volume of noise. Within the roar and the flash and the smoke, she saw the dog hurled sideways by the force of the bullets slamming into it, saw its midsection disintegrate, its body fold and then fall, lifeless as a sack.

It was only then, as the firing continued, that she realized the dog was not alone, that there were others in the room, and that now, with a flash of eyes and a clatter-scrabble of claws, they were turning tail, streaming away, towards whatever hole they had used to enter the building.

At last the firing stopped, leaving a pulsing pain in her ears. Through a soup of smoke and half-light she saw Steve and Sue scrambling over to Greg, saw torchlight weaving from side to side, half illuminating Max, who was heading towards Abby. Libby, realizing she was the only one not doing anything, forced her own legs to move. She too headed towards Greg's prone form, and was almost there when her foot skidded from under her.

Looking down she saw that the floor was a lake of blood. For a couple of seconds the room spun, the world grayed out. She dug her fingernails into her palms and took several deep breaths. Then she went to see what could be done for Greg.

Steve was holding the torch, directing the beam into Greg's face. Under the torchlight Libby thought Greg's blood was the deepest, brightest red she had ever seen. He was coated in it from jaw to belly, but despite his injuries Steve and Sue did not appear to be tending to him, did not appear to be trying to staunch the flow. Steve was sitting on his heels, his head bowed and his shoulders slumped. Sue was kneeling on the floor—in the blood—beside Greg, and resting a bloodied hand lightly, almost tenderly, on his grizzled cheek.

Then Libby looked at Greg's face and immediately she knew he was dead. Though his eyes were bulging in panic and pain, there was no life in them; they were fixed, glazed. His mouth was also open, and Libby realized that the reason he was covered in blood was because a flap of his lower jaw, from his bottom lip down, had been torn away, taking a sizeable chunk of his throat with it.

She turned away and retched, at first producing a thin gruel and then a splash of more solid stuff. She was straightening when she noticed the dog, the one she had seen annihilated in a hail of bullets. It was twitching, and flickers of blue-white light were dancing in its black fur. And then, before her eyes, Libby saw it begin to change. . . .

Although she screamed with enough force to taste blood in her throat, her ears were still so blocked that she barely heard it. Steve and Sue did, though, and as they spun round Libby saw Sue's face turn from slack anguish to absolute fury. Next moment the ex-policewoman was on her feet, her blood-smeared hand grabbing her gun, aiming it, firing. . . .

To Libby, the creature's transformation seemed almost instantaneous. One second it was a dead and mangled dog, tics of light jumping in its fur, and the next it was a mass of . . . what? Black jagged shapes, strange dark angles, flickering filaments of bluish and somehow *negative* light. It looked awkward, cumbersome, *wrong,* and yet despite that it moved quickly, and in such a way that Libby could not tell whether it was slithering or floating or crawling. But that was partly due to the fact that, try as she might, she couldn't quite focus upon it. There was something about the creature that baffled her perceptions, disengaged her eye. It was like a distant radio signal, a staccato image cast by a bad projector, a phantom. One second it was there, and Sue was firing at it, and the next it was gone.

Sue continued firing until her gun clicked empty. Then she simply stood there, her body taut, her dark hair hanging around her face in sweaty ropes. Her combat pants were covered in Greg's blood, her teeth bared in rage.

She dropped her gun, which hit the blood-slicked floor, no doubt with a sharp thud, though Libby couldn't hear it. Then, abruptly, she was crying, tears streaming down her grimy cheeks.

Libby went to her. She wrapped her arms around her and she held her tight.

And as the two women clung to one another, Libby thought, *Another one gone, another one of us dead.* She couldn't help but wonder who would be next.

TWENTY-EIGHT

Tuesday, 24th October

In the last week we've done about 120 miles, all the way up the M1 to Leeds, and from there on to the A1. We're now at the Washington Birtley Services, a few miles south of Newcastle. It won't be long before we're in Scotland—though we'll still have a way to go even when we cross the border. We're all knackered, and we're having to be careful about our feet cos we've all got blisters (and Max has got athlete's foot). We've got disinfectant cream and foot powder, which we put on every night, even if we're exhausted. It always goes quiet when we're doing it cos I think we're all thinking about Greg and how he always said it was important we didn't get infections. In a funny way, looking after ourselves and being careful to treat any cuts or scrapes that we get sort of feels like honoring Greg, cos we're taking his advice, keeping ourselves as healthy as possible.

Talking of infections, Dad's arm seems to be healing up okay now, and the scar on Sue's back, which she got when she was attacked by that creature in London all those weeks ago, SEEMS all right, tho the skin's gone bluish, and she says it's still tender like a bruise. She doesn't complain about it, tho. In fact, she doesn't complain about anything. Sue is a tough cookie, tho I know Dad's worried about her, and I am too.

She's changed quite a bit since Greg died. She's angrier now, less approachable, and there's a kind of wildness in her eyes, which is scary sometimes. After Greg died she wanted to go straight back to Whitthorpe and kill all the baby aliens in their eggs. Dad and Libby said that would be suicide, but Sue didn't care. She said we were fooling ourselves if we thought we could get through this, and that we might as well go down fighting. For a while it looked as tho she was going to go off and do it by herself, but in the end Dad, Libby and Max persuaded her not to. She's been okay since then, but she doesn't talk much, and like I said, she seems angry most of the time. Dad says it's a pity Greg isn't here, because Greg was always the voice of reason and he could always weigh everything up and think of the most sensible thing to do. Dad says that Greg was the steadying hand on the tiller, and it's only since he's gone that Dad says he has been able to appreciate how influential Greg was.

It's weird, cos there are now more women than men in the group. When we started we had 5 men and 4 women, and now there are 3 women and 2 men. Dad calls it the "group dynamic," which is a pretty cool phrase. Every time someone dies the "group dynamic" changes. That's cos when you get together with people you all adopt certain roles, and so when the group changes, either the roles change with it or the group becomes unbalanced. I suppose in a way it's like 'Big Brother' or 'I'm a Celebrity, Get Me Out of Here,' where the group gets smaller and smaller as people get voted off.

I don't know if our group has become unbalanced or whether it's just that things are more desperate than they were. We don't argue all the time or anything, but we don't sit around chatting like we did before. Dad and Libby get on, and me and Max get on, and me and Dad get on (of course), but Sue has become a bit of a loner, which is sad. It was not long ago that me and her had a really good chat. I've tried to start a conversation a couple of times, but I never get much back. I always feel like she doesn't want me bothering her.

Part of it could be that we're just tired cos we're walking further now without the oldies to slow us down (Dad's the oldest at 40), and part of it could be that we're hungry cos food is not as easy to find as it was. We've had to cut down a bit recently, and we've all lost weight. None of us look bad on it (in fact we all look pretty lean—tho I can't say we actually look GOOD cos all of us have got messy, dirty hair, and Dad and Max have got these scruffy beards, and we're all wearing blood- and dirt-stained clothes, which are getting a bit ragged round the edges), but if it goes on like it is, it won't be much longer before we go from LEAN to THIN, and then from THIN to EMACIATED.

We're trying not to think too much about that, tho, and in fact, in the last 2 days, Max has come up with this snare thing and we've managed to catch 2 birds with it—a seagull and a pigeon, which we've cooked and eaten. Sometimes, tho, we only have 2 tins to feed all of us, and cos we don't know what's in them we could end up with something like sweetcorn and mushy peas (which is what we had 4 days ago, by the way. Totally gross).

The birds are getting more vicious. They'll have a go at your ruck-sack, cos they know there's food in it. We've taken to carrying sticks to fight them off. It was a bit of a joke at first, but it's not now. Dad says it's like that old Alfred Hitchcock film, 'The Birds.' I've never seen that movie, and now I don't suppose I ever will.

At least there have been no more aliens, which probably just means their babies haven't been born yet. They're probably in the towns and villages all around us, waiting for their young to hatch out. That's a creepy thought, but there's not much we can do about it. We've de-cided that the monsters are evil now, or at least that they want to wipe us out. If Greg was here he'd probably say that the dog attack doesn't prove anything, that there could be evil aliens and nice aliens, but Sue says we have to assume that they're hostile, and we all agree with her.

Our theory is this: The aliens somehow caused the flood and then they came down to Earth on the blue lightning. We don't know HOW they caused the flood, but Dad thinks maybe they've got some machine, like a giant water magnet or something, which draws up the water and moves it about ("displaces it," he said). It's a pretty simple theory, I know, but, like Sue says, we need to make some sort of sense of things, and this is the simplest thing that everyone can understand. What's a bit MORE complicated is our theory about the dogs, but it's not THAT complicated. It goes like this:

On the night Greg was killed, all the dogs that attacked us were *the same breed (Dobermans, we think). It wasn't until later, when Libby pointed this out, that we all realized how weird it was. We know that the dogs weren't really dogs, but aliens. But what we'd always thought before was that the alien had to "absorb" you before it would change into you. But none of us can believe that the aliens found a whole pack of dogs to absorb. So what we think is, they found one, which had somehow survived, and then they copied it, downloaded it into themselves, sort of. Dad says they must have used the first dog as a template that all the aliens could then tap into. We reckon they must have a group mind (a "hive mind," Sue called it). What's scary, tho, is that if the aliens can become dogs, they can probably become birds, insects, anything. All the birds we see flying above us could be aliens, spying on us, and we'd never know.*

We still don't know how the aliens can be killed. We know they don't LIKE bullets, but guns don't actually seem to kill them. Dad and the rest have shot at 2 now, and both times they've got away. From the dog it looks as tho they can sort of be killed when they're not aliens, but then they can change back into aliens and come alive again.

Apart from guns, the other weapons we've been carrying are petrol bombs—which, with the guns and the camping stove and the food and everything else, means our packs are really heavy. We haven't used any petrol bombs on the aliens yet to see if they work, but sometimes I wish we WOULD see an alien, just so I can chuck a few and get rid of some of the weight.

Me and Dad had a long chat last night. We were staying at yet another service station—Junction 61 at Durham. I was huddled up in my sleeping bag cos I was really tired, and everyone else was sitting a little way away, talking and drinking a bottle of Jameson's whisky that Libby had found poking out of the mud at the side of the road, when Dad stood up and came across.

"Hey, babe," he said, "how you doin?"

"Okay," I said. "You?"

He smiled at that, like it was a question so big and crazy he didn't know how to even begin answering it. Then he said, "Yeah, okay, y'know. All things considered."

I could smell the whisky on his breath, and that made me realize that I missed the warm, sort of homey smell of his rolling tobacco,

which used to linger about him. It was funny, but I hadn't even no-
ticed when Dad had stopped smoking. I guess it must have been when
his tobacco ran out.

"I thought I'd pop over for a chat," he said. "We haven't talked
for a while."

"We talk every day," I said.

"Yeah, but not properly," he said. "It's always just nuts and bolts
stuff. We haven't had a good old natter for ages."

I looked across at Libby. I couldn't help it. I didn't mean to be
bitchy, but that's probably what it sounded like when I said, "Well,
you've been busy with other things, haven't you?"

He sighed, and I wasn't sure whether that was cos he thought I
was being a pain or cos he felt guilty. Then he said, "I know I've been
spending a lot of time with Libby, but that's cos she went thru an aw-
ful thing at that farmhouse. I know you did too, but—"

"But I wasn't raped," I said before I could stop myself.

He winced, as if someone had jabbed him in the stomach. "I know
you were terrified too," he said. "I'm not saying that what you went
thru up here"—he tapped his head—"wasn't as traumatic as what
Libby went thru."

Suddenly I felt like a silly, spoiled kid. I took his hand and said,
"What I went thru wasn't so bad, Dad. I was scared at the time, but
they didn't do anything to me. I'm over it now. It doesn't bother me.
And I think it's cool that you're helping Libby thru this."

He looked at me then, and at that moment I could tell he really
loved me, and was proud of me, and was scared for me too, scared of
what might happen to us. Funny how you can tell so much just from
the look in someone's eyes. He squeezed my hand and said, "You're
an amazing girl, Abby. You've grown up so much these past few
weeks. I can't believe you're only 13."

I wasn't sure what to say, so I just said the first thing that came
into my head: "Max asked me out."

"Did he now?" said Dad. "And what did you say to that?"

"I told him he was too old for me," I said.

Dad laughed.

"Is Libby your girlfriend?" I asked him.

He stopped laughing and said, "Would it bother you if she was?"

I shrugged, then I asked, "What about Mum?"

He didn't answer straightaway. Then he said, "Me and your mum get on OK, but we're never going to get back together. We're too different, Abs."

"You weren't different once," I said. "You were together for 17 years."

"We met at college," he said. "We were kids. We didn't know what we wanted. But Mum was always more ambitious than me. I was into my music, just wanted a quiet life, no hassle. Apart from my records and my guitar, I've never been a material person. But Mum always wanted a bigger house, bigger car, better job. I wasn't into all that, but we stayed together for the sake of you and Dyl."

"But you LIKED each other," I said, suddenly upset. "You were friends—you got on."

"If we'd stayed together we'd have ended up hating each other," he said. "It wasn't easy to split up, believe me. We both cried. But it was the best thing to do."

"Not for me and Dyl," I said, knowing that would hurt him and hating myself when it did.

He looked really sad and his voice went quiet, but he said, "You might not believe it, Abs, but it was."

"But things are different now," I said. "Everyone's the same. You can start again."

"It's not that simple," he said.

"Yes it is!" I said, loud enough to make Libby and Max look at me. I lowered my voice. "It's very simple. You just have to start from scratch. I'm not saying you have to LOVE each other straightaway."

"I love Libby," he said, as if he were apologizing for it.

His words upset me. In the 3 years since Mum and Dad had split up, and Mum had taken me and Dyl to Scotland after she got offered a job as a local TV presenter, I'd never seen Dad with another woman. I know he'd been out with other women, but I just told myself that none of them were serious.

"But you can't," I said.

"Why not?" he said.

At first I couldn't think of a reason, but then I said, "Cos you've only known her a few weeks."

"So?" he said.

"So . . ." At first my brain wouldn't work. Then I thought of something to say. "If you love Libby, why are we going to Scotland to find Mum and Dyl? I thought it was cos you wanted us to be a family again."

He sighed and said, "Dylan is my son and your brother. I care about the 2 of you more than anyone in the world."

"More than Libby?" I said.

"That's an unfair question, Abs," he said, and the way he said it made me realize I'd overstepped the mark.

"Sorry, Dad," I said. "It's just . . ." But I didn't know what else to say. I was scared and lonely and I guess I just needed to know he was always going to be there for me, whatever happened. (Is that selfish? I don't know. All I can say is that I can't help how I feel.)

But he seemed to understand. He gave me a hug, breathing whisky breath on me, and said, "I know, sweetheart."

I had to ask him something. Even tho I was scared of what the answer might be, I HAD to ask him.

"Dad," I said.

"Yes, hon?" he said.

I couldn't look at him. I looked at my hands instead. "When we find Mum and Dyl . . ."

"Yes?"

My mouth went dry. "When we find them," I said, "you will stay with us, won't you? You won't go off somewhere with Libby?"

His hug was even tighter this time. "Of COURSE I'll stay with you," he said. "I'm never going to let you out of my sight ever again."

For a few seconds my eyes went hot and there was a choking feeling in my throat. I felt happy enough to make a joke of it. "That might be embarrassing," I said.

Dad laughed. For a minute or 2 we sat there, happy to be quiet and together.

At last Dad said, "You do know, Abs, don't you, that there are no guarantees?"

"What do you mean?" I said.

"About Scotland," he said. "About finding Mum and Dyl. If things are as bad there as everywhere else . . ."

I didn't want to hear him say it. "We'll find them," I said.

He looked sad and worried. "I just want you to be prepared," he said, "just in case."

"We'll find them," I said again. "Definitely. They're alive, Dad. I know they are. I can feel it in my bones."

TWENTY-NINE

"That's something you don't see every day," Sue said.

There was a wrecked yacht on the partially collapsed road bridge. The aft section was almost intact, but the stern was all splintered wood and shattered fiber glass, as if it had been dropped on its end from a great height. The bridge itself was buckled and there were jagged cracks in the concrete buttress on the northbound side. Even so, they could still all make out the graffiti, carefully rendered in yellow print on the sagging support fascia: CRY GOURANGA—BE HAPPY.

"It's like Tom's," Libby said quietly.

Steve looked at her in alarm. "It's *not* his, is it?"

She smiled and tugged on the straps of her rucksack, shifting the weight. "No. At least . . . I don't think so."

It was October 30, the day before Halloween. Newcastle was a hundred miles behind them, and they were now close to Tranent, just outside Edinburgh, almost at the end of the A1. From here they could either take the quick route and tramp through the city, with all its concomitant dangers, or they could shift down onto the A720 and follow what would probably be a safer route around its southern outskirts. Though they still had the sprawl of Edinburgh to negotiate, what they were hoping was that the Forth Road Bridge at Queensferry would be intact and crossable. If not, they would have to follow the M9 inland, past Falkirk and Stirling and Dublane, in order to loop round the long curling tongue of the Firth of Forth. This would mean adding several unwanted days to a journey that was now beginning to take its toll on them all.

They had crossed the border into Scotland at four fifteen on the afternoon of the twenty-sixth. Perhaps it should have seemed more like a victory, but after a full day's trudging only Abby had been in the mood to raise her arms and tiredly say, "Hooray for us." The metal sign declaring WELCOME TO SCOTLAND had been draped with dried seaweed. A rook had been perched atop it, strutting back and forth like a diminutive border guard. It had looked healthier than any of the group felt, its feathers blue-black and glossy as engine oil. It had regarded them balefully until Max had flung a rock at it, whereupon it had taken to the air with a disdainful *skraak*.

The thirtieth dawned cold enough to turn their breath to mist the instant they emerged from the increasingly stale depths of their sleeping bags. After a breakfast of watery porridge and crunchy apple-flavored fruit bars, they set off into the concrete-colored light of day with numb fingers, sore feet and aching muscles. A frost had settled overnight, lending everything an austere sparkle, turning the ruts of silt brittle underfoot. Max slipped at one point and went down with a bellow of pain, banging his knee; Libby walked with one mittoned hand clamped to the left side of her head, nursing an earache.

It had been twenty minutes to midday when Sue spotted the smashed yacht on the motorway bridge. Walking had warmed them up by this time. Tattered flags of vapor still spumed from their mouths and the chill of the ground still throbbed coldly in their aching feet. They admired the yacht for all of thirty seconds before moving on. The A1 was narrowing now as it neared its end, and an icy wind was blowing in from the North Sea, turning their journey into a test of endurance.

Once again it was Abby who heard it first. Ten minutes after seeing the yacht she came to a halt and pulled down the fur-lined hood of her parka. She raised her head and looked around. The sky was the color of old plaster, flecked with birds, which wheeled lazily, like vultures in the desert.

"What's up?" said Max, who had fallen a little behind in the last hour or so, hampered by the grinding itch of his athlete's foot.

"I can hear something," Abby said.

"Like what?"

"You tell me. Maybe I'm imagining it."

Max pulled off his woolly hat, and immediately his hair—cropped close to his skull when she had first met him—sprang up in wiry tufts. He listened for a moment, frowning; then his eyes widened. "It's that helicopter again!" he said.

"Well . . . I don't know if it's the *same* one," Abby said.

"Where is it?" Max spun round in a circle, scanning the sky. "There, look! Hey, everyone! It's the helicopter!"

As before the chopper was nothing but a silhouette at first, a giant black dragonfly moving across the featureless sky. It was too distant to wave to this time, though still close enough for Sue to identify it as an R44, the same make as the one they had seen in London.

"It *can't* be the same one," Libby said, unwittingly echoing Abby's words.

"Why not, man?" shouted Max. "It's fate, that's what it is!"

This was the first indication of life they had seen in almost three days. The last had been a middle-aged woman in filthy rags who had been lying at the side of the road. They had all assumed she was just another corpse until she had leaped to her feet and scuttled away. They had tried calling after her, but she had ignored them, and they had not seen her again. Later Sue had wondered whether the woman was an alien on watch for weary travelers like themselves.

"Maybe I should have put a bullet in her just to be on the safe side," she said.

"Shoot first and ask questions later?" said Steve. "Is that what we've come to?"

"It's one way to survive."

"It's not my way, and it never will be."

Sue had merely shrugged at that and said nothing.

"It's getting lower," Libby said now. Suddenly her body stiffened with excitement. "It's landing!"

"How far away?" Steve asked.

"A few fields? Just over those trees somewhere."

"About a mile and a half," said Sue.

Max looked at her. "How do you know?"

Sue pointed back the way they had come. "About half a mile back there was a sign for Falside Hill Airfield. I'm guessing our man will be stopping to refuel. The tanks on those things hold about a hundred and eighty liters, and they burn something like sixty liters an hour. He'll have to refuel a lot."

"How long will that take?" asked Steve.

"I'm not an expert. I've never refueled a helicopter before. Not long though, I'd guess. Ten, fifteen minutes?"

"We'll never make it before he's up and away again," said Steve.

"Well, that depends on whether he takes off straightaway, doesn't it? He might stretch his legs, have a bite to eat."

"Come on, let's give it a try," said Max.

"But what would we do if we *did* catch up with him?" asked Libby.

Steve shrugged. "Ask for a lift?"

"Thought you said it was a four-seater," said Max.

Sue shrugged. "We're not exactly porkers, are we? Tell you what, Maxie, if he says yes, I'll let you sit on my knee."

Max grinned, embarrassed.

They decided to give it a try, scaling the banking at the side of the road and setting off across open countryside. They moved in a slow jog, their feet first squelching through an area of marshy gorse and bracken, and then across a number of churned farmers' fields strewn with debris. After a quarter mile or so, Steve, Libby and Abby began to fall behind, sweating and panting, their backpacks dragging them down.

"Come on, you lot!" Sue shouted.

"We're knackered," Libby replied.

Steve flapped a hand. "You and Max carry on and we'll follow at our own pace. We won't be far behind."

"Okay," Sue said; then she and Max headed off, moving faster than ever, despite Max's athlete's foot. Abby stumbled along with her dad and Libby, watching Max and Sue pulling ahead of them. It struck her how military they all looked nowadays, how much they resembled commandos in the battlefield, with their guns and their rucksacks.

They plowed doggedly on—across two more fields, over a narrow road, through a straggly area of woodland. They lost Sue and Max somewhere around the mile mark, the duo shrinking to black specks moving across the brownish landscape before being swallowed by the larger mass of a clump of trees.

They were trudging up the slight incline of yet another field, heading for a stile in the thorny hedge that bordered it, when they heard the crack of a gunshot. Libby pushed her windswept hair out of her face. "That didn't sound good."

"Come on," said Steve. "Everyone up for a jog?"

The girls nodded, and the three of them clumped across the field, the wind in their faces, adrenaline and exertion making them pant.

Abby was first to the stile. She hauled herself up the slippery steps and onto the wooden platform at the top.

"I can see the airfield!" she shouted.

"What about the helicopter?" said Steve. "And Sue and Max?"

"I can see the helicopter. Oh, and I can see Sue and Max. They've got their guns out. They're walking towards a man by the helicopter who's got his arms in the air."

"Oh dear," Libby said.

"Come on," said Steve. "Let's get down there."

They climbed over the stile and thumped down the gentle incline on the other side. The airfield, positioned on a natural plain at the bottom of the hill, consisted of a couple of long landing strips and several buildings, all enclosed within a now sagging and rusty chain-link fence. The fence had been flattened in places, allowing them easy access to the site. Abby, Steve and Libby ran across one of the landing strips towards the buildings a couple of hundred yards away. They saw the helicopter pilot, hands on head, move away from his aircraft and over towards the smallest of the buildings. Outside was what appeared to be a picnic area or beer garden, evidently a place where people had once sat with sandwiches and coffee to watch the planes come and go. The picnic tables and benches had been cemented into the ground, so were still in place, albeit black with water damage. Prompted by Sue, the pilot walked across and perched on the low wall surrounding this area.

"What's going on?" shouted Steve as soon as he was within earshot. "I heard a shot."

"It was only a warning shot," Sue said curtly.

"What happened?" Abby asked.

"He saw us coming and tried to get back to the helicopter," said Max. "Sue fired into the air, but told him she'd put the next bullet in his leg."

Steve came to a halt beside Sue and palmed sweat from his brow. "We're quite friendly, really," he said to the man.

"Is that so?" the man said dubiously. "Does that mean I can take my hands off my head?"

" 'Course you can," said Libby, embarrassed. "You're not our prisoner."

"So you wouldn't stop me if I got back into my helicopter?" he said, the hint of a teasing smile on his face.

"Well . . . no," Steve said, "but we hope you won't. We've just run a mile and a half to talk to you."

The man sighed, albeit good-naturedly, and settled himself into a more comfortable position. "Okay," he said, "I guess I owe you that, at least. In the past four weeks, you're the only people to have caught me, so to speak. Mind you," he added, flashing Sue a facetious grin, to which she failed to respond, "you're the first mob I've come across who've got guns. Where did you find them?"

"None of your business," Sue snapped.

Steve scowled at her. "I apologize for my friend. We've had a tough few weeks. We've lost some people along the way."

The man nodded thoughtfully. "I haven't seen you lot before, have I? When I flew over earlier I thought a couple of you looked like people I'd seen in London weeks back. But I told myself I must have been mistaken. There were more in that group—nine or ten."

"That *was* us!" said Abby. "We waved to you, and you waved back."

The man grinned again. He was around thirty, with blond hair and a neatly trimmed beard of the same color. He was well-spoken, with an easygoing manner. He didn't seem put out that he had finally been "caught," despite Sue's hostility.

"Well, well," he said, "small world. I'm amazed you've made it this far on foot."

"Because of the aliens?" Libby asked.

"Aliens? Is that what you think they are?"

"We don't know," said Steve. "We just call them that for the sake of convenience. Is there anything *you* can tell us about them? Presumably you've spent the past few weeks observing from on high? What does it look like from up there?"

The man puffed out his cheeks. "Well, much as I hate to be the bearer of bad tidings, it's not good. I'm guessing you've been traveling on the motorways, stopping . . . what? At service stations?"

They nodded.

"So you haven't taken a detour in the past two or three weeks? Checked out any of the surrounding towns or cities?"

"We know about the eggs, if that's what you mean," said Libby. "We went to this town called Whitthorpe about two weeks ago. There was a pile of bodies covered with this sort of . . . blue jelly, and these . . . egg things. They had *creatures* moving inside them." She shuddered. "It was disgusting."

"Believe me, it's worse now," the pilot said grimly. "Those mounds of corpses are everywhere. I see dozens every day. There's at least one in every town, usually several in the big cities. And they all have people guarding them day and night—"

"They're not people," said Steve faintly.

"No," the pilot said. "I know. But they look like people most of the time. Strange, really."

"So the eggs haven't hatched yet?" Libby said.

"No, but I suspect it'll be any day. As the blue jelly has expanded, the corpses beneath have been shrinking down. The eggs themselves are much bigger now—each about the size of a child, I'd say. And even from the air you can see things moving in them."

"What do you think'll happen when they hatch?" Max asked.

"Who can say? Maybe they'll stay where they are. Maybe they'll swarm. If I were you, I'd find somewhere you can defend stoutly, then stock up and sit tight."

"And what will you do?" Libby asked.

"Stay airborne as much as possible, I expect. The sky's the safest place at the moment, and will no doubt remain so, unless these bloody things learn how to fly—which, incidentally, I wouldn't put past them."

"What's your name?" asked Abby.

"Adam," he said. "Adam Holland. What's yours?"

"Abby Marshall," Abby said. She introduced each of them in turn. Sue scowled when Abby told Adam her name, as if he could somehow use the information against her.

"So, what's your story, Adam?" Steve asked. "How did you escape the flood?"

"Pure luck, really," Adam said. "Up until a few weeks ago I was managing director of CCS—Cameron Computer Software?"

They all looked blank.

"Ah, well, there's a big pin in *my* ego balloon. Not that it matters a fig anymore. Anyway, on the night of the flood I was in my office, conducting a major deal. Real Premiership league stuff. I had guys on the line from America, Australia, Japan, Germany—big hitters all. It was three, four in the morning, and we'd been at it for hours, but after a tricky start I was finally seeing dollar signs *ker-chinging* in front of my eyes. And then—sod me—the lights went out and the phone lines went down."

Max nodded. "Then the water came, right?"

"Then the water came," confirmed Adam. "My office was on the eighth floor. The lifts weren't working, so I went down the stairs to find out what was going on. Got to floor four, and . . . *splash!* I was up to my ankles in water.

"It didn't take long to work out that the water was rising—and bloody quickly too—so I ran up to the roof, where we kept the company chopper. Bloody extravagant, I know, but there you are. I'd been out in it a few times, even had a couple of pseudo-lessons from Bob, our pilot, but I wasn't qualified or any of that. Once the water reached the roof, though, my only option was to jump aboard and take off. It was a bit hairy at first, but I soon got the hang of it. Trouble is, these babies can only go three hours or so before you have to refuel. Soon as I realized the water was here to stay I plopped down on the highest roof I could find to wait it out. Over the next couple of days I did a few recon flights to see what was what, but I didn't stray far from my roof. I thought I was done for until the water started to go down. Since then I've been hopping from here to there, refueling where I can. Luckily, there was a list of refueling stops in the cockpit, so I was able to work out a rough route of where to go. My aim was to recon the whole country, get a picture of the overall situation, and then decide what to do from there."

"And have you done that?" asked Steve.

"Pretty much. Like I say, I've stayed airborne as much as possible, but I've had to touch down a few times to sleep and find food and whatnot. Had a few hairy moments with the natives, but until I met you lot I'd been lucky." He shrugged. "Ah well, I was bound to get caught eventually. All good things, and all that."

Libby smiled. "But like *we* said, you're not our prisoner."

Adam winked at her. "Ah, but at the same time, there's no way you're going to let me get back into my machine and take off, is there?" He nodded at Sue. "She's not, at least, and I can't say I blame her. If I was in her position, I'd feel exactly the same. I mean, what have you got here? Only means of transport for miles around? The chance to do a journey in a few hours that would take you days on foot? You're not going to let something like that go, are you?"

"Are you open to negotiation?" Steve asked.

"Try me," said Adam.

"Okay, here's the thing." Steve told Adam where they were headed, and why.

"Sounds reasonable," Adam said. "So am I presuming you'd like me to take you there?"

"More than that," said Steve. "Personally, I think we should join forces. I mean, you've got the helicopter, but there's not a lot you can do with it on your own. You can fly around, see what's what, try to keep out of trouble, but the fact remains you're incredibly conspicuous in that thing, and as you admitted, extremely vulnerable when—out of necessity—you're forced to land. Which happens—what?—three or four times a day?"

"Sometimes more," said Adam.

"Exactly. So three, four, five times a day you're putting yourself at risk. You admitted you've been lucky until now, but if you ask me, you're *still* lucky because you've run into us."

"And we're very *nice* people," said Libby, giving him a grin.

"Albeit weird," said Steve dryly. "But no, Libby's right. I'm sure there are groups out there who are desperate enough to cut your throat for that machine of yours before even *thinking* about how they're going to fly it. I mean, the only way any of us have ultimately got any chance of surviving is by being able to move around a large area quickly, and by being able to defend ourselves." He gestured towards the helicopter. "In that thing we can check out the lie of the land, pinpoint the most likely areas where we can get supplies and the best places to avoid. And when we *do* land we can at least defend ourselves. All right, so bullets don't seem to kill the aliens, but they *do* hurt them enough to drive them away. And of course, guns will work against other humans—though hopefully we won't have to demonstrate that."

"Three meals from primitivism," Adam said.

"What?" said Max.

"Isn't that what they say? That no matter how civilized we are, the human race is only ever three meals away from reverting to savagery?" To Steve he said, "So this place you're heading for—"

"Castle Morton."

"Right. You say there's somewhere there we could use as a base?"

"The clue's in the name," said Steve. "In Castle Morton there's—"

"A castle," supplied Abby.

"An old ruin, you mean?" Adam said.

"No, we're talking a solid, beautifully restored castle, complete with thick walls, narrow windows, moat and drawbridge."

"It's my school," said Abby. "It's called St. Catherine's."

"And you think we can live there permanently?"

"We can at least check it out," Steve said. "Though it wouldn't surprise me if people were living there already. Think how delighted they'll be when we turn up with a helicopter and guns."

"Yeah," said Sue heavily. "Like an invading army."

"I'm not talking about taking over," said Steve. "I'm talking about cooperation, building a proper community. We'll get nowhere as a species if we stick to our little cliques. We've got to unite against the common enemy."

"You have a very idealistic view of human nature," said Sue.

"Idealism and optimism is all we've got left to keep us going," Steve countered.

"So, what do you think?" Abby said to Adam. "Are you going to join us?"

He shrugged as if the issue had never been in doubt. "Why the hell not? So, tell me, how far away is this castle of yours?"

"About two hundred miles," said Steve. "Just north of the Kyle of Lochalsh."

"So we should be able to make it on a full tank," said Adam.

"How long will it take us to get there?" asked Max.

Adam shrugged. "Ninety minutes. We should be there for afternoon tea."

They looked at each other in wonder. Ninety minutes. On foot it would have taken them ten days, maybe two weeks.

" 'Course, we'll have to make two trips," Adam said. "She's only a four-seater."

"Can't we just cram in?" asked Libby.

"Maybe in an emergency, but it's not advisable. I wouldn't like to—"

"We've *got* an emergency," Sue said suddenly.

"What?" Steve said. He followed her gaze and saw several dark objects moving towards them across the runway. From this distance, with the noonday glare in his eyes, he couldn't make out what they were.

"What—" he said again, but already she had turned and was running back towards him.

"It's the dogs!" she shouted. "It's *them!*"

Suddenly Steve could see them, a pack of identical Dobermans, tearing across the tarmac. They were still several hundred yards away, but closing in fast. The six of them began to run towards the helicopter, which was maybe fifty yards from where the group had been clustered around Adam on the low wall. Steve trailed at the rear, his legs hollow and heavy, his backpack dragging at his shoulders. Sue reached the helicopter first and hauled open the door. Steve fancied he could hear the dogs right behind him—the rapid patter of their feet, the snarling rasp of their breath.

Max scrambled aboard the helicopter behind Sue, then hauled Abby inside. That done, they each grabbed an arm of Libby's and lifted her into the aircraft. As Libby pitched forward, Steve saw Abby look up, her eyes widening.

"Come on, Dad!" she screamed. *"Run!"*

He didn't need to look behind him to know that the dogs were closing the gap. Sweat was bursting out all over him, running out of his straggly hair, down his face and into his beard. In his lurching vision he saw the rotor blades of the helicopter begin to turn, slowly at first. He didn't know how close the dogs were, but he felt sure they'd be on him before he could make it to safety, leaping at his back, bearing him to the ground. There was a clattering in his ears, a rumbling vibration in his chest. He was yards from the helicopter now and Abby was yelling at him, urging him along, like an over-competitive parent at a child's sports day. He threw out his hands and touched the sides of the helicopter, but the door was too high; he couldn't possibly make the step, not with lead boots and hollow legs and the pulverizing weight of the rucksack. Then hands were grabbing him, one closing around his injured arm and wrenching, making him scream. But the hand didn't lessen its grip, and Steve felt himself yanked upwards. He lifted his foot, scrabbling for the step. Then he was falling into the helicopter, across the lap of Libby, who was fumbling with the strap of her seat belt, fear on her face.

As he lay there, panting, Steve was half aware of Sue stepping around him and raising her gun. The gun roared and something squealed. There was a tilting sensation and Steve raised his head and peered through the transparent domed window of the cockpit. He was surprised to see that they were airborne, the ground rushing away. Above the howling wind and the whirring clatter of the rotor blades he heard Adam shouting, "Close the door! Close the door!"

Then Sue's voice: "We've got a passenger!"

Abby screaming at Adam: "It's hanging on to the runner thing!"

Sue again: "Move out the way!"

Adam: "Don't hit the ski, whatever you do!"

Then there was a shot, a sudden lurch, a bang as the door closed.

Then Adam's voice again, calmer this time: "Is everyone okay?"

And then nothing but the sky.

THIRTY

Despite the many horrific sights they had seen over the past weeks, looking down on the world from above still came as a shock. Edinburgh resembled a war zone—many of its buildings damaged, with several in a state of complete or partial collapse; the streets littered with wrecked cars, uprooted trees and human detritus; and everything coated in a thick black silt that looked like the soot from some colossal fire.

Plus there were the alien "eggs," dotted here and there like splotches of glistening blue fungus. Adam had been right. Even from up here they could see that the eggs had swelled since their encounter with the inhabitants of Whitthorpe two weeks earlier.

Abby leaned forward to get a better look. Because of the lack of space in the helicopter she was sitting on Max's knee, and he grunted as she shifted her weight.

"Watch it, girl," he muttered. "My legs are numb enough without you making it worse."

She elbowed him gently. "Don't be a wuss. Besides, if your legs are numb you shouldn't be able to feel anything."

"Okay, you got me there."

She pointed downwards, through the transparent bubble of the cockpit. "Those things look ready to hatch any second. What's going to happen when they do?"

Max shrugged. "Maybe if we're lucky they'll leave us alone."

Abby thought of the dog leaping onto the helicopter ski as they were taking off, hanging on with its front legs until Sue shot it in its snarling face. Abby had watched it fall, twisting and trailing blood, to the earth below.

"Yeah," she said without any conviction, "maybe they will."

Having taken off in a jumble of arms and legs several minutes earlier, they were now settled, their rucksacks heaped in the cramped space behind the seats next to Adam's limited provisions. Sue was in the passenger seat next to Adam, glowering down at the ruined and deserted city. Dad and Max had taken the back seats, and she and Libby had perched themselves on their laps without any discussion.

In front of her, Sue leaned towards Adam. "Can you take us in lower?"

He glanced at her. "Sure. Something in particular you want to see?"

She pointed at one of the mounds of glistening blue jelly. "Something I want to try. Abby, pass my rucksack, would you?"

Abby snagged one of the straps of Sue's rucksack behind her and, helped by Max, swung it over. Sue unfastened it and extracted two of the carefully-packed petrol bombs.

"Are you thinking what I'm thinking?" Steve asked.

Sue grinned. It was the first expression of real glee Abby had seen on her face since Greg's death. "Let's see how flammable these bastards are, shall we?"

Libby stood up so that Steve could unstrap himself from his seat.

"Try not to move around too much," Adam said. "This isn't a passenger plane, you know."

Libby sat back down as Steve moved across to help Sue unpack more of the petrol bombs. Nervously, Libby asked, "Are you sure this is wise?"

"What are they going to do?" replied Sue. "Fly after us?" She asked Adam, "How low can we go?"

"Low as you like. Fifty feet?"

"Perfect. And we're okay to open the door?"

"As long as you wait till I'm in position," he said, easing the aircraft into a gentle descent arc.

Libby felt a vertiginous thrill as the ground seemed to swoop towards them. The blue mound of gelid eggs—which reminded Libby of a mass of festering boils the color of bread mold—was situated slap bang in the middle of Princes Street Gardens. Libby had come here as a student, had spent an idyllic August, in fact, helping out at Theatre Workshop during the Festival. She had earned extra cash face-painting in the Grassmarket with her best friend, Claire Fleetwood (who used to pretend that her uncle was Mick, of Fleetwood Mac fame). Libby remembered the gardens being full of flowers and statues, remembered the many happy hours she had spent here. She had marvelled at the glory of the famous Floral Clock, had sipped white wine spritzers as she listened to a Dixieland jazz band playing in the summer heat. She had sat beside Ross Fountain and looked up at the Rock at twilight and watched the sun setting spectacularly over Edinburgh Castle.

Where is Claire now? she thought. Probably lying dead somewhere, rotting away with the other 99 percent of the population. As Adam leveled the helicopter, Libby looked down at the gardens again. They had once been a haven of beauty and tranquility, but were now nothing but a debris-choked mud bowl. Rubbish clung to the denuded branches of the water-blackened trees; the statues, caked in silt, had a formless, molten appearance. Ever since that summer—what?—thirteen years ago, Libby had been promising herself that one day she would come back, do the whole Festival thing again. But she never had, and now it was too late.

Though the sky was not bright, the helicopter was now close enough to the ground to be casting a dragonfly shadow across the mud. Adam had maneuvred the aircraft so that they were hovering directly above the blue mound. From this distance the shadowy creatures shifting inside the semitransparent sacs looked to Libby to be in torment. They reminded her of insects trapped by predators, struggling to break themselves free.

All at once, in her peripheral vision, she glimpsed movement on the ground, and looked towards the trees lining the edge of the gardens. There was a woman there, a young woman with long red hair, wearing only a miniskirt and a sleeveless T-shirt despite the cold. The woman was running towards the mound, a look of intense concentration on her face. And immediately Libby saw others, some emerging from the trees as the young woman had, some crossing the road that led to the park, having presumably appeared from the cafés, restaurants and retail outlets on the north side of Princes Street.

"Here they come," Libby said. "Hurry."

But Sue was grinning, relishing every second. She crossed to the door and opened it, knees bent to maintain her balance. Although the helicopter was more or less stationary, a chill wind immediately sprang into the cabin. The din of the rotors doubled so they had to yell to make themselves heard.

"Enjoy the barbecue!" Sue shouted at the ground below and held out her hand. Steve, his hair blowing about his face, handed her the first of the petrol bombs. A tight funnel of fuel-soaked cloth jutted from the sloshing contents of a Tizer bottle. Sue lit a match and touched it to the cloth, which flared with a fierce and sudden flame.

A second later the bottle was falling, not thrown but dropped, to prevent spillage. Libby saw it become a ball of whiteness and exploding glass an instant before it struck the mound. Yellow flame spread across the cluster of glistening blue birth sacs as though they were doused in alcohol.

Instantly the "people," gathered below or rushing towards the mound, began to scream. It was an awful, chilling sound, high-pitched and somehow metallic. Libby had to remind herself that these were monsters, not people, and that they, or their kind, had been responsible for the cold-blooded killings of Mabel and Greg. Even so, she felt the hairs standing up on her arms, felt distress gnawing at her gut, and felt compelled to raise her hands to her ears to block out the sound.

Sue had no such misgivings. Even though the creatures were screaming as though they themselves were on fire, she held out a hand for another petrol bomb. This one exploded in midair, raining white fire and shards of glass down on the mound. As the birth sacs swelled and burst like blisters, releasing a blackish liquor in which shapes thrashed feebly, the screaming of the "people" intensified. Some even collapsed and writhed in the mud, as though in grotesque imitation of their offspring. Others began to change, their human bodies seeming almost to *fold* inwards, the flickering black formlessness of their true shapes pushing out from the inside.

For Libby, watching the transformations was a disorientating experience. She could see the people clearly enough, but try as she might, she couldn't focus fully on the creatures they were becoming. Her gaze kept skidding away from them, and afterwards, when she tried to recapture that exact instant of transformation in her mind, she could only liken it to a reversible glove puppet she had owned as a little girl that had been a dog until it was turned inside out, whereupon it became a cat.

If Sue was having similar problems of perception, she was not showing it. She was lost in her own joyous vitriol, screeching insults down at the creatures. She dropped another petrol bomb, and then another. When she stretched back her hand for a fifth, Steve shouted, "I think that's enough."

She turned on him, scowling. Before she could say anything, however, Steve held up another of the bottles— Gordon's Gin, this one had once contained—and shouted, "We've done the job. No point wasting any more of these."

Sue looked with longing at the burning mass of blue goop below, and then, albeit reluctantly, she nodded. She closed the door of the helicopter, and though the rotors still made a racket even with the door closed, the cockpit suddenly seemed a bubble of tranquillity. For Libby, the best thing was that the stomach-churning screams below were muffled to a thin, high-pitched keening, like the passage of wind through the crevices of an old house. And as Adam took the helicopter up and away, an angel of vengeance rising into the heavens from whence it had come, even that sound faded into nothing.

THIRTY-ONE

They flew across the Firth of Forth, where all manner of flotsam bobbed in the water. They passed over Dunfermline, where they spotted three more of the alien mounds. After that it was mainly moorland and lakes, dark green forests and craggy black mountains, until, at around three P.M., they reached Inverness.

Though they had enough fuel to get them to Castle Morton, Adam decided it might be an idea to call at the airport here and top up. After all, he said, it wasn't as though they would have to make much of a detour, and as they would be heading over some bleak country from now on, he didn't believe in looking a gift horse in the mouth.

The approach to the airport was a tense affair. As it came into view, a gray-black patch of ground across which three passenger planes (one of them upside down) and around a dozen vehicles were scattered like children's toys, they fell into a nervous silence. The reason for this was not the potentiality for trouble, however. Rather, it was the fact that Inverness Airport was integral to their long-term plans and well-being. If they were going to use the helicopter on a regular basis, they were going to need a refueling outlet fairly close by, and for them Inverness was pretty much it. "If the fuel pumps are out of action here, we're buggered," Adam had said. Beyond Inverness, the closest airport was Aberdeen, or maybe Wick, both of which were a good hundred miles in the wrong direction.

As it turned out, however, luck was with them. Not only were the storage tanks intact, but two of the pumps, though crusted with silt and dried salt, were operable. As the fuel began to gush, Adam said, "We're in business." Max and Abby high-fived each other. Steve, Libby and Sue exchanged relieved grins.

Within twenty minutes they were airborne again. They flew over Inverness, over the site of the Battle of Culloden, which now, as then, was strewn with the leavings of the dead. Their first sight of Castle Morton, or rather the building that dominated the town and gave it its name, came less than half an hour later.

"There it is!" Abby squealed, grabbing Max's arm. "Look, Max, that's my school!"

Built on a high hill, the medieval fortress jutting through the surrounding pine forests was gray and impressive.

"It's a weird shape," he said. "Kind of like . . . I dunno . . . a wonky car."

Abby laughed. It was true. Viewed from the air, St. Catherine's *did* vaguely resemble a cartoon car. Its "wheels" were the two rounded towers flanking the huge main doors (in days gone by this would have been a drawbridge and portcullis), and its "bonnet" was the square chunk of buildings built on to the right-hand side of the main structure. These buildings had originally comprised the banquet hall, extensive kitchens and a whole rash of stables, and Abby knew their present-day function was not so very different. The school kitchens and dining hall were more or less on the same site as their medieval counterparts, though where the stables had been there was now a gymnasium and swimming pool.

"The main bit dates from the twelfth century," Steve said,

"but they kept adding bits on until the seventeenth, which is when the family who'd owned it for six hundred years moved out. What was their name, Abby?"

"The Tavistocks," she said.

"So how did it come to be a school?" Libby asked.

"After the Tavistocks moved out or died or whatever, no one could afford to keep it going," replied Steve. "Even the Scottish Tourist Board and the Heritage Commission weren't really interested—too remote to attract tourists, you see. So for two or three hundred years the place was abandoned, falling to rack and ruin. Then in the 1950s a bunch of local rich folk got together and decided to turn it into a school for girls. They did the place up, enticed staff out into the middle of nowhere by paying them top wages, and within a few years the place was paying for itself. They started with thirty pupils, and now they have three hundred. Two-thirds are boarders and a third—like Abby—are day girls. You get girls coming here from all over Scotland—Dundee, Montrose, Oban, even as far south as Stirling and Falkirk."

"Did, you mean." said Libby, quietly enough so that only Steve could hear.

"What?"

"They *did* have girls coming from all over Scotland. You're talking as though the flood never happened."

"Oh, yeah," said Steve, suddenly somber. "Even now I sometimes forget. Stupid, isn't it?"

Libby shook her head and squeezed his arm. Steve smiled at her and glanced at Abby. She was leaning forward, eyes shining and cheeks red, and Steve thought that, for the moment at least, his daughter had forgotten too.

"Where do you want me to land?" Adam shouted over his shoulder.

"There's a courtyard right behind the main doors," answered Steve. "There's a fountain over to the left, but if the area's clear it should be big enough if you can take us straight down."

"I think we should check the place over before we think

about landing," Sue said. "Can we circle the place a few times, Adam?"

Adam made an *OK* sign with his fingers and took them in for a look-see. They flew round the castle several times, their eyes peeled for any indications of life.

"I can't see anyone, but the castle looks okay," Abby shouted. "It hasn't got that black stuff all over it anyway, like a lot of buildings we've seen."

"There's plenty of flood damage in the town below, though," Sue replied, pointing straight down.

"She's right," said Max. "There's wrecked cars and all the usual stuff down there. Where's your house, Abs?"

The town was in a dip beneath the castle, sheltered from the biting winds that tore down from the Atlantic by a surrounding mass of pine forest. Abby pointed to the left, away from the main cluster of buildings, towards a patchwork of boggy-looking fields threaded through with a black tangle of single-lane roads and farm tracks.

"See those four fields and those five houses just above them that look like barns? Well, that one on the end is ours—oh!"

"What's the matter, honey?" asked Steve.

"The trampoline's gone. And look, Henrietta's greenhouse has collapsed. And Mum's garden and our drive and the patio . . . it's all underwater. And there's a tree on next door's roof. . . ." She put her hands over her mouth, as if half believing the devastation might somehow disappear if she stopped talking about it.

"You okay?" asked Max, slipping his arms around her waist.

"Yeah, it's just . . . a shock, that's all. Seeing everything messed up, knowing that the flood has been here too." She was silent for a moment as she strained forward to look. "One good thing is that I can't see any bodies."

"That's probably because they've been collected up and used for food," said Sue.

Steve didn't think she *intended* to sound callous, but her lack of tact infuriated him nonetheless. "Thanks for that, Sue," he said as Abby's face fell.

Sue shrugged. "What's the problem? Would you rather not face up to reality?"

"Of course not. I just think you could have been a bit more sensitive, that's all."

She shook her head. "We're living in a shitty world. You can't shield her from what's happening out there."

Steve looked ready to argue further, but Abby said, "I'm all right, Dad. Really. And Sue's right. You shouldn't try to protect me from what's going on."

Sue gave a nod of approval. "Well said, girl."

Steve raised a hand in acknowledgment, but he didn't look entirely convinced.

"Hold on to your Stetsons, guys," Adam announced. "I'm going in."

He took the helicopter in low. So low that Abby felt herself drawing in her knees, half afraid that he would scrape the underside of the machine across the crenellated turrets of a tower. As they sank towards the stone courtyard behind the stout main doors, she couldn't help thinking there was something a bit James Bond about all this. She looked around at the internal windows, which now rose around them on all sides, half expecting to see the astounded faces of her school friends pressed against them. It all looked so normal, so unaffected by the disaster that had befallen the rest of the world, that she believed she would have been only mildly surprised if her headmistress, Mrs. Beecham, had suddenly appeared from the archway that led to her office, dressed in her trademark blue blazer, demanding to know the meaning of this intrusion. But all Abby saw in the black windows were reflected white chunks of the R44 sliding past as it slowly descended.

Of course, if the flood had happened during term time, she *might* have seen girls' faces pressed against the windows. Then again, if it had happened during term time she wouldn't have been in London with Dad in the first place. She would have been here in school, doing maths with Mr. Gordon or geography with Miss Whittaker. She would probably have been staring out the window and thinking about riding Flash at the stables later, or maybe just wondering what was for tea. How would she have felt if she had seen the water creeping up through the trunks and branches of the pine trees below, filling in the gaps with an almost tarry blackness? If the girls had felt the rumbling that had preceded the water, no doubt they would have assumed it was an earthquake. Abby could almost hear Mrs. Beecham's voice: *"Sit tight, girls* (she would have pronounced it gurruls), *there's nothing to be alarmed about."* But for once she would have been wrong. On this occasion there would have been *everything* to be alarmed about.

The helicopter touched down with barely a bump. Adam turned off the engine and for the next minute or so, while the rotor blades slowed and eventually whickered to a stop, the six of them merely sat in silence, looking around. It was almost, Abby thought, like taking a breather at the end of a long day, like coming home, dumping yourself in your favorite armchair, and for several minutes just sitting and doing nothing. Taking stock.

Now that they were on the ground, Abby saw that the school had not been *completely* unaffected by the flood, as had appeared from the air. Water had evidently seeped beneath the main doors, and had left deposits of the all-too-familiar silt crusted between the cobbles like black cement. What this meant was that, if the water had risen so high, then the entire town below must almost certainly have been engulfed. The only way anyone down there could have survived, therefore, would have been by somehow making it up to the refuge of the castle. Abby knew what a tall order that was, especially given the time of the flood, but she consoled herself with the fact that it was not *beyond* the realms of possibility. And particularly heartening was the evidence that a clear attempt had been made to shift as much of the silt as possible. In her mind's eye Abby pictured a team of townspeople, among them Mum and Dyl, hard at it with shovels and bin bags and sweeping brushes.

"It all seems pretty quiet," Steve said eventually. "Shall we look around?"

Sue was scanning the windows that looked down on the courtyard. "Yes, but stay alert and keep your weapons ready."

Abby shared her observation about the silt, and Sue nodded. "Yeah, I noticed that too. Well spotted, Abby."

Libby raised herself off Steve's lap so he could open the helicopter door. When Abby jumped down, her feet went from under her on the slippery cobbles, and she would have fallen if Steve hadn't grabbed her arm. Adam slammed the helicopter door shut behind them, then turned with an easy smile, palming blond hair back from his forehead.

"Not sure whether getting you here in one piece qualifies me as a member of the Scooby gang," he said, "but I just thought I'd point out that I'm the only one without a gun."

"And?" Sue said, her expression unreadable. "You think you need one?"

"Well . . . it might come in useful."

"Don't you trust us to protect you?"

"It's not that I don't *trust* you," Adam replied, "it's just that I'd prefer my destiny to be in my own hands."

Sue regarded him, eyes narrowed, as if weighing up her options. Adam bore her scrutiny with apparent good humor for maybe fifteen seconds; then he laughed and raised his hands. "Listen," he said, "I don't want to get confrontational here—it's not my style. If you're not prepared to trust me with one of your guns, then okay—I understand your reasoning and I respect where you're coming from. But the thing is, I'm a businessman, which, contrary to my easygoing manner, makes me a bit of a pigheaded bugger. I've spent my whole working life negotiating deals, and one thing I've discovered is that for a relationship to work there has to be give and take on both sides. But at the moment, Sue, you're doing all the taking and none of the giving, and if that's going to remain the case, then maybe we ought to cut our losses now and say toodle-oo."

He tilted his head and smiled at Sue to let her know the ball was back in her court.

It wasn't Sue who replied, however; it was Libby. "Well, *of course* you should have a gun," she said. "Don't you think Adam should have a gun, Steve?"

Steve pursed his lips, but nodded almost immediately. "Yeah," he said, "I think he should. I know what you said after Mabel died, Sue, about not trusting anybody, but sometimes I think you have to take a leap of faith. I mean, if we never trusted anybody ever again, the monsters would win, wouldn't they?"

"Divide and conquer," said Libby.

"Exactly."

Sue said nothing for a moment, simply stared at Steve without expression. Then she abruptly turned to Adam. "Have you ever fired a gun before?"

Adam couldn't have looked more put out had she asked him whether he had ever kissed a lady before. "Of course I have," he replied. "I'll have you know I was vice president of the South Cambridge Clay Pigeon Shooting Society. I've even bagged the odd grouse on occasion."

"So I take it you'd rather have a rifle than a handgun?" she said dryly.

"Oh, I think so. A real gun is a two-handed weapon, isn't it? Handguns are for hoodies and the like. No offense, Max."

Max looked so comically surprised that Abby whooped with laughter. "What's that supposed to mean?" he said to Adam. "You think I'm a gangsta rapper or somethin'?"

"Well, *aren't* you?" Steve said innocently. "*We* all thought you were."

"Swivel on it," Max said, flipping him the finger, and suddenly they were *all* laughing.

Adam was given his gun and they made their plans. They would head off in pairs to look around. Because Abby knew the school inside out, and because Steve had been here a few times (it had been a hell of a journey from London to Castle Morton even in the good old days, but he liked to keep in the loop of his kids' lives as much as possible) and had a rough idea of the layout, it was decided that Abby would accompany Sue, and Adam would go with Steve. That left Max and Libby as the only couple with no prior knowledge of the place, but Abby did her best to give them directions.

"Okay," Sue said, "we'll have a ten-minute poke around and then meet back here. Any trouble, fire your gun and the rest of us'll come running. Keep your wits about you and trust no one. Steve and Abby, even if you see the people you've come looking for, remember it might not be them, so don't drop your guard. Okay?"

Abby nodded, though the thought of having to point her gun at Mum and Dyl instead of throwing her arms around them made her feel sick. Then again, if Mum and Dyl were aware of what was going on—which she was sure they would be—they would probably be just as cautious. And at least, if it *did* come to that, it would mean that they were alive and well, which, at the end of the day, was all that *really* mattered, wasn't it?

"Okay," Sue said, "let's go." She and Abby stepped out from the shelter of the rotor blades and headed across the courtyard towards the main building, which contained the bulk of the dormitories and classrooms; Steve and Adam peeled off right, towards a walkway sheltered beneath a series of small arches, at the end of which was a door leading to the dining hall and kitchens; and Max and Libby headed left, where a larger archway led to the main administration offices, including the head's study and staff quarters.

It was not yet four o'clock, but just enough daylight had leeched from the sky to rime the hard angles of walls, roofs and windows in solid black lines of shadow. Similarly, the rotor blades of the helicopter threw long black streamers of shadow across the cobbled ground.

Abby was trailing Sue, and still brooding about how she might react were she to come face-to-face with Mum or Dyl, when the sound of breaking glass yanked her back to full alertness. For a moment she thought one of the others must have dropped a bottle of water or a jar of food—but then there came another crash, followed rapidly by another, and another. Within seconds these individual crashes had escalated into an overlapping cacophony, appallingly strident after the previous cathedral-like hush. It took a moment or two of disorientation before Abby was able to even *think* about reacting, and by then it was too late.

Attempting to haul her senses back to some sort of equilibrium, she became aware of several things happening in quick succession. First she saw what appeared to be giant raindrops falling from the sky before realizing they were bottles or jars, flashing in what remained of the failing light. As each of these jars (or bottles) hit the ground, they shattered on the cobbles, spitting glass splinters over a wide area (and Abby was glad of her thick trousers), and releasing some kind of pungent yellow smoke.

At the same time Abby was vaguely aware of upper-floor windows all around the courtyard opening and just as quickly closing.

Additionally she was aware of Sue's movements, first out of the corner of her eye (the ex-policewoman spinning around, pointing her gun, then apparently changing her mind and lowering it again), and then directly, as Abby shifted her glance from the windows and turned towards her (Sue starting to run back through the smoke towards the helicopter, but only managing to get about halfway before clutching her throat and dropping to her knees).

After that, as she herself started to choke, Abby was aware of nothing but her own discomfort. The yellow smoke rose all around her, seizing her lungs so tightly that a bright, juicy spark of panic leaped into jittering life in her brain, threatening to obliterate her ability to think.

And then she could no longer see anything at all because her eyes were streaming and stinging, and the yellowish smoke from the broken jars and bottles was billowing around her in ever-thickening clouds. *Mustard gas,* she thought feverishly, even though she had no idea what mustard gas was or how it worked. What she *did* know, however, was that the smoke was *like* mustard—yellow, acrid and pungent, burning her sinuses and her eyes.

A few seconds later—and maybe fifteen since the first jar had smashed on the ground—Abby found she could no longer breathe. Her lungs had locked, become inoperative; her throat, which had shrunk to the size of a pinhead, had now closed up completely. She began to flail in panic, her arms moving instinctively, spasmodically, as if the gas were an assailant that her beleaguered body was trying to fight off. She felt her legs going, turning to needles and water, collapsing under her weight.

I'm going to die! she thought, and the thought was a terrible final flare in her dwindling consciousness. She was receding from her body, yet was simultaneously aware that she was clawing and scrapping for life.

Then the blackness closed in, like a wave—like *the* wave—silent and deathly, annihilating everything before it. And now, at the end, she was not even aware that she *needed* to breathe, was aware of nothing but a fading sense of disappointment.

Is this it? she thought. Her last thought. Her last words.

Is this really . . .

THIRTY-TWO

. . . it?

The world rushed back at her, and with it came the pain. Her lungs felt full of wet cement and broken glass; her throat felt raw, bloody, *scoured*. She groped at the pain, as if it were something she could remove with her hands—and then from somewhere above her an infinitely kind and gentle voice said, "Here. Drink this."

Her head was lifted and something was pressed between her lips. Something that was pottery-hard but not sharp. Thin and rounded, like . . .

The rim of a cup.

The cup was tipped, and liquid sloshed gently against her upper lip. Abby drew it in, let it trickle down her barbed-wire throat, and oh, it was good. Cool and smooth and sweet. Manna from heaven. The balm of the gods.

Maybe I'm dead, she thought suddenly. *Maybe I'm dead and in heaven and an angel's looking after me. . . .*

"There you go. Is that better? Don't answer, just nod."

An angel with a voice like Dylan!

She tried to open her eyes, and felt more pain, sharp and

stinging. Her eyelids didn't come apart like eyelids; they came apart like a wound which hadn't yet knit together. And her eyeballs were all nerves and raw flesh, and this time she couldn't help crying out. And the cry was rusty and birdlike, not human at all. And it hurt like she was swallowing broken glass and stinging nettles. And it wasn't *just* a cry of pain, but also of fear, because she could feel hot blood running out of her eyes and down her cheeks. And blood was not supposed to *come* out of her eyes, was it? And that was scary because it meant she might be blind, here in heaven, forever and ever amen. And then she saw light, flickering light, somewhere beyond the swimming, stinging pain. And she realized it wasn't blood running down her cheeks: it was just water, just tears.

Just tears.

She sank back. She hadn't even realized she'd raised her head until the weight of it dragged her back down and the soft plumpness of a pillow cradled her skull. As she settled, the pain still throbbing in her eyes and throat, like a triangle of red lights marking out the battleground of her face, she heard her hair rustle against her ears as someone bent down to speak to her, and then her angel (*her angel with Dylan's voice*) said, "It's okay, Abs. I know it hurts, but you'll be fine. I promise."

She felt a cool, rough hand on her sizzling cheek (*Weird that angels should have rough hands,* she thought), and the cup being pressed to her lips. She drank again (*the sweet balm, the nectar*), and then the angel said, "I need you to open your eyes for me again, Abs. Just a tiny bit. I know it hurts, but I need to put some drops in them. They'll sting for a second, and then they'll feel better. I promise."

Angel drops, she thought, and she made herself open her eyes. For the tiniest fraction of a second (which was still *much* too long) she felt fire pouring into the slit between her lids (or maybe it was the tip of a red hot poker being pushed into her socket). She arched her back, her fingertips clawing at the mattress, her barbed-wire throat getting ready to scream. But before she could dredge up a sound her hot eye was turning deliciously cold, the pain extinguished like a camp fire doused by a bucket of crushed ice. She heard a long exhalation of breath whistling through her throat—the throat which still hurt, but not as much as before; the throat which had been soothed by the balm of the gods.

"Good girl," her angel said. "That's one. Now the other. You ready?"

She wasn't, but within seconds it was over, and it wasn't as bad the second time.

"Okay," her angel said, "there we go. You rest now for a bit."

She drifted. Time passed. Her angel came back and poured more nectar down her throat and into her eyes. She got out of bed and ran round the school, looking for her dad's Jimi Hendrix guitar string, knowing it was vital she find it before the wave came. She didn't realize that was a dream until she opened her eyes and became aware of two things: one, that she was still in bed, and two, that her eyes no longer felt full of hot coals, but were now merely sore in a manageable way, as if she had been standing too close to a bonfire.

From her prone position she looked around, taking in her surroundings. Her vision was still a little blurred, but clearing all the time. The first thing she registered was that it was night. The room was illuminated by the soft, honey-colored glow of candlelight. From the profusion of toast brown shadows, Abby guessed that there was probably only one candle burning in the room, two at the most. The flickering flame made the walls and high ceiling appear to sway and shift, as if the room were breathing.

The candle itself was somewhere to her left, and quite close by. For the first time she realized that she was lying in a proper bed, which, after weeks of hard, damp floors cushioned only by the thickness of her sleeping bag, seemed impossibly soft, impossibly comfortable. As she looked from side to side, she saw the tops of various items of furniture—a wardrobe, a bookcase (with proper, undamaged books on it!), and a mirror in a wooden frame, which presumably crowned a dressing table or a chest of drawers.

Her thoughts turned to her angel—and suddenly it was as

if she had had a shot of adrenaline to her system. She sat up, feeling ridiculously weak, and peeled the duvet away from her bare legs. She noticed, with some consternation, that someone had removed her boots, walking socks and waterproof trousers (but thankfully not her underwear) before putting her to bed, and then she swung her feet to the floor.

She looked around the room in the light of its one flickering candle, and although she didn't recognize it, she realized there was something in here she *did* recognize. She recognized the trio of windows in the far wall—or at least their shape. They were not regular windows, but deep-set slits, arched at the top, and they were designed like that to reduce the risk of enemy arrows entering the room and causing injury to its occupants. So she was still in the castle, and during the day these windows must look out over the grounds or the slope of pine forest that marched down to the town below.

Still looking about, it suddenly occurred to her what *kind* of room this was, and she felt a curling sense of disorientation and, oddly, guilt in her belly. It was a staff member's bedroom, and back in the old world it would have been forbidden for her to have set so much as a foot in here, never mind crawled under the duvet and caught a few z's. In fact, a matter of weeks ago, just being found in this part of the school would have been punishable by suspension.

How times change, she thought, not knowing whether to laugh or cry. Then she thought of her angel again, and suddenly, as if just *thinking* about him was akin to summoning him, the door opened and there he was.

Dylan's hair was longer than she'd ever seen it, beginning to curl at the edges. He looked thin, almost gaunt, and his cheeks were coated with a scruffy fuzz of beard. But he was grinning in that slightly crooked way that Abby always told him looked goofy, but that, for some reason, made most of her friends go giggly and stupid.

"Hey, stinky," he said softly (he had called her that since she had proclaimed it her favorite word at the age of three), "how's it going?"

She tried to reply, but a bubble of emotion rushed into her throat and burst, taking her by surprise. What emerged instead of words was a wailing cry and a sudden flood of tears. Forgetting Sue's warning entirely, Abby stumbled forward and wrapped her arms around her brother's neck. She dragged his face down to hers and, still crying, planted dozens of slobbery, snotty kisses all over his face.

Dylan laughed beneath her onslaught, and hugged her back hard enough to make her ribs ache. As the first wave—the first *tsunami*—of her tears subsided, she re-discovered her croaky, tear-laden voice.

"It's so good to see you," she said. "I thought I'd never see you again."

"Can't get rid of me that easily," he said jovially; then his own voice dropped to a wavery murmur. "I've really missed you, Abs."

Eventually they broke apart, though continued to stare into each other's flushed faces, into each other's bloodshot eyes, as if barely able to believe what they were seeing. Too late, Abby remembered Sue's warning.

"It is *you*, Dyl, isn't it?" she asked.

He gave a throaty *huh* of mirth. "'Course it is. Who do you *think* I am? Bob Geldof?"

She responded with a shriek of laughter, which she immediately smothered with her hand. Forcing herself to calm down, she said, "You know what I mean. You *do* know what I mean, don't you?"

"You mean am I a slug?" he said.

"Slug?"

"It's what we call them."

She nodded. It was a pretty good name. "We just call them aliens."

"How retro," he said, complete with snooty expression and raised eyebrow. Then he became serious again. "I'm not one, by the way. Or I wasn't last time I looked."

"But how do I know you're telling the truth?"

"You don't. Though you could always gas me—but I don't really fancy that."

"Gas you?" said Abby.

"It's how we knew none of you lot were slugs. If slugs are disguised as humans, and they get attacked, they turn back into slugs again. Dead giveaway."

"Do they?" said Abby.

"Well . . . *duh*," he said. "Haven't you found *that* out?"

Abby thought of the times they had engaged the aliens (or slugs, as Dylan called them) in combat. There had been the Marco one that had killed Mabel—though that had already been in its alien form when Dad, Sue and Max had started shooting at it. Then there had been the dogs—and certainly the one Sue had shot had changed back into an alien before scooting off. Then there had been the eggs they'd firebombed in Edinburgh—and she still shuddered as she recalled how the people below had run around, shrieking in pain and anguish, before (in some cases, but not all) transforming into the monsters they really were.

She shrugged and said, "I suppose. We hadn't really made the connection."

"I don't think *we* did until Mr. West pointed it out."

"Mr. West? You don't mean—"

"Your old chemistry teacher, yeah."

"Oh, God," Abby said, "he's not here, is he?"

As soon as the words were out of her mouth she felt ashamed of them. Was she *actually* bemoaning the fact that Mr. West (Fred, the girls called him, though his grouchiness probably didn't quite warrant being named after a sexually depraved serial killer) had survived the flood? Would she honestly wish him drowned in favor of a teacher she liked better? Kindhearted Mrs. Pagett, say, or the ever-cheerful Miss Cheever, who had been only a decade or so older than Abby herself?

"Yeah," Dylan was saying, "he decided to stay at school for half-term, so he was all right. It's him who made that gas that knocked you out, by the way. It was only supposed to be used against the slugs, but when you arrived in that helicopter it threw everyone into a panic. None of us had ever considered an attack from the air."

"It wasn't an attack," Abby said. "It was an arrival."

"Yeah, well, we know that now, don't we?"

"So what was *in* that gas?" Abby asked, wondering about long-term effects.

"God knows," Dylan said. "It's pretty strong stuff, though, isn't it?"

"That's an understatement," she said. "So how many of you are there?"

"Eleven. There were fourteen, but five of us went out on a scavenger hunt and we got ambushed by slugs. Only two of us got away—me and Andy Poole. He's a couple of years older than me."

"Don't his mum and dad own the Malt Shovel?" asked Abby.

"*Did*. Not anymore."

" 'Course," Abby said. "So who else is here I might know? There's you, Mum, old Westy, Andy Poole . . ."

The sudden look that Dylan gave her made Abby feel as though her guts had turned inside out.

"What is it?" she said. "Dyl, don't—"

"Mum's dead."

His voice was flat, toneless. Abby gaped at him.

"No, she isn't," she said angrily. "What do you mean? How can she be?"

"She died in the flood," he said dully. "I mean, I never actually saw her body, but . . ." his voice tailed off.

"But *you're here*," Abby said. "How can *she* be dead if *you're* here?"

He looked at her with something like exasperation. "We weren't joined at the hip, you know."

"But if you were both at home—"

"I wasn't at home."

She glared at him almost accusingly. "Where were you then?"

"I was staying at Callum's. Except me and Cal had come up here to smoke some blow. We were sitting out by the tennis courts, looking over the valley, when the flood came. It was dark and we couldn't work out what it was. There was this sort of rumbling, then a whooshing sound. Then the water came and it was . . . just black. . . ." He shivered and shook his head.

"What happened to Callum?" asked Abby. It was maybe not the most pertinent question to ask, but her mind was in turmoil.

"He was okay," Dylan said. "We both got wet, but compared to most people . . ." He shrugged and then almost casually added, "He's dead now, though."

Abby made a small sound. So much death, so much misery. "What happened?" she found herself asking, aware she was talking simply to avoid having to think about Mum, about the terrible, impossible fact that she was gone.

"The slugs got him," said Dylan. "He was one of those who died on the scavenger hunt."

"Oh." It was all she could think of to say. On a subconscious level she sensed there was a dam inside her, a dam which was holding strong for now, but which was liable to collapse at any moment. She touched her brother's cheek, noting almost detachedly that her hand was trembling.

"My poor Dyl," she said. "How have you managed here on your own?"

"I haven't been on my own," he said. "The people here have been looking after me . . . or, what I mean is, we've been looking after each other. They're a good bunch, Abby. You'll like them."

"I'm sure," she said. "But how have you managed without *us,* without your family? I don't know how *I'd* have got through this if Dad hadn't been with me."

Dylan shrugged. "You just . . . do, don't you? I mean, what else *can* you do? You can't just . . . lie down and die."

"No," she said. "No." When she next spoke her voice seemed to have been dredged from deep inside her. "I can't believe Mum's gone. I felt sure you'd both be okay. I felt it in my bones."

She slumped forward. Dylan leaned towards her until their foreheads were touching.

"That was a good feeling to have," he whispered, "because it was the feeling that brought you here. I thought I'd lost everything . . . and then you and Dad showed up, and suddenly it's like . . . I've found something worth carrying on for."

She felt the dam crumbling then, and suddenly she was scared. "Hold me," she pleaded, reaching out blindly for him.

He put his arms around her, and she clung to him as if he had just dragged her to safety from a collapsing building or a raging inferno. She thought about what she had found and what she had lost, the miracle and the tragedy, and she found herself crying with such ferocity for both that pretty soon she could no longer distinguish one from the other.

THIRTY-THREE

It's funny how quickly people adapt to new stuff and settle into routines. Dad says it's the human instinct for order and structure. Probably not all people are like that, but I think on the whole we don't like messes. I don't mean untidy rooms and stuff, I mean bigger messes—chaos.

I haven't written since the day after I found out about Mum, which was a week ago. Sorry, but I've been too upset. It's weird how the horrible things affect you most. The brilliant things, like finding Dyl alive, are just kind of, not taken for granted exactly, but got used to really quickly. The horrible things, tho, like finding out about Mum, stay with you and make you feel upset and awful all the time. It's not fair how good things only make you feel good for a little while, but bad things make you feel bad for a long time.

Dyl's been brilliant, and so has Dad, and so has everyone, really, but it doesn't help. Mum's still gone, and every night, on my own, I've cried, knowing I'll never see her again. Part of me still can't believe it, and it's that part, I think, that lets me carry on doing normal stuff. But even that feels weird. When I'm getting dressed or eating breakfast or talking to someone, I feel guilty, as if being able to do those things means I don't care enough about Mum. There's a part of me that thinks I should just lie on my bed crying all day and refuse to eat and wash and all that. I even feel guilty writing this diary.

Does this make any sense or am I just odd?

Anyway, we've been here for a week, and like I was saying, it's funny how quickly we adapt and settle into routines. The people here are pretty nice, tho I don't know some of them that well yet. They've accepted us, tho, and Mr. West appreciates what we've brought to the community (the guns and the helicopter), tho he usually only tells us when he's got something he wants to moan about. He'll say, "We appreciate what you've brought to the community, but," and then he'll have a go at one of us for not doing a job properly or something.

He's all right on the whole, tho. He just likes to organize everyone. Dad and Adam and some of the others make fun of him behind his back, which is funny but sometimes a bit cruel. Max calls him "the walrus" because he's fat and bald with a big gingery moustache. Sue and Mr. West don't get on AT ALL, but then Sue never gets on with ANYONE who tries to tell her what to do.

Altho Mr. West is the only teacher here, he's not the only person from the school. Mr. and Mrs. McGregor, the caretaker and his wife, are here too. They're both about 60 and they're really nice, tho Mr. McGregor's got such a strong Scottish accent that I can't tell what he's saying half the time. I don't think he likes Mr. West much either, tho he gets on with everybody else, and he and Sue get on great. Although Mr. McGregor is quite old, he's very fit and he's practical and sensible (he can fix things and come up with ideas for stuff). He was in the army for a long time, and he's like a friendly sergeant major.

Mrs. McGregor is plump and she's always trying to give us food. Even now, when we haven't got that much (altho the school kitchens are well stocked with tins and stuff), she's always trying to give us biscuits and making us cups of tea. She's like a mother hen, and when I was at school all the girls thought she was cool. Her and Mr. McGregor never had any kids (I don't know why), but there are 3 girls here who stayed at school over half-term cos their parents were abroad or something, and Mr. and Mrs. M have become sort of parents to them. Well, what I mean is EVERYONE looks after them, just like everyone looks after everyone else (Dad says it's like a hippy commune from the 60s), but Mr. and Mrs. M look after them the most.

I don't know the 3 girls all that well cos they're younger than me. I'd seen them at school, but I hadn't really spoken to them before. 2 of them, Marcie Willets and Victoria Teague, are 11, and are in year 7 (or were before the flood). They seem nice, but they're both really quiet (tho Marcie is quieter than Victoria—she hardly says ANY-THING). The other girl is called Portia Paige-Harvey, and she's a good laugh. Her dad's a Scottish MP and her mum was once an African Miss World contestant or something. Portia's got lovely light brown skin (caramel-colored, Dad says) and curly black hair. She's only 12 (year 8), but you can tell she's going to be really beautiful when she grows up. She's dead nice and cheerful and we get on really well (it's SO NICE to have someone more or less my own age to hang out with), and altho her mum and dad are probably dead (they were in Holland when the flood came, at a political conference or something), she says until she finds out for sure she'll keep thinking they're alive. She says I should think the same about Mum. She says it's like dissing your parents to think they're dead when they might not be. She says thinking of her mum and dad alive, maybe living with other survivors, is what keeps her going.

She's right, I suppose, but I find it hard to think that Mum might still be alive. I keep thinking that if she was, she'd have managed to get to the school. After all, there's nowhere else to go around here. Plus things would have been against her from the start. Our house is on such low ground that the fields around us always used to flood just when we got heavy rain for a couple of days. So when the wave came it would have hit Mum and our neighbors pretty much before anyone else. Also I'm sure Mum wouldn't have been awake at 4 in the morning, or whatever time it was. She always sleeps well and doesn't set her alarm for 7. And even if she had been awake she didn't have a boat she could have escaped on or anything (that's how most of the others got here, but more about that in a minute).

The thing is, if Mum lived far away, then maybe I WOULD be able to think about her in the same way Portia thinks about her mum and dad. But being here and seeing the flood damage, and hearing from Dyl about how the water rose above the town and the forest and came right up to the castle, makes it all much more real. I think if Portia went to Holland and saw the place where her mum and dad had been she might feel differently. I'm not going to tell her that, tho. Why should I be the one to spoil her dreams?

Like I said, there were only 6 survivors from the town (6 we know about anyway) and 5 of them arrived crammed into the same boat. They were really lucky, but then I suppose everyone who escaped the flood was lucky. On the other hand, I sometimes think we survivors are the UNlucky ones. Plus what about those who survived the flood, but have died since? Were they lucky, then unlucky? Or does luck even come into it?

The 5 survivors (tho there are only 4 of them now) are the Poole family—Andy, who was with Dyl when they were ambushed by aliens (or slugs, as everyone here calls them) a few weeks back, and his mum and dad, Joe and Moira, and their neighbors, Daphne McIntee and her son, Gregory. Mrs. McIntee is 67 and Dyl told me her husband died 15 years ago. Dyl says he was in the shower on holiday and it suddenly went "live" or something and he was electrocuted.

The reason the Pooles and McIntees survived the flood was because a) they lived a bit outside the town, in 2 cottages next to each other on one of the steep roads thru the forest that leads up to the castle, and b) Mr. Poole and Andy had got up early to go fishing that morning, and happened to be loading their rowing boat onto their trailer when the wave came.

Mr. Poole told us that the water rose so quickly that even tho they had the boat they still nearly drowned. He said that by the time they'd woken up Moira and Daphne and Gregory, and they'd all got into the boat, the water was up to their knees, and they had to form a human chain to avoid being swept away. He said the boat got thrown about all over the place, and that as the water carried them up they were nearly impaled on trees further up the hill a few times. He told us there was all sorts of stuff in the water that bashed into the boat, and that it was a miracle they didn't capsize. He also said that when they arrived at the castle they were all as bruised "as old bananas."

We were all sitting round the big table, having a meal, and when he said that (not the thing about the bananas, the thing about the miracle) Mrs. McIntee said, "Miracle is right. It was God who kept us alive that night."

"And why would he do that?" asked Dad, who I know doesn't believe in God (and after everything that's happened, I don't think I do anymore either).

Mrs. McIntee, who's very fat (sorry, but she is) and can't walk very well, looked at him as if he'd asked a stupid question and said, "Because He is merciful."

"Not to 99.9 percent of the population, he isn't," Dad said.

Max (who was sitting next to me and whose Mum had also been quite religious, I think) laughed quietly and whispered, "Way to go, Steve."

Mrs. McIntee huffed and puffed at what Dad had said, and said something about us being Saved for a Special Purpose and that it was not our place to Question His Judgment. She seemed to speak in capital letters all the time, which is why I've written what she said like that.

(By the way, this version of the conversation is taken a bit from my memory, but mostly from Dad's.)

Dad laughed (at this time we didn't know that Gregory had been killed in the alien/slug ambush) and said, "There IS no judgment. It's just law of averages. It doesn't matter how devastating a disaster is, there will ALWAYS be survivors, even if it's only a handful of people out of millions. But the REASON those few survive is nothing to do with God. It's purely down to luck, which in most cases boils down to being in the right place at the right time and being favored by a particular set of circumstances." He pointed round the table with his fork and said, "Look at us. You're not seriously telling me we're God's chosen ones? And don't say that God works in mysterious ways, because that's just a way of trying to explain the randomness of what happens on this little planet of ours."

I could tell he was quite angry, even tho his voice was calm. Libby knew he was angry too, cos she put a hand on his arm. It was weird seeing that, cos it was what Mum used to do when they were together, and it made me feel sad for Mum, and angry at Libby for taking Mum's place, but also kind of thankful to her, cos it meant that Dad had somebody who really cared about him (and I know how weird all that sounds, with all those different feelings jumbled up, but that's how it was).

I'm not sure why I'm writing all this. It just seemed important somehow. It made me feel proud of Dad and it also made me think that maybe there isn't a meaning to everything, even tho we always keep trying to find one.

Mrs. McIntee said she felt sorry for Dad, and that she was sure he would eventually see the Light or whatever. And Dad, who I know didn't really want to argue and had been feeling upset about Mum even tho they weren't a couple anymore, said that he doubted that very much, but that he hadn't meant to cause any offense and that it must be nice for her to have her faith to fall back on.

It wasn't until the next day that we found out one of the other people who'd died in the alien/slug ambush was Mrs. McIntee's son, Gregory. It's funny that both groups should have someone called Greg killed by aliens, but maybe that's one of God's "mysterious ways." Maybe it also explains why Mrs. McIntee is so religious. I wonder whether she was religious before her husband died or whether she just took it up to try and make sense of stuff.

The only other person I haven't mentioned is the 3rd person who died in the alien/slug ambush. It's funny to be talking about someone I've never met and who I'm never going to meet, but if I don't leave a record of who he was, I don't suppose anyone else will.

His name was Peter Atwell and he was an art student from Glasgow. He was doing a project or something, traveling round Scotland, painting a load of castles. He had permission to camp in the castle grounds over half-term and was there in his tent when the flood came. I don't know much else about him except that he was 22 and that (according to Dyl) he was a nice guy.

So that's it. For the past week we've been catching up on our sleep, sorting out our various aches and pains, and making new friends. I've been talking to Dyl a lot and (like I said before) thinking about Mum and crying and stuff. There are SOME jobs to do here, like keeping the place clean and washing clothes and sheets and preparing food, but not that many. Portia and I have been hanging out, and we've even been playing board games and listening to music (they've got a stock of batteries here, so my iPod's working again) and I've been reading.

Like I said, the kitchens are pretty well stocked, but Adam's taken teams out in the helicopter a few times, either to try and pick up things we keep running short of (bottled water, toilet rolls, gas canisters for the camping stoves, booze (!!), petrol for the petrol bombs, cleaning stuff, matches, candles etc) or to see what's happening with the aliens/slugs, and firebomb as many of their eggs as possible.

Actually things have been quiet on the alien/slug front since we've been here, by which I mean they haven't attacked US even tho we've been attacking THEM. I think it's cos they've been preoccupied with their babies hatching out (if you can CALL them babies) to fight back. Alex took Dad and Mr. McGregor out on a firebombing mission this afternoon, and cos they weren't landing, and cos I kept nagging at Dad to let me and Portia come along cos I said it was important for us kids to know what was going on, we were allowed to sit in and watch.

There are now so many egg hills that we didn't have to go far to find ones that hadn't already been firebombed. Dad said that altho we've been making a stand, we've hardly even scratched the surface. I'm not sure how many aliens/slugs come out of each lot of eggs, but I'd say it was a few hundred. The places where the aliens have already hatched out are pretty gross. The egg hills aren't shiny and blue anymore, they're just black pools of goo with human bones sticking out of them. In some places the baby aliens are moving about near the egg hills in big groups, surrounded by huge circles of adult aliens in human form. The babies are packed so tightly together that looking at them is like looking at a bluey black moving carpet of kind of lumpy electricity. It's hard to look at them full on, even tho there's loads of them. If you try too hard your eyes ache, as if you're looking into the sun.

I couldn't watch the aliens/slugs being firebombed and dying, cos it was too horrible. Even above the noise of the helicopter I could hear them screaming, and that was bad enough. When I put my hands over my ears, Portia looked at me as if I was a wuss and said, "They're vermin. They're like rats. They deserve to die."

"They're cleverer than rats," I said. "And anyway, even rats have feelings."

"Don't tell me you feel sorry for them?" she said.

"I just don't like to hear things in pain," I said.

When we got back, me and Dad had a cup of tea in what was the

6th form common room and was now a chill-out room for whoever wanted to go in (there was a dartboard and a football table and stuff). I asked him whether I'd been a wimp and he said I was "empathic" and "sensitive," which was no bad thing.

"I wish they were friendly," I said. "I wish we could talk to them. Why do aliens always have to be evil?"

He laughed and said, "You talk as if you've met lots."

"I just mean on the telly and films they always seem to be evil," I said. "You know, Daleks and Cybermen and that big monster in 'Alien' and that kind of stuff."

He looked thoughtful for a minute, then said, "I'm not sure that the aliens are actually EVIL, Abs. I'm sure THEY don't think of themselves as evil. They're probably just trying to survive like us."

"But this is OUR world," I said, "and they invaded it. Why can't they go and find their own world?"

"How do you know they're from outer space?" Dad asked.

"Well, they weren't here before, were they?" I said.

"Not that we know of," said Dad, "but how do you know our scientists didn't create them in a laboratory somewhere? Maybe what we're dealing with is mankind's folly."

"But if you don't think they're evil, why do you kill them?" I asked.

"I didn't say I didn't THINK they were evil," he said. "I just said I didn't know. And as to why we kill them . . ." He looked uncomfortable and then he said, "I suppose it comes down to increasing OUR chances of survival. The likelihood is we'll be overrun by these things eventually, but I think it's our duty to try and delay that as long as possible."

"So do you think we'll lose then, Dad?" I asked him. "Do you think they'll kill us in the end?"

He stroked my hair and said, "Let's not dwell on that for now, sweetheart. Let's live from day to day. Let's do what we can and see where it takes us."

About 6 o'clock this evening me, Dyl, Max and Portia were playing cards in the dormitory that Portia, Marcie and Victoria sleep in and I was telling them about my conversation with Dad. "I just wish we could talk to the aliens," I said. "Find out what they want."

Dyl looked at me with a weird expression on his face.

"What?" I said.

"There's something I'm not supposed to tell you," he said.

Max chucked his cards down. We were all sitting in a circle on the floor. "So tell us, man," he said.

Dyl looked around, as if he was afraid we might be overheard. "Best if I show you," he said. "Come with me. But be really quiet."

"Cloak and dagger. What a laugh," said Portia. She was well-spoken and she sometimes said things that made her sound spookily grown-up.

Dyl led us downstairs thru the castle and out into the courtyard. It was dark and there was a ring of torches burning down there, like big fire-brands propped in wooden stands. Mr. McGregor had made them and they made the courtyard look like a medieval film set—the sort of place you'd see in 'Robin Hood' or something. It was cold outside and spitting with rain, but despite that it was a clear night. You could see every star. As I looked up I realized I hadn't seen any blue lightning for about 10 days. I wondered again whether the aliens and their eggs had come in on the blue lightning, and whether it had stopped now because its job was done.

We saw a few people on the way down the stairs—Mr. McGregor talking to Adam in one room, and Libby walking past with Moira Poole. Adam winked at me, and both Libby and Mrs. P smiled, but none of them asked us what we were doing. They were used to us us-ing the castle as a playground, especially this time of the evening, an hour or so before dinner. All our jobs (if we had any) for the day had been done and the adults were either preparing the meal or chilling out with a glass of booze and talking about stuff.

Out in the courtyard, Dyl said, "Wait here. I'll be back in 2 min-utes."

"Where you going?" I asked him.

He sighed and said, "Don't ask me loads of questions, Abs. You'll find out soon enough."

He went thru the archway that led to the head's office and the staff bedrooms and came back 2 minutes later looking pleased.

"Right," he said, "come on," and he led us across the courtyard to the base of one of the towers next to the big wooden front door. This was known as the Muniment Tower and in its wall was a thick wooden door, which, when I was at school, was always kept locked.

"Okay," Dyl said, looking around again, "this is where we have to be careful."

"Of who?" Max asked.

"Well . . . Mr. West, mainly," said Dyl.

"I'm not scared of him," said Max.

"Neither am I," said Dyl quickly. "It would just save a lot of hassle if we didn't see him, that's all."

He reached into his pocket and took out a big, old-looking key, which he put into the lock of the door and turned. He pushed the door open and had a quick look around the courtyard again, and said, "Come on, quickly, everyone inside."

We squeezed through the door, Portia giggling and Dyl shushing her. "Don't go too far forward," Dyl said. "There are some stone steps in front of you, which you'll fall down if you're not careful."

He pulled the door shut and suddenly we were in total darkness. Portia giggled again and said, "Are we going ghost hunting? When we were at school everyone used to say this tower was haunted. They said a woman committed suicide by throwing herself off the top and now she drags her mangled body up and down the stairs."

Even tho I'd seen worse things than ghosts over the past few weeks, I felt a bit nervous and wanted to tell Portia to shut up. I was trying to think of a way to do it that would make it sound like I was bored when Max said, "Anyone got a—"

Then Dyl switched on a torch.

"Never mind," Max said, and we all laughed.

Dyl shone the torch around, but there wasn't much to see. We were in a circular stone chamber. It was chilly and damp. Just as Dyl had said, about 10 steps in front of us was a sort of rounded alcove, and there were stone steps in there, going up and down.

Dyl shone his torch into the alcove and the beam slid around on the stone steps. On either side of the beam black shadows leaped up and down the stairwell.

"Cool," said Portia. "Which way are we going?"

"Down," said Dyl.

"What's down there?" asked Max.

"Oh, don't tell us," said Portia. "I bet there's a really cool leisure complex, with a swimming pool and a pizza place and a cinema and

*a Starbucks." Her voice became dreamy. "God, I would pay, like, a
million pounds to have a caramel macchiato right now."*

"Then again it could just be a torture chamber," said Max.

"Close," said Dyl. "It's dungeons."

"Ooh, dungeons," said Portia in a bored voice.

"Yeah, but it's what's IN the dungeons that we're interested in,"
said Dyl.

"Which is?" I asked.

"You'll see," he said.

He took us down the steps, shining his torch. It was a curved staircase, quite narrow, and the steps were uneven and slippery. There was
a smell of wetness and something like rotten vegetables that came up
to meet us. It wasn't as bad as the smell of bodies we'd had to put up
with for the first few weeks after the flood, but it was gross all the same.

When we got to the bottom there was a wall to our left and a narrow stone corridor to our right. There was light at the end of the
corridor—candlelight, which was throwing shapes and shadows on the
wall. You could tell from the block of light there was a room at the end
of the corridor, or at least that the space opened out.

Apart from us lot shuffling around, there was no sound but the
drip of water. The walls were wet and slimy, and I wondered whether
they'd been that way before the flood, or whether it was because seawater had soaked down through the grass and soil. The corridor that
led to the candlelight at the far end was so narrow that we had to go
down it in single file. Dyl went first, shining the torch ahead, so that
the beam mixed with the candlelight and made it doubly bright. After Dyl went Portia, then me, then Max. Max kept touching my
shoulder and giving it a little stroke in a kind of 'It's okay, I'll look
after you' way, which was typical of him—sweet, but trying to keep it
quiet, to act tough and not embarrass himself.

Altho the room at the end was a bigger space, it wasn't THAT
much wider than the corridor. The ceiling was low and made of rock
and covered in slimy green moss. There were 4 cells on each side of the
room, 8 altogether. The cells were just black holes cut into the rock
with thick metal bars across the front. The bars looked old and rusty,
but also solid, as if they'd never come loose, no matter how much you
pushed and pulled and shook them. The floor was wet stone, covered

in puddles, and inside the cells it was just as wet, which meant you wouldn't be able to sit or lie down without getting cold, wet and filthy. There were 2 candles in holders on the floor next to the far wall, sending shapes dancing up the walls. Without the candles it would have been pitch-black, not to mention freezing and silent except for the drip of water. I tried to imagine what it would be like down here in one of these cells with no light, and just the thought of it made me panicky and tight-chested. Dyl walked to the cell at the far end on the left-hand side and shone his torch into it.

We all crowded round to look. Inside the cell was a young man. He might have been good-looking once, but now his face was like a skull—white with dark hollows around his eyes. His hair was long and plastered to his head as if it was wet, and he had a stubbly beard. He was wearing jeans and trainers and a gray hoodie, and he was squatting on his heels, with his back against a shelf of rock that came out of the wall and was probably meant to be a table or a bed, or maybe both. There was a blanket in yellow and brown tartan draped over his shoulders.

"Who is he?" Portia whispered.

I looked at Dyl and I could see that his jaw was tight, as if he was angry or disgusted.

"It looks like Cal MacDonell," I said. "He was Dyl's best friend. Except it's not him, is it, Dyl?"

Dyl shook his head.

Behind me I heard Max breathe out hard. "It's one of them, isn't it?" he said. "An alien."

"A slug," Dyl said, loud enough so that the thing that looked like Callum would hear.

It didn't react, tho. Didn't look up at us or even flinch from the light when Dyl shone his torch into its face.

"What's it doing here?" Max whispered, as if he didn't want it to hear him.

"We caught it," said Dyl.

"How?" I asked.

"We went into Castle Morton on a scavenger raid," said Dyl, "to see what we could find. We hadn't seen much slug activity at this point, so we were a bit cocky. We split up, all going into different shops

*on the High Street. Me and Andy went into Price-Cutter's—you re-
member, Abs, the supermarket?"*

I nodded.

"We were loading up our rucksacks with stuff when we heard
shouting," Dyl said. "We ran out and there in the street was Pete
Atwell, and this big bearded bloke was holding him from behind,
twisting his arms behind his back. Pete was yelling, and at first I
thought the bloke was the shop owner and that he thought Pete was
a looter or something—stupid, I know. I was about to explain who
we were, maybe even invite the guy back to the castle, when he
changed. First he went all . . . bluey white, like a negative photo.
Then he sort of . . . shimmered or dissolved or something and became a different shape. It's hard to describe."

Me and Max both nodded. "We know what you mean," I said.
"We've seen it."

Dyl said, "And there was this fizzing sound. And then Pete
started to scream."

He stopped for a minute, looking at the Cal thing in the cell as if
he really hated it.

"Then it ate him," he said. "Just sort of sucked him in, like he
was . . . a piece of spaghetti or something. Pete folded in half and we
heard his bones breaking. We knew we couldn't do anything for him,
so we ran down the street to warn the others, just in case there were
more slugs around. I went towards the chemist's, which was where Cal
had gone, and Andy went down to Jackson's Hardware—you know,
Abs, next to the stationer's, across the road from the Market Hall?

"I was s***-scared, going into that shop. The place was a wreck,
and it was knee-deep in mud and all the things you get in chemist's
shops—packets and boxes and bottles, full of pills and tablets and
cough sweets and stuff. I couldn't see Cal anywhere. And I kept
thinking something was going to come out of the mud and grab me, or
was maybe going to grab my ankles and pull me under. And it was totally silent, and all I could hear was my own breathing, and my own
heart, going like f***ing crazy . . . sorry Portia."

"What for?" Portia asked.

"Swearing," he said.

Portia rolled her eyes and said, "Not a f***ing problem, squire."

Dyl gave her a quick grin and carried on, "So I was in the shop and I'd just decided that Cal definitely wasn't in there when I saw that, behind the counter, at the back of the bit where they sort out the prescriptions and stuff, there was an open door. I could see daylight thru the door and realized it must lead into a backyard. I was going to shout Cal's name, but something stopped me—I suppose I didn't want that thing that had eaten Pete to hear me. So I walked forward, wading thru all the . . . crap and stuff, and I got to the door and looked round it."

He paused again and gave the Cal thing another hateful glance.

"Cal was there, all right," *he said,* "but that thing was eating him. Sucking him in, just like that other one had sucked in Pete. There was no screaming this time. I could see Cal was already dead. Could see from the blood . . . and . . . all that kind of stuff.

"Luckily the thing didn't see me. I managed not to shout or scream or anything. I pulled my head back through the door and got out of that shop as quick as I could. Out in the street I saw Andy running towards me, looking scared, and I asked him whether he'd seen Gregory. He said no, but he'd found his rucksack on the floor with stuff spilling out of it. Also he said there were 3 more of those things up there. I told him about Cal and said that we should get back to the castle. I said that if Gregory was okay, that's where he'd make for. Andy agreed and we started back, looking all around for slugs. Then we heard a shout behind us— 'Hey, guys, wait for me.' And I knew that voice straightaway, and . . . Jesus, it scared the s**t out of me. I turned round and there was"—*he jerked his torch at the alien in the cell*—"that thing, looking like Cal, walking towards us."

"And did you know it was an alien?" *Max asked.*

"Oh, yeah," *said Dyl.*

"So what did you do?" *I asked.* "If it had been me I'd have run like hell."

Dyl grinned again—or showed his teeth, at least. You couldn't say he looked as tho he was finding this funny. "That was my first thought," *he said,* "but then I remembered what we'd been talking about the night before—a bit like what you and Dad were talking about earlier, Abs. Old Westy had been saying how much he'd love to know what made these things tick, what their physical makeup was, all that stuff. And Andy's dad said jokingly, 'We'll have to pop out and catch you one then.' Except Westy took it seriously, and he started wondering HOW we could catch one. And someone—Pete, I think—said it might be best to try when they were in human form cos that was when they seemed at their weakest, just as weak as real people, in fact.

"We didn't think we'd ever really get into a situation where we'd be able to catch a slug, but when this one turned up pretending to be Cal, I suddenly realized that, first, it was doing it to get into the castle, and second, it didn't know that we knew it was a slug.

"So when it started running up to us, I gave Andy a sort of 'go along with me' look, and luckily Andy seemed to understand straightaway and he gave a little nod. So the slug came up and I went, 'All right, Cal?' and he went, 'All right.' And I asked him whether he'd seen any slugs and he said, 'I saw them, but they didn't see me.' I told him Pete and maybe Gregory were dead and he said he'd heard the screaming and how awful it was and all that. And then I asked him where his rucksack was, cos he wasn't carrying it, and he said he'd chucked it cos it was weighing him down and he was scared, and then we started walking back up the hill to the castle."

Dyl had been talking nonstop for a few minutes and his cheeks were burning bright red. He looked at the alien again, and grinned again, and I was suddenly shocked by how nasty that grin was, and it made me realize, probably for the first time, how much everything that had happened had changed him too, how hardened he'd become, and that made me feel sad.

"Do you want to tell them what happened next, slug boy?" Dyl said to the Cal thing in the cell. "Do you want to tell them how dumb you were? How easily we got you?"

The Cal thing just stared straight ahead and didn't say anything. I didn't like the way Dyl was glaring at it, his face full of hate. I touched his arm and said, "Why don't YOU tell us, Dyl? He's not going to say anything."

For a moment Dyl looked at me, and the expression on his face didn't change. "IT'S an it, not a HE," he said.

I didn't know what to say to that, but luckily Max must have known how I was feeling, cos he said quietly, almost like he was talking to a wild animal, "Come on, Dyl, tell us the rest, man."

Dyl looked from me to Max, and suddenly it was as if he realized who he was talking to and a bit of the meanness went out of his eyes. "Yeah, sorry," he said. "We were walking up the hill road to the castle, and there were branches and bits of trees and stuff all over the place, and I picked up this big branch, about the size of a baseball bat, and I started swinging it, hitting bushes and things at the side of the road as we were talking—you know how you do sometimes?"

Me, Max and Portia all nodded.

"And I just . . . dropped back," Dyl said, "started walking behind slug boy here. And then I just went up behind it, swung the branch round and . . . WHAM! Right on the top of its head. It didn't suspect a thing."

"And he went down, yeah?" said Max.

"Oh yeah," said Dyl. "Went down like a ton of bricks."

"So what did you do then?" asked Portia.

"Andy grabbed its arms and I grabbed its legs and we carried it up to the castle," said Dyl. "At first the others found it hard to believe it was a slug, but we persuaded them to let us bring it down here. We put it in this cell and sat and watched it. As soon as it came round, they knew."

"It changed?" said Max.

"Oh yeah," said Dyl. "Opened its eyes and WHOOMPH! Just like that. One second it was Cal, the next it was throwing itself around, spitting sparks like a Roman candle."

"But it can't get out?" said Portia nervously.

"Well . . . obviously not," said Dyl.

"But I thought they were, like, really powerful," she said.

"Well, they're strong, yeah," said Dyl. "Stronger than us. But they haven't got special powers or anything. They can't pass thru solid objects."

Portia looked at the Cal alien as if it was some weird and exotic creature—which in a way it was, I suppose.

"How come it's changed back into a human?" she asked.

"Westey thinks it does it to make us uncomfortable," said Dyl.

He turned to the alien and raised his voice. "Not that it does. Whatever it looks like, we know it's still a slug."

"Has it spoken since you put it in here?" I asked.

"Off and on. Westey comes down every day to try and speak to it, but it hasn't said much to him. It basically just tries to mess with your head. The main thing it says is that we're making a big mistake and it means us no harm." He snorted, his face turning ugly and mean again for a second. "That's probably what it said to Cal before it ate him."

"What do you feed it?" asked Portia, still looking at the Cal thing with fascination.

Dyl looked at her as tho she was being annoying. "It's not a pet rabbit," he said.

"Nah, man, it's a fair enough question," said Max. "Anything we find out about these things has gotta be good, yeah?"

Dyl shrugged and said, "I suppose," but he didn't seem as tho he really believed it. "We're not starving it if that's what you think. We just bring it normal food, but it doesn't eat much. We've asked it what it wants, but it just keeps saying, 'I'm like you,' so we give it what we're eating. I mean, what else can we do? It's not like we're torturing it or anything."

"So what else have you found out about it?" I asked.

"Not much," said Dyl. "It hasn't told us what it is, or where it comes from, or what the blue lightning is. Westey took some samples from it—blood, hair, that sort of stuff, and tested them as best he could in the school lab. As far as he could tell, when the slug was in human form, it was just . . . human. I mean, we can't analyze its DNA or anything, but Westey said it looks as tho the slugs can take in whatever they absorb and just sort of . . . become that thing. On the outside, at least. Which means they can shrink whatever the body part of themselves is down to something really tiny, to fit inside the . . . disguise or whatever."

Max was nodding. "But if the disguise gets damaged, then it affects the aliens too, right? I mean, if the disguise only gets damaged a little bit then they can change back to their real selves straightaway. But if the disguise gets damaged a lot it takes a while for the thing inside to recover. It's like the disguise is a kind of . . . vehicle for them. Like a stolen car, yeah? They crash that car, and if there's not much damage, they walk away. But if they smash that car up real bad then maybe they get knocked out for a bit, real shaken up, you know, and they can't get out straightaway."

"That's good," Dyl said. "I like it."

"I'm not sure how it helps us, tho," I said. "I mean, sorry to . . ."

"P**s on my parade?" said Max.

I smiled. "Something like that."

"Yeah," he said, "I know what you mean." He stared at the alien. "So, what are you gonna do with it?"

"I don't know," Dyl said. "It's not up to me."

"Why didn't you tell us about this before?" I asked.

"Westey told me not to," Dyl said, looking embarrassed. "He said the fewer people who know about this the better. He said some people might not approve."

"Does Dad know?" I asked.

Dylan shook his head.

"Who does?" asked Max.

"Me, Andy, Westey, Mr. and Mrs. Poole, Mr. and Mrs. McGregor . . . Mrs. McIntee, I suppose," said Dyl.

"So your group was keeping this secret from our group?" said Max. He shook his head. "Thanks a bunch, man. What did you think we were gonna do? Set it free or something?"

"No," said Dyl, looking REALLY embarrassed now. "It wasn't up to me. And I'm telling you NOW, aren't I?"

"Your dad should know about this," Max said.

"Yeah," I said. Dad could decide whether to tell the others, I thought.

"You said you wanted to talk to one," Dyl said to me. "That's why I brought you here. So you could."

Everyone looked at me. Suddenly I felt uncomfortable. "Yeah, I know, but if you lot have been talking to it and it hasn't said anything, why would it talk to me?" I said.

"Cos you're pretty?" said Max.

I blushed and said, "We probably all look the same to them."

"You could try," said Portia. "You never know."

I looked at the alien, the Cal thing. He (it) hadn't moved since we came in. He was still squatting there, still staring straight ahead. He looked as tho he was in a trance or something.

"Hello," I said, trying not to sound nervous. "Can I ask you some questions?"

The Cal thing said nothing. "See?" I said. "He won't talk to me."

"Just ask your questions," Max said.

I didn't want to be there. But I turned back to the alien and said, "I just wondered what you wanted. Here on Earth, I mean."

It sounded stupid put like that. There, I thought, I've asked. Now let's go.

But then the Cal thing raised its head. There wasn't anything weird or different about it (it didn't have hypnotic eyes or anything), but it gave me a shivery feeling all the same.

"To survive," it said. Its voice was quiet and raspy, like it needed a drink.

"Is that all?" I said.

The Cal thing seemed to think about my question. "What else is there?"

"But that's all WE want to do," I said. "We just want to survive and live in peace. But your lot keep trying to kill us. Why?"

The Cal thing stared at me and I stared back at it, trying not to look scared. "We become you," it said.

"What does that mean?" I asked.

"We become you," it said again. "You thrive by subjugation. You destroy and consume. We become you, so we can survive."

"But . . . why can't we all survive together?" I said. "Why can't we live in peace?"

"Yes," said the Cal thing. "Let's live in peace."

I was confused. I didn't know what to say. "Where are you from?" I said. "Are you from outer space?"

The Cal thing looked at me as if it didn't understand the question, or as if it was PRETENDING not to understand the question. Then it said, "Isn't this outer space?"

Dyl shook his head. "It's tying you in knots," he said. "It always does that. Messes with your head."

"Maybe it just doesn't understand," I said.

Dyl snorted, but he didn't say anything.

"This is Earth," I said. "It's our planet."

"Is it outer space?" the Cal thing asked again.

"It's IN space, yeah," I said.

"In space," the Cal thing said. "Is that where you're from?"

"I suppose so," I said. "I'm from Earth. From here. Where are you from?"

"In space," the Cal thing said. "We're all in space. That's where I'm from."

"But what's the name of your planet?" I said.

The Cal thing just looked at me, as if I were talking a foreign language.

"Did you come on the lightning?" I asked.

"Did you?" it said.

"No," I said. "We were already here. We live here."

"We live here too," said the Cal thing.

"But where did you live before?" I asked.

"In space," said the Cal thing. "Like you."

"Did you make the flood come?" I said.

"The flood," the Cal thing repeated. It wasn't actually a question, but it said the word as if it had never heard it before.

"The water. Did you make the water come?"

"The water was already here," said the Cal thing. "The water has always been here. No water, no life."

Dyl was right. It was messing with my head, refusing to answer my questions properly. Or maybe it honestly and truly didn't understand.

"This is pointless," I said. "Let's go."

Dyl put his face up to the bars of the cage and said, "Shall we blow the candles out as we go, slug boy, and leave you in the dark?"

"Dyl," I said in a sharp voice, which I was glad to see was enough to make him look ashamed.

We left. Portia actually wiggled her fingers at the Cal thing in a little wave. I wasn't sure whether she meant it in a sarcastic way or not. No one said anything as we retraced our steps along the corridor and up the slippery steps.

You know that thing people say about the s**t hitting the fan?

Well, when we opened the door of the Muniment Tower and stepped out into the courtyard that's pretty much what happened.

Sue was crossing the courtyard as we came out of the door and she saw us. "What have you lot been up to?" she said.

"Nothing," said Portia. She couldn't have looked more guilty if she'd tried.

"I thought this tower was inaccessible," Sue said. "A couple of days ago I suggested we could park the helicopter on top of it and was told there was no key."

"There wasn't," said Dyl. "We found it."

"Found it where?" asked Sue.

"Just . . ." I could see Dyl's mind had gone blank ". . . around," he said.

Sue looked at me, then at Max. "Max, what's going on?"

Max sighed, then said, "I swear, Sue, we only found out about this, like . . . 10 minutes ago. It wasn't our idea to keep it secret."

"Keep what secret? Show me," said Sue.

Uh-oh, I thought.

THIRTY-FOUR

"You had no right to keep this from us!" Sue shouted.

Steve sighed and leaned back in his chair. In essence he agreed with her, but he wished she didn't have to approach every situation with all guns blazing. Why couldn't she be diplomatic now and again? Didn't she realize that antagonizing people only made them defensive, uncommunicative, resentful? Wouldn't she have had this instilled in her during her police training?

If so, she had forgotten it now, had long ago reverted to type. Exceptional circumstances, he supposed. Wasn't it often said that extreme situations tended to bring out the best and worst in people?

If that were true, what had he learned about himself these past six weeks? He guessed he'd turned out tougher, braver and more resourceful than he would ever have imagined. On the other hand, he had come to realize how much he craved a quiet life, a life filled with order and routine. The week or so since they had arrived at the castle had only underlined this fact. If he hadn't had to cope with the news of Jackie's death and provide emotional support for Abby, he would have been in his element here. Apart from an electricity supply the castle had pretty much everything Steve could want from life: private rooms with comfortable beds, a reasonable stock of provisions (despite shortages in some areas) and generally good company. There was even a gym where he and whoever wanted to join in could forget things for an hour with some circuit training or a game of football or badminton. Plus (glory of glories) there was a music room, to which Steve had been able to retreat at quiet moments to play the piano and guitar. In fact, he had appropriated the guitar to serenade Libby by candlelight, and on one occasion had sat with Abby, strumming away whilst softly singing Jackie's favorite song— Burt Bacharach's "I Say A Little Prayer" (his ex-wife had particularly favored the Aretha Franklin version). That little singsong had reduced them both to floods of tears, but they had been *good* tears, or at least cathartic ones.

Although he had been half-expecting it, news of Jackie's death had hit Steve harder than he had let on. He and Jackie might have been estranged for a couple of years now, but that could never alter the fact there was a hell of a lot of history (mostly very good; mostly *wonderful*) between them, a vast and precious library of cherished memories. In essence he and Jackie had grown up together, had undertaken the journey from naive and idealistic teenagers to confident adults hand in hand. And not even the fact that they had eventually grown apart had sullied that too much. Their relationship since the breakup had certainly never been worse than civil, and indeed there had still been a great deal of affection between them— which was precisely why, even after two years, Abby had still harbored hopes of a reconciliation between her parents.

Realizing his mind was wandering, he turned his thoughts back to the matter at hand. Sue had called the meeting (*war conference*) fifteen minutes before, after it had come to light that Brian West and his group had been secretly harboring an alien in the castle dungeons. Now twelve of the seventeen current inhabitants of the building were gathered around the long central table in the dining room. The only five not present were the two youngest girls, Marcie and Victoria, Jean McGregor, who was keeping them occupied elsewhere, Adam, who was on top of the Watch Tower (the Muniment Tower's twin), undertaking his weekly maintenance routine on the helicopter, and no doubt up to his elbows in grease and muck, and Daphne McIntee, who had simply opted out of the proceedings and was in her room.

The meeting had started badly—with Brian West and Sue going at each other hammer and tongs. Despite Steve's advice to her to play it cool, Sue had immediately all but accused Brian of consorting with the enemy and of recklessly endangering their lives.

Brian, inevitably, had snapped back in his customary pompous and blustering manner, and for the first few minutes it appeared that the discussion was destined to degenerate into a slanging match between accuser and accused.

To Steve's surprise it was Joe Poole who eventually waded in to break-up the combatants. Joe was a slight man, maybe three or four years older than Steve, and was well liked by everybody. He was quiet and easygoing, albeit with a sharp, occasionally laconic, sense of humor. Following Sue's latest outburst, he raised his hand and calmly asked, "Sorry for being a bit thick, but can I get it clear exactly what you're angry about, Sue? Is it that the slug is there at all, or just the fact that you weren't told about it?"

Sue turned on him. She made Steve think of a savage dog which wasn't fussy who it bit, but would simply go for whichever moving target was closest.

"Both," she snapped. "That thing is bloody dangerous. If it got out it would kill all of us, probably starting with the kids. Is that what you want?"

Alex McGregor scowled. "Don't be bloody daft, girl."

"That thing is locked up," Moira Poole said. She was a tough, sinewy Irishwoman with strikingly pale eyes. "It can't get out."

"How do you *know* that?" said Sue. "That thing down there isn't human. How do you know it hasn't got . . . acid saliva or something? How do you know it can't melt metal? How do you know it's not strong enough to smash through those bars?"

"It hasn't so far," said Joe reasonably.

"Maybe it's just waiting," suggested Max. "Biding its time."

"What for?" said Brian witheringly. "No, if that thing *could* escape it would have done so by now."

"How did you know the cell would be strong enough to hold it in the first place?" asked Steve.

Brian pushed his lips out pugnaciously, making his mustache bristle. "We felt it a risk worth taking. We took suitable precautions."

"Such as?" demanded Sue.

"For the first forty-eight hours we had people armed with gas bombs watching the creature day and night."

"Forty-eight hours? You need someone watching that thing all the time. You can't get complacent with these bastards."

"You could be right, girl," Alex McGregor conceded. "And now that you're here mebbe we can arrange that."

Brian tutted. "I'm sure it's not necessary. The young lady is scaremongering. The creature can't get out."

"What I was saying before," Max muttered, "about that thing biding its time . . ."

"Go on, Max," encouraged Libby.

"Yeah, well, it's just . . . what I was going to say is . . . that thing can change shape, right?"

"Right," said Steve.

"So what's to stop it changing into something small—a cockroach or a fly, say—and getting out like that? Maybe it's just waiting for the right thing to come along."

"That's . . ." Brian began, then lapsed into silence. It was clear the possibility hadn't occurred to him.

"You see?" said Sue. "You see how f—um, effing stupid you've been?"

Portia rolled her eyes. "Oh, puh-*lease*. Don't hold back on my account. It's not as though I haven't heard it all before."

There was a ripple of laughter around the room, a momentary release of tension. Taking advantage of the lull, Steve said mildly, "You haven't explained why you kept this from us."

Moira Poole crossed her arms and glared at her husband. "*I* said we should tell them, didn't I? *I* said it would blow up. in our faces if we started keeping secrets from one another."

Joe sighed. "You did, Em." He looked across the table—at Sue, Steve, Libby and Max. "All I can do is say sorry," he said. "We *should* have told you. It was wrong of us not to."

"So why didn't you?" demanded Sue.

Joe glanced at Brian. "Well, far be it from me to cast aspersions, but Brian here thought it might muddy the waters. Too many cooks and all that."

Brian West sighed as if he was finding the whole affair tiresome. "I've made a significant amount of headway with our guest," he said. "You might say the two of us have established something of a rapport."

"So basically you didn't want anyone muscling in on your love affair?" said Sue contemptuously.

Brian reacted as if stung. "Don't be so bloody puerile! The reason I didn't tell you was because I didn't want to deal with the kind of ludicrous tripe I'm hearing now. For your information, not that I expect you to display the slightest interest in anything that doesn't involve blowing what you perceive as the enemy into little pieces, I've discovered what I consider to be some fascinating, not to say potentially useful, facts about our visitors."

"Such as?" asked Libby.

"Well, for instance, they appear to have no inkling where they come from, and no concept of space, planets, the universe. Their motivational force seems to be simply to survive. And their means of achieving and maintaining that appears to be an instinctive observation and emulation of what they consider the most efficient and ruthless life-form they encounter— which in this case is us."

He sat back and folded his arms, looking smug. Dylan said, "But the slug pretty much told *us*—well, Abby—all that in, like, ten minutes."

As though encouraged by her brother speaking out, Abby said, "We also all got the feeling it was holding back."

She looked at the others for confirmation and they nodded.

Sue turned triumphantly to Brian. "So much for your *rapport*," she said.

Brian flushed a deep crimson. "I can't believe you're giving more credence to the immature witterings of a few school-children than you are to my own considerably more thorough observations. Or, on the other hand, perhaps I can. And perhaps this justifies my decision to withhold the information of the presence of our guest."

"Hey, *I'm* not a school kid," Max grumbled.

Sue looked about to respond to Brian's outburst, but before she could Steve raised his hands.

"Okay, guys, let's calm it down and discuss this reasonably. Trading insults won't help anyone. It seems to me that the creature is clearly a danger to us—potentially, at least. So the question we should be asking is: What do we do about it?"

"Kill it," said Sue.

Brian looked appalled. "Kill an intelligent creature? What are you, a savage?"

"An intelligent *predator*," corrected Sue. "Give that thing half a chance and it would kill the lot of us."

"Nonsense," spluttered Brian. "I believe that by establishing a dialogue with these creatures we may be able to—"

"It's *not* nonsense," said Dylan suddenly. "Sue's right."

Everyone looked at him. His eyes were blazing. Steve felt a stab of unease. He had never seen his son like this before. So troubled. So *haunted*. Dyl had always been a laid-back kid—sometimes *too* laid-back. There had been times in the past when even Steve had thought he needed a rocket up the arse.

He's seen too much, Steve thought. *Too much, too young*.

"That thing *would* kill us all if it got out," Dylan said. "I've seen the slugs in action—I've seen what they do. They don't care about us." He gestured towards Andy Poole, who was sitting beside his parents, silent and withdrawn. "We should never have brought that thing back here. I should have bashed its brains out. I thought maybe we could learn stuff from it, but I was wrong."

"Nonsense," snapped Brian. "As I think I've ably demonstrated, I've learned a great deal from the creature."

"You've learned nothing!" Dylan shouted, jumping up from his seat. It was only when Abby put a restraining hand on his arm that he sat back down with a thump.

In a more reasonable tone, Libby said, "I do think Dylan's got a point, Brian. Nothing you've told us so far actually seems that . . . *concrete.* Maybe if you tell us what else you've learned, we might be more sympathetic. As it stands, I think we all need a bit more convincing."

Brian was clearly exasperated. "It's not as simple as that," he said. "Who knows what will become useful and what will remain irrelevant in the long run? But if it'll keep you all happy . . ." He was silent for a moment, gathering his thoughts, and then he said, "I believe from talking to our guest that it and its kind are not inherently hostile. I believe they act mostly on instinct and that their main motivation is survival. They're intelligent, but I don't believe they're particularly sophisticated. I believe they can process memories and information enough to produce a fair simulacrum of whichever human personality they have absorbed, but I think they insinuate themselves among us not out of guile or cunning, but in the way that a parasite or a virus will affect an organism—simply in order to survive."

"So you're saying they have no emotions?" said Libby.

"Well . . . not as we understand them," said West. "They can derive emotions from us, which they assimilate and reproduce more or less appropriately, but I don't think their own emotions are complex. They feel pain and hunger, and distress when their young are threatened, but those emotions are purely instinctive, motivated by their overriding desire to survive and flourish as a species."

"I'm not sure whether knowing they don't actually *hate* us makes things better or worse," said Steve.

"Doesn't make any difference to me," muttered Sue.

"Nor me," said Max.

"*I'm* not sure whether any of this actually helps us much either," said Joe. "You said earlier, Brian, that you thought we could . . . what was it—establish a dialogue with these things?"

"I believe that's a possibility, yes."

"But to do what?" said Steve. "Persuade them that killing us is wrong?"

"Well . . . naturally," said West.

"Do ye think that'd work?" asked Alex McGregor.

"Who knows?" said West. "But it's worth a try."

"It *wouldn't* work," Sue said firmly. "If you think we can ever make friends with these things, you're living in cloud cuckoo land."

"Oh, *you'd* hate it if we found a way to make peace, wouldn't you?" said Brian. "It would give you nothing left to destroy."

Sue shook her head. "Believe what you like. I'm a realist, that's all. I think those things caused the flood, and I think they aim to wipe out those of us who are left. You say they're not cunning? I think they are. I think they're cunning, ruthless and manipulative. I think they know exactly what they're doing, and I think the one you've got in the cells down there has been twisting you around its little finger."

Brian looked disgusted. "I would hate to be as cynical as you."

"I'd rather be cynical than naive," she retorted. "It's cynicism that's kept me alive these past six weeks."

"You'll note we've all managed to survive one way or another," said West.

Sue snorted. "And how have *you* done it? By skulking in here. You wouldn't last five minutes out there."

The argument was broken up this time by the door bursting open. They all turned to see Adam standing there, face flushed with excitement.

"Got a . . . radio message," he panted, and jabbed a finger above his head.

Steve was already pushing his chair back. "What do you mean, a radio message?"

Adam bent double and put his hands on his knees. He had clearly run all the way down from the top of the Watch Tower. "Since the flood," he gasped, "there's been . . . nothing on the radio . . . just static. But I try it every . . . now and again, just in case. And today I . . . turned it on, and . . . there it was . . . a message. Someone speaking in French. Not very good reception . . . and it lasted . . . twenty seconds maybe. But it was definitely there."

"French?" Libby's eyes were gleaming.

"Can you call them back?" Joe asked. "Can you let them know we're here?"

"Possibly," said Adam, "if I can find the frequency again. Does anyone speak French?"

"Un peau," said Libby.

"Ah," said Adam, *"moi aussi. Peut-etre* we can come up with *une message* together?"

Abby nudged Steve's arm. "You see, Dad," she said, "maybe they won't beat us, after all."

Steve smiled at her, knowing that it didn't really mean anything, that all it proved was that there was someone alive in France with a working radio. Even so, it was hard not to get caught up in the optimism of the moment.

"Maybe they won't," he said.

THIRTY-FIVE

It took only the lightest touch for Steve to be instantly and fully awake. He sat up to shield Libby, who was sleeping on the other side of him. Blinking into the darkness, he said, "Who's there?"

"It's me," came a hiss not three feet away.

"Who's me?"

"Max."

Steve felt his shoulders relaxing. "Jesus, Max, why are you skulking in the dark? You nearly gave me a heart attack."

"Sorry, man, but I think something's wrong."

"Wrong how?"

"I was supposed to be on four-to-six sentry duty," Max said, "taking over from Alex? But he never woke me. My brain must have known there was something wrong, cos I woke up suddenly at twenty past four. I went down into the courtyard to see what was happening, but there was nobody there."

Steve was already swinging his legs out of bed. "You got a torch, Max?"

"Yeah, right here in my hand."

"Could you turn it on? But point it at the ceiling, not into my face."

Max did so. Steve blinked at the sudden light. He turned and shook Libby gently. Like him, she came awake instantly, letting out a startled gasp as her eyes opened. She looked at Steve, then Max. "What's wrong?" she said.

"Hopefully nothing," said Steve. Briefly he told her what Max had said. "We're going to wake up Sue, Joe and Adam and check things out. Can you round up the rest and take them to the top of the Watch Tower? Do it quickly, but make sure everyone's properly dressed, boots and everything. Don't go outside, use the internal corridors. I know it takes a bit longer, but it's safer. Oh, and make sure you and Abby have got your guns loaded and ready."

Steve was hauling on jeans, a sweatshirt and jacket as he was talking. Libby was nodding as she sat on the side of the bed, pulling on thick gray hiking socks.

"Go to Sue's room first. She's got two boxes of petrol bombs in there. We'll take some, but we'll leave some for you. Take your rucksack so you can carry them."

"What about provisions?" asked Libby. "Should we grab some food and stuff just in case?"

"No time. Just get everyone up to the helicopter and make sure you can defend yourselves if need be. That's the priority for now."

"Okay."

Steve was now fully dressed, boots laced up. He pulled open the bedside drawer and took out his gun and ammunition, his torch, and a big box of matches. He stuffed them into his pockets, then swiveled round on the bed, took Libby's face in his hands and kissed her.

"Good luck," he said. "I love you."

"I love you too," she said. She gave his hand a quick squeeze. "Be careful."

He tried to laugh. "It's probably a false alarm. Alex'll most likely be snoring somewhere." He patted Max on the shoulder. "You ready?"

Max looked apprehensive, but he gave a single determined nod.

"Then let's go."

THIRTY-SIX

Steve, Max, Sue and Joe crept down the wide, plushly carpeted staircase. All four were armed and carrying torches. As they descended, their heads darted from side to side, as though snagged by the plunge and sweep of their torch beams. The overlapping cones of light on the red carpet made it look as though the stairs were bathed in blood. The oily eyes of the portraits on the walls seemed to follow their progress. A gleaming figure standing silently at the bottom of the stairs caused momentary alarm before Max's torch beam revealed it to be the suit of armour they all passed a dozen times a day.

Steve briefly wondered how Adam was getting on. The helicopter pilot had split off from the group two floors up. If all was going to plan he would now be working his way, via a series of internal corridors, around the outer walls of the castle to a padlocked door that led directly into the Watch Tower. Steve prayed he wouldn't encounter anything nasty on the way. In many respects Adam was the most valuable member of their group, because if the castle had been breached, the helicopter would be their only realistic chance of escape.

He tried not to wonder how sixteen people would cram

into a helicopter designed for four adults. Tried also not to think about Libby and his children, about what might happen to them and whether he would ever see them again if all their worst fears were realized. He kept telling himself that this was a false alarm, that they would laugh about it later, but at the same time he knew that Alex McGregor was one of the most disciplined and reliable members of the group.

"So far, so good," Joe murmured as they reached the bottom of the stairs.

"Don't get complacent," Sue said. "Stay alert."

They crossed the wooden floor—once kept brightly polished, now scuffed by boots and dulled by tramped-in dirt—to the arched doorway ahead of them. This led out onto the stone-flagged walkway, supported by pillared arches, which edged two sides of the courtyard. Sue slipped her torch into her jacket pocket and curled her hand around the brass doorknob.

"Steve, Max, you go to the left and take cover behind a pillar," she whispered. "Joe, go to the right and I'll join you there. Okay?"

They nodded.

She tugged open the heavy door, and as soon as the gap was wide enough the men slipped out. Five seconds later Sue had pulled the door shut behind her and was huddling behind the pillar with Joe.

"Anything?"

Joe shook his head. "All seems quiet."

The four of them swept their torch beams across the cobbled courtyard. The double doors at the far end, which in medieval times would have led out onto a bridge across a moat, still appeared to be closed, which was a good thing. Perhaps not so good was the fact that there was no sign of life whatsoever. Even if Alex had fallen asleep, he still should have been visible. But when Sue directed her torch across to where he should have been sitting, on one of the stone benches beneath the left-hand walkway, all they saw was his crumpled tartan throw rug and his metallic red coffee flask standing upright on the bench beside it.

"There's no sign of a struggle," Joe hissed. "That's something."

"His gun's gone," noted Steve. "I'm not sure if that's good or bad."

Sue grunted and swept her torch slowly across the courtyard, left to right, like a searchlight. Rain was falling thinly, making the cobblestones gleam, darkening the four stone nymphs atop the pedestal in the center of the fountain. After weeks of inactivity the water in the fountain had turned green and oily with stagnation. The cone of light slid across the stonework and came to rest on a patch of ground ten yards beyond it.

"What's that?" she said quietly.

Steve linked his torch beam with hers, shining it on to the rain-glossy cobbles.

"Oh, fuck," Max said, "that's not blood, is it?"

"I'm afraid it might be," said Sue grimly.

They broke cover and moved in a half crouch across the cobbled ground, their eyes checking every archway and window, every shadowy alcove. It became clear as they neared the patch of illuminated ground that the reddish gloss was not *only* blood; it was *a lot* of blood.

"Mary, mother of Jesus," said Joe. "What happened here?"

Sue was stone-faced. "I think this is where Alex died."

Joe stared at her, aghast. "Died? How?"

"Eaten," said Sue. "Absorbed." She took another look around. Calmly, she said, "I think the enemy is in here with us."

Joe looked ready to ask more questions, but she was already speaking rapidly to the others.

"Max, Steve, check the main doors, make sure they're secure. I'll check our friend in the—"

Her words were interrupted by the sudden crack of a rifle shot.

Steve ducked instinctively, suddenly and horribly aware that he was out in the open. As he looked around for the source of the shot, he was just in time to see Joe's body falling lifelessly forward. He had the momentary but awful impression that

Joe's head was the wrong shape. Then the body hit the floor with the weighty gracelessness of a flour-filled sack, and Steve's gaze shifted to the figure standing behind it.

It was Andy Poole, Joe's son. He was framed by the arched opening that led to the staff quarters and administration offices. He was holding a gun (*Alex's gun,* Steve thought) and he was pointing it at them.

Steve threw himself to the ground as Andy fired for the second time. As his knees hit the cobbles with a jarring crunch he fancied he saw a flash of white from the gun muzzle. He was aware both that he had dropped his torch, which was spewing light across the cobbles, and that he had landed on his gun, which was now trapped between the floor and his body. He was aware also that he had a rucksack full of petrol bombs on his back and that Sue had told him (unnecessarily, he had thought) to keep them upright to prevent spillage.

He also became aware, as he swiveled his head, that although it was Sue who had been hit, it was Max who was yelling. He was bawling a denial at the creature which had almost certainly killed Andy Poole and which had been living quietly among the survivors in the castle ever since the day of the disastrous scavenger hunt. It now seemed that Dylan had been the only survivor from that day.

Sue was down. She was down but she was not dead. Judging by the blood and the mess, she had been hit in the left shoulder, or maybe the collar bone. She was lying on her back, and the bulk of her rucksack gave her the appearance of a stranded turtle. *Keep those petrol bombs upright,* Steve thought crazily as he watched (and admired) the way she was rocking from side to side, trying, even now, to raise her head, perhaps even to get to her feet. Her face was so pasty that her lips looked livid, almost maroon, and her eyes were black, glittering jewels. There was pain on her face, but also a furious indignation, a fierce and absolute sense of purpose.

Even as he was screaming at the creature, Max had been running to take cover behind the fountain. He fired at it now, a couple of his shots going wild but one hitting it in the chest, another in the left temple, ripping a good quarter of its head away. The thing that had taken on the form of Andy Poole fell backwards, its legs folding under it like the collapsing supports of a rickety table. Its gun fell from its nerveless fingers and clattered on the blood-streaked cobbles. Max ran up to it and fired another bullet into its chest, making the seemingly lifeless body jerk.

"Max," Steve called, and was amazed at how croaky his voice was.

Max turned, eyes staring wildly, like a sleepwalker waking up in an unexpected location.

"Don't waste your bullets," Steve said. "Burn it. It's the only way to be sure."

For a moment Max looked at him uncomprehendingly; then he nodded and swung his rucksack from his back. As he lit the strip of cloth and hurled the bottle savagely into the creature's face, Steve was already scrambling to his feet, retrieving his gun and his torch from the wet cobbles, turning to give what aid he could to Sue.

But someone was already there, crouched beside her, holding her head in his hands. For a split second Steve thought it was Dylan, but then his vision cleared and he realized the newcomer's resemblance to his son was nothing but superficial—similar build, roughly the same age. Even as his mind adjusted, he saw the door into the Muniment Tower standing open—and at once everything fell horribly into place.

Leave her alone! he tried to scream, but all that emerged was a wordless screech. He rammed his torch into his jacket pocket and scrabbled to aim his gun, but the grinning creature in the form of Cal MacDonell was already fizzing and changing. By the time Steve fired, the thing was a bewildering mass of black energy, jagged and overlapping shapes, glittering fronds of light. It *absorbed* the bullets he fired into it with barely a ripple, and then it began to absorb Sue.

Still wearing that same expression of clench-teethed intensity, Sue's body began to convulse. Her back arched and slammed down, and at first Steve thought she was doing it involuntarily, her dying brain shooting out random signals like sparks from a Catherine wheel. But then he heard the tinkling of glass, and saw her hand scrabbling in her jacket pocket. It emerged clutching a match box, which she tore open with both hands (one wet and bloody from the bullet wound in her shoulder), causing long-stemmed matches to scatter across her stomach and chest. She grabbed several and scraped them down the sandpapery side of the box, and a bloom of flame appeared, delicate and ephemeral. As the flame met the fumes of the petrol soaking into her clothes and the ground beneath her, there was a soundless sound, an *absence* of sound, like a sucking in of air, and all at once Sue and the Callum creature were encased in a raging pillar of flame.

Sue did not cry out, but simply lay there, turning black and withered and less human as she died. The creature, however, thrashed and writhed, trapped within the fire as it had been trapped within the cell below, screaming its shrill and somehow *electronic* screams. Steve stood and watched, shocked beyond reason and yet at the same time full of vitriolic triumph and savage pride. The creature seemed to take a long time to die, and by the time it did, Steve's skin was black with greasy ash, his body drenched in sweat. There was a stench in the air, like scorched rubber and roasted meat and smelted iron and something else. Something sickening and indefinable. Something alien.

He felt a hand on his arm and turned to see Max, his hair flecked with ash, his skin glossy with sweat.

"Did you see what she did?" Steve mumbled.

Max nodded and tugged at his sleeve. "Yeah, man, but we gotta go. We still got stuff to do."

THIRTY-SEVEN

There was someone in the room. Jean McGregor knew that as soon as she opened her eyes. She knew too that it wasn't Alex. Alex's was a *big* presence—tall, broad-shouldered—and even in the darkness she was aware of the space he filled. This, though, was someone small and light. She reached out unerringly in the blackness, found the matches, lit the candle. A face appeared, glowing yellow. An angelic face, framed by a halo of golden hair.

"Marcie!" Jean exclaimed. "What are you doing here?"

Marcie looked at her without expression. "I want a story, Aunty Jean."

Aunty Jean. Both little girls had taken to calling her that. Even Portia did sometimes, in her more vulnerable moments. Jean couldn't deny that it gave her a warm glow.

"A story?" she said. "My goodness! Whatever's the time?"

She consulted the battered alarm clock which she and Alex had owned for donkey's years.

"Ten to four! Your uncle Alex will be back soon. What do you think he's going to say when he finds you here?"

"Just one story, Aunty Jean," said Marcie.

Jean knew she was a soft touch; knew that Marcie and Victoria could twist her round their little fingers. She only hoped *they* didn't know it too.

"Just one then," she said firmly. She pulled aside the blankets. "Come on, dear, climb up beside me. Don't stand there catching your death."

A moment later she said, "Dear me, your wee feet are cold. Like little ice blocks."

Marcie looked at her. In the candle's glow her eyes seemed lit by a strange and avid light.

THIRTY-EIGHT

Although the cry woke her, Daphne couldn't rightly say whether it was part of her dream or outside in the real world. Whichever, her heart was going nineteen to the dozen, and it was hurting too, each pulse bringing a spasm of pain that radiated out from her chest and rippled through every part of her fleshy body.

Perhaps this is it, she thought. *Perhaps the Lord is finally calling me.* She was not afraid of the prospect. This world had collapsed beneath its Weight of Sin, had become the Devil's Playground, and she wanted no further part in it. Thus far, her Lord had seen fit to spare her, but perhaps He had now decided that the world was Beyond Redemption, that the time had finally come to call His Children home. Whatever His decision, Daphne was happy and willing to comply with it. She trusted implicitly in the Word of her Lord.

And so she lay in the dark, her swollen heart thumping in the corpulent mass of her body, and she waited patiently for His Judgment. As she waited she thought about her husband, Alastair, and her son, Gregory, his flesh (but not his Immortal Soul) destroyed by the minions of Satan, which had crawled up from the Pits of Hell to lay waste to Mankind's poisoned realm.

Would they be waiting to greet her, her loved ones? She pictured Alastair with his arm around the shoulders of their son and her eyes pricked with tears. Gregory had been a wee boy when his daddy had died, little more than a baby, in fact. Perhaps she could picture them so clearly now because they were calling to her, because the veil was thinning between this Fallen World and her Lord's Eternal Kingdom.

Another cry came tearing out of the darkness, shattering her reverie. No, more than a cry this time—a scream. The sound of a mortal soul in appalling distress.

Daphne wished she could close her eyes and ears to this Babel, but perhaps her Lord was Testing her? Perhaps it was her Christian duty to ease the passage of His children from this world to the next? If so, she would fulfil it, she would not turn her face from Suffering. She would go forth and be the Lord's Good Samaritan on this Fallen Earth.

The scream came a third time, a hideous, guttural sound, full of agony. Daphne squeezed her crucifix briefly with her pudgy fingers, then took several deep breaths and began to rock herself from side to side, trying to gain enough momentum to swing her purple-blotched, elephantine legs to the floor.

She was a large lady with bad hips, a weak heart and poor circulation, and rising from her bed was not a simple task. At last, however, she managed it, and fumbling open the drawer of her bedside table, she groped inside for the small torch she kept there. Using its narrow beam of light, she fed herself two aspirin from the blister pack she kept on her bedside table, washing them down with a mouthful of bottled water. That done, she reached for the stick propped against the wall at the head of the bed and used it to raise herself into a standing position.

Since that last terrible scream perhaps a minute ago there had been nothing but silence. Although it was hard to tell where the scream had originated, Daphne was almost certain it had come from the McGregors' room, farther down the corridor. There were only two occupied rooms aside from her own on the ground floor, and one of those belonged to Brian West, who was in his old room, way down at the opposite end of the corridor, close to the headmistress's office. The room occupied by the McGregors (who had been forced to move out of their cottage in the school grounds) was just a few doors down on Daphne's right. Of course the upper levels of the castle were also occupied, but the staircases were steep and the walls thick and she doubted whether a sound from up there would have been loud enough to have woken her.

Shining her torch along the corridor, Daphne saw that the McGregors' door was ajar. However, although her heart was pumping madly, she could honestly claim that she wasn't *frightened* by what she had heard. She was concerned for Jean, certainly, but she felt comforted, as ever, by the presence of her Lord. As she puffed her way closer to the McGregors' door, she thought steadfastly, *Yea, though I walk through the Valley of the Shadow of Death* . . .

She was a few feet from the partly open door when she became aware of a faint sound coming from beyond it. It was a hissing; no, more of a *fizzing*. Rather like the sound of soluble painkillers dropped into a glass of water, or chips into a deep fat fryer.

"Jean?" Daphne ventured. "Are you there, dear? I heard you cry out."

There was no response but the peculiar fizzing noise. With the fist that was holding the torch, Daphne pushed open the door.

The thin torch beam sidled around the edge of the gap and probed into the room ahead of her. The beam seemed drawn to the bed, which was where the fizzing was coming from. There was something there all right, but at first Daphne could make neither head nor tail of it. It was blackish and big, like an inky shadow that had come alive, and it seemed to glow, but also to bounce light away from it at the same time. Although she had never seen one, Daphne had no doubt that this creature, this abomination, was what her fellow survivors referred to as a slug. They professed not to know where these horrors came from, but Daphne had no doubt at all. A creature such as this could only have been sent by the Dark One himself. She looked around for Jean and then, with a jolt that sent her heart into wild and chaotic arrhythmia, she saw a pair of blood-streaked legs jutting from what she could only assume was the creature's maw.

The legs jerked, shedding droplets of blood, which sprayed through the funnel of her torch beam like a scattering of tiny jewels. White feet waggled obscenely at her; Daphne clearly saw blood dripping from the ragged yellowed end of a toenail. Then, with an awful crunching of bones, she saw one of the feet swivel around, so that it was facing in the opposite direction to its twin.

The haphazard booming of Daphne's heart grew louder, filling her head. Her eyelids fluttered and she became aware of the sensation of falling, and then of a thump that seemed both jarring and distant. When her eyes drifted open again, she was vaguely surprised to find herself lying on her back. She was equally surprised to see a dark ovoid rising into her frame of vision, a blot of darkness that she realized was a head, attached to which, presumably, was a face, peering down at her.

Aware that she was still holding her torch, she shone it onto the face and saw that it belonged to Andy Poole. She tried to speak his name, but couldn't get the words past the bludgeoning cacophony of her heart, which had become so loud that it seemed to fill every hollow and vessel of her body.

Perhaps Andy *had* heard her, though, because he was grinning. Daphne tried to smile at him, but then noticed that blue sparks were dancing around his teeth. An instant later the sparks zigzagged from his mouth, tracing spidery lines of icy light across his face. His skin turned ashen and then dark, like a photo negative. As she heard the fizzing sound again, Daphne used the last of her strength to grasp the tiny silver crucifix at her throat and hold it up towards the creature that Andy Poole was becoming.

Her lips moved, mouthing words that her failing heartbeat prevented her from hearing: *Get thee behind me, Satan. . . .*

THIRTY-NINE

Libby and Moira met in the corridor. Moira normally wore her mousey hair pulled back from her sharply boned face in a tight ponytail, but now it was loose and tousled, which made her look softer, more feminine. Her pale eyes were wide with the startled expression of someone who had just jumped straight out of bed, but despite appearances Libby knew the Irish woman was anything but a helpless female.

"Hi. You okay?" Libby asked.

Moira gave a swift nod. "You got your gun and your rucksack?"

Libby nodded, tapping her gun pocket with her torch and holding up her empty rucksack at the same time.

"Come on then, let's fill these and go get the kiddies," Moira said in her broad accent.

As Steve had promised, a dozen petrol bombs had been left behind for the girls. They were standing upright in a cardboard box against the wall in Sue's room. As they loaded up their backpacks, Moira said, "We should give the matches to the kids. Then if we do meet a slug they can light the bombs as we grab 'em."

Libby hauled her rucksack onto her back and smiled wryly. "I thought as a parent you were supposed to tell your kids *not* to play with matches?"

"So y'are," said Moira, "but that's only if you're not setting fire to a big fecking monster."

Libby laughed and they moved along the corridor towards the head of the stairs. They were almost there when someone below started screaming.

It was an awful sound, high-pitched and ragged. "That's one of the girls," Moira said, and broke into a run.

Libby had momentarily frozen, but now she forced her legs to move and followed Moira. The screaming continued as the two women pounded down the wide staircase, the bottles in their packs jangling. Mixed in with the screams were other voices. Libby clearly heard Abby yell, *"Let her go! Leave her alone!"*

As they reached the foot of the stairs, they heard a gunshot, then another, and seconds later, a third. The two women ran along the corridor, torch beams jolting ahead of them, towards the open door of the younger girls' dormitory.

They burst in, the white cones of their torch beams leaping crazily into the room. Libby's beam picked out Abby. She was standing on Portia's unmade bed, dressed in a long gray T-shirt and underpants. Portia was behind her in a pair of yellow pajamas, crouching on the floor, clinging on to Abby's ankle. Abby was pointing her gun at the fully transformed alien on the far side of the room, which was absorbing the little blond girl, Victoria.

The bottom half of Victoria had disappeared into the jagged black space in the center of the creature. Her top half, and the bed from which she had evidently been plucked, was covered in blood, but horribly she was still alive. She was no longer screaming, but her mouth, drooling blood, was opening and closing, as if she were impersonating a goldfish. Her eyes were bulging, as though about to burst from their sockets; the left one was full of blood.

Libby took all this in within seconds, and then she became

aware that Abby was swinging towards her, leveling her gun. Libby realized that she and Moira must be nothing but black shapes behind the dazzling whirl of their torch beams.

"It's us, Abby!" Libby shouted. "Don't shoot!"

Abby's eyes were wild, and Libby thought for a terrible second that she was too far gone to listen. She was bracing herself for the bullet when Abby lowered the gun. In fact, her shoulders slumped, her arms came down and the gun slipped from her grasp and bounced once on the bed before coming to rest.

With no preamble, Moira crossed to the bed, picked up the gun, turned and fired at the creature. Unused to the recoil, her first shot went wild, thwacking into the wall, and she grunted in surprise. She advanced a couple of steps, shone her torchlight directly onto Victoria's bloated face, and aimed the gun again. This time when she fired, the top of the little girl's head ripped away in a lumpy splash of red. What remained flopped forward, blood and brains leaking from the hole in her shattered skull.

Libby felt faintness wash over her, and she stumbled backwards and plumped onto her ass. Abby dropped to her knees on the bed and tried to scream, but could produce nothing but a high-pitched wheeze. Still training her torch on the creature, Moira lowered the gun and turned to face her companions.

"I had to," she said. "I couldn't let the wee thing suffer any more."

Libby nodded, still trying to fight the swimming sensation in her head, and swung her rucksack from her back. She placed it on the floor between her knees, pulled it open with shaking hands and lifted out one of the bottles. Moira swiftly followed suit, putting her rucksack on the edge of Portia's bed. As she pulled on the cord, she glanced at Abby.

"Listen, sweetheart," she said, "go into your room and get dressed. Take Portia with you. Try and find something to keep her warm."

Abby looked at Moira as if she didn't understand what the Irishwoman was saying. But then she gave a quick nod and led Portia from the room.

Libby took deep breaths to fight off the dizziness in her head. She had risen to a kneeling position now, and was un-screwing the cap on what had once been a bottle of elder-berry cordial. Warily eyeing the creature on the other side of the room, she hissed, "Why's it just sitting there?"

"Maybe Abby injured it," Moira said.

"Or maybe it's digesting its meal," said Libby.

"Wonder where Marcie is," Moira said.

"Maybe she escaped. Or maybe that thing ate her too."

"Or maybe," said Moira, "that thing *is* her."

"What if—" Libby said, and then the creature began to move.

Fizzing and crackling, it rolled towards them. In motion the creature was even harder to focus on than usual. It ap-peared to leave a series of fading afterimages as it flowed across the room.

"Fuck!" Moira shouted.

Libby leaped to her feet, instinctively switching the bottle to her right hand and drawing back her arm.

Seeing what she was doing, Moira tossed her torch onto the bed and delved into her pocket for matches. She had the box in her hand even as Libby dashed her bottle to the ground a meter or two in front of the advancing creature. The bottle hit the carpet and bounced, petrol sloshing out of it—though to Libby's horror, it didn't break. A split second later Moira threw her own bottle down, and whether by luck or design, it hit Libby's bottle, causing both of them to shatter in a spray of glass and petrol. The creature flowed over the broken glass just as Moira scraped a fistful of matches down the side of the box. The creature was less than five meters away when she flung her handful of flaming matches at the crackling blue-black mass.

Libby was scooping up her rucksack when, suddenly and spectacularly, the creature became a sheet of flame. For an in-stant it seemed to shrivel into itself, and then it began to shud-der and thrash about, hurling itself this way and that, as though attempting to shrug off the fire that engulfed it. In the enclosed space the stink of the burning creature was awful, and within a couple of seconds the two women were choking on thick black billows of rubbery smoke. As the creature ricocheted off beds and walls, it left black burning smears of itself behind.

Moira tugged at Libby's sleeve as a bed erupted into flame. "Come on," she shouted above the tortuous squeals of the creature, "let's go."

Libby was already on her way out, but had stooped to grab a pair of Converse trainers from the floor at the foot of Portia's bed. Taking one last look at the dying alien, she followed Moira from the room, slamming the door behind her.

FORTY

There was blood up the walls, across the bed, on the carpet. Steve looked around in disbelief. It was as if someone had come into Brian's room with buckets of the stuff, intending to cause as much mess as possible. He spotted Brian's specs on the bedside table; there was blood on them too. Some of the streaks on the carpet were already drying to a black crust.

"Nothing we can do here," Max said dully.

Steve nodded. Even with the stench of the burning alien still in his nostrils, he could smell the blood; it was meaty and coppery, and it turned his stomach.

He followed Max from the room and the two of them jogged down the corridor to check on Daphne McIntee and Jean McGregor. A quick sweep with the torch revealed the older woman's room to be empty. Any hopes she might still be alive, however, were dashed when they entered the McGregors' room. There was even more blood in here than there had been in Brian's, and it seemed to be concentrated in two areas—on the bed and on the carpet by the door. Lying in the blackening blood on the floor was a walking cane with a black plastic handgrip.

"Fucker got them all, didn't it?" Max muttered.

"Looks like it," said Steve, sickened. "Come on, let's get up that tower."

"At least we got the cunt," Max said, as the two of them hurried back towards the door that led out into the courtyard.

"Yeah, but there may be others," said Steve.

"I know it," said Max. "It's like on *The X-Files*. We can't trust no one now—except each other."

It was an awful thought. Assuming they survived this, how long would it be before Steve was able to look at his children again without suspicion? And what about Libby? Could he sleep in the same bed as someone who he couldn't be *entirely* sure wasn't some alien predator in disguise?

After Sue's death, Steve and Max had discovered that not only were the main doors to the castle unlocked, but also that all the padlocks and keys that had previously secured them were now nowhere to be found. Additionally, the huge top and bottom bolts had been ripped clean from the wood, which effectively meant that the castle was now defenseless. The two of them had briefly discussed building a barricade, but had quickly come to the conclusion that the idea was impractical. In the end they had decided that the best solution was simply to round up as many of their fellow survivors as they could and head for the helicopter.

They exited the block of buildings housing the now empty staff quarters and moved back out into the open. Despite the incessant drizzle, the stink of cooked alien was still heavy on the air, and ash still swirled like black snow among the silver raindrops. Glancing left and right, Steve and Max moved across the small cobbled square towards the arch that led into the larger area of the main courtyard. Steve was in the lead, torch in one hand and his Glock in the other.

Suddenly he stopped. "Listen," he said.

Max halted by his shoulder. They both heard it—a faint but telltale fizzing sound coming from the courtyard ahead.

"It's one of them, isn't it?"

Steve nodded. "Grab a bottle out of my rucksack."

He felt Max unbuckling the top flap and tugging at the cords of his rucksack. But before the younger man could even reach in for a bottle the fizzing sound abruptly increased and the crackling blue-black mass of an alien appeared in the archway.

Steve and Max backed up, leveling their guns. For the next few seconds the night air rang with the echoing din of gunfire. The alien shuddered under the barrage of bullets, but continued to move forward, forcing the two men back.

"There's another one!" Max yelled.

Directly behind the alien that was taking most of their flak they could see another of the creatures.

"This is hopeless," Steve shouted, lowering his gun.

"Let's torch the bastards!" said Max.

"We haven't got time. Come on, back this way."

Together the two men retreated, forced back in the direction from which they had come. Inexorably, like shapeless, shambling masses of negative energy, the creatures now swarming into the castle through the open main doors flowed after them.

FORTY-ONE

Adam cautiously made his way through the castle corridors. Five minutes after saying *au revoir* to the others, he had heard gunfire—at least half a dozen shots, maybe more. A couple of minutes after that he had heard *further* gunfire, closer this time, perhaps only a couple of floors below. Which could only mean that the aliens, or slugs, or whatever you wanted to call the vile buggers, had finally managed to breach their defenses.

Now that it had actually happened, Adam couldn't help thinking there had been a whiff of inevitability about it from the start. They must all have been crackers (himself included) if they had honestly thought they could stay here indefinitely, ensconced within their magical kingdom.

Ah well, he thought, it was fun while it lasted. But what was it they said? Onward and upward. Literally, in fact, if he could make it to the copter without being gobbled up by some ghastly monster en route.

It was funny in a way, because although he felt distanced from the firecrackers below, there was a part of Adam that genuinely *wanted* to be down there in the thick of the action. There was, after all, something to be said for standing shoulder

to shoulder with his friends, fighting for the right to survive—
besides which, it was bloody creepy up here on his own. It was
quiet, and there were great long shadows all over the place, and
he kept thinking some horrible beastie was going to jump out
at him. He wasn't generally the sort of chap to suffer from the
heebie-jeebies, but it was different when the monsters were
actually *real*. Even having a torch wasn't much of a blessing.
All right, so without it he would have been as blind as a bat,
but on the other hand it made him a sitting target; in fact,
rather than creeping about, he might just as well have been
wearing a luminous suit and announcing his whereabouts
through a megaphone.

The route he was taking to the Watch Tower was convo-
luted (Jean McGregor had described it as being "all up hill
and down dale"). It involved working his way along various
corridors, up a couple of staircases and even through several
rooms, all of which would eventually bring him to a long
stretch of corridor known as the Whispering Walk. At the end
of this corridor was a section of curved wall inset with a
wooden door, which opened directly onto the halfway point
of the Watch Tower's spiral staircase. Adam knew the route by
heart; he had walked it regularly, in preparation for such an
eventuality as this.

He was currently about halfway to the tower and, despite
all the commotion below, had not yet encountered a soul. *So
far so good,* he thought, creeping up a narrow flight of stairs
and entering what had probably once been a bedchamber, but
had now been converted into an IT suite, complete with
ranks of now obsolete computers. Looking at them, gathering
dust, their screens a pearly gray in the light from his torch,
Adam felt a brief pang for his old life. He wondered what had
happened to his girlfriend, Lisa. No doubt drowned along
with almost everyone else he had ever known. He quashed
the thought. In general he was a pragmatic man who coped
the best he could with whatever life threw at him, and who
tried not to dwell on his failures and disappointments. *Onward
and upward,* he thought again, passing through the IT suite,

and opening the door in the opposite wall onto yet another red-carpeted corridor.

Sweeping his torch side to side to satisfy himself nothing was lurking in the shadows, Adam turned left. The wall on his left-hand side was inset with doors at regular intervals. On the sections of wall between the doors was a series of Gothic-looking portraits, all murky browns and forbidding expressions. To Adam's right was a thick outer wall occupied by wide, evenly spaced windows in deeply recessed alcoves. Curtains were pulled across each of the alcoves, and it occurred to Adam that the deep, wide windowsills provided ample space for someone to hide. He glanced nervously at each one as he walked by, half expecting the curtain to suddenly billow out and something to leap at him. His rifle was over his shoulder, and he wondered whether he ought to carry it, ready to fire, just in case. He was still wondering when he heard a creak from the far end of the corridor.

Instantly he switched off his torch and pressed himself against the wall on his left. There was a wavering light up ahead, splashed across the wall like an elongated moon where the corridor took a sharp turn to the right. It was evidently torchlight, and whoever was casting it was maybe halfway along the next corridor, heading in Adam's direction. It crossed Adam's mind to call out, but then he decided it was best for now to keep a low profile. Even if this did turn out to be someone he knew (and Adam assumed they had made it up here via the courtyard), how would he know it was really them? For that matter, how would he know whoever made it to the helicopter was the genuine article? The simple answer was, he wouldn't. He would just have to play it by ear.

Thinking quickly, he darted across the corridor to one of the alcoves. He fumbled with the long curtain in the dark, searching for the opening in the center. After a moment of panic he found it and slipped through the gap. A little hampered by his gun and rucksack, he clambered onto the knee-high windowsill, trying to be as quiet as possible. He crouched there in the dark, facing the back of the curtain, trying to breathe as shallowly as he could. It was dusty in the recess, and he felt a desperate urge to clear his throat. It would be typical, he thought, if he did that clichéd thing of sneezing as the newcomer walked past.

For perhaps thirty seconds it was pitch-black, and then Adam saw the faintest glimmer beyond the curtain. The glimmer became brighter as the figure approached. Adam held his breath, listening to the pad of footsteps, the occasional creak of a carpeted floorboard. When the beam of the torch swept directly across his hiding place, he couldn't help but hunch his shoulders. The involuntary movement caused the gun to shift on his back, its butt tapping the windowsill. Adam winced. It had only been a gentle tap. Maybe whoever was out there hadn't heard it.

There was a moment of silence—and then the curtains were yanked back and a torch was shone full in his face.

He threw up his hands, dazzled. He couldn't remember ever feeling more scared or helpless.

Then the figure behind the torch said, "I thought you'd be around here somewhere."

Adam squinted, but the light of the torch was still blinding him. "Who are you?" he said.

"It's me," the figure said, sounding surprised that he had to ask. "It's Dylan."

FORTY-TWO

"Which way?" Libby said.

Moira flashed her torch up the corridor. At the far end was the beginning of a curving staircase, the first three steps fanning out from the central spindle like overlapping wedges of cake before disappearing around the corner.

"I think we go up there and turn left."

"You *think?*" said Libby. "Don't you *know?*"

Moira glared at her. "Don't *you?*"

"You've been here longer than I have."

"That doesn't mean I know the place like the back o' me hand, though, does it?"

"Please," said Abby, "don't argue." Her voice sounded tired and strained. As instructed by Moira, she had rushed back to her room and dressed in double-quick time, dragging on jeans, sweater, jacket, socks and boots. Portia was less ideally clothed, in Abby's blue hoodie, which came to her knees, over her yellow pajamas. At least, though, thanks to Libby's foresight, she had shoes on her feet.

After checking the boys' rooms, and finding no sign of them, the four girls had headed upwards, trying to remember

the route that led to the tower. It hadn't seemed too complicated in the daylight, but at night it was a different matter. It
made Libby realize how little of the castle they utilized, how
much of it remained abandoned on a daily basis.

"I think Moira's right," Abby said. "I think we go up that
staircase. At the top I think there's a sort of hall, and then another corridor where the IT suite is. This is like the back way
to it, which we never used, did we, Portia?"

Portia looked at her solemnly and shook her head, though
Libby got the impression the younger girl had not even heard
the question.

They hurried along the landing and up the staircase, torches
in their left hands, guns in their right. Moira still had posses-
sion of Abby's gun. When the women had met up with the
girls in the corridor, Moira had offered her gun back to her,
but Abby had told her to keep it.

At the top of the staircase was what might once have been a
baronial hall, just as Abby had said. It had a wooden floor and a
huge fireplace at the far end and there was an impressive collection of shields and swords and medieval breastplates on the
right-hand wall, which reflected their torchlight in steely
flashes. There was a long table, with perhaps two dozen chairs
arranged around it, in the center of the room. It was difficult to
imagine what the hall had been used for prior to the flood—a
boardroom, perhaps?

They were hurrying across the hall towards the door in the
far corner, their feet clomping on the floorboards, when a
croaking voice shouted, "Mum."

They whirled in unison. The voice had come from a particularly dense clump of shadow at the base of the wall beyond the central table. It was only when they shone their
torches upon it that they realized the shadow was in fact a
crumpled figure. Now, in the harsh light, they could see its
white face, the eyes screwed up and blinking, and the hand
reaching out to them. And they could see the blood, which
the figure wore like a glistening bib on the chest of its black
hooded jacket.

"Oh my God," Moira gasped, and stumbled towards the figure. "Oh, sweet Jesus, Andy, what happened to you?"

Andy Poole tried to rise. He grimaced, and they saw he had blood on his teeth too.

"It was Dylan," he said weakly. "He attacked me."

"Dylan?" repeated Abby. "No . . . why?"

Andy glanced in her direction, but his eyes were glazed. "He's one of them. He went for me. I managed to fight him off. I came up here and hid."

Abby was shaking her head. "No," she said in a tiny voice, "not Dyl. He can't be."

Moira ran over and crouched beside her son. It wasn't until she reached towards him that she seemed to realize her hands were already occupied. She put her torch and gun on the floor and tried again, reaching towards his blood-soaked jacket to unzip it, assess the damage. In one fluid movement Andy sat up and shoved her hard in the chest. Even as she was rolling over backwards, he snatched up the gun and shot her in the face.

Moira's feet jerked wildly for a moment and then the life went out of her. Andy raised the gun again, but Libby, astonished by her own reflexes, shot him in the chest. He made an *urk* sound and the gun flew out of his hand.

"Grab it!" screamed Libby, but Abby didn't need telling. She went for the gun like a cricketer diving full-length to take a catch. Andy was already beginning to transform, sparks fizzing and flickering around his darkening face. Libby shot him twice more, and then Abby, her gun back in her hand, pumped several more bullets into the writhing form.

Libby grabbed Abby's gun arm. "We need to burn it before it can get up," she shouted.

Abby nodded, but even as the two of them were reaching towards their rucksacks, there was a familiar fizzing noise from the far side of the room. Portia screamed as a fully-formed creature came sliding through the door they had recently entered.

"Run!" Libby yelled, and turned towards the far door.

Abby fired once at the new arrival, and then she grabbed Portia's hand and the three of them ran for their lives.

FORTY-THREE

Steve and Max ran back into the wing of the castle that housed the administration offices and staff quarters. Steve was trying to work out how they could escape, where they could go. This building was pretty much a sealed unit. As far as he knew there were no secret doors or hidden staircases leading into other parts of the castle. The upper floors could only be accessed via what had now become the no-go area of the courtyard.

Thinking furiously, he shoved open the door of the former head teacher's office. Max, who had been about to run straight past, skidded to a halt.

"What you doing, man? Those fuckers are right behind us. We can't hide in here."

"We're not going to hide," Steve panted.

"What we gonna do then?"

"Jump out the window."

Max looked at him for an instant as if he were crazy, then gave an abrupt nod. "Okay."

There were two windows at the back of the room—thankfully not the narrow archways that proliferated in most parts of the castle, but wide square modern windows that let in plenty of light during the day.

"Aw, man, they're locked," Max moaned, trying them both.

"Stand back." Steve picked up the heavy swivel chair under the desk and hurled it at the left-hand window. The explosion of shattering glass momentarily drowned out the angry fizzing of their pursuers. The chair went through the window, trailing chunks of frame and glass fragments. Max began to bash out the last potentially lethal jags of glass and spars of wood with the butt of his rifle, whilst Steve swung his rucksack from his back and grabbed a petrol bomb.

"You get out!" he yelled. "I'll slow them down!"

Max shone his torch out the window, drizzle falling across the beam. "It's a fucking long drop."

Steve was moving across to the door, bottle in hand. "But we're on the ground floor."

"Yeah, but there's a dip and, like, a banking. There used to be a moat out there, remember. Must be . . . twenty feet down, at least."

Steve was at the door now, pulling it open. "What do you want, a ladder? It's either jump or engage these guys in hand to hand combat."

"Yeah, I know, man, it's just . . . aw, fuck," Max said and climbed onto the windowsill.

Steve never saw him jump. He was preoccupied with the creatures flowing up the corridor towards him, filling it from side to side. It was impossible to tell how many there were. Trying to focus on them for too long hurt his eyes.

He had left his torch and gun on the desk to avoid having to juggle too many items at once. Trying to stop his hands from shaking, he lit the taper of cloth drooping from the neck of the bottle and hurled it at the wall a couple of feet in front of the advancing aliens.

It shattered, dousing the creatures in liquid fire. As one they shrank back, shriveling into themselves. Clots of flaming petrol landed on the carpet and began to burn merrily. For maybe half a second Steve considered lighting another bomb, then decided he had bought himself as much time as he could reasonably expect. He turned back into the room and ran to the window, snatching up his torch and gun as he passed. Flurries of wind and rain were blowing in through the jagged-edged hole, making the curtains billow and flap. Steve shone his torch into the darkness. Shit, Max had been right. It *was* a long drop.

He picked out Max, lying on the damp grass a little way up the banking. He was on his back, his rucksack on the ground to his left, his gun within reach of his right hand. He didn't seem interested in picking it up, however. His face was creased in agony.

"You okay?" Steve shouted.

"Fucked my leg." Max's voice was high and breathy, almost a scream.

Steve redirected his torch and his stomach turned over. Though the light was diffused, he could see the teenager's left leg below the knee was soaked in blood. And tearing a hole in his combats was what appeared to be a sharp white stick, but was almost certainly a bone.

Compound fracture, Steve thought. *Oh fuck, oh fuck.* What chance did Max have now? What chance did *either* of them have? Because he sure as hell wasn't leaving the poor kid on his own.

"I'm coming down!" he shouted, and before he could dwell on Max's injury any longer he climbed onto the sill and jumped. He felt a moment of exhilarating terror as the ground rushed at him. Then he hit the banking and tried not to brace his legs as Max must have done, tried to let them crumple beneath him, carry his momentum into a sideways roll.

He overcompensated slightly and felt himself tumbling head over heels down the hill, the bottles clashing and sloshing in his rucksack, a hard edge of glass occasionally slamming into the muscles of his back or whacking into his spine, though thankfully—as far as he could tell—not breaking.

He dug heels and elbows into the ground, trying to slow himself down, terrified that if he carried on he would smash into the castle wall below and end up with his brains spattered all over the ancient stonework. At last he managed it and slithered to a halt, bruised and battered, but more or less intact.

Dazed, he rose to his feet and staggered back up the banking. He was not only grimy with sweat and ash now, but also caked with mud. Max's breathing was loud and fast, and in the light from Steve's torch, which (unlike Max's) had mercifully survived its impact with the ground, Steve saw the boy's hands opening and closing, his fingers digging deep into the soft earth.

"Hey, mate," he said softly, dropping to his knees on the grassy slope beside Max, "how you doing?"

"Not good," Max said. His face was drenched with sweat, and there was a grayish tinge to his dark skin.

Steve looked around. They were in the shadow of the castle. The top of the slope was still a dozen feet above them. It was not a good position as far as potential rescue was concerned.

"We've got to get onto flat ground, otherwise the helicopter won't see us to pick us up. Which means I'm going to have to carry you or drag you. Okay?"

Max's eyes were rolling. "Just leave me, man," he gasped.

"Yeah, like that's gonna happen. If I leave you, I'll feel a shit for the rest of my life—and I'm sure you wouldn't want *that* on your conscience."

Max tried to smile, but managed no more than a grimace. "No way," he muttered. "Your happiness is important to me."

Steve patted his cheek. Though Max's skin was boiling hot, the boy was beginning to shiver. As carefully as he could, Steve slid his right arm under Max's legs, his left around Max's waist. "Okay, big feller, here goes. I'm afraid this is probably going to hurt a bit. Can you put your arm over my shoulders?"

Max did so.

Steve counted to three, then lifted. Max's grip on his shoulder suddenly became so tight that Steve knew he'd have bruises there the next morning—if he lived that long. Max didn't quite faint, but his eyes rolled back in his head and he made an awful, almost animal-like moaning sound.

"Hang on in there," Steve muttered, feeling a little faint himself as Max's splintered tibia thrust farther up through the material of his trousers. He carried Max up the banking, only managing to avoid dropping him through willpower alone. At last, however, they were at the top of the slope, on what might once have been a sports field. Steve walked maybe another thirty yards, then sank to his knees, lowering Max gently to the muddy ground.

Max was only semiconscious now, muttering incoherently. His eyelids fluttered as if he were desperately trying to remain conscious. Steve felt like lying on the cool grass himself. How nice it would be to close his eyes and drift off. Just for five minutes. But of course he couldn't. Very faintly he heard the unmistakable fizzing sound of the aliens. They were out there somewhere, in the darkness. He wondered whether they were aware of himself and Max. He wondered how they hunted, what senses they employed to pinpoint their prey. Could they see the light of his torch? Smell Max's blood? Detect the vibration of their movements? There was so much he didn't know about them, so much that mankind had to learn, to understand—not that it was likely they would ever get the opportunity to do so.

"I'm just going for the gear. Back in two ticks," he said to Max, and ran back across the grass in a half crouch, shining his torch ahead of him. The fizzing seemed to be coming from all around him, though as yet there were still no aliens in sight.

As he gathered up the rucksacks and Max's gun he decided that if worst came to worst he would put a bullet through Max's head and then his own. Better that than to be gobbled up alive by the intergalactic equivalent of a great white shark.

For one jolting moment when he got back, Steve thought that Max was already dead. The teenager was motionless, his eyes half-open, a crust of dried foam on his lips. . . .

Then he jerked, and swallowed whatever was in his throat with a gulp, and—though he knew how ludicrous it was under the circumstances—Steve felt a surge of relief. Deciding that the only remotely useful thing to do was prepare their meager defenses as best he could, he squatted beside Max and opened the teenager's rucksack.

"Shit," he muttered, shining his torch onto the heap of shattered glass sloshing around in several inches of petrol. He lifted the rucksack up. He hadn't noticed before, but petrol was leaking out through the bottom in a steady trickle. He looked at the escaping liquid in despair—and then he had an idea. He grabbed a bottle (all but one of which were still remarkably intact) from his own rucksack, pulled the material plug from the neck and lifted Max's rucksack again, holding his bottle underneath, so that the escaping petrol trickled into it.

Taking a quick look round, he ran across the grass until he was twenty yards from where Max was lying. Only then did he remove the bottle from beneath the stream of petrol, allowing the liquid to trickle freely. He began to walk around Max in a wide circle, drizzling petrol as he went. Eventually the stream from the rucksack slowed, turned to drips and then dwindled to nothing. Steve gave the rucksack a final shake—scattering the last drops of fuel and jangling the slurry of broken glass inside—and dumped it on the ground. He continued walking in a circle, now pouring petrol from the bottle. When that too was empty, he ran back across to his own rucksack and grabbed two more. Five minutes later all the petrol he and Max possessed had been poured onto the grass.

Dropping the last bottle on the ground, Steve took his torch and gun from his jacket. He shone his torch around, trying to locate the source of the faint crackling. Was it his imagination or could he see blue-white glints concealed within the silvery veils of rain? He had the impression the creatures were massing out there in the blackness, just out of range of his torch beam. He shivered, and pushed grimy clumps of hair out of his eyes. Standing beside Max's deflated rucksack, he wondered whether pouring the last of their petrol on the ground had been such a good idea. Maybe the fuel would evaporate, or soak into the earth, or become so diluted that it would not catch fire. Or maybe it would only burn for a moment, then peter out.

The fizzing was getting louder now, and seemed to be coming from somewhere over to his left. Was something moving out there, a bulk blacker than the screen of trees on the perimeter of the playing fields? He dropped his gun back into his jacket pocket and fumbled for his matches. He felt sick with anticipation, exposed out here in the open.

All at once he smelled smoke and turned to look behind him. The castle was on fire, yellow-white forks of flame rising from some unspecified area towards the rear of the structure, stabbing at the night. He thought of the petrol bomb he had thrown in the corridor leading to the head teacher's office. Surely it hadn't caught so quickly? Then he thought of Libby and Abby, and remembered that they had petrol bombs too. The prospect that they had been forced to use them made his stomach clench.

As though agitated by the drifting smoke, the fizzing took on a more urgent tone. Steve turned back to face the rain-flecked darkness—and suddenly he could see them, the aliens, the slugs, moving forward in a wave, shedding light that was simultaneously an absence of light, cloaked in a wave of energy that was impossible to ignore and equally impossible to focus upon.

Trying to stay calm, he lit a match, hoping the rain wouldn't douse it. As a bud of flame appeared, he glanced once more at the mass of energy bearing down on him (and received a fleeting image of jagged and overlapping black shapes moving like loose scales or a mass of pecking beaks); then he stepped back, stretched out his arm and dropped the match.

It hit the rucksack and tumbled down its side to land on the grass below. Though it remained alight, nothing happened, and for a moment Steve felt a wave not so much of despair but of regret, of shame even for not having provided his injured friend with better protection. He glanced back at Max, as if to apologize for his failure—and the rucksack soundlessly bloomed with flame. So quickly that Steve registered it as no more than an impression, the fire ignited the petrol and spread outwards in both directions, burning first with a delicate blue flame, and then with a fiercer white one.

Steve walked back a few steps, then turned and jogged over to Max. Despite the wet grass, he sat cross-legged beside the unconscious teenager, trying not to look at the spike of white bone protruding from the tear in his blood-soaked combats. The ring of fire burned around them, feeding first on the fuel, then the grass and earth beneath. The ring maintained its integrity for perhaps a minute, and then—to Steve's horror—the flames began to die. Steve saw breaks appearing in the circle, saw licks of fire fizzling out, leaving nothing but patches of scorched earth and curls of oily black smoke.

"This is it, Max," he murmured as the fizzing of the encircling aliens reached a new pitch. He tightened his grip on his gun and waited for the end.

FORTY-FOUR

Portia had almost fallen twice—unable to match the longer strides of Abby, whose hand she was clutching—and had had to be literally yanked back to her feet. Because of this, the aliens were still close behind them, no more than half the length of a corridor away. It might have been her imagination, but Abby thought that the fizzing sound they were making was hungrier, more eager than ever.

As if being chased by monsters wasn't stressful enough, Abby felt it her responsibility to ensure the three of them kept going in the right direction. It was her school, after all, but though she knew its layout pretty well, she had never run through its corridors at night, and certainly never in fear of her life. The place looked different in the dark, particularly as their torch beams made the walls sway and lurch like the inside of a funhouse. Trying to stay focused, she blurted instructions as they ran, knowing that if she made a mistake and they ended up running into a dead end, then that would be it. Game over.

When they rounded a corner into the Whispering Walk, therefore, and she saw the door in the curved wall at the end, she felt like sobbing with relief. Instead she yelled, "There it is!" and taking a renewed grip on Portia's hand, she put on a last burst of speed.

It was Libby, however, who reached the door first. Wrapping both hands around the brass doorknob, she clenched her teeth and gave it a twist. Nothing happened, and for a bone-freezing second Abby thought the door was locked—even though it was supposed to be kept *un*locked, for such an eventuality as this. Panic leaped into Libby's eyes, and she twisted harder—and suddenly, with a grinding *chunk,* the door swung open.

They filed through the gap, Abby tugging Portia behind her. She resisted looking over her shoulder, even though the crackling now seemed to be almost upon them. The immediate thing that struck her about the inside of the tower was how cold it was. Icy air swirled up the stairs, drying the sweat on Abby's body, making her shiver. She followed the beam of her torch onto the stone steps as Libby pulled the door shut with a boom, muffling the sounds of pursuit.

They pounded up the stairs, their feet slapping the worn steps. Abby's torchlight slid around the curved wall, rippling over the stone like a wave over shingle. Though the top of the tower was spacious enough to accommodate the helicopter, its walls were thick, which meant that the spiral stairs were tight and narrow. For this reason the three of them could see no farther than seven or eight steps ahead. Their echoing footsteps and amplified breath made it sound as though the tower was full of people. They had climbed no more than twenty steps when the fizzing of the aliens suddenly increased in volume, seeming to fill the air with static.

"They're in," Libby wailed, as if she had believed the door might have proved an effective barrier against them.

"Come on," Abby said, her voice booming, "we're almost there."

She only hoped, now that they had got this far, that Adam would be there too. If he wasn't they would be trapped on the roof with nowhere to go. What would they do then? Fight back until they had used up their bullets and petrol bombs, she supposed. She didn't want to consider what might happen beyond *that*.

Rounding the curve and seeing the little girl sitting half a dozen steps above her brought Abby up with a jolt. Her torch beam jerked across the girl's hunched figure and stricken face. The girl gave a squeal of terror, scrunched up her eyes and buried her face in her hands.

"Marcie!" Libby blurted, pushing past Abby and Portia and climbing a step closer to the girl.

Portia spoke for the first time since Libby and Moira had burst into the girls' dormitory. "That's *not* Marcie," she said, her voice low and fierce.

Libby glanced at her uncertainly. Below them the fizzing was getting louder. "How can you be sure?"

"Marcie's dead. That's one of those things, pretending to be her," Portia said.

Libby grabbed Portia's arm. Portia looked at Libby's hand encircling her wrist as if it were a curious bracelet.

"But did you *see* Marcie change?" she said. "Did you actually *see* it?" Her eyes flickered upwards, to Abby's face. "Did *you?*"

"No," Abby said. Portia shook her head dumbly, but she continued to glare at the girl on the stairs.

"But that's just it, isn't it? We can't be *sure*. How do we know Marcie didn't wake up, see what was happening to Victoria and simply run away?"

"She didn't," said Portia.

"But we can't be *sure*, can we? And for that reason we can't leave her behind."

The fizzing was reverberating all around them now. Any second Abby expected to see the flickering, jagged shape of an alien appearing around the curve behind them. Her gut instinct was to agree with Portia—she didn't think this *was* the real Marcie—but on the other hand, she understood Libby's dilemma. Because what if, against the odds, this *was* Marcie? What if Marcie *had* fled from the dormitory before Abby had got there, and what if she had worked her way through the castle to this point? And what if it was the echoing sound of their footsteps, or even the fizzing of the aliens, that had frozen the little girl in place, made her too terrified to climb any farther?

The fizzing was close behind them now. Abby couldn't think of anything else to do except take the risk and allow Marcie to accompany them. "Okay, bring her," she said to Libby, but just then Portia turned and pressed herself against Abby as if wanting a hug. Abby frowned. She understood Portia's need for reassurance, but there wasn't time for this now. And then Portia turned with the gun she had taken from Abby's jacket and she shot Marcie in the chest.

The bullet slammed into the little girl and flung her backwards. Her arms flew up and her chest erupted, blood splashing on the steps as she bounced back from the wall and crumpled forwards like a broken doll. She landed on the steps face-first, then slithered down several, leaving a trail of blood behind her. Libby looked down at the body for a second, then turned to Portia, her eyes and mouth stretched into such an expression of horror that it made her look ugly.

"What have you done?" she breathed. Her voice became shrill and chalky. *"What have you done?"*

Portia's face was composed. She handed the gun back to Abby, who took it dumbly.

"It wasn't her," she said.

There was fury in Libby's voice. "How do you *know?*"

"She's fully dressed," said Portia.

It took a moment for Abby to register the comment—and then she realized that what Portia had said was true. Marcie was wearing a sweater and a ski jacket, jeans, trainers, even socks. But if she had fled in terror she would have been wearing pajamas or a night shirt, and her feet would almost certainly have been bare.

"She's right!" she shouted, giving Libby a nudge. "Go on, get going!"

Libby looked bewildered, but she did as Abby said, delicately but swiftly stepping over the sprawled body of the dead girl, avoiding the streaks and splashes of blood. Portia pounded up behind her, and Abby, now clutching her gun instead of Portia's hand, brought up the rear—though this time not before taking a quick peek behind her.

The blue black mass of alien flesh (if it *was* flesh) was sliding around the curve of the stairs. If she had descended three steps she could have reached out and touched it. She saw its filaments waving like wheat in the breeze, shedding their strange nonradiant light; she caught the merest glimpse of beaks or mandibles or thick scales rippling, moving in tandem, and somehow *over* one another. And then, as though the alien and her own senses were like repelling magnets, she felt her vision being deflected away. For a moment her head felt muzzy, and then she blinked and shuddered and turned, all in the same movement. Skipping past the sprawled body of the creature that had been mimicking Marcie, she ran after Libby and Portia.

Abby heard it then—the sound she had been desperate to hear, the sound that meant there *was* hope, after all. It was the roar of the helicopter's engine, the whickering of its rotor blades. Despite the situation she felt a savage joy surge through her.

But . . . hang on . . . wasn't the sound moving away? Fading into the distance? "*No!*" she screamed, and though she wouldn't have thought it possible, she forced her legs to move faster. She shoved Portia in the back, and when the younger girl glanced back at her, fearful, even a little resentful, Abby screamed, *"It's going away! Listen! Adam's going without us!"*

Both Portia and Libby got the message. The three of them pounded up the last dozen steps, the beams of their torches again jolting and swooping ahead of them. Abby knew they were nearing the top when the steps became slippery with water. She glanced up, saw the opening ahead, the rain, the blackness of the night sky.

And then they were out on the flat roof of the tower.

And the helicopter was gone.

Abby could still hear it, though, somewhere above them.

"There!" Libby shouted, and pointed over Abby's shoulder. Abby spun round, saw the helicopter maybe a couple of hundred feet in the air. It was a vague outline, a dazzle of rain-blurred lights. It was circling the now-burning castle, its spotlight roaming over the stonework as though searching for survivors. She began to shout and wave her arms, to jump up and down, her rucksack—stuffed with her diary and whatever clothes she had been able to grab—jouncing on her back. Libby too began to leap and shout. Her rucksack clinked with the petrol-filled bottles it contained. The beams of both girls' torches cleaved the night sky, darting like birds, sparkling with rain.

Suddenly Portia screamed, and instantly Abby redirected her torch beam, following Portia's eye-line and illuminating a shadowy area on the far side of the tower's roof. Within a curtain of rain she saw yellow eyes flashing, saw the lean, muscled shapes of four . . . no, five black Dobermans creeping from the darkness which had concealed them. The Dobermans had their heads down, their hackles up, their jowls curled back to reveal long yellow teeth. They might have been snarling, but there was too much noise—from the helicopter, the rain, the pursuing aliens (now rising from the opening of the stairwell)—for her to tell.

As Portia cowered behind her, Abby pointed her gun and started firing. She hit one of the dogs with her first shot, which went down in a twitching, yelping heap. Her next two shots went wide, but by this time Libby was beside her and firing too. The dogs began to pick up speed, strings of drool trailing from their jaws. Libby hit one square on, and it gave a horribly human scream as it twisted in the air and crashed down on its back, limbs pedaling.

Portia, who had been clutching Abby's rucksack as though it were a shield, suddenly broke away in panic. Abby screamed her name as the girl ran towards the low crenellated wall at the edge of the roof. Portia ignored her, and Abby thought fleetingly of animals so terrified by pursuing predators that they would leap to their deaths from cliffs or other high places to evade capture. She felt her stomach tightening in anticipation of Portia doing exactly that, even briefly considered putting a bullet in her friend's leg to bring her down—but then, six feet from the edge of the roof, Portia slipped, her feet skidding from under her on the wet stone.

She went down face-first, though it was her hands, which she put out instinctively, which took the brunt of the impact. Abby imagined rather than heard the rough slap as they hit the ground—her ears were still full of the overhead roar of the helicopter, still ringing from the crashing din of gunfire. She saw one of the dogs veer towards Portia's prone body and raised her gun again. Knowing she had to make the bullet count, she took careful aim and fired. More by luck than judgment, she hit the dog broadside, just behind the shoulder. The impact, coupled with the animal's own momentum, took it right off the roof in a flailing mass of limbs.

Abby neither saw nor heard it hit the ground below. She was already running across the wet roof towards Portia. The girl was sobbing, hands and knees scraped and bloody, clothes filthy and wet. Abby fell to her knees beside her, then turned, anticipating the next attack.

It didn't come. The remaining two dogs had evidently decided to make Libby their primary target. Abby was just in time to see one of them leap through the air towards her. Before Libby could swing and fire her gun, the dog had closed its jaws on her arm, toppled her backwards with the weight of its body. Instantly both animals were upon her, snapping and biting, going for her face. Libby screamed and writhed, her arms windmilling as she fought them off. Just beyond her, almost looming over her, were the aliens, which had flowed out of the stairwell and now seemed to be spreading across the roof like a flickering, blue-black carpet of fuzzy static.

Abby didn't have time to think. She jumped to her feet and, screaming incoherently, ran back towards Libby and the dogs and the aliens, her gun clenched in both hands. There had been seventeen rounds in her pistol, but she had no idea how many were left. She ran up to one of the dogs and

kicked it as hard as she could in the ribs. It gave a surprised, almost indignant yelp and snarled at her. Abby saw it had blood
on its teeth; then she raised her gun and blew its head off.

The dog fell across Libby's body, spattering her with blood
and brain tissue. The other dog continued to savage her for a
second until Abby put her gun against its steaming flank and
pulled the trigger. The dog's spine and most of its hind-
quarters ripped away, and seemed to become instantly absorbed by the wall of alien flesh behind it. The front of the
dog looked almost surprised, its eyes widening and its tongue
unrolling from its blood-smeared jaws, before its remaining
legs gave way and it crumpled, shuddering, to the ground.

Libby, her arms still over her face, was shaking and sobbing.
She was covered in blood, but Abby couldn't tell how much
was hers and how much had come from the dogs. She saw the
sleeves of Libby's jacket were shredded and that there were
bite marks on her hands. She didn't have time to examine her
closely, however. The aliens were almost upon them. They
sounded like a swarm of bees, hovering just behind Abby's left
shoulder. She grabbed Libby's arms and attempted to pull
them away from her face. Libby screamed and tried to fight
her off.

"It's okay, Libby. It's me. It's Abby. We need to get away."

No sooner were the words out of her mouth than she felt
an odd sensation ripple through her. Her back and shoulders
felt suddenly cold, numb, and the world seemed to recede. For
a second or two the feeling was almost pleasant, like drifting
into sleep. But then she felt an uncomfortable dragging in her
shoulders, a dragging that quickly became a painful tightening, as if her flesh were being forced into too small a space. It
made her think of newspaper stories about people being
dragged into industrial machinery. She felt herself panicking
and tried to pull free, but her body was heavy, unresponsive.
Although she was still holding her gun, Abby found she could
no longer lift it. Indeed, her hand seemed far away, as if she
were looking at it through the wrong end of a telescope. Her
bones began to ache; she imagined them bending, straining. It

would surely be only a matter of seconds before they cracked and splintered. She tried to scream, but she couldn't make any sound. Far away, at the end of a long tunnel, she saw another hand reach out and tug the gun from her unresisting grip.

Then her head erupted with sound, a series of explosions that deafened her. For an instant the tension in her shoulders increased; she thought her spine would be ripped from her body. But immediately the feeling of pressure, of being dragged out of herself, lessened and she slumped forward. She felt faint and horribly sick. She lifted her head and vomited. She became aware that someone was tugging her arm, trying to drag her upright. She heard a voice, and though she knew the tone was urgent she couldn't make out the words. All she wanted was to sleep, to be left alone. But something—some nugget of self-preservation—made her force herself to her feet, stumble away on legs that felt boneless.

If she hadn't had help, however, she might not have managed it. For the first dozen steps she was in a daze, oblivious to her surroundings. It was the rain splashing on her face that revived her. She looked around and saw Portia on her left—wet and dirty, blood trickling from her grazed knees—and Libby on her right, sleeves in shreds, cuts on her face and hands, the front of her jacket covered in blood.

"What happened?" Abby asked. "I felt so . . . weird."

"It nearly got you," Portia said. "One of those things. It was pulling you in, but I shot it and it let go."

Abby reached out and grabbed Portia, drew her into a hug. "Thanks," she said. "You saved me."

"For now," Libby said, her voice strained and hollow.

Abby turned. They had put maybe twenty yards between themselves and the aliens, but there wasn't much farther to go. It was another ten yards to the edge of the roof and then that was it. Abby glanced around, still a little disorientated. The fire Libby and Moira had started in the girls' dormitory was spreading, flames devouring the rear section of the castle. Abby could smell the smoke and feel the gusts of heat. As for the helicopter, it was circling again, tilting in an arc that would bring it back in their direction. She wasn't sure whether Adam and whoever else he might have with him had seen them. They could only hope.

"We've got to hold them off as long as we can," she said, but Libby had already swung her rucksack off her back and was routing through it.

"Some of the bottles broke when the dogs knocked me over," she said. "There are only three left."

"One each then," said Abby, and thought, *Come as you are. Bring a bottle.*

Libby lifted out one of the bottles, dripping with petrol, and handed it to Abby, who passed it to Portia. Abby herself took the next one and Libby kept the last for herself. As Abby placed her bottle on the ground and reached in her pocket for matches, she realized that her hands were empty. A quick glance revealed that Portia was still holding her gun after shooting at the aliens with it, but as for her torch, Abby guessed she must have dropped it when the alien had tried to absorb her.

Praying that the matchbox wasn't too damp, she pulled it from her pocket and opened it. To her relief the match that she dragged down the side of the box flared immediately. Hand shaking, she used it to light the thick fuse of cloth protruding from the neck of Libby's bottle. Coated in petrol, the bottle became an instant fireball in Libby's hand.

"Fuck!" Libby shouted and hurled the bottle at the approaching aliens. It fell short, but smashed on the ground in a gout of flame. Portia held out her own bottle, her jaw clenched tight. Abby saw the angry determination on her face, and touched the still-burning match she held to the dangling cloth taper. Again the petrol coating the bottle caught fire, but despite the fact that her hand was gloved in flames, Portia calmly drew back her arm and threw her bottle as hard as she could. Trailing fire like a comet, it landed close to Libby's and shattered, spilling fiery nuggets as though they were precious stones.

Bracing herself, Abby picked up her own bottle and lit it

with the guttering match. Once more the entire bottle became a sudden and silent ball of flame. Surprised and relieved
that it wasn't as hot as she had anticipated, Abby threw the
missile and scored a direct hit, fire spilling down the buzzing,
flickering wave of alien flesh. The foremost alien (though she
couldn't honestly tell if it was one of many or whether the
army of creatures had now somehow coalesced to form a single vast entity) released a burbling electronic howl of pain and
distress, and flinched back, like a slug jabbed with a stick.

Abby knew the fire wouldn't burn for long, but at least it
would buy them a few more seconds. The blatting beat of the
helicopter blades was getting louder now. She saw the chopper swooping in low, and at such an angle that it now seemed
its occupants must have seen them. Though she was exhausted, and though her shoulders were burning where the
alien had latched onto her, she began to jump up and down
again, waving her arms frantically.

The spotlight of the helicopter swooped over her, blinding
her for a moment. When the glare passed, she saw someone
leaning out of the machine, which was now hovering less
than forty feet above them. With a sudden rush of joy she realized it was Dylan. He was holding something in his hand,
something that glittered. When the helicopter was directly
above the aliens, he let the glittering object go. Abby recognized it as a petrol bomb a split second before it landed
amongst the rippling blue-black mass and erupted into flame.

Instantly the aliens began to writhe and judder. Even
though they gave the impression of nothing so much as a
flickering, shapeless expanse of dark matter, Abby couldn't
help but think of a panicking crowd, targeted by gunmen or
fleeing from the effects of tear gas.

Dylan dropped another bottle, creating further agitation in
the ranks. Though it hurt her eyes, Abby forced herself to focus on the creatures, and saw them begin to flow, like thick
sludge down a drain, back into the staircase opening.

"They're retreating!" she screamed, jumping up and down.
"They're going away!"

The helicopter drifted lower, almost but not quite landing on the tower roof. Dylan was leaning out the open door.

"Come on!" he shouted. "Grab my hand!"

The three girls ran towards the helicopter. Together Libby and Abby lifted up Portia, who was grabbed and pulled inside. Then Abby clutched Dylan's hand and he hauled her up and in too. Finally Libby, resembling an extra from *Night of the Living Dead*, was dragged aboard. Once all three were safely inside, Dylan pulled the door shut and the machine rose into the air.

Lying in the cramped space of the helicopter cabin, Portia crushed up against her, Abby let her head fall back for a moment. She was lying on her rucksack, but stuffed only with clothes and her diary it was almost comfortable.

"You okay?" Dylan said, leaning over her. His dark mop of hair hung over his face.

Abby nodded and sat up with an effort. Looking around she said, "Where's everyone else?"

Dylan shrugged. "We haven't seen anyone except you three. We've been flying around and around, but . . ."

"So no sign of Dad?" Abby said anxiously.

Dylan shook his head. "All we know is Andy Poole turned out to be a slug—he came for me in my room, but I scarpered and was making my own way up here until I met Adam—and we saw two bodies in the courtyard. One was Joe Poole, but the other was too badly burned to recognize."

Abby clenched her fists as if that could contain her emotions. Dully she said, "Moira's dead too, and so are the two girls, Victoria and Marcie."

Dylan blew out a long sigh. In the pilot's seat, Adam turned briefly and shouted above the whirring hack of the rotors. "I'll circle around the outside of the castle, see if we can spot anything. You never know, someone might have got out."

The girls strapped themselves into the passenger seats, Portia sitting on Abby's knee. Dylan took the seat beside Adam. Abby leaned her head back and closed her eyes, and didn't open them again until Dylan shouted, "There, look!"

At first Abby couldn't work out what she was seeing. In the darkness below was some sort of shimmering wave with a black hole in the center. It wasn't until they got closer that she saw intermittent flickers of fire around the edges of the hole. And it was only when Adam shone the searchlight directly into the center of the circle that she saw—and instantly recognized—the two figures.

One was standing protectively over the prone (possibly dead) body of the other. The standing figure had its arms stretched out and was firing at what Abby now realized was a remorseless, shimmering wave of oncoming aliens.

"It's Dad!" she screamed.

Dylan already had a rucksack clinking with petrol bombs in one hand and a box of matches in the other. He scrambled across the floor of the cabin towards the door, dragging the rucksack behind him. Tossing the matches to Libby, he shouted, "Can you light me up, Libby? It's quicker if someone else does it."

Libby nodded and unstrapped herself from her seat.

Adam took them in so low that Abby could see the jaw-clenched expression of determination on her dad's grimy face. For the moment he seemed unaware of the presence of the helicopter. He was swinging this way and that, letting off shot after shot, as the aliens closed the circle.

Max, lying between his feet, was unmoving, oblivious. Abby could see there was something wrong with his leg, but before she got a chance to focus on it properly the helicopter tilted as Adam took them to within thirty feet of the ground.

Dylan held out the petrol bomb and Libby lit it. As soon as the bottle had left his hand he was reaching into the rucksack for another. The two of them worked with grim efficiency. There was no whooping and hollering, no misplaced triumphalism. Whatever happened now, this would not be a victory. There were too many people dead for that.

Doused by flames, the aliens screeched and scattered, falling into disarray. Like cockroaches emerging from a plughole, they spread outwards from the circle of dwindling flames that Steve had created, seeking security in the surrounding blackness.

When the fire had started to fall from the sky, Steve had lowered his gun and was now standing, arms dangling at his sides, staring up into the beam of the spotlight. Perhaps, Abby mused, he thought this was the mother ship, come to abduct him. Or maybe he even thought he was already dead and this was the fabled tunnel of light, come to carry him to the next world. If so, he was going to be sorely disappointed.

Dylan held up his hands, showing them his empty palms. "That's it," he said, "all out."

Adam circled the area, checking out the terrain. "I'll take us in as close as I can. But you're going to have to move fast, gang. Guns at the ready."

He brought the helicopter down right on the edge of the charred circle. Even before the runners had fully settled, Dylan was leaping to the ground, running in a crouch towards his father.

Steve was hunkered over Max's body like a mother bird protecting its injured chick. He had a hand on Max's chest and was talking to him. From the way that Max's head was thrashing from side to side, Abby—who had jumped to the ground behind her brother—guessed that Dad was trying to soothe or reassure him. Dylan was half a dozen feet from Steve, scanning left and right through the thick smoke from the smattering of petrol fires, when Max raised his head from the ground and looked directly at him.

For an instant Abby thought that Max was not only conscious but fully aware, and then his eyes started to roll and his lips began to move in a feverish jabber, and she realized he was away in his own little world. Even so, that didn't stop him from reaching out and, with unnerving accuracy, suddenly grabbing the rifle lying on the grass beside him. Next moment he had swung the rifle round and was pointing it at Dylan's chest.

"*I see one!*" he screamed. "*I see one, Steve! Coming right at us!*"

"No, Max," Steve said, raising a hand, "that's—"

Max pulled the trigger.

Abby saw Dylan close his eyes and throw himself to one

side. Even so, she was still expecting the bullet to hit him even a second or two after the gun had been fired. The relief she felt when she realized he *hadn't* been hit was just beginning to kick in when Portia started screaming. She half turned and was just in time to see Libby, blood gushing from her mouth, drop her gun, stagger a few steps forward, and crumple to the ground.

For a second or two Abby literally didn't know what to do. She stood motionless, rain drumming on her shoulders and back, staring down at Libby's bleeding body.

It was Adam, appearing at the door of the helicopter, who got her moving again. "Get her inside quickly," he yelled, whereupon she ran across to Libby, shoving her gun into her pocket as she did so.

Adam was there at the same moment. He dropped to his knees beside Libby, and together he and Abby gently turned her over.

At first Abby thought that Libby's entire bottom jaw had been shot off. But almost immediately she realized that although there was a lot of blood, her wounds were mostly superficial. It appeared that the bullet had skimmed her cheekbone and nicked her earlobe before zinging harmlessly away into the night. Libby was not badly hurt (even now her eyelids were fluttering), but the passing kiss of the bullet must still have felt like being socked in the jaw with a burning fist.

"She's going to be fine," Adam shouted. "Let's get her into the helicopter."

Together the two of them carried Libby over to the helicopter and, with Portia's help, lifted her inside and placed her on the floor of the cabin.

"Where are you going?" Adam said when Abby immediately stood up and headed back across to the door.

"I'm going to tell Dad that Libby's okay, and help him and Dyl with Max."

Before Adam could comment or argue she jumped down to the ground. Certain that she must now be functioning on her last reserves of adrenaline, she ran across the saturated grass. Dad and Dyl were already lifting Max, who now appeared to be unconscious. As she approached them, Dad—for the first time that she could recall seeming older than his forty years—looked at her in anguish.

"She's fine, Dad," she said quickly, and touched her cheekbone with the tip of her finger. "She's got a little nick here, that's all. She'll have a cute little scar and maybe a bruise for a day or two."

Abby looked down at Max's leg, registering the extent of the injury for the first time, and for a few seconds the world grayed out.

"I know," Steve shouted above the noise of the helicopter, "it's a mess, isn't it?"

Determined to neither pass out nor throw up, Abby took several deep breaths. She saw that Max's ankles were bound tightly together with her dad's jacket and asked, "Will he ever walk again?"

Steve glanced at Dylan, then, evidently deciding that the time for sweetening the pill had long gone, said bluntly, "He'll have to survive first. He's lost an awful lot of blood."

Together the three of them, running, carried Max across to the helicopter. Abby glanced up and saw Portia, wearing a glassy, shell-shocked expression, peering at them from the open door as they approached. Then she saw Portia's expression change, her head turn to the right.

"Look out!" she screamed.

All three looked to their left. A flickering, fizzing wave of creatures, newly emboldened, was surging towards them. Steve had Max's rifle over his shoulder and his own handgun in his pocket, but, supporting the weight of Max's upper body, couldn't get to either. Abby was only taking a nominal amount of Max's weight, acting more as a support for his midsection, and her weapon was therefore more accessible. She started to fire at the approaching aliens even as she, Dad and Dylan were slithering and scrambling across the rain-slick ground.

"Come on! Come on!" Portia screamed.

They reached the helicopter and all but rammed Max in head-first. Abby fired off a couple more shots as Adam grabbed the shoulders of Max's muddy, soaking jacket and hauled him inside. Abby jumped in, then Steve and Dylan scrambled aboard just as the aliens surrounded the aircraft in a crackling wave.

"So long, suckers!" Dylan yelled, pulling the helicopter door shut as the machine, bearing more weight than it was designed for, lifted sluggishly into the air. Soon they were climbing into the night sky and away, the burning castle and the shimmering carpet of aliens growing distant behind them.

"Where now?" Abby said.

Steve had moved across to a groaning Libby, who had a wadded-up T-shirt from Abby's rucksack pressed against her bleeding jaw. "We need to find medical supplies for Max—splints, painkillers. Lots of painkillers." He shook his head.

"Is it *really* that bad?" Abby asked, once again eyeing the jacket bound tightly around his legs like a restraint.

Steve nodded wearily. " 'Fraid so. When he comes round he's going to be in agony, and it's going to stay that way for a long time. Even if he survives he'll probably be a cripple. And then of course there's the danger of gangrene. The wound's already filthy as it is. . . ." He tailed off and his face twisted with anguish. "This fucking world . . ."

Abby crawled over and put her arms around him, put her arms around both him *and* Libby. "We'll just have to do what we've always done," she said. "Keep going. Stick together. Help each other as best we can."

Adam, sitting at the controls, turned to glance at them. "Don't know how you chaps feel," he shouted, "but I was wondering, once we get Max sorted out, whether you all fancied a little trip to France?"

Steve glanced up, shrugged. "You really think it'll be any better there?"

"Who knows? Couldn't be any worse, though, could it? And someone somewhere's got radio communication, so they may be in *slightly* better shape than us. And the weather's better."

Dylan smiled slightly at that. "Hey, maybe we can go sun-bathing in Saint-Tropez."

"Well . . . it's a plan," Steve conceded.

They flew on.

Into the rain.

Into the darkness.

Into an uncertain future.

DEMON EYES

L. H. MAYNARD
&
M. P. N. SIMS

Emma had just started her new job as personal assistant to Alex Keltner, the charismatic and powerful head of Keltner Industries. So when he asked her to attend a party he was throwing that weekend at his secluded estate, she knew better than to refuse. It would be her first party amid the extremely wealthy and powerful elite....

It will be a party she'll never forget...if she survives. At first it will be simply odd. Mysterious warnings. Strange, seductive guests. An atmosphere of lust and sexuality. Video cameras in the rooms. But as the weekend progresses, Emma will slowly learn the true nature of the guests and her mysterious host—and the real, grotesque purpose of the party.

ISBN 13: 978-0-8439-5972-7